BEFORE I WAKE

This book belongs to:

Christina L.
Anderson

Before
I Wake

DEE HENDERSON

TYNDALE HOUSE PUBLISHERS, INC.
CAROL STREAM, ILLINOIS

Visit Tyndale's exciting Web site at www.tyndale.com and the author's Web site at
www.deehenderson.com

TYNDALE and Tyndale's quill logo are registered trademarks of Tyndale House Publishers, Inc.

Before I Wake

Designed by Beth Sparkman

This novel is a work of fiction. Names, characters, places, and incidents are either the product
of the author's imagination or are used fictitiously. Any resemblance to actual events, locales,
organizations, or persons, living or dead, is entirely coincidental and beyond the intent of either the
author or publisher.

Library of Congress Cataloging-in-Publication Data

Henderson, Dee.
  Before I wake / Dee Henderson.
    p. cm.
  ISBN-13: 978-1-4143-0815-9 (pbk.)
  ISBN-10: 1-4143-0815-9 (pbk.)
  1. Women private investigators—Illinois—Fiction. 2. Illinois—Fiction. I. Title.
  PS3558.E4829B44 2006
  813'.54—dc22
                                                    2006009264

Printed in the United States of America

11 10 09 08 07 06
7 6 5 4 3 2

Prologue

The movers had gutted the house of her furniture and belongings. Rae Gabriella doubted she could find even a throw pillow remaining. She sank down on the living-room carpet to use the fireplace hearth as a backrest.

Stones dug into her back. The house had felt sunny and welcoming when she had moved in; now it felt ready to expel her too. Too much violence had happened here.

"You want the last piece of pizza?" Bruce Chapel asked, stretching out where her sofa had been.

"I can't eat another bite. Go ahead." Sweat had dried on Bruce's blue sweatshirt and his jeans had picked up cat hair. Rae wished the movers had taken the cat too, but the Siamese she was watching for a friend was still prowling around here somewhere.

Bruce tugged over the open cardboard box and picked up the last slice of pepperoni pizza. "What time did you say your friend was coming by?"

"Late."

He waited, but she didn't offer more. "When we were dating, you weren't this quiet with details."

She smiled at him. "I've acquired a few bad habits in the last eleven years." She finished her soda and then slid out one of the ice cubes to crunch. "I already miss being a cop."

"I bet the FBI would ignore the resignation if you want to change your mind. And I know the Chicago PD would welcome you back."

She trusted Bruce implicitly, but she wasn't ready to talk about the last undercover assignment yet. "No, I'm done. I just want to equivocate now that the decision is made. I'm joining my uncle's crime-scene-cleanup business at least part-time and I'll see where I want to go from there."

She'd seen her first dead body before she was seventeen and helped clean up her first murder scene when she was twenty. At least the work saved relatives of the dead from having to deal with the mess—and maybe for her it would be a bit of redemption through service. She studied the bottom of her glass and didn't want to think about her motivations that deeply.

The cat came into the room hugging the baseboards. Bruce held out a corner of the pizza crust and the cat swished his tail and stalked over to check it out. Bruce deftly got his hand around the cat and pulled him over to pet. "I was thinking on the drive out here that I might do something more than just help you pack."

"Oh? What?"

"Offer you a job."

Rae crunched another ice cube and shoved it to the side of her mouth. "What did you have in mind?"

Bruce smiled.

It was the way he smiled. She blinked and dropped the ice cube into her hand. "You're dangerous to my health, you know that? I about swallowed it."

"You said you'd be my partner one day."

"We were talking about getting engaged, not being business partners. Besides, it was eleven years ago and I seem to remember we were sitting on my uncle's front porch at 2 a.m. when we had that discussion. A statute of limitations should apply."

Her phone rang, the sound echoing through the hollow rooms. She got to her feet. "I'll think about it, okay? But no promises."

"None expected. The idea's going to grow on you."

She laughed at his confidence. "Maybe." She went to answer the phone.

Spending more time with Bruce—it had an interesting appeal to it. The phone rang a third time and she picked up her pace, afraid it was news she did not want to hear. Mark Rivers was dead and she just wanted to get out of town before the next chapter in that story was written.

§⊗§   §⊗§   §⊗§

Bruce listened to Rae take the stairs two at a time. She was coloring her hair to keep away the gray, and her glasses were new, but for a former girlfriend, she was in a lot better shape for the years than he was. He'd added thirty pounds and another break in his nose since leaving the Chicago PD. He was glad friendship covered a lot of flaws, for it appeared their relationship was going to pick up where it left off as if the years in between hadn't happened.

But the secrecy was new. Bruce rolled onto his back. Rae hadn't patched over the two bullet holes in the living-room wall well enough; he could still see the outlines of the impact in the plaster. He studied the painted white spots and a grim resolve replaced the casual expression he'd kept around her.

Rae hadn't explained; he hadn't asked, but he knew how to read the remaining trace evidence. The grit between the ceramic tiles of the kitchen floor had been bleached, but there were still faint traces of pink in the corners, suggesting blood had pooled and soaked in before someone had been able to clean it. Two of the kitchen cabinet doors had been replaced, the wood stain used not quite matching the older wood.

A weapon—a knife, a bat, something not small or fragile—had been swung to injure or kill. From the area involved, it looked like the bullet holes had come toward the end of the fight.

Someone had tried to kill her in her own home.

What had happened here?

He let the cat have the last of the pizza crust and got to his feet. He'd supported Rae's move from the Chicago PD to the FBI, thinking it would keep her away from the trouble he saw on the streets and let her do more white-collar work. It had been that or else present her with the ring he had carried in his pocket and convince her to stay.

It wouldn't have been the best thing for her; he'd been a bit too career intense back then and the chances he took on the job hadn't meshed well with the idea of a wife expecting him to come safely home.

Rae had graduated from the FBI Academy, gone to Dallas, and then moved to Washington, D.C., where she had become involved with another agent. He'd let her go and wished her the best. But seeing this, it was obvious he had made the wrong choice.

A case gone bad? A relationship? He could speculate and contemplate, but he wouldn't ask. Rae would tell him when she was ready. He had his own memories from the last eleven years that would not easily find words even with Rae. She hadn't been that religious years ago; neither had he for that matter, but getting shot at might have changed things. It had for him. So much needed to be understood to know how he could best help.

"The Realtor will be over in the morning."

Bruce turned as Rae came back into the room. She joined him by the window to look out at the night. She didn't bear the visible signs of a fight, but her sweatshirt and jeans covered a lot. He settled his hand on her shoulder. He felt her weight shift to lean into his hand. "It's a good clear night for driving."

She smiled at him and he could feel the emotional hole that was her absence in his life fill a bit. The doubts he'd had about coming east, minor and merely whispers of regret, faded. He rubbed his thumb on her shoulder blade and then lifted his hand away. There was time and that was the best news he had. Time could fix about anything. "Traffic's light. I should make good progress once I'm out of the city."

Rae walked him to the door. "I should be ready to follow by noon tomorrow, once the Realtor has what she needs."

"Call me occasionally as you travel."

"I will."

Bruce unlocked the door of the van packed with Rae's more breakable pieces. Snow hadn't stayed this far south yet, but the January night had a cold bite to it. At least Rae had called him, out of the blue and late at night, but when she needed a friend she'd still had his number. He could build on that. Whatever had happened here, it would best be dealt with by getting her onto his own turf.

1

Rae fingered the edge of the worn business card as she drove, her handwritten directions on the back faded after lying on the car dash in the sun. She turned the card over and read the raised black type.

> *Bruce Chapel*
> *Chapel Detective Agency II*
> *Justice, Illinois*

Bruce's cousin, Sam Chapel, had formed the first Chapel Detective Agency over in Brentwood years before. Bruce had decided a few years ago to follow in his footsteps. If working for Bruce was anything like dating him, she was heading into unpredictable terrain.

She didn't have to do this. She looked at herself in the rearview mirror, into calm blue eyes that masked the accumulated turmoil of the past few years, and accepted that she had to do something.

She needed somewhere quiet to let the stress of the last years drain away, and it didn't get more anonymous than working for Bruce in a small town she'd struggled to find on the map.

The town of Justice was south of Chicago and east of the Mississippi River; it had a population of twelve thousand six hundred four, and had the distinction of also being the county seat for Justice County: it sounded like a good place to disappear.

She reached around to the boxes in the backseat for another CD. Years of FBI service had been reduced to a few private files, paperwork on her future pension, phone numbers of friends and colleagues, and a pile of past daily calendar books noting appointments she could no longer remember. At least the music CDs were still useful. Rae pushed aside the regrets. If she had to start life over again at least it would be with a friend.

Justice, Illinois.

At least it had the sound of being an interesting town.

𐠲 𐠲 𐠲

Justice was a quiet town; all his friends said so. Sheriff Nathan Justice drove down Main Street watching a group form on the east side of the street in front of city hall. He slowed.

Teenagers congregating on corners were his normal problem on a Saturday morning, but today it was the adults. He scanned the backs of jackets for union logos and sought out faces. Several were long-term union members and in the center of the closing circle was the union treasurer.

Nathan pulled over to the curb and let the squad car idle. He watched his patrol commander Chet Peterson leave the coffee shop and walk over to join the group, his bulk and uniform parting the crowd.

Chet had been a union member before joining the police force, and his presence had the desired influence. The group spread out even as the discussion grew louder. The strike at the tile plant had entered its fifteenth day and stress was growing in proportion to the days without a paycheck. The union contract had expired, a new one to replace the rolling extensions wasn't in place, and emotions were rising.

Chet glanced his direction and quietly motioned that he had it covered. Nathan put the car back in gear. *May the day just end without violence. . . .*

Nathan parked in the nearly empty parking lot behind the Justice Police Department and unbuckled his seat belt, but he did not open the door. He sat and looked at the chipped paint on the hand railing leading to the back entrance and he waited, hoping for any sense of optimism to return.

The town bore his family name and he was the one on duty watching it crumble.

If only he were wealthy and wise, he'd buy the tile plant and keep it open, keep employees paid, and keep this community together. If the plant closed, the stress of losing fifty-two direct jobs, as well as the work that flowed to local businesses, would decimate the town economy and trigger a cascade of business failures.

Those failures would ripple through the downtown area, forcing people to move to find work, collapsing housing prices, and weakening the tax base. The mayor was his mother; Nathan knew in excruciating detail how the plant's closing down would impact the town budget.

If there was optimism to be found, he couldn't find it. He pushed open the car door. Someone had to keep the peace and he had sworn the oath to do so. He just hoped this didn't end with his having to arrest his friends.

Nathan entered the police department and took the stairs two at a time up to the second floor where officer desks dominated the open space. His small office tucked into the corner had a door for privacy, but it was open, a box fan in the doorway turned on high. Winter outside meant the building's old furnace created a sauna inside. He stepped around the fan. His deputy chief was waiting for him.

"I heard it was a bad wreck," Will Rickker said, offering the transfer sheet Nathan had come back to sign.

"The SUV went down the embankment on the east side of the river and slammed into the railroad bridge. The gas tank punctured, and the fireball scorched the wood to the second level of crossbeams. It could have been a disaster. I've got railroad engineers out there now assessing the damage."

Nathan shed his gloves but not his coat and searched for a pen. "If we don't get warning lights ahead of that curve, it's only a matter of time before there's another fatal accident out there. The state highway department is promising action before the end of next week, but I've heard that before. I want us to step up patrols and start issuing speeding tickets a mile ahead of that curve until the problem is resolved."

"I'll talk to patrol."

Nathan scrawled his signature approving Noland Reed's application to the county narcotics task force. Every department in the area was vying for the precious slots on the task force, for once there, an officer had access to better resources and his salary was paid for by a federal grant. He hoped Reed got accepted.

Drugs flowing from the south up to Chicago were coming through the county in ever increasing volume and it was creating a cottage industry of safe houses and homegrown labs. Nathan had been diverting ever larger portions of his department's budget to keeping the problem out of his community. He handed the papers back to Will.

"The posting for the opening is going up at ten and I'll be there to hand over the paperwork," Will promised.

"You could send Carol."

"I could, but we need the radio upgrades and shifting Noland's salary is how we pay for it. If there are problems with the paperwork that I can't solve on the spot I'm tracking you down."

"I'll stay reachable."

Nathan moved around to the credenza to pour himself a cup of coffee. He'd fixed the pot at 1 a.m. and it was almost gone. "What's the latest here?"

"The contract talks broke down about twenty minutes ago. The union team walked out first. Adam looked mad as a hornet and he pushed through the gathered men without stopping to comment."

"He'll go steam somewhere in private rather than spread that anger to his men. What about management?"

"Zachary paused to make a short statement to the newspaper. The bottom line is still the health-care cost increases. There was some pushing and shoving between the picket-line guys and the company guys when word spread there were no new talks scheduled."

Nathan drank his coffee and let himself worry. "There's going to be trouble."

Will nodded. "The union is riding close rein on their guys, but if no new talks get scheduled soon, we're going to start losing control. We've already had some minor vandalism of plant trucks: graffiti and slashed tires. We need to avoid either side having a press conference and digging in their positions."

"I'm more worried about management trying to bring in strike breakers next week. Can we get through Monday with the officer rotations we have now?"

"We've got three officers at the plant, another two monitoring the picket lines, and we've stepped up patrols around the homes of the negotiators and plant managers. Short of having to start making arrests, we can handle it."

"How's morale?"

"Officers are wondering when this will end, but for the most part keeping their opinion of the strike to themselves and doing their jobs."

Nathan studied the duty board. The names ran out before the assignments did. He had four ladies with protection orders against ex-husbands and boy-friends, two unsolved rapes, five open burglaries, and the county task force suspicion that there was at least one clandestine meth lab operating some-where in his area.

He had more problems than he did men to solve them. The department only had twenty-six officers and some of those were part-time. "I don't want to ask for more overtime unless it's a crisis; we're already pushing the men hard. What else happened in town overnight?"

"We had three calls reporting a prowler out on Kerns Road that haven't been resolved. Someone took Goodheart's pickup again; officers found it out of gas down by the lake pavilion. Overall, it was a pretty quiet night."

"We needed one. I need to have a frank talk with the union steward today. If a man can't pay his bills, he gets angry. If a man can't feed his kids, he gets desperate. The other side of desperate is dangerous. We need a better handle on how guys on the picket lines are doing."

"I'll see what I can arrange."

Nathan spotted the chief dispatcher. He leaned out the office door. "Eileen, how's your voice doing?"

"Raw, but there. Just don't come near me and catch this."

"The pharmacist has your prescription refill ready. Call over, and he'll de-liver it here."

"What did you do, bribe him?"

"Anything to keep my favorite lady answering my radio calls."

She laughed. "Thanks, Nathan."

He looked at the clock. "Will, after you deliver that file, why don't you head home and get some sleep. You can spell me around dinner."

"I can take tomorrow morning for you."

"I'll take you up on it." Nathan had yet to find a substitute to take his Sunday school class of junior high boys and the last day he had off—it had been before the strike started. "If you need me in the short term, I'll be patrolling on the highway, keeping speeds down while they clear that wreck. After that, I'll be over at the plant."

Will nodded. Nathan pulled on his gloves and headed back out to patrol.

※   ※   ※

Death was such an interesting process. Nella's eyes flickered open. She tried to focus on him. Her eyes began to water as they widened. Her hand pushed against the blanket to slide out but didn't have the strength to push the heavy weight aside. Her breath began to come in gasps. He watched, interested in the way her nerves reacted as the seizure hit. Her neck stiffened and tilted back. Her blue eyes filmed over as membranes broke. She bit her tongue. As seizures went, it was small and lasted less than a minute.

Her breathing stopped.

He watched for death changes, in her eyes or in her muscles, and saw her go slack. A double dose of the new formula killed; there was no surprise there. The tougher question would be to find a dose that gave the euphoric high without killing as it wore off.

He turned away and swung his legs to the floor, sitting on the side of the bed and stretching. He picked up his shirt.

He tugged against her weight to free the sheet; her limp body settled into the bed and pillow. He tossed the blanket back up and made his presence in her bed less obvious. He buttoned his jeans and bent to pick up his shoes.

He had to force the window to get it to rise in the aged frame. The window screen had numerous tears in the wire mesh; he used his finger to widen a few of them. He let the window come down under its own weight and it jammed off center, half an inch from closed. He rocked the frame with his hand and it just jammed tighter. Good. Let the bugs come in.

He turned on the ceiling fan and closed the bedroom door. In the hallway, he turned the thermostat to eighty-four. Nella liked to keep her rooms warm; she complained to everyone about the heating bills and how her poor circulation gave her cold feet. He'd attest to the fact that her feet were cold; it had annoyed him for the last four years.

In the kitchen he retrieved the last of the wine he'd brought and poured himself another glass. He walked to the window. The rising sun left the woods between the house and the town of Justice in dark relief.

He could go home or back to work or to meet the guys at the union hall. He considered that and the absolute senseless way this weekend was going. Had she just been able to keep her mouth shut, he could have had another couple hours of sleep. But she liked to talk to strangers.

He finished the wine, took the bottle with him, and closed the front door, letting it lock behind him.

2

What did she know about being a private investigator? Cheating spouses, missing child support, employee theft, insurance fraud . . . Rae winced just thinking about the cases she'd likely see in her first year working with Bruce. The shift from the intensity of undercover work to working small jobs for the public was going to be an abrupt change of pace. She'd learn to enjoy the work or she'd suffer the boredom.

She rubbed at her right forearm. She didn't care if there was a scar; she just wished the gash would stop itching as it healed. She had dealt with a lot of violence in her undercover career, but never before at the hands of another agent.

Reaching down, she changed the radio station. She could tell she was nearing her childhood home. The talk radio had turned conservative, snow-covered fields dominated the landscape, and she grew accustomed to passing semis and tanker trucks that stacked in the right lane in long convoys. She loved the Midwest even though she'd not been back very often in the last decade.

Sirens interrupted her thoughts.

She instinctively looked ahead at the heavy interstate traffic and then looked in the rearview mirror and saw flashing lights.

She checked her speed and immediately eased up on the gas. She had a faint hope those lights were not for her but as the police car closed the distance it moved into the lane behind her.

Rae sighed and turned on her blinkers, acknowledging she saw him. She slowed. There were no exits ahead she could see but there was a wider shoulder where the railroad joined to flow alongside the interstate. She pulled to the side of the road, activated her hazard lights, and put the car into park. She'd made it all the way to her home state before getting pulled over; she didn't know if that was a blessing or a curse.

She touched a button to lower the window. The temperature immediately dropped. The radio was blaring outside and she hit a button to shut it off. In the rearview mirror she could see the officer sitting in the police car, talking on his radio, likely calling in her license-plate numbers and location of the stop.

The officer got out of the squad car, a tall man with dark hair blowing in the stiff breeze, his jacket a deep blue and designed for the cold.

She left her hands on the steering wheel as she watched him walk toward the car. He was watching her as well as studying the car. She waited until he drew even with her before moving to rest her arm on the open window frame.

"Good morning, Ma'am." He scanned the interior of the vehicle. "Do you realize you were speeding?"

"When I heard your sirens I did. I'm afraid my thoughts were elsewhere. My error."

"I clocked you crossing eighty miles per hour. May I see your license and registration please?"

"My purse is in the backseat."

He nodded and she turned to retrieve it. She fumbled unzipping her purse. He patiently waited while she figured out how she had zipped fabric into the zipper teeth and got the inside compartment open.

Her leather case that had held her badge for so many years was empty, but she didn't think she'd have tried to ask for a law enforcement courtesy to get out of the ticket even if she still carried it. Speeding was her own private little demon and she paid for it regularly. She handed over her license and car registration.

He added it to his clipboard. "Washington, D.C. You're a long way from home."

"Yes."

Explaining everything was in storage or in transport, her house was with a Realtor, and her friend was picking up her mail, seemed like more information than was warranted. She'd also lost twenty pounds since that license was printed. She wanted to mention that too but didn't.

She slid off her sunglasses being used to block the sun's glare off the snow and read the officer's name tag. *Sheriff Nathan Justice.* The town of Justice was just ahead. That was too much of a coincidence not to be connected. It had to be so strange to live and work in a town your family founded. "I don't suppose there's any way you can not write that."

"Sorry. You were speeding."

"Just checking."

"No problem with checking," he agreed easily. His face wasn't pretty, too prominent cheekbones and chin, his skin weathered by too many days in the sun and wind, but his smile was nice and the brown eyes kind.

He wasn't missing details; the pause when he had seen the scar on her arm had narrowed his gaze, and the stack of coffee cups piled together in her cup holder had brought a smile. Altogether the man who led the Justice Police Department left a nice impression. He finished the registration card and handed it back but held on to the license. "I'll be back in a minute."

Rae watched him in her rearview mirror as he walked back to the patrol car. She would be working with the man in the coming days or at least trying to get information out of his department. Why was a sheriff out making traffic stops? The Justice jurisdiction was that small?

The sheriff reached inside his squad car for the radio and stood leaning against the car as he talked with dispatch. The way he leaned to shift his weight—maybe it was just projection on her part—but the man looked like he was, like her, also ending a very long week.

He must live around here somewhere, eat at the local restaurants, shop at the local mall—running into the man under less awkward circumstances shouldn't be that hard to arrange. She needed to make a better impression than this before she asked for her first favor.

He signed off the radio and leaned into the car to replace it, then walked back to join her. A semi rolled past and the wind rocked her car.

The sheriff offered her the clipboard. "Sign at the *X* and I can return your license. If you wish to contest the ticket or raise any mitigating points with the court, you have ten days to do so, by mail if you wish. The address is on the back of the form."

She nodded, read his neat handwriting listing her name and information, and signed where indicated.

She handed back the clipboard. He gave her a copy of the ticket and returned her license. She wrestled with her purse zipper pocket again to put away her license. "Could you by any chance give me directions to the Chapel Detective Agency?"

Her question surprised him; he took his time putting his pen back into his pocket before he responded. "As you head into town, the third stop light is Tremont Road. Turn right. You'll find Bruce's office between the pharmacy and the bank. If you pass the Fine Chocolates Shop you've gone too far. If he's not at the office, at this time of day you'll likely find him at Della's Café."

"Thanks."

"You have business for Bruce?"

"Possibly."

"He's a good guy. Just for reference, the speed limit in town is twenty-five."

She smiled.

He smiled back. "The road might appear clear, but it's deceptive; there are still patches of smooth ice under the underpasses around here. Drive safely, Ms. Gabriella."

He stepped away and she lifted her hand, then closed the window.

She'd planned to drop her things at her uncle's home and get some sleep, then see Bruce tomorrow. She hadn't realized Justice was so close to the interstate that she actually entered the town's jurisdiction for a brief stretch of highway. Her uncle was not expecting her until Monday and it would be easier to talk schedules with him once she had details with Bruce worked out.

She put the ticket into the glove box to deal with later. "Sixty-five dollars. We're going to have to talk to Bruce about an expense account that covers speeding tickets." She put the car back in gear. "Welcome back to Illinois."

෫෬෩ ෫෬෩ ෫෬෩

Nathan watched from his squad car as the older-model Lexus reentered the flow of traffic. He knew just about everyone in town and Gabriella wasn't a family name he recognized.

What trouble did she have that needed Bruce's attention? Or was she one of Bruce's friends from days past? He was still meeting them. Something specific had her coming to Justice. Nathan couldn't remember the last time someone from Washington, D.C., had intentionally come to visit their town.

He put away the paperwork and glanced at his watch. He was hoping to meet up with the union steward to see if they would limit the number of men walking the picket lines over the weekend. A reasonable request, asked in a reasonable way . . . as his dad said often, you couldn't get a yes if you weren't willing to risk hearing a no. It would let him give one more officer an afternoon off.

Another car sped past. Nathan groaned. He punched on the lights and pulled out into traffic. The Porsche was red and in a hurry.

I'm going to take away the car keys. Get his license revoked. Slice the car tires. . . . His grandfather was eighty, his wife had died last year, and he liked to drive fast. If his grandfather didn't voluntarily slow down this was going to be a long chase and he'd be arresting his grandfather. That Porsche could accelerate.

Nathan passed Rae Gabriella now doing the speed limit and wondered what she'd think about his town after she met some of its residents.

෫෬෩ ෫෬෩ ෫෬෩

Rae found the building easy enough and a parking place just a space off the front door. She stretched, studied the quiet street, and nodded to herself. It fit.

Rae pushed open the door to the Chapel Detective Agency II and stepped into the receptionist area. The room was empty. She tugged off her gloves. The thermostat must be cranked toward eighty degrees; the heat in the room was oppressive.

The receptionist desk was clear but for a phone, a day-calendar, and a paper-back book (Sam Whitmere's *Murder at Midnight*) left resting facedown to mark the page. Salt tracked in by snow-covered shoes had left a white trail on the low-pile, blue-and-gray carpet. Three fabric-backed chairs along the wall looked nice if uncomfortable, and the magazines on the table were current.

Rae shoved her gloves into her coat pocket and turned to look at the window where an Open/Closed sign was turned to Open. Saturday hours were listed as nine to two.

She walked through the receptionist area with no interest in waiting there to the hallway that disappeared toward the back of the building. It was bright-ly lit, the fluorescent bulbs making a soft electrical hum.

She headed down the hall, listening to the quiet sounds of her own footfalls on the carpet, checking doorknobs on either side as she passed them. The doors were locked. Framed photographs of the Chicago skyline, the White Sox ballpark, pedestrian-packed sidewalks lined the walls in an unexpected display of nostalgia.

Bruce wouldn't have an office with windows near the front of the building when he could have one with windows facing the alley where he could safely park his precious restored Jaguar. The odds were solid that he still had the car.

The hallway ended with a closed door. Rae tugged the yellow phone slip from the door crack. *Bruce, call Heather.* Heather's name was written in caps and underscored. Rae pocketed the slip and tried the doorknob. She wasn't surprised to find it locked.

She slid a case from her handbag, selected a pick, and several seconds lat-er turned the doorknob. *Bruce, Bruce, the things you teach your friends.* She pushed open the door and found the light switch.

Nice. Bruce had himself an extra-large office, twenty by eighteen, done in a rich cherry paneling and deep blue painted trim. She cluttered up the desk by adding the call slip.

Rae crossed to the windows and moved aside the blinds. The alley was empty but for a gray painted industrial-size Dumpster, but someone did park out there regularly; the snow had a clear spot and the area around it had been square-cornered by someone with a snow shovel.

Rae let the blind fall back in place and turned to study the office. He'd brought in stereo equipment and a guy-size leather chair. She ran a finger along the black leather of the couch. Back when he worked for the Chicago PD she'd helped move this couch into his first undercover apartment. She'd promised him the leather would wear well and it had.

She read the list of cases written on the whiteboard in Bruce's neat handwriting—*Heather Teal's husband, Larry Broderick store robbery, Tretton Insurance claim, Karen Elan's sister, Laura's ex-husband, Nathan's inquiry.* It was a pretty sparse work list.

He said he needed her help, but it looked more like he was offering her a graceful way out of her own troubles.

What do I know about being a private detective, Bruce? And why do you really want to hire me? Knowing Bruce, his reasons would be layered and shared only when he thought them relevant. She just hoped she learned to like the job.

The small refrigerator had nothing decaffeinated. Rae closed it. She could wait for Bruce to come back, but nothing indicated what case he was working on or how long he would be gone. She found a piece of paper.

> *I arrived early. I'm going to get a room at the Sunburst Hotel and take a nap. I'll find you in the next 24 hours.*

She didn't bother to sign it; the man had received hundreds of notes from her over the years, most from when they were dating, and he would know her handwriting on sight. She relocked the office door behind her.

3

Nathan walked toward his grandfather's car, breathing deep and watching the horizon where a hawk was circling in the sky, doing his best to get control of his temper before he reached the driver's-side door. He pulled his pen from his pocket and opened the ticket book, slipping a blank form onto the clipboard. The back of the Porsche was spotted white as the salt and snow streaked the red panels.

Nathan stopped beside the driver's door and gestured for his grandfather to lower his window. It was grudgingly lowered. "Henry, you know the speed limit; you know how dangerous this road can be. Do you have a death wish to go along with the new car?"

"If I'm going to get the lecture every time I pull over to let you catch me, I'm not going to stop next time. Just write the ticket."

There were roses wrapped in cellophane in the passenger seat. It was likely Henry was going to the cemetery, but Nathan didn't have the courage to ask. He accepted the driver's license and registration offered and wrote the ticket, keeping part of his attention on his grandfather. Arthritis had stiffened Henry's knuckles and fingers, the glasses had thickened, and his hearing had become selective. The man grew noticeably older with each passing month.

The days they had played ball together, trekked through the family land deciding what trees to clear, gone out at dawn to fish in the river—they were good memories now swallowed up by years of back and forth irritations within the family and this latest round of pushing the limits of the law. Nathan missed what they once had. He handed over the ticket. "Are you still coming over for lunch Sunday?"

"I invited myself, didn't I?" His grandfather folded up the ticket and pushed it in his pocket. "Are we done? I've got things to do."

"We're done. Just please, slow down."

His grandfather pulled smoothly away from the side of the road. Nathan sighed and turned back to his squad car. Maybe his father could reason with Henry. The two men had both been sheriffs before him and until the last couple years Henry hadn't been acting this way. The radio interrupted his thoughts. Nathan listened to the tones and picked up his pace back to the car to a jog.

છ૭ૐ   છ૭ૐ   છ૭ૐ

Bruce Chapel watched the flow of people in and out of the bus depot. A mom with two kids struggled to pass their luggage to the baggage handler while keeping the boys close. They danced around the others in line, and the youngest tugged against her jeans. "You said I could have a window seat."

The voice already had the petulance in it of a tired little boy. Bruce read the signs on the bus they were moving to board. Milwaukee, a good four-hour drive if the roads were clear and today the roads were not clear; snow already in the air was growing and accumulating.

He drank his coffee and kept scanning. The car didn't allow him room to stretch out his legs and surveillance without a partner to talk to felt like prison time for its pace at flowing by. He watched an old man get passed by younger folks and keep going on his slow journey inside to the ticket counter.

The work didn't change, just the signature on the paycheck. Most of his life as a cop had been waiting, watching, followed by moments of too much adrenaline. He pulled an apple from the paper bag and bit into it.

Rae was going to need a place to stay. The odds she'd last in the small town of Justice were maybe ten to one. It was a quiet place and she was big city.

But the idea of her working for her uncle doing crime-scene cleanup—she needed a break and that job bent the will of even strong cops. One problem at a time. At least in a place like Justice no one could easily slip into town to make trouble for her without him getting early word of it. He should have married her when he had the chance and avoided the last decade of wondering about her.

Bruce sat up. He punched in the speed dial on his phone and on the second ring the dispatcher for the Justice Police Department picked up the line. "Eileen, get me the sheriff."

"He's on a pursuit, Nathan."

"If he's chasing his grandfather again, tell him to break it off and get on this channel. I've got my eyes on Kyle."

"Oh! Yes, hold on. I'll patch you through."

She'd drop him more likely, connecting a call to a radio frequency was still too many switches on the new console for her to remember, but he waited while she tried.

"Bruce, go ahead," Eileen said.

"Nathan?"

"I'm on."

"Kyle's made an appearance." Bruce watched the denim-shirted man cross the parking lot and reach the entrance doors. Kyle opened a door and stood there scanning the inside of the building. The door slammed against the frame as he went in. "I'm at the bus depot. We're going to have some trouble here."

"I'm on the way."

"Keep Chet away."

"I've got him assigned on the east side of town."

Bruce retrieved his oversize gym bag. He slung the bag over his shoulder and headed into the bus depot. Ex-husbands gave cops and PIs nightmares. He wasn't interested in making it a fair fight if he had to stand between Laura and the man.

The bus on the way to Milwaukee pulled out, belching diesel exhaust. Now if all the civilians would get out of the way and the security here didn't shoot the wrong guy, maybe he'd be able to finally mark one case off his whiteboard list this month.

❦   ❦   ❦

Nathan silenced the sirens and threw his squad car into park beside Bruce's blue Caprice, reaching to open the door even as his seat belt released. A crowd of adults at the east side of the bus-depot building surged back and two men spilled out into the gravel parking lot, locked in struggle. They crashed into the newspaper stands and trash canisters, sending cigarette butts and fine white sand bursting into the air. "55-J, 10-97, requesting two more units, Code 2."

"10-4."

Nathan spotted a deputy at the bus-depot doorway providing a buffer for the lady watching the fight. Laura's arms were wrapped around her chest and her face was pale; she looked scared, but at least not bruised this time. Bruce had done his job; Kyle had not gotten near her.

A wildly thrown fist caught Bruce in the mouth. Nathan winced. "Move back, people. Let me through." Bruce had a former cop's instincts and experience, but Kyle had height and weight and mean on his side: the fight was coming out a draw.

Nathan chose his point of contact to take Kyle's feet out from under him. It was like kicking steel, but the man went down. Bruce seized the moment of advantage and pinned the man with a knee in his back. Nathan pulled out his handcuffs and secured a hold on Kyle's left wrist to lock them on. "Welcome home, Kyle. We've been looking for you."

"She ain't marrying him; I ain't having my kids raised by no black."

Nathan brought Kyle back to his feet with a jerk. Laura was marrying one of his best officers. "She can marry whoever she likes, and you've got a court order not to come around and be harassing her."

"She's mine. You hear that, Laura? You're mine! I'll be out in hours and back here."

"Not this time. The judge is learning."

Squealing tires braked hard as a squad car came to a stop. Nathan saw Chet surge from the car. "Stop him!" He forced Kyle to turn, putting his own body between the two men. There hadn't been a murder in Justice in six years and Nathan didn't intend one of his officers to be the next one accused.

Bruce moved to cut Chet off.

"Get out of my way; he was warned about coming around here," Chet ordered.

"Sorry, buddy." Bruce kept himself in Chet's way in a dance of bodies bordering on shoving.

"Back off, Chet," Nathan ordered.

"You aren't marrying her, you hear me! I'll bury you first."

Nathan physically muscled Kyle back. It was like shoving a brick wall. Racist and stupid seemed to go together; Chet would bury Kyle in a fight. Two more squad cars pulled into the parking lot and officers poured out of the cars to help. They separated the men by shear numbers.

Ignoring the venom spewing from Kyle, Nathan handed him off. "Get him downtown." Nathan turned to Chet. His officer had backed off two steps, but he still looked ready for an opportunity to finish this with his fists. "Take Laura back inside and stay with her; I'll need her statement. She needs a jacket if she's going to be out here," Nathan ordered.

Chet didn't immediately move. Laura tugged at his arm. His officer finally nodded and wrapped his arm around his fiancée to take her inside.

Nathan knew it was a temporary reprieve. If he didn't get Kyle put away for a long time, next time might not be so controlled an ending. Chet had seen Laura bruised too many times to risk letting Kyle get close to her again. And Kyle was the kind of guy who would shoot a cop in the back if he thought he could get away with it. This situation was a mess.

Nathan turned his attention to Bruce. "I'll get a statement from Laura first; then I want to hear yours."

"No problem. The file is at my office. He got vocal when he saw the wedding announcement and I've got it on tape. He made good on his threat. The DA can get it to stick this time."

"Let's hope you're right; I thought we had enough last time. Did you enjoy going back undercover?"

"Not particularly. Kyle hangs around some bars that give bars a bad name."

Nathan offered Bruce a handkerchief. "You might want to find a clean shirt before you head to your office. You've got a new lady client looking for you."

Bruce's look turned skeptical. "I took this domestic case as a favor; I'm not interested in making it a habit."

"I doubt if it's a domestic case; she looked self-assured enough to take care of herself. I'd tell you what I know but you're a man who enjoys a surprise."

Bruce touched his lip. "Go talk to Laura while I clean this up. You owe me a steak dinner seeing as how the department can't afford my bill."

"I'll make it a thick one," Nathan promised. The rumbling of buses told him he was in danger of witnesses leaving before they were interviewed; he slapped his friend on the shoulder. "Thanks for the help. I'll catch up with you at the agency." He turned back to the task at hand.

ℤℝℤ ℤℝℤ ℤℝℤ

Rae slid the key card for room 3723 through the lock and heard it click as the light turned green. She turned the handle and used her foot to push open the door. Elbowing her way into the room with her two suitcases, briefcase, and can of soda tucked under her elbow, she cleared the doorway and dropped the bags to catch the soda before it fell.

Two queen-size beds took up the majority of the room. There were a desk in a corner and a small couch, two chairs, a small table, and a large TV able to turn to face either section of the room. The bland decorating in greens and blues would eventually get on her nerves, but there was a complimentary fruit basket on the table and a set of towels with a ribbon around them on the dresser beside a pool pass. The hotel staff had done what they could to make it welcoming.

"Home sweet home," she whispered to herself and got down to the business of unpacking. It would be home for a while; she was in no hurry to settle on more permanent living arrangements until the house out east sold. She turned down the thermostat dial on the unit under the window.

It looked like the hotel was one of the tallest buildings in town. The town had a symmetrical square look to it as the roads extended into nearby neighborhoods. In the near distance the bell tower of the church she'd passed marked downtown. She rested her hand on the window glass.

The distraction of the journey and the trip back to Illinois were over, and the weight of the stillness in the room around her began to press in. With the silence and stop came the resurgence of painful emotions shimmering just below the surface. Hundreds of miles hadn't changed the weight of the memories. There were days when peace with all that had happened in the past year seemed impossible to find. "Jesus, I need hope back," she whispered.

The last undercover investigation had turned terribly wrong. She'd accused an innocent man of murder and now he was dead. That others in the agency had been convinced he was guilty too didn't ease the pain or change the outcome. She'd been so certain Mark was guilty, so sure of the truth—and it had all been a lie.

The pain wasn't new, the self-doubt. She'd failed. It made her wonder about every decision now. *I just want the pain to end, Lord.*

Rae turned away from the window. It felt like the rest of her life was going to be restitution for something she still didn't know how she could have prevented.

Eventually the memories would fade, but they were raw now, and quick to reappear in the silent slices of her life. Filling that silence in the days ahead would be a matter of survival she thought, and the idea of burying herself back in work of some kind was a welcome one, for the silence would be her own judge and jury if she gave it space.

She tossed pillows against the headboard and picked up the phone, determined to start filling in the blanks of her new life. While she listened to it ring, she opened her soda and then stretched the phone cord and picked up her briefcase. Her cousin answered.

"Frank, it's Rae. I'm in the state. I stopped off at Justice."

"It's good to hear your voice and have you nearly home."

"I think I'll settle in here and talk to Bruce first, before I come up to see your dad. Is Matt around?"

"You just missed him. A guy used a shotgun to kill his boss before turning it on himself; it's an awful mess. The cops are releasing the scene this afternoon. I'm just finishing packing up the van to go join him. Want me to have him call you?"

"Sure." She pulled over the phone to read off the direct number. "If we end up playing phone tag, just let him know I'll be there for dinner Monday as planned."

"I will. It will be good to see you, Rae."

"Same here. I'll see you soon, Frank."

Rae hung up the phone. A murder/suicide. Working with her uncle even part time was going to be a heavy task.

She thought about a nap but the desire for a good meal was stronger. She pocketed her keys, license, and cash and headed out to explore her new town.

4

The Chapel Detective Agency II was quiet, the receptionist desk empty. Nathan followed Bruce down the back hall. His friend retrieved the phone slips tucked in the doorframe, unlocked his office, and turned on the lights inside. "Come on in. I'll find the tape of Kyle shooting his mouth off about what he was going to do."

Nathan dropped his jacket across the chair. "I guess I was wrong about the prospective client. Or is one of those phone slips from a lady?"

Bruce picked up the note on his desk and smiled. "Relax. She's been here. And she's not a client."

"Rae Gabriella?"

"Yes."

Nathan stretched out on the couch, avoiding the one hard spring that tended to dig into his left shoulder, and wished he had twenty minutes to close his eyes and catch a catnap. It was hard to set aside the job and stretch out on the couch in his own office when the men he commanded were right outside his door.

"If she's not a client, who is she?" Nathan remembered blue eyes and a nice voice and long dark hair pulled back by a silver ribbon. The clothes had been expensive, and the wristwatch high priced. The lady struck him as a bit above both of them for class.

"An old friend and hopefully my new partner. I need your help to move the last of the boxes out of the next room and up to the attic. It's going to be her office."

Nathan lifted his head to turn and look at his friend. "You're serious?" He hadn't seen this ground shift coming. "When did you start thinking about a partner?"

"About the time I took the case for Mrs. Breck and stood out like a sore thumb trying to keep track of her attending the women's bridge club meetings. Rae's a good cop; she'll be an asset to this place." Bruce slid his hand into a sided file folder and pulled out a small cassette tape. "Kyle's eloquence, captured for all to hear."

Nathan accepted the tape and the report, wishing Bruce would stay on the subject of Rae Gabriella a while longer. "How's the tape quality?"

"I was wearing a mike in a crowded bar. The conversation is buried in the mud, but it's there. A competent sound guy should be able to clean it up." Bruce wiped the case off his whiteboard.

Nathan read the report, wishing his own officers were as concise in what they wrote. Bruce had identified Kyle's new job, residence, and drinking buddies and done it with swift efficiency. When you could pay for information, life did get simpler. Not for the first time Nathan wondered if being a private investigator was as liberating as it appeared to be from the outside.

"Rae will need a carry permit."

Nathan glanced up from the report. "It will take some time."

"I'd appreciate it if you would expedite it."

"Any particular reason? Is there trouble you know about?"

"She's been working for the FBI for longer than I care to think about and with that innocent-looking face of hers, most of the time has been spent working undercover. I'd rather not take chances. Rae's kind of like your grandfather; she keeps her own counsel. I'll get you her prints and background paperwork and her last shooting qualification date."

"That will help. I'll see what I can do," Nathan promised. He studied the whiteboard. "Speaking of my grandfather, has anything turned up?"

"No."

"He bought that car for cash; it had to come from somewhere. There isn't a life-insurance policy that got cashed in or some bonds?"

"Not that I can find. Why don't you just ask him where the money came from?"

"I have. He says, 'Sonny, you should mind your own business.'"

Bruce smiled. "Annoying, isn't it? I'll keep looking. I think the car dealer knows more than what he's saying, and I'll eventually find something I can use as leverage to get him to tell me what he knows."

"I hate spying on family."

"Which is why you have me." Bruce picked up the phone. "I'm going to track Rae down. Do you want to join us for a late lunch?"

Nathan looked at the clock and groaned, then sat up. "I'd love to, but I'm pressed for time. I was supposed to be somewhere ten minutes ago."

"I'll tell her you said hello."

"Do that." Nathan tugged on his coat. "I gave her a speeding ticket the first time I met her."

"How bad?"

"Sixty-five."

"She'll get over it."

That was easy for Bruce to say. Nathan enjoyed working with Bruce, even if they did sometimes find themselves at cross purposes when a police investigation and one of Bruce's client's interests overlapped. Nathan thought he'd enjoy working with Rae too if given the chance, but he was hardly off to a good start with her. "What hotel is she staying at?"

"The Sunburst. She likes to read the East Coast newspapers in the morning."

"Thanks."

"Hey, you two have to get along. I'll be sending her to do the diplomatic work like getting license plates run and tugging police reports out of you." Bruce lifted a hand in farewell and turned his attention to the phone call, asking for Rae's hotel room.

Nathan made a mental note to make sure he introduced Rae to his chief assistant. Most of Bruce's requests were answered with a no, but it would definitely be an improvement having Rae Gabriella do the asking. Nathan turned up his jacket collar as he stepped outside.

He held down the transmit button on his radio as he unlocked his car. "55-J, 10-98. Mark me 10-7 to the union hall."

"10-4."

If he managed to get to the paperwork on his desk before the late-night news came on he would be surprised. Former FBI moving into his town—it would at least generate a new topic of conversation at the café once word of Rae's arrival spread.

§◊§   §◊§   §◊§

Rae saw picket signs as she passed the town's city hall. She didn't see many of those on the East Coast; the sidewalks and roads were too crowded and the unions not as robust.

At the stop sign she rolled down her window. A striker on the picket line stepped over. His gloves were frayed and his jacket zipped against the elements; the cold had chapped his exposed skin suggesting the man had been outside for a couple hours. "I'm new to town. Where's the best place to eat a late lunch?"

"There's a little diner over on Franklin Road that has great steaks and fries; for hot chili the place to go is the Chili Den. There are also a couple pizza places that are worth a visit."

"How about directions to the diner?"

He motioned to the next streetlight. "Take a right at the stoplight, two blocks will be Franklin, and you'll want to go north half a mile. The M&T Diner—it stands for Mabel and Tom—is tucked in beside Sir Arthur's. Be sure to try the onion rings."

"Thanks." She nodded to the picket signs. "How long has the strike been going on?"

"Fifteen days."

She read the stitching on his jacket, *Mark Yates*. "What do you do at the tile plant, Mr. Yates?"

"Control the firing temperature for the tiles. Do the first oven walk-in to see how they baked."

She could see the aged scars on his calloused hands. The man was old enough to be her father and she liked him for no reason other than he had a nice voice and smile and took time to chat with a stranger. "If you stop by the diner later, there'll be a cup of coffee waiting with my thanks. You've got a cold day for walking the picket line."

"If I happen to see you there, I'll buy you a piece of Mabel's famous pie."

They shared a smile.

She followed the directions he gave. She found a parking place down the street and walked back to the M&T Diner. She stepped inside and was welcomed with the smell of warm bread, french fries, and the yeasty smell of donuts.

The sign said *Welcome. Take a menu and seat yourself. A waitress will find you.*

Rae took a laminated menu several pages thick from the stand and scanned the seating options. The food must be good for the late-lunch crowd was heavy.

She waded into the mix of men in work boots, jeans, and heavy jackets draped over the chairs; of women in groups of two and three crowding around small tables.

A waitress met her with a smile and pointed to a back table. "There's a relatively quiet table that's open in back, or if you want to chat strike politics you can sit at the counter where the guys are debating things. We're always like this on a Saturday."

Rae smiled back. "Thanks, I'll take the table." She slipped the waitress a folded five-dollar bill as an early tip. "While I scan the menu, would you bring me a cold Coke and keep the refills coming?"

"I'll be glad to."

Rae walked back to the table.

ജ   ജ   ജ

Nathan noticed the Lexus with Washington, D.C., plates parked down the street from the M&T Diner. Rae Gabriella was either exceptionally lucky or a piece of good advice had led her to one of the best restaurants around.

He debated stopping in for coffee to say hi to her and hear what the guys were saying about the contract talk breakdown, but those discussions would be better had at the union hall where the rank and file were free to say what they wanted without it becoming a community discussion. Nathan drove on.

The union hall was beside the VFW hall, in what Nathan thought of as the civics corner of Justice, for it was next to the old courthouse that now served as the county-records depository. Nathan pulled into the union-hall parking lot, squeezing in between two trucks.

Three men were loading picket signs in the back of a pickup truck. Nathan lifted a hand in greeting but didn't pause.

The union men saw this as a life-and-death struggle for their future and for every one of them the outcome of this strike was critical. That kind of lack of control over their own future worried Nathan, for they were proud, hardworking men, and without a job, anger and despair would set in. And that was a bad recipe for the officers who were charged with trying to keep the peace in this town.

Nathan scanned the tables set up in the union hall looking for Larry Sikes, the number two man at the union, who had direct responsibility for membership and morale.

"Nathan, come over and join us."

He changed directions toward the back table where a group of guys were eating lunch—hot dogs and potato chips and take-out bowls of chili from the Chili Den. The old guards were here, the men who had worked at the tile plant for twenty-plus years.

Nathan slapped shoulders in welcome and greeted the men with a smile. These were the ones who would keep the others settled and balanced. "How's everyone doing?"

"On this beautiful day, we're doing just fine. Your dad was by earlier, playing checkers and talking baseball."

"I can always count on him to know the inside scoop on things."

"Are you over here to tamp down trouble, or here to stir it up?"

Nathan laughed and helped himself to a hot dog. "Martin, you know trouble just seems to come my way on its own. So what's the biggest issue under discussion today?"

"It's a tough one, Nathan," Lewis replied, joining the conversation. "For the last three years, the company has paid half the costs for prescriptions filled at the local pharmacy. Management is threatening to stop the payments for anyone who doesn't cross the strike line."

"And those who immediately need the prescription-cost help are either ill or have family members who are ill," Nathan finished for Lewis, finding the hot dog hard to swallow as the implications registered.

"Of all the threats they could put down, this one strikes at the most vulnerable among the union membership," Martin said.

"It's just words so far. Maybe they won't do it," Jim added.

"Then they should stop threatening to do it. It's cruel," Martin insisted.

Nathan nodded, agreeing with Martin. "I'll make sure that message is passed on when I see Zachary," he offered, knowing he would see the chief management negotiator in the morning.

"It's got to be coming down from headquarters to him, for there is no way Zachary would be for this move. His brother is one of the guys on strike and he's diabetic. Zachary knows what this would do to the family finances."

"I agree; it's not like Zach." Nathan raised a hand in greeting as he spotted Larry Sikes coming through from the office. "I appreciate the update. Let me talk with Larry about it a bit."

"How's it going, my friend?" Nathan offered his hand, and Larry took it. They had gone to high school together and had been both track rivals and basketball teammates.

"Are you getting any more sleep than I am?" Larry asked.

"Probably not much."

Larry motioned to the office. They walked back to where they could talk in privacy.

"Is this suspension of prescription payments a serious threat?" Nathan asked.

"Adam thinks so. The strike is over health-care issues and management knows it's a key place to apply pressure. We could probably make acceptance of a deal contingent on them making up the payments they owed, but in the meantime members will have to come up with the money out of their own pockets and we're already seeing the first mortgage payments missed."

Nathan settled into a chair and stretched out his legs. He turned his left foot slightly to see the bottom of his boot. He'd walked through some dog droppings somewhere and crushed a few dead leaves into the goo. It matched the kind of day it had been. "Does the union have contingencies in place?"

"We've got some reserve funds, but they won't last long. Walter Sr. was over this morning to give us some numbers—how many prescriptions the current union membership has with his pharmacy, what kind of costs the company has paid out in the last two months. If the union has to make up that payment, he's offered to cut his costs as low as he can, but there are only so many days he can carry the debt before the pharmacy also runs into cash-flow problems."

"We can't lose the only pharmacy in town. And those who are sick need the prescriptions filled without a delay." Nathan leaned his head back and looked at the ceiling. "This is a mess."

"Tell me about it. Does the company still want to have a tile plant in this town? That's what it's coming down to, Nathan. Adam thinks the conglomerate is ready to use the strike as a reason to get out of the slow-margin-growth tile business and simply shutter the plant. They can't make up their mind on that question, so the negotiations go in circles. We're not far apart. If they wanted a deal, there would be one with about twelve hours of negotiating the language."

"How many days can the union carry the costs if they do hold back the matching funds?"

"Two, maybe three weeks, and that's optimistic," Larry replied. "That's my day, so what's on yours?"

"My budget is stretched to the edge of what the town can afford; the overtime is killing me. Would you be willing to reduce the number of guys on the picket lines Sunday, so I can give one of my guys an afternoon off? Some of them haven't had a day off since before this strike began."

Larry slid a pencil through his fingers from the tip to the eraser and back again. "What if we suspend the picket line downtown and have men walking only at the plant?"

Nathan scraped at dirt under his thumbnail, thinking about it. Larry would take some heat from the rank and file for making the offer. "It would let me give two men the day off."

"Done. We'll call the picket line at nine tonight and pick it up again at 7 a.m. Monday."

Nathan leaned forward and offered his hand. "Thanks."

"Today it feels good to have any decent agreement on which to shake hands."

"Did you get a chance to take Marla out for her birthday?"

Larry smiled. "We went out for Chinese, and she got a fortune cookie saying Happy Birthday. It made her day; personally I had heartburn from eating the pork."

Nathan smiled as he got to his feet. "She loves you, man."

"I know it."

"I'll see you tomorrow, Larry."

౷౩   ౷౩   ౷౩

Rae listened to the conversations flowing around her in the diner, putting faces together with voices and topics that concerned them. The couple by the window were talking about their grandson, the table of three to her left were discussing where to go skiing next weekend, and the rest immediately around her seemed to be talking about different issues surrounding the strike.

So who in this diner might make a good neighbor? She studied those around the restaurant as she ate.

Safe neighborhoods were nice, but people who lived in safe neighborhoods rarely knew anything useful about what was going on in the town. She preferred to call neighbors those who had a friend or relative who had brushed through trouble with the law, for it was there that a pipeline of useful information flowed.

Families affected by crime cared a lot about stopping it, but they were not always willing to talk directly to the police, making it fertile grounds for her and a stack of agency business cards.

"Rae Gabriella, you are hard to track down." Bruce pulled out a chair across from her at the table. "I heard a rumor that you were in town, got to my office, and found the proof."

She looked up and bit the inside of her cheek to stop herself from reacting to the fact that someone had beat him up and recently. It had to have been a polar bear of a guy to get past Bruce's head-snapping right hook.

"A hotel room is not a place I like to hang out." She accepted the ring of keys Bruce held out. The back of his hand looked bruised, so he'd given some of what he had received.

"Your new office key is the blue-tabbed one, not that you'll need it."

She smiled at the quiet dig and pulled out her own ring of keys to add them to.

"Couldn't sleep?" Bruce asked.

"I'll catch a nap later."

He helped himself to one of the remaining onion rings.

She returned her attention to her lunch. "This steak is as good as advertised."

"Everything here is good, especially the cheeseburgers. How was the trip?"

"It was nice to have the time to think. Are you going to explain that face, or should I guess?"

"A restraining order needed to be enforced and I was the closest when it came time to do it."

"It looks like it hurts."

Bruce smiled. "Only when I smile. I've closed up the office for the day. Would you like to look at housing or take a drive around town? I'm yours for the afternoon."

"Actually, you're just in time to join me for dessert. I want a slice of choco- late cream pie. Let's go to the Dessert Palace."

Rae reached for her cash, taking advantage of the fact that Bruce had just given her an excuse to move them out of here. The lady at the next table over had just angled her chair to make it easier for her to overhear their conversation. The teenagers had started whispering, and one was craning her neck to see Bruce. Her friend was a bit radioactive at the moment. This was probably not the place to talk details of her job or the cases Bruce was working on.

"The Dessert Palace is more than an hour north of Chicago."

"Yes. So?" She slid bills to pay for dinner onto the tray with the ticket and left a large tip on the table. "I'm driving."

Bruce laughed. He got up and picked up his jacket. "You haven't changed, Gabriella. I'm getting the lemon meringue, and when my blood sugar goes high enough to kill me, I'm blaming it on you."

"Can we take your Jaguar?"

"After the snow clears you can have a set of keys. Until then, we rough it in yours or take my Caprice."

"I'm upgrading the Lexus to something with less miles on it just as soon as I get settled in here. I didn't want to pay the district tax."

Rae picked up a toothpick at the counter and a copy of the free town advertiser in order to read the ads later. She pushed open the door. She pointed to her car and dug the keys out of her pocket.

"It's going to take a while to adjust to a small town where everyone listens in. You were getting a lot of attention back there and speculation about that bruised face."

"You'll get use to the attention. The best defense is to never explain; they add to the facts anyway."

Rae drove at the speed limit through town and turned toward the highway. "So what do you see me doing this next week and month?"

"Whatever interests you. This is a job, Rae, but it's also a slice of freedom. You can acquire your own cases or share the work on mine. We'll be partners all the way down the line. I figure it will take a couple weeks for you to decide on housing and get an office up and put together. Your work with your uncle is going to be event driven, so we'll let that govern how you split your time during the week."

"They've got a murder/suicide cleanup to deal with; I figured I would join them Monday to help out."

"All I ask is that you carry a good cell phone so I can find you."

"I turn it off when I'm having an interesting discussion with someone."

"I remember. I can shout at your voice mail."

She laughed and sorted out change for use later on the toll roads around Chicago. "It's good to be back, Bruce." There was something so comforting about the oldest of friends. For the first time in months she was with a friend she knew cared more about her than a case outcome. And there was something refreshing knowing Bruce had already encountered most of her bad habits, and would be more amused than offended when they inevitably reappeared.

"I'm glad you decided to say yes. I've missed having a partner who can talk through the cases, debate the details, and keep me company when the stakeouts last all hours. You're going to let me pick up the tab for really nice office furniture too and not fuss about it."

"That kind of welcome gift I'll accept." And it fit his nature; he was generous with his friends.

Rae glanced over at him. In years past she had been able to read him, but it was a skill she would need to reacquire. She felt a sudden uncertainty, that the gap between what she was certain of with him and what would have to be rediscovered after eleven years apart, might be vastly wider than she realized. People changed. Not allowing for that would be devastating if they took a misstep. "Bruce, one caveat? For now, it's just business."

Bruce just smiled. "Noted. Give me a few months to catch up on your last eleven years and then I'll think about changing your mind."

She wondered if when he knew the details, if he would still be of that mindset. He had an image in his mind that was frozen from years ago, and so much about her had changed in those years. Maybe not in appearance, in habits, or in the memories they shared, but inside—she was nothing like the lady he remembered. She knew the changes had gone too deep in how she saw things in the world around her. Too many betrayals and hurts and failures had left their scars. The optimist he remembered had died a long time ago. "I hope you're not disappointed with what you find."

"I won't be," he reassured.

She studied the road and traffic ahead of them and smiled. That self-confidence fit what she remembered. He probably hadn't changed as much as she had, which was a good thing.

5

Rae strapped on her watch and reached for her worn tennis shoes. This hotel had to have some sort of exercise room with a treadmill or bike. She shoved her room key into her pocket, picked up a large white hotel towel, and went to explore.

She'd turned down Bruce's offer of company tonight, thinking she would catch a nap, watch some TV, and make it an early night after a long day of traveling. A two-hour nap had taken care of the desire for sleep, there was nothing on TV, and she was bored. Staying in the hotel room was not a workable option.

She found the workout room on the first floor just past housekeeping. The one occupant, a lady Rae recognized by sight as having a room a few doors down from her own, was walking at a fast clip on the treadmill.

Rae set the tension wheel on the stationary bike and cleared the mileage counter.

"Do you happen to have the time? The wall clock's dead."

Rae looked at her watch. "Seven twenty-two."

"Thanks. I've got a late-night movie date."

Rae settled into a smooth pace on the bike. "What's playing these days?"

"We're going to go see *Holiday Park* with James Roberts. I heard it was good. If not, at least Roberts is cute."

"I'll agree with that." Rae slowly increased her cadence.

"Do you happen to know Joe Prescott?"

"The name isn't familiar," Rae replied, paying a bit more attention to the lady on the treadmill, as it became obvious she was looking for some conversation.

She was in her late twenties, in good shape. Her workout clothes were plain, but the jacket draped over the chair had a logo on the pocket from a gym Rae recognized as one that marketed itself as the LA gym of the stars.

"I know he lives somewhere near Justice but I haven't been able to locate him."

"I've met only a handful of town residents, but it strikes me that most know each other. Maybe someone at the café can help."

"I think word is out that I'm a reporter; they don't say much when I start asking questions."

If she had realized it, she would have probably done less talking as well. "You work for the local paper?"

"I'm freelance with the *Chicago Daily Times* and the *National Weekly News*." The lady slowed the treadmill pace. "Five miles. That's plenty. Have you tried the hotel sauna?"

"They have one?"

"Down past the pool. I'm going to risk it."

"I hope the movie turns out to be good."

"So do I. First dates tend to be unpredictable."

Rae understood exactly what she meant and shared a smile. The lady left.

Rae did fifteen minutes at a brisk pace on the bike and then slowed to cool down. She thought about visiting the sauna, but she wasn't that desperate to talk to someone to want to search out a reporter. She returned to her hotel room.

A shower helped kill another twenty minutes of her evening. As Rae paced the hotel room towel drying her hair, she flipped through the channels on the TV again.

It was after 8 p.m. on a Saturday night; there was nothing on TV worth her time, and while she wasn't lonely, the emotions were flittering just below the surface. She needed conversation and people and something happening around her. She tossed the remote back on the bed. She picked up her room key, cash, and a book.

The best way to understand a town was at night, when some of the surface clutter of businesses and shoppers faded away and most people were at home. Finding out what the nightlife was like would help her understand the pace of the town. She took the stairs down three flights and exited through the south doorway into the parking lot.

It was a cold night, but the wind was calm. Rae left her car in the hotel parking lot and walked across the street, retracing the way she had come through town earlier that day.

She headed toward the M&T Diner. She didn't know how late it stayed open, but there had been a place next door to it that had also looked interesting. The lit sign had said Sir Arthur's, and there had been a suit of armor visible through the tinted window.

Where did the cops in this town hang out when they were off duty? That would be an interesting place to find.

Rae crossed streets void of any traffic and others that were busy. She noted streetlights and alleyways. Soldiers called it reconnaissance. Cops called it patrol. She called it being smart. She very much wanted to start this job with her feet on the ground, knowing the territory and the people who lived here.

The white-collar-business guy who might drain a company pension fund, or snap and murder his wife, tended to go home every night. It was the guys who swiped wallets, did petty burglaries, had short tempers, and got into fights, who would hang out late on a Saturday night at a local establishment. She needed a network of people in that group who would talk to her about what they heard. The faster she had that network identified the better off she would be.

Rae opened the door to Sir Arthur's, stood for a moment absorbing the music and the movements of people and with a smile walked inside. She'd spent a lot of time in such places over the years for they provided a convenient place to meet her FBI handler and pass along information. If she could get someone to take her up on a game of pool, she'd be right back in her comfort zone.

ⓖ ⓖ ⓖ

Nathan spotted the town's new resident sitting at a round table to the left of the jukebox at Sir Arthur's. He stopped. Rae's car hadn't been in the lot; he'd scanned license plates out of habit as he found a place to park. A small pile of peanut shells on the bread plate suggested she'd been here awhile.

Nathan looked around the room. He was on the prowl to find his mother. His report for the city council meeting was finally done and the lobbying to protect his budget was just beginning. She said she'd be over here to chat with the town's fire chief, but Nathan didn't see them. He changed his plans. He could pass on the report in the morning.

Rae was reading a book in a pub full of people. That piqued his interest, for in this group were several whom he knew would have taken a moment to stop by her table and say hello once they saw she was alone. She must have politely turned them all down. Nathan pocketed his gloves in his leather jacket and maneuvered through the crowd toward Rae's table.

Rae slid out a chair for him with her foot without looking up. He changed his opinion of how aware she was of the room. He draped his jacket over the back. "Is it a good book?"

"My grandmother gave it to me and since I'm going to visit her tomorrow, I figured I ought to be able to say I actually read it."

He smiled as he sat down. "Which ducks the question I asked."

"I'm not into flowery historical prose. But the underlying true crime is interesting." She marked her page and closed the book. She looked directly at him for the first time. Her blue eyes caught his attention again, for they were beautiful in their clarity. "You look tired, Sheriff."

"Make it Nathan? I'm finally off duty."

"Nathan it is." She raised her hand, caught the waitress's attention, and held up two fingers.

"What are we drinking?"

"Hot tea and honey, because I like it, and because if you don't start babying that hoarse voice, you're not going to have it tomorrow."

He nodded at the practical assertion. "We'll see if it works. I've got six ten-year-old boys in my Sunday school class; I'll need more than a whisper." He picked up a laminated sheet from the stand and thought about an appetizer from the diner next door to go with the drink. "I see you've found our town hangout. Were you also able to find Bruce?"

"I did."

"He didn't start the fight."

Rae laughed. "I've known Bruce a long time; I imagine he didn't avoid it either." She leaned closer and confided, "He used to be better at ducking."

She did indeed know Bruce well. "Am I by any chance stepping on his toes by sitting here?"

If they were involved, he would keep his distance out of respect for the friendship he had with Bruce. But if they weren't . . . this town didn't get many single ladies his age moving into town. A lady who understood his profession was a rarity, let alone one with a smile that made a man want to smile back.

"Bruce and I dated seriously eleven years ago. Now is an open question."

Nathan remembered Bruce's comments this afternoon; his friend wanted to revive the relationship. But eleven years—Nathan wavered on whether he should concede to his friend before he even made an effort to get to know Rae. A statute of limitations should apply. And tonight the idea of getting to know her better appealed to him a great deal. "That's good to hear."

Rae smiled back but let the remark pass.

The waitress brought over their drinks in heavy mugs and Nathan ordered a basket of onion rings from next door. "Are you settled okay at the Sunburst Hotel? I saw your Lexus there when I made rounds this evening."

"It's a comfortable place, a newer hotel than I expected to find in town."

"We have a good amount of tourism. The Amish community, botanical gardens, Lincoln museum, the old Indian trading post—they are all within twenty miles of Justice." He stopped his answer. "Sorry. I sound like the tourism director."

"Your name is on the town; I figure you have a vested interest in seeing it prosper."

"I do. And the name is both a blessing and a liability. Rae Gabriella—I'm guessing Spanish is in your background, maybe Italian. Am I close?"

"Yes to both." She rested her chin on her fist. "You're English? Scandinavian?"

"Probably both. If I go back four great-grandparents or so, a Neil Justice arrived in this area and started a trading post here in the 1800s. Legend has it he was a gunman who served in the army, was dishonorably discharged, and started working for the highest bidder. When those kinds of stories pass through the generations, it doesn't inspire a lot of interest in tracing genealogies."

"A case of too much family?"

"In this town, I never get away from family." And given the status of things with his grandfather, he'd rather stay off the subject.

Nathan worked on the hot drink as his conversation with Rae drifted through nonconsequential topics. He ignored the amused glances from friends who saw him chatting with her, but who were wise enough not to wander over and interrupt.

He remembered what he'd thought early he needed to tell her. "Bruce asked if I'd arrange a carry permit for you. You'll need to stop by and sign some paperwork at the office, but it should be ready by Tuesday."

"Thanks. Is there a shooting range in town?"

"At the old concrete factory, the manufacturing floor has been turned into an indoor shooting range for the department. You're welcome to use it once you have the carry permit; you just need to pick up your own brass."

His order of onion rings arrived.

Nathan waited to see where Rae wanted to take the conversation, but she didn't offer a topic. Bruce had said she had worked undercover and Nathan bet that was where she had learned to listen like this, to make the other person desire to talk just to break the silence.

He smiled slightly at her and obliged with another question. "Bruce said you've been with the FBI for a long time. Why the change to join a private firm?"

"Bruce asked me."

Nathan waited for more, but she offered nothing more. It probably was that simple when it came right down to it. "I'm glad you said yes."

"I expect I'll learn to enjoy the work; it will certainly have a different pace to it." Her expression opened up. "Do you play pool? I'm two-for-three tonight. I'm a bit rusty."

Nathan picked up the basket of onion rings and rose. "The third table is my home away from home. I'll play you for who buys dessert."

"Deal."

Nathan watched Rae rack the balls solid-stripe-solid and roll the group to the center dot with a brisk snap. In her actions she was precise and quick. He wished she was as easy to read overall. She liked being alone with her thoughts.

Part of him really liked the mystery that presented, but he was very aware how tight his schedule would be over the next weeks until the strike and its aftermath were settled; time was precious and turning this from acquaintances to friends didn't look like a simple endeavor.

He slipped his friend Ben a folded ten-dollar bill and whispered another request; the young man watching their game rose from his chair and headed toward the M&T Diner.

"Another order?"

"Potato skins are coming next."

Rae looked past him, her eyes narrowing and her attention locking in on something for several seconds, and then she relaxed and looked back at her task.

Nathan glanced around but saw no one out of place in the crowd. Saturday nights at Sir Arthur's stayed pretty packed and tonight was no exception. He was beginning to suspect she had worked undercover so long she didn't know how to turn off the caution when she was in a crowd.

He wanted to tell her all was fine, but she didn't know him well enough to take his word for it.

She rolled the cue ball to him. "Your break."

He obliged and placed the cue ball. Hefting the pool stick in his hand to the balance point, he braced his fingers on the cloth. He struck the cue ball and pocketed a solid and a stripe on the break. "Solids." He set out to do his best to run the table.

Rae leaned against a post and watched him, slowly eating a handful of pretzels. "Do you ever miss?"

"Not if I can help it."

He pocketed the six ball. Most cops eventually brought the conversation around to talk about work, for it was a common language with another cop. Rae never brought up the subject. He'd been probing all evening.

He'd known Bruce for over a year before he learned he'd spent most of his career working undercover focusing on the wholesale drug dealers working out of the south side of Chicago. It looked like Rae was going to be equally hard to crack. "Did you chase counterfeiters?"

"That would be Secret Service, not the bureau."

"Bank robbers?"

"That fun was reserved for agents more senior than I."

He was running out of suggestions. "I bet you weren't giving out parking tickets."

She picked up one of his onion rings. "I was probably watching one of you give them out."

"You've done a lot of stakeouts?"

"It helps if you bring gum that keeps its flavor." She stepped forward as he missed the seven ball and set out to run the table in reply. When she missed the twelve ball, she set aside her pool stick and drank her refilled tea, then absently rubbed her right arm as she watched him try again to pocket the seven ball.

"What happened?"

"What?"

He didn't like the look of that scar. "Your arm. That cut looks defensive."

She looked down at where she was rubbing. "Blocking a knife does that. It itches like crazy."

A knife . . . it was a wonder she had use of that hand if the blade had hit as it appeared, striking deep into the muscle of her arm. "You should talk to Walter at the pharmacy; he could patent the cream he has for sunburns. He probably has something that will deal with an intense itch."

"I may do that."

"What happened that led to the knife fight?"

She finished her tea and picked up her pool stick. "A friend got upset. I'd rather not talk about it, Nathan."

"Fair enough, but answer a question first. Is he likely to show up here in Justice and cause problems?"

She took so long to answer he wondered if she would. "He's dead."

Nathan accepted reality. Her expression had closed; the urgent questions he now had would not be getting answered. He raised a hand and caught the waitress's attention, signaled for two more refills for their tea. "You're up two to one; let's see if I can even out the score with the next game."

Ben came back through the crowd carrying a large plate, and Rae shook off the sadness to smile at the young man, causing Ben to blush just a bit. "Just what did he order?"

"Jumbos," Ben mumbled.

"I can tell."

"I haven't had dinner yet," Nathan added mildly.

"Now you have."

Nathan held open the door at Sir Arthur's for Rae, aware it was past midnight and he was pleasantly tired. He'd forgotten the strike, let go the urgency of the budget crisis, let dinner be hors d'oeuvre eaten between turns with the pool cue. He hadn't had such a relaxing night in weeks. "I'm surprised Bruce didn't join us tonight."

"If he's smart, Bruce is probably soaking his sore ribs," Rae replied, shifting her book to under her arm so she could tug on her gloves. "I enjoyed tonight."

"So did I. Let me give you a lift back to the hotel."

"There's no need. I haven't been surprised by trouble during a walk at night in years."

"It's still my town." Nathan tugged on his own gloves, content to walk with her.

"Are your nights often like this? A steady stream of people with requests and information they think you should know?"

Nathan looked over at her, curious as to what she had noticed. "Were there that many requests?"

"A cow that keeps getting out is police business?"

"The cow is a few hundred pounds of stubbornness and it belongs to my mom, Linda Justice. We fix the fencing; the animal just leans against a post of her choice until the fence goes down again. If the strike hadn't interrupted my plans, I would have been replacing a few posts this weekend."

"Okay, I buy the cow is a special case. The lady with the cracked dining-room window?"

"One of my Sunday school boys caused it. So tomorrow I'll be arranging an apology from him and an agreement that will satisfy Mrs. Remstein regarding her window."

"The missing petty cash at the library?"

"I see your point. I do hang out somewhere easy to find on weekend nights so people can tell me what is going on. So yes, this night is typical. It's part of being elected sheriff. They vote for you; you work for them."

"I think it's nice."

Her quiet words of praise made him smile. He did try hard to be accessible to folks in town and it wasn't often people noticed, for it was just expected now. "Thanks. And just FYI—if you ever need to pass on news, don't wait for a weekend. Pick up the phone."

Rae laughed. "I'll keep that in mind."

They walked to the hotel, a comfortable silence between them. They crossed the last strip of grass and stepped into the hotel parking lot.

"The strike has me working some odd shifts, but if you have a free evening this week that works out, I'd like a rematch at the pool table," Nathan offered.

"I'd like that too." She dug out her hotel-room key. "I appreciate your time tonight, Nathan. It was a nice welcome."

"Anytime, Rae. Sleep well."

※   ※   ※

Rae dropped her book and room key on the dresser beside her things, comfortably tired. Sleep would come now.

Nathan was good company. He was going to be asking more questions about her past than she was comfortable with, but there was no way to avoid them. She just had to resolve how much she wanted to say about those days.

The message light on her phone was blinking. Rae dialed the front desk for the message. A fax had arrived for her. "I'll be down in a moment."

She picked up her room key and went downstairs again.

The cover page of the fax was from her former boss. Knowing it was being sent by a public fax, he'd kept the note general. They had found a bank safe-deposit box belonging to Mark Rivers. There were several pictures of her with him. Would she contact him at her earliest convenience? They could either be destroyed or sent on to her.

That Mark had kept photos didn't surprise or concern her; that he'd thought them important enough to put into a bank safe box did. She'd have to think about this before she answered. Rae returned to her room and added the fax to her briefcase to follow up on Monday.

What was she going to wear to church in the morning? She shifted hangers, looking for something pretty and yet simple. Her attendance at her local church in Washington, D.C., had been sporadic due to the undercover assignment. She was determined to change that now.

This last year had rocked so much of what she thought about God. She had to start rebuilding that relationship somewhere. She would start with finding a new church home.

Nathan had mentioned he taught Sunday school, but she hadn't thought to ask which church he attended. She hoped Bruce had begun attending church, but she wasn't going to call at this hour of the night to ask.

She found the phone book. The town had four churches with yellow page ads. All the ads welcomed families, mentioned free coffee and said services started at eight, with First Catholic also saying ten. It was a town that liked to get up early.

No matter which church she chose, she'd have to endure standing out as a stranger, for she doubted there would be more than a handful of visitors. She studied the directions for the Justice Christian Church and then closed the phone book. It wasn't going to be an easy morning, but it was necessary.

Rae set her alarm clock for six-thirty. A knock on the door interrupted her.

It was late for a visitor. She peered through the security hole, saw the manager who had checked her in that afternoon standing in the hall, and opened the door. "Yes?"

"Ms. Gabriella, I apologize for the hour. I was asked if we would deliver these when you returned, no matter what the hour." A clerk joined him carrying a huge bouquet of roses.

"Oh, my." She pushed open the door and took the vase, counting more than two dozen roses. "Please, give me a moment to get my purse. I appreciate the trouble you both took." She thanked them both generously.

Rae closed the door with her foot and carried the vase of roses over to the dresser. They were absolutely gorgeous against a sea of green. Perfect deep red roses in the winter—someone had gone to a lot of trouble. She pulled out the card, suspecting Bruce was following his own plan for how to welcome her to Justice. She opened the envelope. *Welcome to Justice, Rae. Nathan.*

She blinked. Nathan.

She smiled. He'd just spent much more on the roses than she would on the speeding ticket. She read the card again and slid it back in the bouquet of roses. It had been a long time since someone sent her roses. She drew one of the roses toward her. A nice welcome message, as well as being a spot of beauty in the winter. She'd remember them to his favor.

6

Cars crowded the parking lot of the Justice Christian Church and people had begun parking on the side streets. It had snowed overnight. Rae didn't want to be walking far in these shoes. She found a parking place behind a red Toyota on a side street within sight of the church building and picked up her Bible and her purse.

She joined others walking toward the building, aware her nerves were stretched tight this morning.

How much did she want to say when someone said hello and struck up a conversation? She wanted to make a good impression and the truth had so many layers to the full story.

Did she want to talk about D.C. and the FBI or simply focus on the fact that she was new to town and would be working with Bruce? How much did she want to say about her history with Bruce and how she knew him? She'd be most comfortable hiding behind the safety her connection to Bruce provided her, and the fact that they were good friends. She wasn't above using his relationships with folks in town to smooth her own introductions into the community. Her life would be so much easier right now if she had chosen to be a homemaker rather than a cop.

She slowed. Nathan was across the street, heading away from the church at a fast clip. She watched him tug off one glove and pull out keys from his pocket. Headlights flashed on a Mercury Sable. Rae remembered him mentioning he had a Sunday school class to teach, yet he was leaving in a hurry. Where was he going? As he pulled away from the curb he reached out and put a canister light on the roof. Police business.

She stopped. She wavered on the decision and then turned around. She walked back to her car and got in, set her Bible and purse on the passenger seat, and started her car.

She didn't plan to spend her next months chasing ambulances or cops, monitoring scanners, or otherwise being a police groupie, but she did have a fine sense of priorities. Something was wrong.

With the strike Rae knew the Justice Police Department was stretched very thin. There was always a possibility that another pair of hands would make the difference between a good outcome and bad. She was still a cop in her heart. There were church services tonight; she could come back.

Rae followed Nathan.

⋯ ⋯ ⋯

Nathan followed the Sunburst Hotel manager down the hall to room 3712. The first responder to the scene stood before the closed door.

Several guests were clustered out in the hall watching what was going on. Nathan didn't need them hearing the report or seeing this scene. "Sergeant, close off this wing of the hall and task the arriving officers for the perimeter; then come give me your report."

"Yes, Sir."

Nathan pushed open the door of the hotel room. "Step inside so the door can close, but stay there," he instructed the hotel manager. Nathan stepped toward the king-size bed and the body lying still beneath the covers.

He touched his radio transmit button. "55-J, 10-97. Confirm 10-54. Notify appropriate."

"10-4."

The lady looked asleep, her head resting square on the pillow with her right hand limp atop the covers.

Nathan simply stood and looked for a long time, absorbing the details from the eyelashes against her cheek to the way her mouth slackened on the left side. There were possibly the faintest signs of a seizure—a touch of dried spit on the corner of her mouth, the jaw a little off for a natural slacking of the muscles in sleep. Her hands were open, fingers curved, her left hand partially caught in the sheet.

The covers were disrupted only slightly, suggesting it had been her own movements disturbing them. There weren't signs of violence marring her face as it recorded the circumstances of her last breath. Her hair had been brushed before she turned in, for while it showed the disruption of movement during sleep, it still had a brushed-in shine. Death had come early in the morning?

"Did the maid come into the room, touch anything?"

"No. Lucinda knocked, came in to deliver the towels and toiletries requested on the form last night, and got a shock when she saw this. She closed the door and used the hotel radio to call down to my office. She wasn't very coherent, but she was real insistent that she just shut the door."

"I can understand her shock; this isn't something you expect to walk in and see. Where is Lucinda now?"

"My assistant manager took her down to her office. We'll see that she doesn't talk to anyone else before you speak with her."

"Good." Guests died in their sleep of natural causes, it happened even in a small town like Justice, but rarely to someone this young. A suicide? A drug overdose? He needed definitive answers on this one, and the sooner the better.

"Please get the room records, anything she signed, how she paid for the room, if there were calls made. Bring them up here."

"I'll get them," the manager agreed, looking relieved to be able to leave the room.

Nathan scanned the tables and dresser: no prescription bottles to be seen, no drinking glass. Her things were in order, with a random carelessness that suggested they remained where she had set them down. There was no ring on her hands, and he saw none that she had removed. A book rested on the bedside table, near the edge.

Nathan stepped to the bathroom door and turned on the light, studying the counter. A toothbrush, washcloth, makeup, hair dryer. No sign of a prescription bottle or pill case. Numerous towels were draped over the shower rod and the side of the tub to dry. She'd used the pool on Saturday? He could faintly smell chlorine.

There was nothing visible that caused him concern.

Lord, she just died?

He didn't like the feel of that answer, for it made him feel so small. She didn't wake up. It brought back the vividness of the child's prayer: *Now I lay me down to sleep, I pray the Lord my soul to keep. . . .* Only he had always said it differently, *I pray the Lord my soul to leave.* A child's fear of the bogeyman in the night, of going to sleep and never waking again.

Death came suddenly; that was God's business. But when death came with assistance; that was his business.

Who was she?

Why had she come to town?

Nathan needed answers to both questions. Two Chicago newspapers were on the table, one from Friday, another from Saturday. There were no signs of a laptop or briefcase, making him doubt she was here on business.

Nathan pulled on latex gloves and picked up the trash can. She liked Diet Mountain Dew, granola bars, and had tossed away the last two bites of a bagel with cream cheese. A small empty sack from the Fine Chocolates Shop downtown confirmed she'd visited at least the downtown area since she had arrived in town.

He moved to the dresser. He found a slim clutch billfold in the top drawer, picked it up, and opened the clasp. A single key with a rental car tag, a set of cards including a phone calling card, and a credit card. He found a driver's license.

Peggy Worth, 433 Greenbriar Drive, Waukegan, IL. She'd signed her license to be an organ donor.

He looked toward the bed where she lay, a silent witness to his search. She was twenty-eight years old.

She was so incredibly young to be dead.

She was also staying at a hotel less than three hours from her own home. That struck him as odd.

He counted the cash she was carrying. Three hundred and twelve dollars in small bills, mostly tens and twenties. It seemed a bit much, but it fit with a tourist. The billfold yielded a card for a hairdresser appointment, a slip from a dry cleaner, but no photos. *Who was important in your life, Peggy? Who is wondering what has happened to you; why you are late to arrive or to call?*

"This is unfortunate."

His deputy, Gray Sillman, head of the investigative division, joined him. Nathan offered the license. "I'm getting a mixed sense of this; I haven't seen anything particularly alarming yet, but it just doesn't feel right."

"Pretty lady."

Nathan nodded. "See if you can find a scanner in this hotel, enlarge the photo, and get a couple dozen copies made. Let's get officers canvassing to find out who saw her before a guest who might have useful information checks out."

"I expect she'll be remembered." Sillman stepped out to make the arrangements.

Nathan checked through her suitcase.

The hotel manager returned. "Her name is Peggy Worth, and she registered with a Visa card."

"How many nights?"

"Four. She checked in Thursday evening and was scheduled to leave Monday. There are room-service charges on her bill but no outgoing long-distance phone calls. Local calls wouldn't show up." The manager handed over the paperwork.

"Thank you. The coroner is on the way. Would you arrange for him to come up through the service entrance?"

"Already arranged. Do I need to move the guests who stay on this wing to different rooms?"

Nathan closed the suitcase, not finding anything particularly helpful. "You might want to clear the two rooms on either side of this one as people will be coming and going for a few hours, possibly the rooms by the elevator as well. I'll also be down to talk with the maid in a few minutes. Your assistant's office is located where?"

"Behind the check-in desk."

"Would you also pull the security log for this room; let me know when she came and went from her room since the time she arrived."

"I'll start work on it," the manager agreed and left.

"Sir." The initial responding patrol officer stepped into the room to offer a folded note. Nathan took it as two more officers joined him.

He held out the car key. "Let's see about finding her rental car in the parking lot; maybe we'll find something there to get us to next of kin."

"Yes, Sir." The officers headed out to get the search started.

Nathan opened the note.

5'7", blonde hair, green eyes, designer eyeglasses. She has a workout jacket with an LA gym logo above the pocket. She left the exercise room about 7:40 p.m. Saturday heading for the hotel sauna and after that said she had a late-night, first-time date to see the movie Holiday Park. *She's a freelance reporter with the* Chicago Daily Times *and the* National Weekly News.

He turned over the note. It wasn't signed.

Nathan stepped to the door. "Who gave you this?"

The officer pointed down the hall to a group of guests watching what was going on. "The lady in blue."

Rae Gabriella.

She was talking with a young teen, making notes on a pad of paper. She was dressed for a morning out in a simple and elegant dress, her hair pulled back by a red ribbon and the high heels accentuating her graceful posture and long legs. Nathan watched her for a moment, making herself at home in the investigation with the ease of an officer assigned to the case.

Rae had a room at this hotel, and Nathan had never met a cop yet who wasn't curious. She'd probably stepped out of her own room and into this scene. Nathan walked toward the group, not sure what he wanted to say to her, deeply appreciating the note she had passed him, while knowing this was probably a crime scene she shouldn't be involved with.

Nathan paused as the elevator opened. The coroner stepped out; a spry man at sixty, the doctor and former medical naval officer was one of the county's irreplaceable personnel. Nathan had never seen Franklin Walsh lose his focus even at the most awful of crime scenes.

"What do we have, Nathan?"

Nathan glanced down the hall at Rae and left that conversation for later.

Nathan turned back to room 3712 and held the door for the doctor. "She's young. Peggy Worth, twenty-eight, according to her driver's license."

Franklin set down his bag and walked over to the bedside to lean down and study her face. "Tell me what you've found in the room."

"No medication of any kind, not even an aspirin. The only food in the room are the remains in the trash of a bagel and cream cheese, granola bar wrappers, an empty Diet Mountain Dew can, a chocolate sack from the shop downtown."

"Bag them for me. I wouldn't think food allergy, but we'll rule it out. Any inhaler for asthma, a medical card?"

"Nothing so far. We believe she was working out in the hotel exercise room last evening around seven-thirty, and then may have visited the sauna. The damp towels in the bathroom suggest she might have also gone for a swim at the pool."

"Anything that looks like performance-enhancement drugs or even simple vitamins?"

"Not so far. We're still looking for her car and any more luggage."

The coroner loaded film in his camera and took several photos; then he set it aside and pulled on gloves. He moved back the blankets. "There's no gross sign of physical trauma, no bruises on her neck or her arms."

He opened her eyelids to study her eyes. Using a tongue depressor, he opened her mouth and studied her tongue and gums.

"Maybe a seizure, rather than a heart attack. Her shoulders are a bit drawn under her like her chest had lifted up, and these look like bite marks on her inner lip. Her eyes are a little cloudy but that could be the time until the body was found. You called for the transport?"

"Yes."

"I'll do the autopsy this afternoon and put a rush on the toxicology." Walsh stepped back. "To die in your sleep the reflex to breathe has to be suppressed or blocked, and in someone this young—something massive has to go wrong to make that happen by natural causes. When we move the body, let's keep it simple. Wrap the sheets over her and put the entirety in the body bag. Send the blankets over as well."

"I appreciate the expedite." Nathan stepped out to the hall as he heard a stretcher being maneuvered from the elevator. "They are here now."

Rae was no longer with the group by the elevator; she was farther down the hall talking with an elderly lady watching what was happening. Nathan headed her way. Rae nodded and closed her pad, thanked the lady. Rae came to join him.

"You've been busy."

"I'm not trying to step on your investigation. It just felt really strange just standing here not doing anything."

Nathan raised a hand to pause her words. "You're fine, Rae. I appreciate the note you sent to me. What else do you know?"

"Everything I'm sure of is in the note."

"I'm the kind of guy that likes to hear the less-than-certain maybes too." He scanned the top page of her notes and saw a neat orderliness. He could either encourage her away from talking with guests, or he could trust Bruce's judgment that she was a good cop and knew how to do a field interview that didn't suggest the answers by the questions she asked. "Keep taking notes. As soon as I get things organized here, I'm buying you a cup of coffee and I want to read that notepad."

"Thanks, Nathan. If I'm not here or in the lobby downstairs, I'll be in my room—" she pointed—"that one —3723."

Five doors down. "I shouldn't be long; I've got an interview to do downstairs. If for some reason I get delayed and you need to leave the hotel, would you mention it to an officer?"

"Sure."

He paused long enough to smile at her. "For what it's worth, this kind of thing doesn't happen often in my town."

"It's a quiet town; I've been assured of that many times."

His words were getting echoed by others . . . it was a bit disconcerting. Nathan went to interview the maid who had found the lady.

7

Nathan tapped on Rae Gabriella's hotel-room door forty minutes after their brief hallway conversation. He heard the chain slip off and Rae opened the door holding a phone in her hand. "Come in, Nathan. I'm almost done." She turned away from the door and back into the room. "Is there any indication of what kind of chemical it is in the vat, Frank?"

Nathan hesitated before stepping into the room, not sure he wanted to eavesdrop on her conversation. Rae had changed from her dress to jeans and a sweatshirt. Her hotel room was neat, the bed made, a well-read newspaper folded back together on the table, and a cup of coffee cooling on the desk.

She paged through a thick book on the desk, pausing to spell out a chemical name. "That's closer. Does it have a phosphorus base?"

It sounded very much like a work conversation, and Nathan wondered again what Rae had specialized in while with the FBI.

The bouquet of roses he had sent dominated the hotel dresser. Nathan walked over, pleased with it. The roses were two days away from perfection as they opened, the blooms perfectly formed. Beside the roses rested a pair of earrings and her sunglasses.

Nathan studied the three photos set out on the dresser. Rae Gabriella had at least a couple men in her life who qualified for framed photos. They looked to be roughly Rae's age. He noticed, because life went smoother when he noticed the details. The mere fact she'd taken the time to set out the photos in a hotel room told him they were more than casual relationships.

"Maybe drain it to glass flasks? I don't know that you want to use anything made of rubber or plastic unless we know exactly what it is. What quantity are you dealing with?"

Rae pulled out a calculator from her briefcase and punched numbers. "I can stop at the medical-supply company on my way into town Monday and get some flasks if you can work around it for another twenty-four hours."

Nathan gave up trying to appear not interested in the one-sided conversation. Hazardous chemicals caught any officer's attention. She was working another job besides her work with Bruce? Was one of these photos the man she was talking to?

"Okay, I'll do that, Frank. Expect me about nine." Rae hung up the phone and marked the page in the book before closing it. "Sorry about that."

"No problem. Trouble?"

"My uncle owns a crime-scene-cleanup business and occasionally the unexpected surprise shows up at a scene. My cousin has got something neither of us has seen before." She switched pads of paper. "I've got my notes."

"Let's get a cup of coffee at the restaurant downstairs."

She picked up her room key. "Thanks for the roses."

He wasn't sure but he thought that was the faintest hint of a blush forming with her smile. He smiled back. "You're very welcome." He held the door for her. "Elevator or stairs?"

"Stairs."

Nathan nodded toward the restaurant café. The room was still being set up for the Sunday lunch crowd, with a few guests finishing a late breakfast.

Rae took a seat at a table away from the other guests. "I spoke with nineteen people, four of them staff, twelve that have rooms on the third floor, the rest guests who expressed various levels of interest and had questions in what was happening."

Nathan smiled as she started her report as soon as she sat down. He held out his hand. "Let me see," he asked, and she offered the pad of paper.

The waitress joined them. "Two coffees," he requested. She nodded, and came back with coffee mugs for them both.

Nathan scanned Rae's notes. He turned a few pages, seeing a common format she had followed. Name, date, and location at the top of the page, any time reference people made pulled out to the left edge of the page for quick reference.

Most of her notes were verbatim quotes of phrases as someone answered a question, but occasionally a paragraph appeared in a fast shorthand he would have to ask her to translate in its entirety. Full contact information for the person was circled at the bottom of the page. She'd done this out of habit, and he wondered again at what her day-to-day job had been at the FBI. The completeness of the interviews, when they had been informal conversations in a hallway, told him she was good at teasing out information without witnesses feeling pushed by the questions.

"Two guests were especially helpful; they spoke with Peggy at lunch and knew some of her itinerary for Friday and Saturday."

Nathan went back to the front of the pad and began to scan the quotes from different people, finding a reassuring consistency in the information from various guests. When these notes were matched up with the broader number of interviews being done by his officers, there would be a good record of Peggy Worth's movements since she arrived at the hotel.

"From what I see here, you were one of the last ones at the hotel to see her. Talk me through your meeting with Peggy Worth, Rae."

"She was in the exercise room Saturday evening when I arrived and looked like she had been working out awhile. I recognized her as someone I had passed on the third-floor hallway and I think she also recognized me. She asked me if I had the time, which is why I know it was seven-twenty-two when I got to the exercise room, and she didn't stay more than another fifteen minutes or so."

"What else did she say?"

"That she had a late-night, first-time date, and she mentioned the movie *Holiday Park*. She wasn't sure how successful a date it was going to be; I got the impression she didn't know her date that well."

A late movie—that suggested an eight or nine o'clock start time, which gave him an eleven or twelve o'clock finish. "Did she say who she was meeting?" Nathan asked.

"No. Nor did she mention if she was meeting him somewhere or if he was picking her up here."

"You got back to the hotel last night about 12:30. Did you happen to see her then? Or anyone else in the hall?"

"When I got to the room I found there was a fax waiting for me so I went back downstairs again. A few minutes after I got back to my room with the fax, your roses arrived. I didn't see Peggy during those trips, although I passed a few people. I didn't notice enough about them to be helpful to you."

"The fact you didn't tense to someone that appeared out of place is itself helpful. Peggy talked about an upcoming date, what else?"

"It wasn't a long conversation; I didn't even know her name until today. She did ask if I knew a Joe Prescott."

"Joe? That's interesting."

"Why?"

"He's dead, about three months ago now. He lost a grandson to a drug overdose at one of those millennium New Year's Eve rave parties in Chicago and he had been battling depression ever since. He drove his truck into a tree, likely on purpose."

"I'm surprised Peggy didn't learn that quickly," Rae said.

"Those who knew Joe knew how strongly he resented the press that came around asking questions after his grandson died. I'm not surprised they avoided talking with a reporter about him.

"Twelve teenagers died at that rave party from some new designer drug and it was a sensational story around here. Joe didn't even want an obituary run in the paper announcing his passing; that's how contentious it became with the press. Peggy would have eventually learned he had passed away, but it wouldn't have been volunteered once she said she was a reporter."

Rae turned her coffee mug in her hands. "If she were working on a drug-use story and doing a follow-up on the rave deaths . . . does this in any way look like a suspicious death?"

"Peggy Worth died in her sleep; we're going to have to wait for the coroner to say if it was natural causes or not. Everything I saw suggests it's natural causes."

Nathan lifted a hand, acknowledging the detective at the café entrance. "I'll call you tonight with a general update and to see if you heard anything else around here that might be useful. How late is too late?"

"I'll be up through the late news."

Nathan nodded. He left money on the table for the two coffees and a large tip and got to his feet. "Thanks for the help, Rae."

8

Nathan pulled into his driveway Sunday afternoon and parked behind the rusted truck his grandfather drove when he wasn't hurling by in that new sports car. The backyard gate was open and as Nathan opened his car door, he smelled charcoal. Barking erupted and two fast black dogs darted out to meet him.

"Yes, it's me." Nathan knelt to greet them, their bodies wiggling in joy and their tongues lapping at his exposed skin. "Are you two enjoying the company?"

His grandfather appeared at the gate. "They are eating your flower-bed edging."

"I know." Nathan accepted it as the cost of having young dogs. Digit and Black chewed on their gnaw bones when in the house, but outside they ate the flower-bed edging, the tarp over his planters, and just about anything that let them cut their teeth.

Nathan opened the passenger door of his car. The deli had fixed a quart of coleslaw, baked beans, and a batch of deep-fried chicken hearts for him. "Sorry I'm late."

"I heard the scanner traffic. She's dead?"

"Yes."

"That will do wonders for tourism. The café crowd will be talking it up."

Nathan waved his dogs ahead of him and walked into the backyard where his grandfather had the grill ready to accept two thick-cut steaks. "What can I help with?"

"I've got the meat handled, assuming your dogs don't jump me for it."

"They'll listen to a no."

Nathan entered his kitchen. *Lord, give me patience.* His grandfather taxed his ability to be polite, for the man knew how to get under his skin. Mom said he was lonely and mad, and it came out as being cranky. Nathan understood her point, but it didn't make the situation any easier. He could have ducked out of the lunch arrangements today pleading the case to work, but he was worried about his grandfather. If Henry wanted to invite himself for lunch, he would be here.

He opened the deli items, found serving spoons and a large tray to carry everything outside so they could eat on the back patio. The day was freezing, but his grandfather preferred a coat and a view rather than sitting around a kitchen table.

Nathan pushed open the patio door with his foot. His life revolved lately around eating with someone and catching up on news—at this rate he was going to have to figure out how to run during the winter or pay for it come spring.

"How long are you planning to maintain two homes? I need your tongs to do these steaks properly and you don't have anything here but big serving forks."

"As long as I'm sheriff, I have a place in town," Nathan replied. He'd made it a campaign promise, and he didn't regret it. It minimized how long calls at night cut into his sleep.

"Well it's a waste of money now that you've been reelected. I know this town. You'll be sheriff for life until you decide not to run for reelection again. I was by your main place yesterday and it's obvious no one is home much. The drive needs attention, you've got tree limbs down from the last storm, nothing has been done to repair that fence your mom insisted was perfect."

"I'll get to it, Henry. I was out there a day ago, and Dad is by to get the mail if I don't have time. Once the strike is past I'll be spending the weekends out there again."

For topics of conversation it was family, the strike, or what was happening in Bruce's life, and the only one of those subjects that Henry didn't have a preset position on was Bruce. Nathan sacrificed his friend without a qualm. "Bruce Chapel has brought in a partner."

"I heard she's already gotten involved in police business with that hotel death."

"Her room is a few doors down; it's hard to miss the cops and coroner traipsing by. She's a retired cop; she was useful."

"Is she single?"

Single, pretty, and had him intrigued. "Yes. I think she and Bruce go way back." Nathan watched his dogs come around from behind the garage, both with noses brushing through the snow on the ground and tails wagging fast. One began to dig at the woodpile.

"Bring over the tray. These steaks are done."

Nathan brought over the tray. They were two beautifully cooked steaks. "Thank you, Henry." He waited until his grandfather took a seat at the table. "Would you say grace?"

His grandfather put his rugged hands together in an old-fashioned sign of respect. "Lord, You made us and gave us breathe. May we do justice, love mercy, and walk honorably before You this day. By the precious name of Jesus, I ask for Your help to do this. Amen."

Nathan blinked away unexpected moisture in his eyes. "Thanks."

"I'm not so old I forget who I'm about to meet one day soon. Pass the salt."

Nathan passed it over, knowing the salt was bad for Henry's blood pressure but that he'd also lived long enough he didn't care. "I talked to Larry over at the union hall yesterday. I'd like your advice."

His grandfather reached for the baked beans. "What's the latest wrinkle?"

"Prescription costs." Nathan cut into his steak and explained what he had learned the day before.

⓪〃 ⓪〃 ⓪〃

Rae closed the book she was reading and slid it over onto the hotel table beside the couch. Her Sunday was ending back at the hotel where it had begun.

Are you happy when you first awake? Her grandmother knew how to get to the heart of the matter. The lady was ninety-two, had lived in a nursing home for the last seven years, and was at peace with life.

Rae envied her grandmother. Mornings when Rae woke were often the heaviest point of the day, the moment when she opened her eyes and saw a good day, and then the memories of the past returned. . . . She didn't know how to be happy anymore or if she even deserved to be again. She'd failed so miserably, and Mark was dead. That would never change.

Sunday was at least ending. She'd spent the afternoon with Bruce painting her new office, left to see her grandmother, and returned to town too late to make the evening church services. Her only contribution to the world today had been to get in Nathan's way this morning even though he'd been nice about her interference. Tomorrow, working with her uncle, she'd be too busy to waste time thinking.

She wanted to be needed again, to fit in, to have a place and a job she could do. Happiness—maybe someday she could let herself hope it would return.

She reached over for her Bible. The book traveled with her as one of her most important possessions, but for all the handling and hours spent reading it, the words had felt dry this last year, the words not reaching past the confusion and hurt she was feeling. Her fault probably, but a reality she had come to expect. She let the Bible open to the middle and found herself in Proverbs, on a familiar page marked with underlined verses she had discovered and noted in years past.

> *He who gives heed to the word will prosper,*
> *and happy is he who trusts in the Lord.*
> *Proverbs 16:20*

Not for the first time in the last year she read the words and found they hurt. They held out such promise and she just couldn't seem to take hold of it and see it come true.

Lord, I just don't understand anymore. I tried my very best to take care in what I did, to do my job with honor, and I ended up destroying Mark's life and my own. Why didn't You stop what was happening? You could have laid me out with cancer or a busted leg or done something to change the course of events. But You didn't.

I prayed daily about that case and the work I was doing. I trusted You to help me to get it right, and that didn't happen. Was it wrong to expect that of You? How did I fail with You? What did I do wrong? I still don't understand, and I need to understand.

The words ran out and left too much emotion behind them. Life hurt, and she couldn't figure out how to pick up the pieces anymore. *I feel so lost, Jesus.*

She had dreamed about being a cop since she was a child, and that dream was gone now. There wasn't a dream to replace it, just a huge void and a lot of uncertainty. Half her life was gone and what she had to show for it was failure.

She faced setting up a new home, making new friends, sorting out her past with Bruce, figuring out how to function as a private investigator—she didn't know how to do it without making another serious mistake. She knew God was with her, but as the days stretched by and the weight of the past didn't lift, it felt like she was walking this new journey alone. She was so tired of feeling alone.

She closed the Bible and set it aside, knowing she needed to keep reading, but finding the emotional hit that was waiting for her in the memories too much to bear tonight. The case had happened, and her life was different now. Life was going down this new path regardless of how she felt or if she was up to the change. She had to figure out how to adapt. She didn't have a choice.

She scrunched down on the couch. Nathan had said he'd call with an update and she would stay up through the evening news to see if he did. If he didn't—well, she knew better than most how days as a cop could spin out of control.

She envied Nathan that job he did and the reality he had this place where he belonged. This town and his family history were intertwined, and that was a special fact she wondered if he could truly appreciate. He'd never been without it.

She listened for the phone to ring, monitored the television for the start of the news, and tried to rest without thinking. She was tired of thinking.

છા   છા   છા

Nathan slid open the back patio door of his home late Sunday night, trying to move quietly. His dogs slept in an intertwined pile of legs, tails, and noses on the rug in the kitchen. They untangled themselves in a flurry of movement and fur. He set his Bible on the dining-room table and hitched up his suit slacks to kneel and greet them.

Digit raced away and returned with the doggy teddy bear, the plush bear almost too much to carry. Nathan wrestled it from him and tossed the toy into the living room. Both dogs went racing after it and attacked with a skidding stop. The bear was dropped, picked up again, tossed, and growled at.

Nathan watched with a smile. They gave him some perspective back in life, for they counted on him to feed them, play, take them for walks, and rub their bellies when they wiggled on their backs wanting his attention.

Digit wore out first and came to collapse on his shoes, panting and licking his hand. "Yes, I love you too." Not to be outdone, Black came to sit and lift a paw to be taken. "Give me half an hour, guys, and we'll head out for a while."

He rose and tugged at his tie. Church had been good tonight: William's sermon continued his study in Ephesians, and Sandy had done a beautiful job with the music. He'd stayed for the Communion he had missed that morning and afterwards a conversation with Zachary had them lingering beside his car for twenty minutes while they stood in a cold wind, the seriousness of the discussion leaving them both willing to ignore the chills. He could feel his sore throat intensifying.

Management was serious about ending the strike and bringing in strikebreakers.

Nathan sighed as he climbed the steps to the master bedroom. *Jesus, I'm now deeply out of my league. How am I supposed to act on this information without betraying Zachary's trust in providing me advance warning?*

Would some within the union decide their personal situation left them no choice but to cross the line and return to work, setting off a fight within the union? Would there be violence at the plant when the strikebreakers came in? Nathan wasn't wise enough for this.

He changed into jeans and a sweatshirt and glanced at the time. He owed Rae a phone call, but it was close to being too late. He had Sillman's report in his briefcase; it had been delivered by a courier along with a stack of reading he needed to have reviewed by tomorrow's early conference call with the county DA. Rae would understand if he called her tomorrow.

Nathan went downstairs and whistled for his dogs. He opened the patio door and let them race into the backyard.

He had told Rae he would call. Nathan sighed and reversed course. He got a drink from the refrigerator, opened his briefcase and dug out the correct report, and picked up the cordless phone. He turned on the backyard light and stepped outside, tugging on his coat. Sitting at the patio table, occasionally seeing his dogs as they tracked an interesting scent along the fence, Nathan scanned the report. Digit howled in joy and began digging at the woodpile.

"You're not going to catch it; you know that, don't you?" Nathan called over, amused at the dog's intensity. Black joined Digit and they both began to dig. He was going to have a hole in the ground to fill in before this was over. He turned the pages of the report to find the coroner's update.

৪৬৪৬ ৪৬৪৬ ৪৬৪৬

Rae watched the evening news with her eyes half opened. Peggy Worth's death was not mentioned, the small town of Justice too far out of the city for the television station to find the death worth airtime. The Justice weekly newspaper on Monday would probably have it on the front page. The phone rang as the weather reporter showed a radar trace over the area with an approaching band of light green and more snow. She reached over to answer it.

"Hello, Rae. I'm sorry it's so late."

Nathan's voice was a welcoming break in her evening. "The news isn't over yet. You're fine." She reached for the remote and turned down the volume, pleased he had called. She was glad he couldn't see the shape she was in, a few tear traces having dried on her face, and the lingering sadness apparent. She hoped it wouldn't be conveyed in her voice. "You've got news."

"Some. I've finished reading the deputy's report on Peggy Worth and the summary of what the interviews provided. He hasn't been able to find anyone who remembers seeing Peggy Worth after she left the exercise room."

Rae clicked off the TV and pushed herself up in the couch, startled by the news. "I was the last one to see her alive?"

"So far, yes. She didn't go to the movie theater as planned; the security tape at the theater confirms that."

"Her date itinerary changed."

"Or the date was cancelled and she turned in early. The book on her bedside was half read, and there's a receipt showing she bought it that afternoon. The security code shows her door opens and closes a couple times around 8 p.m. and again around 1 a.m., which doesn't help confirm or rule out either option."

Rae agreed; the facts left more questions open than answered. "If the date destination changed or even if it was cancelled, her date should still know something of her plans."

"The man has yet to come forward. If he's in town, you have to figure he's heard about her death by now. And if the date was cancelled for some reason, you still have to figure he'd be grief stricken at the news and would call in with questions. So far nothing."

She heard pages turn.

"The autopsy showed a seizure and heart attack as the cause of death, but it's not conclusive yet that it was natural causes. The coroner expects to have the rest of the toxicology results tomorrow."

The guy Peggy planned to meet hadn't come forward as news spread of her death—that said foul play. But Rae didn't see how it fit with the other details of the scene. "A traumatic death usually leaves more evidence behind than this."

"I know. She looked peaceful, Rae, like she closed her eyes and simply never woke up. I hope for her parents' sake it was natural causes."

"Have you spoken with them?"

"Yes. Peggy was single. I spoke with her parents shortly after 2 p.m., when we had confirmed the identity."

"That had to be hard."

"It was."

Rae shifted one of the throw pillows behind her head and rested back again. Nathan sounded tired tonight. "I appreciate the update."

"No problem, Rae. Your notes helped today."

"Where are you, Nathan? There's a bit of an echo."

"Sorry. I'm home, I'm on the cordless phone, and I just stepped outside with my dogs. I'm trying to convince them to come in for the night. They like to sleep in the oddest places in this big backyard and then wake me up at 1 a.m. with their mournful cries to come back inside."

"You love them, though."

"I must. One is now trying to eat my tennis-shoe laces and the other just brought a dead something as a gift." She heard the phone shift as he dealt with the unwanted gift. "How did your day go, Rae? Have you gotten settled in at the agency?"

"Bruce and I started painting my office. It's going to be nice when it's done."

"You'll enjoy it. How is your grandmother? Were you able to see her as planned?"

She appreciated the fact he remembered her plans for the day. "She's fine. I spent about three hours with her and enjoyed every moment. She's a wonderful lady who makes me laugh and showers me with love."

"I'm glad you're close to her."

"So am I." She wanted to linger over this call but knew doing so risked her saying more than she should tonight. She'd known the man a couple days, liked him, but that didn't stretch to talking about how her grandmother was handling life well while she was not. "I'll let you go so you can get some sleep. I'm glad you called."

"So am I. Good night, Rae."

"Good night, Nathan."

She thought for a moment about the news he had shared before she set down the phone. What had Peggy done during those last hours before she died? If the death was determined to be natural causes, Nathan would close his file, the body would be returned to her family, and a funeral would end this tragedy. Rae didn't like an unexplained puzzle.

She got up and prepared for bed. She'd spend tomorrow helping her uncle and cousin with the cleanup job, and when she got back to Justice she'd give her office a second coat of paint. Bruce wanted to show her his place and fix her dinner. She'd let him. What she wasn't going to do was let herself have more nights like this one, with too much time on her hands to think, and not a plan to fill those hours. She wasn't sure where she wanted her relationship with Bruce to end up or even how best to figure that out, but she'd start with prowling his place and letting him char a hamburger for her. As a plan, it would do for the day.

She tugged up the covers and thought about Peggy. The idea she had simply died in her sleep was a bit frightening. "If I should die before I wake, please welcome me to heaven, Jesus," she whispered. She clicked off the light.

9

Rae followed her cousin through the bakery to the back offices Monday morning.

"The fired employee shot his former boss in his office, but the first shot didn't kill him. The second blast near the bakery ovens took care of that," Frank said, his voice muffled by the full respirator he wore. "Then the employee turned the gun on himself."

Rae could see the blood in the hallway marking the man's flight, the trail now heavily covered by ants. She stepped into the office. Blood had splattered on the desk and walls and dried into a gory painting.

"Carpet, desk, chairs—it all needs to come out," she assessed. She could likely recover the photos on the desk, some of the awards on the wall, the plants, most of the files. The small things would help the man's wife find closure and the company recover a portion of the work that had been in progress.

"I'll bring in the heavy plastic rolls and tape. We've got the lift truck coming midafternoon to take a load to the incinerator. Under the new rules of disposal, anything we throw away that's got blood on it has to be burned, no matter what the object's size. We'll haul furniture and carpet out once the truck arrives."

"I can handle in here, if you and Matt want to stay focused on the ovens area." The bodies had rested out there on the tile floor for several hours before being discovered and the amount of decay in that heat environment was intense. Even the respirators could not block the stench in there.

"We'll call when we get to the point we're ready to drain that chemical vat. Use the radio if you need us; we'll hear you."

Rae nodded. "I'm set, Frank. Thanks."

Her cousin nodded and made his way back into the bakery.

They were pressed for time to complete this job so the questions Rae had braced herself to answer about Washington, D.C., had been left for another time. Uncle Matt had hugged her in welcome, Frank had brought her a cup of coffee, boots, and protective clothes, and they'd piled into the van for the drive over here. Rae was back, and it was much as if she had never left. The simplicity of that had itself been a blessing.

She hauled in the plastic tubs from the van, lined them up on the clean section of the carpet, and began moving items that might be recoverable after they were cleaned in the tubs. She would take them back to the warehouse, where metal mesh shelves and a progression of bleach baths and fine brushes would let her remove the bloodstains and seeped-in odor and hopefully be able to return items to his family.

Items beyond recovery she put into the HazMat barrel to seal and haul away to be burned.

Frank wanted her to join him in this business when his dad retired. Not just anyone could take on this business and it would be difficult to run without a full-time partner. Rae was glad it was a decision for another year.

She gagged when she picked up the briefcase and roaches scurried away. She hated roaches. They loved scenes like this one.

Kevin Hammond, vice president of B.G. Bakery—she picked up the photo and studied the man who had days ago been going about his life on the expectation he would live another ten years. His blood had splattered on his wife's picture. Life came with no guarantees about its length. She put the picture in the tub and turned back to the desk.

Before the day was done she would be aching in muscles she hadn't used in a while and emotionally tired from looking at the effects of death, but she didn't regret telling her uncle yes, she'd come back to work with him part-time. A janitor or hired cleaning crew didn't need to be the ones dealing with this cleanup. As awful as this was, she had come ready for the job. She added another photo to the stack to clean and moved on to gathering business papers.

❒ ❒ ❒

Nathan braced his elbow against the truck radiator and strained to get enough leverage on the wrench and the old bolt rusted into the engine frame to get it to turn. He'd oiled the bolt, tried heating and cooling the metal, and still he couldn't get movement.

He wished his grandfather would not get so attached to vehicles. The way the truck was running, it was unsafe, and he'd told his grandfather so on Sunday when he'd heard it start. Somehow in that exchange he'd volunteered to try and make the repairs. It wasn't how he'd envisioned spending his snatched Monday lunch break.

"Sheriff." The doorbell rang inside his house and he heard knocking start on the front door. "Sheriff!"

Nathan lowered his hand to keep his dogs quiet. He reached over and turned down the volume on his small radio.

"Sheriff." Mrs. Neel strode around his house. She was wearing her favorite floral dress but with clunky winter boots, coming fast on the stepping stones.

His dogs disappeared into the open garage behind them. "Traitors," Nathan whispered after them. He reluctantly straightened and picked up a rag to wipe his hand.

"That private investigator is sitting in his car down the street from Heather Teal's, watching her house. The entire neighborhood is in a buzz about it."

"Are you sure he's not just asleep?"

"Am I sure he's not . . ." Her voice moved up in shrillness. "This is serious, young man. He's been there for the last two hours and ten minutes and he's disrupting the entire neighborhood."

"I'm sorry to hear that. I'm on my lunch break, Mrs. Neel."

She opened her mouth and closed it again. She took a breath. "Well, I never. Your father would have never made such a lame excuse to avoid his duty."

My father was better able to hide. "Yes, Ma'am, he was a great sheriff." Nathan looked back at the vehicle engine. "What would you like me to do?"

"Tell him to move along."

"It's a public street."

"Well he can't just sit there; it's vagrancy or something."

Or something. Sometimes Nathan thought Bruce enjoyed the fact he could get people so riled up without even trying. "I'll talk to him, Mrs. Neel."

"Now?"

"Soon."

He needed a new timing belt, and since his grandfather was now an hour late being here to supervise, it was probably best to go quietly prowl to find the man. The man missed his wife. Nathan wasn't sure what as a grandson he was supposed to do.

"This truck should be junked; it's falling apart."

"Yes, Ma'am. I'll tell Henry."

"I'll be talking to Mrs. Teal and telling her you're going to deal with this problem."

"I'll talk with Bruce." He closed the truck hood and watched his neighbor walk away. Living in town did have a few drawbacks. He sighed and then snapped his fingers for his dogs. "You can come out now, you two."

They scampered out.

Nathan stopped his squad car alongside Bruce's Caprice and motioned to his friend to lower his window. "This is the strangest stakeout I have ever seen. Practically everyone in town knows your car."

"I figure at least half a dozen friends of Heather have called her to mention I'm parked down the street from her driveway."

"They have, and they've found me as well. What are you doing, Bruce?"

"Getting myself fired."

Nathan grinned. "I told you not to take the case. Heather's husband is not cheating on her; she's just paranoid."

"I know. I suspended my good judgment for the rent money."

"I brought you a coffee." Nathan leaned over and offered through the window the coffee he'd picked up at the hardware store, the owner determined to be known for the best and cheapest coffee in town. Nathan's own cup of coffee came from the deli. He couldn't afford to pick sides in the town's coffee war.

"Thanks."

"You could call her and quit."

"I've tried that. She keeps ignoring my final report and suggests I don't know how to do my job or I'd find the evidence. It's time to make her decide she wants to end my services. I doubt Heather lasts another hour before she's storming out the front door and down the street to fire me in person."

Nathan put his car in drive. "Private investigators have such interesting jobs."

"I notice you're on patrol duty."

"We were short a man for the evening shift," Nathan replied. "You want a real job?"

"And miss out on the Heathers of the world?"

Nathan smiled. "See you later, Bruce. If you happen to see my grandfather, let him know I figured out what was wrong with his truck."

"Will do."

Nathan slowed as he passed Heather's home, saw her at the window with the curtain half pulled back, and offered her a wave. The curtain dropped. He'd get a call from her before long and there were only so many times he could put her off before she called his father to complain. There were days belonging to the town's founding family was not a blessing.

Nathan picked up the radio and called into the dispatcher, then turned east. He would check in with the picket lines and listen to the conversations for a while. Someone getting antsy enough to cause trouble—maybe a friend would think it best to say a quiet word before the trouble actually started.

Sending guys coming off the line over to the diner for steak and fries on him might defuse some idle talk from turning into actions. If he had to buy the peace with cash from his own pocket today he'd do so.

Every day of quiet bought that much more time for the negotiators to find a way to settle the strike. It had to end before strikebreakers arrived and violence erupted around him between folks who had known each other for decades. He feared the town would never recover if that happened.

⁃ʘ ⁃ʘ ⁃ʘ

Bruce watched through half-closed eyes as Heather's husband appeared through the fenced backyard gate and crossed the yard, reached the sidewalk, and turned toward Willow Street. His daughter lived the other direction so he wasn't walking over to see his grandson, and if he was getting out of the house to get away from his wife it was odd he wasn't heading downtown as was his custom.

Two weeks of following the man had convinced Bruce that the man was a creature of habit who just wanted some time away from his wife. He'd eat a piece of pie, walk down to the library, and read a book in peace.

Bruce watched the man walk away and debated with himself. Another few minutes and Heather was going to be out here firing him; the upstairs window curtain was twitching often now as she watched his car and worked up the words to say to him.

Where was Bob going?

Bruce sighed and tugged his keys from the ignition and shoved open the door. Curiosity was a bad character trait for a private investigator to have. It created work. He headed after Heather's husband.

At the stop sign a blue truck pulled to the curb; Heather's husband walked over to the passenger door and opened it. He got inside. The truck, driven by Nathan's grandfather, turned east. In weeks of following Bob, Bruce hadn't even realized the two men knew each other beyond a casual name recognition. And that blue truck looked new. Henry had bought himself yet another vehicle?

Bruce returned to his car. He followed the truck. Snowplows were current with their work and traffic was light for a Monday, making it an easy enough tail but ensuring he would also be spotted. Bruce caught a clear enough look at the back window to see a temporary license-plate tag taped in the corner. The truck did indeed look like a new purchase.

Nathan's grandfather ran a stop sign. Bruce drummed his fingers on the steering wheel. Henry wasn't pleased with being followed. So much for doing this chase the easy way. Bruce followed for another mile and watched the truck turn into the cemetery where Henry's wife was buried. Bruce had a feeling it wasn't the two guys' original intended destination. He drove past and continued on. *Another time, Henry . . .*

Bruce turned back toward his office. He wanted another look at what he had on the car dealer. If that truck was getting titled in Henry's name, that made two substantial purchases in only a few months. Where was the money coming from? One way or another he was going to figure out what was going on.

10

Rae bit the tip of her tongue as she concentrated on painting around her office-door woodwork. This was going to be the place she talked with clients, managed case files, did her research, took a nap when the days were slow, read a novel when she didn't want to leave for home yet ... it was beginning to feel like her space and she liked that feeling. She'd chosen a great color for the walls.

"How was the day with your family?" Bruce asked, pouring more paint into his roller pan.

"Pleasant for catching up on news, not so pleasant for the job. I'd forgotten how physically hard the work is. How did your day go here?"

"I trailed Heather's husband around some more." Bruce started rolling a second coat of paint on the wall.

"I've heard that name several times. Who is she?"

"One of the town's lifetime residents. Heather Teal is sixty-two, the owner of a card shop here in town. She thinks her husband is cheating on her."

"Is he?"

"I very much doubt it. She's got a suspicious perspective on everything in life."

Rae leaned back to study her paint job. "You need to give me an update on the cases you are working on. I saw the list on your whiteboard."

He pulled a rag from his pocket to wipe a paint splatter off the light fixture.

"Tretton Insurance is a possible insurance-fraud case. Several items reported on a robbery report may not have actually been taken. The couple moves a lot—different cities, different states—and there is a string of insurance claims with different companies in their wake. I'm going after their former friends to see if one of them will give me a lead on what is really happening with the items being reported stolen.

"Next item on the whiteboard—Larry Broderick. That is a real robbery case. Someone broke into his hardware store and stole several thousand dollars' worth of inventory, including six handguns. Nathan has that case well in hand, so I'm trying hard not to step on his investigation. We both want the guns found, so it's been a cooperative arrangement so far.

"The last cases on the whiteboard are smaller—Karen Elan is looking for a half sister she recently learned exists, Laura's ex-husband is the one who gave me this shiner, and I'm working on a private item for Nathan."

"They all sound much smaller than what I worked on recently."

Bruce glanced over at her and laughed. "Did you work on anything less than a task force and a case that took a year of your efforts?"

She conceded that point with a good-natured shrug. "I had one case that we wrapped up in six months," she offered.

"A record for the FBI. The cases on the whiteboard are big to the people involved. Remembering that helps."

"How do you get cases? Do people come by the agency? Do you make inquiry calls on businesses that might have work?"

"You'll find in a small town it's not so formal. People will stop you at the hardware store, the diner, at the post office to mention a problem and ask for advice. Some will call and ask that you stop by. I'm content to sit back and let work come in at its own pace. I don't want this to be a large and growing agency, Rae. I had my run at being decorated and famous when I was a cop, and I want something different.

"I keep the files for the active cases in the top drawer of my credenza. Feel free to read through them and make copies for yourself," Bruce offered. "You're welcome to help me with any of the cases that catch your interest."

"I'd like that."

Bruce closed up his paint can and pulled over a chair to take a break. "I've been thinking some more about Peggy Worth. What would you do if you were getting ready for a date?"

Rae didn't have to think about it long. "Buy a new dress, shoes, visit my hairdresser, take time on my makeup, maybe get a manicure. Basically spend money and look great so if the date was a dud I would still feel like the time had been worth it."

Bruce smiled. "I remember the time you took getting ready for a date, but I always appreciated the results. So which of those did Peggy do? If her date was cancelled, she would not have gone through the preparations. There should be something to indicate she actually went on a date—what the coroner says she had for dinner if nothing else."

"Thanks for that image. And you have to figure Nathan has already asked those questions."

Bruce shook his head. "His first question is more simple—does he need to pursue those questions? Unless the coroner says it's a suspicious death, the case will be closed despite the open questions. It's a fact of life when it's the public paying for how the police spend their time."

"Nathan thought he'd hear from the coroner on the toxicology results today. Do you think he would mind if I called him to ask the results?"

"Call him. Nathan can always say no." Bruce gathered up the stack of paint-sample strips and returned them to some kind of order.

"I'm surprised the two of you get along so well."

"I'm a bit surprised that it developed as it did too." Bruce shrugged. "We're friends. Since his election as sheriff, Nathan's friends who are cops now work for him. There's no way around the fact that creates some tension for him."

"You're a former cop who is also an impartial outsider."

"Something like that. When our interests on cases overlap, we work together. When they don't, we make accommodations." Bruce looked up from the paint strips. "With Nathan it's best to tell him not only the facts as you know them, but also what you suspect."

"I've noticed that." Rae stepped down from the ladder and began putting away her paint supplies. "Are you ready for me to wash that roller?"

"Yes, I'm done. You've got your keys? I'll head over to the lumberyard and buy what we'll need to build the bookshelves. If they can deliver the wood tomorrow afternoon, this paint should be dry."

"I've got my keys," Rae confirmed. "I hate to blow a hole in our plans for tonight, but could we move dinner at your place to tomorrow night instead? At this point I'm looking for a long shower and some sleep. I thought I'd copy the active-case files to read and then head over to the hotel."

Bruce smiled. "It's no problem, Rae. I figured that might be the case; you were dragging like a dishrag when you got back from your uncle's. I remember what that business does to your appetite too. I'll burn you a hamburger another night. I plan to be feeding you often in the next month; you'll get tired of hotel food pretty fast."

"I admit, it's kind of strange thinking of you as a homeowner. I look at your office here, and that's what I remember about you—that couch and the neat files, the music. You could be living here and you'd be right in line with my memories."

Bruce laughed. "Eleven years changes a few things. You'll see. I'm actually kind of enjoying this phase of life, being house tied with a driveway to shovel and a yard to mow."

He paused beside her and gently wiped paint off her cheek. "You're freckling in colors now. Try to sleep in tomorrow. I'll find you midmorning and we can talk through the cases and what makes sense as the next move on them."

She blinked at the shift in the man toward a beat in time much more personal and then let herself relax. "It works for me."

Bruce smiled. "Good."

He left to head to the lumberyard.

Rae closed up the paint cans. She smiled. She'd forgotten a few things about the man and why she'd been so very tempted to stay in Chicago years before.

It was casual on the surface with Bruce, friendship and work. The deeper current rarely showed its eddies, but it was there. Strong, deep, dependable. Their relationship years before had begun to touch that depth. She'd been too young then to appreciate all that meant; she'd just enjoyed it. Now—if she let them, they'd flow this relationship along at the deeper level as well as the surface.

It wasn't something she was ready to grasp yet, but the knowledge it was out there for the future—Bruce was helping her recover more than he could realize. Just the hope felt good. She was going to enjoy being grounded somewhere again. Maybe grounded again with him.

Rae stopped by Bruce's office to retrieve the active files. The files he had described were neatly arranged in the credenza in alphabetic order. Rae pulled out the first handful, one of them thick enough it bulged out a two-inch folder. She carried them to the front reception desk and turned on the copier.

The forms Bruce used, how he documented his work, there was a familiar and comforting similarity to it. Rae read his notes as she undid the clasp and removed pages. In many ways they were now a two-person, private police agency. She set the copier to make two copies so she could leave one set in her office and take the other with her to mark up.

Rae looked up Nathan's work phone number and dialed on her cordless phone as she walked back to the break room to retrieve a cold soda. "Nathan, it's Rae Gabriella. Do you have a moment?"

"One sec, Rae." The phone was covered. "Will, see if there's a number for Zachary in there. I need to see him tonight. Tell him to stay put; I'll come to him." The phone shifted. "Yes, sorry about that Rae. I'm glad you called."

"You're busy. I won't take your time."

"No, it's fine. It's always like this of an evening after my assistant has gone home."

"There's news about Peggy Worth?"

"It's been ruled a death by natural causes. Franklin called an hour ago and said the toxicology reports were all clean. He confirmed she had a seizure, which apparently triggered a heart attack. He's not very satisfied with that answer and wants to talk with her personal physician, but he's found nothing suspicious to question the natural-causes ruling."

"She was so young."

"I know." The paperwork she could hear him working on stilled. "You okay?"

Rae sighed. "It's almost harder to hear natural causes than it is to hear it was suspicious." Rae tugged out a chair with her foot and sat down.

"It happens."

"It's just sad. Was there any progress on who her date might have been on Saturday?"

"Not when I last talked to Sillman. Hold on; let me get Sillman's closing report." She heard him moving folders.

"There were a couple calls to the station after the article appeared in the newspaper, but nothing that helps resolve the 8 p.m. to 1 a.m. window or who her date was with. It looks like you remain the last person we've found to have seen her. I'll have a courier drop off your notepad tonight; I've got copies for the file. I noticed you had a to-do list on one of the back pages."

"Since I didn't even remember writing the list, I bet nothing on it was critical, but thanks for the delivery. I appreciate the news, Nathan."

"Anytime. Caller ID tells me you're still at the agency. How's your office coming along?"

"We finished the painting. I'm copying files at the moment. Tomorrow Bruce and I will build the bookshelves."

"If you need an extra hand, give me a call? I can get an hour free."

"If the lumber starts to overwhelm us, I'll do that."

"Talk to you tomorrow, Rae."

"Night, Nathan." She hung up the phone, still smiling. The man went out of his way to be helpful, either because it was his personality or because he wanted reasons to stop by. Either way, she appreciated it. She could use all the friends in this town she could make, and the sheriff was a nice place to start. She walked back to the receptionist area to start copying the next file.

Rae shut off the copier and took the last stack of pages over to the desk. She handwrote the tags for her files in a neat print and sorted out the pages.

The front door of the agency opened as she packed the insurance-company file. Rae looked up.

The couple looked to be in their midsixties. The lady wore a long blue coat and darker scarf, her hair beginning to gray and she moved with the slowness that suggested arthritis. The door was held open by a man wearing a hat and gloves but with only a suit jacket to protect against the cold evening.

As the lady came toward her without waiting for the man Rae assumed was her husband, Rae moved around the desk to greet her. "Good evening. I'm Rae Gabriella. How may I help you, Mrs . . . ?"

"Worth, Lucy Worth, and this is my husband, Richard."

Peggy's parents—Rae had met the family of the dead many times in her life but it never got easier to know what to say. The lady's fingers remained bent and stiff at the joints as she shook hands, and her grip had no strength. Rae lowered her guess at the lady's age to her fifties for she looked remarkably young. "It's nice to meet you both."

Rae offered her hand to Richard and got a solid handshake in return. His eyes were gray and below them a darkness to the skin suggested he had had very little sleep the last forty-eight hours. The suit jacket creases suggested hours of driving.

"Our daughter Peggy . . . she died at the hotel Saturday night, and the sheriff said you were one of the last people to talk with her."

"I spent a few minutes with her about seven o'clock," Rae confirmed, wondering exactly what Nathan had told them.

Richard looked around the office and then back at her. His jaw firmed. "We'd like to hire you to find out who killed our daughter."

11

Rae pushed open the door to Bruce's office and turned on the lights. A conference room didn't fit the conversation she needed to have with this couple. "Please, make yourselves comfortable. May I get you coffee or a soft drink?"

"Coffee, please," Mrs. Worth said.

Richard helped his wife slip off her coat. "It would be welcome."

"I'll be back in a moment."

In the break room she started coffee and then walked back to the reception area to get her briefcase. She retrieved her notepad, glad Nathan had thought it important enough to have couriered over.

She pulled blank forms from the office manager's supplies, not sure which she would need so she took a few of everything. She wished Bruce would swing back by the office and join her for this conversation, but she didn't want to call him and convey the fact she couldn't handle this.

This wasn't a case she wanted.

Lord, I'm not equipped for this coming conversation. Denial is natural in cases of sudden death, and they've had very little time to absorb this loss. If they pursue the idea their daughter was murdered in the face of information that it was a natural death, they will cut off the grieving and mourning they need to pass through in order to go on with their lives. Somehow, please, help me know how to help them turn that corner and accept what happened.

Rae collected the coffee and added cookies to the tray. She very much doubted if they had taken the time to eat, not if they had spent the day making arrangements with the coroner after the release of their daughter's body and had sought out the sheriff.

They had taken seats, Lucy Worth on the couch, Richard Worth in one of the chairs alongside. Rae slid the tray on the table and handed out the coffees, then took a seat near Richard, staying on their side of the desk. Lucy looked near the end of what she could handle today, her hands had a fine tremor as she lifted the cup to drink and her eyes were rimmed red from tears.

"I am so sorry for your loss."

"The police department called to pass on the fact she had been identified. We drove down and the coroner let us see her before the autopsy. Today we made arrangements for her burial plot. . . ." Lucy tried to say it without her voice breaking but her words trailed off.

Rae sipped her own coffee and just listened.

"We want to know what happened to our daughter," Mrs. Worth said. "It makes no sense that this was a seizure that killed her, when there is no history of epilepsy in either of our families; she never had a head injury or anything else which might contribute."

"This case is being closed as natural causes and we don't believe that's the full story. She was young, in good health, wasn't one to abuse her body with drugs or alcohol, and we don't think she drove to this community to sightsee. She was a freelance reporter, a good careful writer, and we think whatever story she was investigating in this town is related to her death."

Rae watched Richard from the corner of her eye while she listened to Lucy. Despite Richard's initial statement, she wasn't sure if he agreed with his wife's conclusions. "When did you last speak with your daughter?" Rae asked Mrs. Worth.

"Peggy called Saturday morning about nine. We made arrangements to see a play tomorrow night; she was going to buy the tickets from a friend who wasn't able to use them. We talked about her ongoing plans to redecorate her living room. She had found two table lamps she thought would be perfect. Peggy sounded fine."

Suicide didn't fit with what Rae already knew, and Mrs. Worth's words reinforced that. No one who initiated a call to her mom, arranged an evening out, would take her life before that day. She'd want one last opportunity to say good-bye.

Foul play . . . it was hard to get past the coroner's report. She hadn't seen the details but the conclusion of natural death had a legal implication and it wouldn't have been made had the coroner not been satisfied he had established both cause of death and the absence of contributing factors. "Do you know why your daughter was in Justice?"

"She often worked freelance on stories that interested her. What she was currently working on—she never said. We haven't found her notes at her apartment or in the belongings at the hotel which were returned to us this evening."

"I spoke with her Saturday evening and she mentioned she was going out on a late movie date. Do you know who she might have been meeting? A friend who lives in this area? A fellow reporter?"

"She didn't say. I have her address book; there might be something there which would suggest a name."

"Did she have a cell phone?"

"Yes. It was with her purse." Mrs. Worth leaned forward. "Please, you were the last person to talk with her that we know of. Don't you wonder?"

Rae studied her notes. Stalling for time wasn't going to work; they wanted an answer tonight on whether she would help them. Rae knew as much as anyone did about what had happened Saturday night, and it was precious little. She looked at Mrs. Worth. "What would set your mind at rest that Peggy's death was natural causes?"

Mrs. Worth reached for a tissue.

"We have questions," Mr. Worth replied. "What she was doing in town, where she went, who she saw. We'd like you to answer those questions for us."

"I would need to see her things from the hotel, and I'll need your permission to visit her home and copy items I might find helpful—phone bills, e-mails, even a diary."

"You have it."

"Mrs. Worth? I don't want to add to the grief you now feel. If my work confirms what the police have already told you, will that be helpful or will it just be more painful? I'll have to ask questions of her friends and coworkers and they may wonder why you asked me to investigate your own daughter. I don't want you to feel like you betrayed Peggy when that happens."

Lucy took a deep breath. "I need to know what happened. Even if the answers you find are not what I want to hear, I want the questions answered."

Rae nodded. She looked at Mr. Worth. "Twenty hours should be enough time to review what the police and coroner have, to complete the interviews with hotel guests and town residents who might have seen your daughter, and to learn what Peggy was working on. Let me brief you in a week on what I've found."

Mr. Worth visibly relaxed. "That would be fine." She understood his relief: he was doing this for his wife and while the costs would be accepted without blinking an eye, he didn't want to set in motion something that was open-ended. "What do we need to do next?"

"Are you staying in town?"

"At the Hilton Hotel."

"I'll need you to sign one form hiring me for the time discussed, and for you to fill out a questionnaire for me about your daughter. I'd like to come over to the hotel and pick up your daughter's things tomorrow morning, say 10 a.m., and also make arrangements to visit her home."

"Thank you, Miss Gabriella," Mrs. Worth said.

Rae took her hand after she rose. "I'll do my best to answer your questions. I'm truly sorry for your loss."

Mrs. Worth tried to smile. "Peggy was the light of my life."

Mr. Worth gestured to the photos on the wall as Rae led Mr. and Mrs. Worth back to the receptionist area. "You lived in Chicago?"

"I grew up about forty minutes from your daughter's home," Rae replied.

"That's good to know. Very good to know," Mr. Worth said.

Rae escorted them to the door and after they had reached their car, she turned off the outside lights and locked the door. She leaned her head against the doorjamb.

She had her first case. She couldn't say it was one she would have chosen; she had just found herself unable to say no.

She walked back to Bruce's office and picked up the coffee cups and tray. She thought about calling Bruce, but what would she say? I'm taking it because it needs to be done?

She had lived through an innocent man being accused, even though all the work had been done with the intent to get it right. Now she was asking was a natural death really something else? Not an intentional mistake by officers or the coroner's staff, but because of something that would change how they viewed what evidence they now had before them.

Bruce was going to raise an eyebrow and warn her to be careful. She wasn't worried about Bruce. Nathan was really not going to like this.

The last few days of enjoyable company and goodwill with Nathan were going to get trashed in a matter of hours when she stepped onto his turf and implied the police had missed something. Rae sighed. She couldn't seem to avoid controversy even when she wanted to keep a low profile.

12

"Tracy, get the Streets Department on the phone again, and tell Scott I want that bomb crater of a pothole on Second Street filled before I go home tonight or I am going to park a squad car in front of his house and leave the sirens on at 2 a.m." Nathan brushed at the spilled coffee on his shirt and tried to remember if he'd had time to do laundry in the last week or if this really was his last clean shirt.

"I'll get him. And you've got someone waiting in your office."

"So I just realized. Good morning, Rae."

"Sheriff."

He smiled and walked around her to dump his newspaper and his briefcase on the desk.

He had a 7 a.m. conference call with the state police beginning in minutes and an emergency meeting of his command staff to talk about protecting strikebreakers twenty minutes after that. He leaned back against the front of his desk. He'd take sixty seconds to enjoy the fact that Rae Gabriella looked wonderful first thing in the morning. She wore a business suit in hunter green and her jewelry was black pearls. Her smile alone was worth a rushed morning. *Bruce, you are one lucky man having her as a partner.*

"A hazardous morning?"

He accepted the Kleenex she offered to help dry his shirt. "Only because I really needed that full cup of coffee to drink. I'm a bit rushed for time, I'm afraid. How can I help you this morning?"

He took the stack of phone-call slips Tracy brought him. The number of them with red underlines would keep him on the phone for better than an hour. He dropped them in his in-box.

"Peggy Worth's parents came to see me last night."

"Did they?"

"You mentioned I was the last one to see their daughter."

Nathan tried to remember the details of the two conversations he had had with her parents. "Yes, I may have."

"They've hired me. They want more information about why Peggy came to Justice, where she went, and who she saw Saturday night. Mrs. Worth doesn't want to believe it was natural causes."

Nathan walked over to the door. "Tracy, would you ask Detective Sillman to stop by my office when he gets in and to bring the Peggy Worth file?"

"Will do."

"I'll have a copy of the file sent to you, as much as can be released to her parents, which will probably be all of it. If something is held back, we'll put in a paragraph summary." Rae's mouth opened and then closed without her speaking. He'd caught her off guard and it was fascinating to see. He had a feeling it didn't happen that often.

"You're not bothered because I'll be going over your department's work?"

"Rae, we do a good job. And for your first case, investigating a natural death will keep you out of trouble. No villain is out there. I've got enough trouble in this town at the moment."

A shouting match erupted out in the open bull pen of desks. "Anything else you need, don't hesitate to ask. If you can't find me and Tracy can't provide it, she'll know who to direct you to."

"Thanks, Nathan."

He paused in the door long enough to look back and share a smile. "Remember, I want a rematch on that pool game this week."

Nathan headed toward the shouting match. "Okay, what happened?"

The officer desperately wiping his eyes smelled strongly of Mace. "Tyler, don't use your shirt material; it makes it worse. Someone get him a water bottle."

"Here." Jim tossed one from the other side of the room.

The officer who caught it doused paper towels and handed them and the bottle of water to Tyler, who tipped his head back and flushed out his eyes. "He Maced me."

The department's youngest rookie looked like he wanted to disappear through the floorboards. "It was an accident. I used it last night to break up a fight, and I didn't get it secured on my belt."

"Tyler?"

"Yeah, it was a mistake. One I'm going to kill him for, but a mistake."

Nathan looked around and the crowd of officers began to fade away as the crisis passed. "Learn not to take down your fellow officers," he advised the rookie softly and offered a reassuring pat on the back. "For what it's worth, you're the third officer this year to catch the latch on his belt; these new canister designs are painfully bad."

Nathan turned his attention to Tyler. "Hold still, and look up. Let's make sure those contacts aren't trashed."

"One's moved to the corner of my right eye; I can feel it."

"Yeah, I see it."

Tyler managed to blink it out. "I'm fine, Nathan. I'm due off shift. I'll go take a shower and find my glasses and give my partner a remedial class in equipment safety."

"Check with Walter and see if there are eyedrops available over the counter that will counter some of that burn."

"I can do that for you, Tyler," the rookie offered.

Nathan took one last look between the two of them and left the men to sort it out.

When Nathan returned to his office he found Rae had gone and the phone was ringing. He'd hoped to get a cold soda before he started this conference call. He answered and set his handset to put the conference call on speaker. His deputy chief joined him in the office as the secretary taking minutes for the meeting began a roll call inquiry of names, her voice over the speaker-phone fading in and out.

"Sheriff Nathan Justice."

"Here."

Nathan held out a grateful hand as Chet arrived and passed over the second cold soda he carried.

"Detective White."

"Here," a faint voice answered somewhere down the line on the call.

Nathan motioned for Chet to close the door. At least this workday had begun with a good-looking lady sitting in his office. He was going to have to find an excuse to get Rae back here when he had more than one minute to talk.

Nathan studied the duty board on his wall as the state-police spokesman who ran these conference calls began the overnight update.

"A tanker truck was hijacked in St. Louis overnight, carrying two thousand gallons of unleaded gas."

Nathan glanced over in time to see Chet wince. That one would fall under Chet's patrol officers' duties. No one had ever told them a safe way to stop a loaded fuel truck.

"We continue to search for a missing ten-year-old girl from Peoria, Kim Louise. An updated flyer will be issued at 9 a.m."

Nathan opened the soda. It got to be a drag to have a job where he heard the bad news all across the state as the way to begin his workday. They cut off the bulletin at sixteen items and began the city roll call.

"Clarksville, do you have anything to issue?"

"No."

"Justice?"

"No."

"Treemont?"

"A 7-Eleven robbery last night killed four. We are searching for a '93 Honda Civic, license plate TRG 3498."

"Brentwood?"

"No."

As tough as a 7 a.m. call was on his schedule, it did help, if only to let him hear the voice of his counterparts in surrounding towns at least once a day. He tried to get over to Brentwood every month or so to do some after-hours chatting with Luke. The police chief over there, Luke Granger, had the big-city problems to deal with that Nathan was slowly seeing arrive in his own town. It helped, having that friend in the business to swap ideas with. The odds were good that before this was over, he'd be asking Luke for the loan of some officers to help with this strike.

The news that the company would bring in strikebreakers would be public in a day or two. Nathan needed a plan ready to implement, but as much as he studied the duty board there just weren't options that didn't leave him vulnerable in other areas.

Patrol, investigations, dispatch, and administration: the duty board showed twenty-six names with two on vacation or sick leave. It was thin staffing for the amount of work under way. The state call began its wrap-up and Nathan hit the speaker button to drop them off. "Will, Chet, let's find a place away from the office to have this strike discussion."

"I vote for breakfast," Will said.

"See if Della can give us the back room for some privacy," Nathan suggested. Nathan saw Sillman approaching the office and waved him in. "Gray and I will catch up with you."

Will and Chet headed out.

"What's up, Boss?"

"Peggy Worth." Nathan closed the door. Sillman wasn't going to like it.

ξ❦ვ   ξ❦ვ   ξ❦ვ

"Rae Gabriella, you don't even have a desk in your office yet and you got your first case."

She half turned from her discussion with Bruce's part-time office manager and was grasped around her waist and swung off her feet. "Bruce, put me down!" She laughed.

Bruce lowered her so her feet touched the floor again but left his arms draped across her shoulders to hug her. "Good job."

"How did you hear?"

"I ran into Nathan and his guys walking toward Della's café. Detective Sillman didn't exactly look pleased with it, but he'll get over it. So what are you going to do first?"

"Finish giving Margaret the coroner-report number so we can get a copy of it, head over to the hotel to finish up a few staff interviews, then meet up with Peggy's parents at ten. Nathan said he'd send over a copy of the police report and that should be here anytime."

"It sounds like a good plan. You can fill me in on what you find over dinner."

"Sure. Where are you heading?"

"I got a call from a guy who may know where those stolen handguns are at. I'll be over at the town rec center."

"You'll be careful?"

He smiled at her. "I will, Partner. Enjoy today. You only get a first case once."

13

Rae spread out the police file on the passenger seat of her car and searched for the call summary. Detective Sillman had retrieved Peggy's cell-phone records for the last couple weeks of her life. The sun warmed the inside of the car and she cracked the window. *Why did you come to town? Who did you see?* The items Peggy had with her at the hotel and in her rental car didn't give many clues.

Rae confirmed that the number Peggy had called Friday afternoon was the pharmacy. She had passed the store three times today for it was literally steps away from the Chapel Detective Agency.

She flipped pages and saw Detective Sillman had put a check mark next to the business, indicating he'd made a follow-up call. Since there was no report on file they had probably been playing phone tag or else the coroner had directly contacted the pharmacy.

Rae picked up the folder and photograph of Peggy and pushed open the car door.

The rich smell of cinnamon and the strong smell of disinfectant both met Rae as she opened the door to the pharmacy.

Peggy had arrived in town Thursday night; she'd visited the Chili Den for dinner, and Friday morning she'd stopped at the café for breakfast. The rest of Friday morning was a mystery and then at 3:12 p.m. she had called this pharmacy. Maybe a prescription refill of some kind?

She saw aisles neatly arranged, lightbulbs and aspirins on sale at the end of the nearest aisle. The checkout register had a young lady in her early twenties ringing up an assortment of shampoo and vitamin bottles for a customer.

Rae walked through the store to the back where the sign Pharmacy covered the wall and an arrow pointed to the prescriptions drop-off and another to order pick-up.

"Do you remember the directions for how to apply it, Mrs. Reit?" the pharmacist asked, leaning over the wide counter to show her the small bottle and the directions.

"Two drops on cotton and press hard for ten seconds, then wash with warm water. I remember."

"Don't use it more than once a day."

"I'll try to be patient, Walter, if you're sure this will work."

"It should do the job for you in about three weeks."

Rae scanned the shelves of vitamins and cold remedies as she waited. Something with zinc was supposed to be good for a sore throat. Nathan needed something; he was really getting hoarse. She picked up cough drops and for herself a pack of Juicy Fruit gum.

The lady opened her change purse and tugged out folded bills. "Would you make my change in quarters? I need some gum balls for my grandkids from that machine up front."

"Sure." The pharmacist made change and handed it across the counter along with her prescription sack. "Come see me next week and let me know how it's doing."

"I will."

Rae waited until the lady had moved down the aisle before stepping to the counter.

"Good afternoon."

She read the name tag and was relieved to find it was the owner. "Mr. Myers. I'm Rae Gabriella; I just started working with Bruce Chapel next door."

"Sure, I heard word at the café Bruce had himself a partner. It's nice to meet you." Walter offered his hand across the counter. He looked in his midforties, blond hair and brown eyes, a nice tan, and a welcoming smile that had her smiling back. "Walter Jr., as opposed to Walter Sr., my father." He nodded toward the man in a white coat working the other end of the counter.

It was a family business, and she didn't figure they had moved to Justice just to open the pharmacy. "Your family is one of the town's lifelong residents?"

"We've been here just a generation less than the Justice crowd, right, Dad?"

"Twenty years less, give or take," Walter Sr. replied, rearranging boxes.

"My father was the pharmacist in town before me, and probably my son Scott will take over one day for me. You'll get used to families in town all knowing each other for generations back. How can I help you today?"

"Could I purchase these items back here?"

"Sure."

"Nathan Justice mentioned you might have something over the counter that could help with an intense itch." She rested her arm on the counter and rolled up her sleeve to show the scar. "The doctor did a good job, but it's healing and driving me crazy when it gets warm."

Walter set aside the cough drops and took hold of her wrist to turn her arm and study the scar. "You may be a touch allergic to the dissolvable stitches they used. I've got a cream that might help, if only to keep the salt of sweat out of irritating it more."

"I'll try about anything."

Walter turned away and opened the refrigerator. He brought back a small cream jar. "Let's see if this helps before I make you a batch. It's basically a bunch of things out there on the shelves mixed together in a skin cream, but those who hit poison ivy during the summer swear by it."

He opened the jar and she smelled a rich vanilla. "Rub in some at one end of the scar and if it's helping in a few hours, stop back by and I'll make you a few days' worth."

"Thanks." She found the cream smooth and cold and it rubbed in easily. "Nathan said you also had a sunburn cream."

"He should market it I keep telling him," Walter Sr. said.

"That's more work than I want, Dad." He rang up her small purchases.

"Most of these come down as recipes from my grandmother and I improve them a bit as new over-the-counter options become available. The mosquito repellent still needs work, but I'm hopeful I'll get it perfected this summer. I like being practical."

Rae pulled folded bills from her pocket for the purchases. "Did you hear about the lady who died at the Sunburst Hotel this weekend?"

"Yes, it's tragic news."

Rae showed him the photo. "Her name is Peggy Worth. I'm working for her parents, trying to trace where Peggy went while she was in town. I noticed she called the pharmacy on Friday afternoon. Would you remember what that happened to be about?"

Walter Sr. came over to take a look at the picture too. "I remember her."

Walter Jr. nodded. "As I told Detective Sillman, she'd walked through a briar patch and wanted to know if we had peroxide or something she could use to deal with the burrs which had gotten under her socks. I sold her tweezers and antiseptic and talked her into getting a package of those ankle guards the guys use when they are out walking pastures to avoid just that kind of thing happening."

"Did she say where she had been?"

"Since she also asked about where to find Joe Prescott's place, I assume she was out east of town getting lost on the unmarked roads down by the river trying to find his place on her own."

"Let me guess—you didn't tell her Joe had died."

Walter winced. "I feel kind of bad about that now. Joe's so ornery, rumor around here has it he faked his death to get reporters off his case. Joe could be living comfortably back at one of his cabins in the woods enjoying the start of the early ice fishing, or so the legend around here goes."

She accepted the good-natured no and smiled. "So Peggy from here probably went where . . . ?"

"Have you tried the newspaper?" Walter Sr. asked. "They would have been closed to the public by 4 p.m. Friday, but there's a chance Peggy talked herself in to see the archives."

"I already did. The editor would love to have a story on my search, but he doesn't remember Peggy and he worked Friday until shortly after 8 p.m."

"She had to eat, and this town loves to notice visitors."

Rae slid the photo back into her file. "I'm counting on that. Thanks, guys, for the help and the cream."

"If it's working in a few hours, give me a call. I can make a batch in about an hour," Walter promised.

"I'll do that."

Rae picked up her sack, nodded her thanks, and walked back through the store.

Rae unlocked the passenger-side door of her car. She was glad she'd arranged to see Peggy's home first thing tomorrow morning. Peggy had to be working on a news story of some kind, either human interest or a more investigative piece. Maybe a neighbor of Joe Prescott had seen Peggy or her car. So far it appeared that Peggy hadn't learned of Joe's death by Saturday night when she died.

Had they been wrong to assume Peggy had been planning to see the movie in Justice? Rae knew she personally thought nothing of driving an hour north of Chicago for dessert. Peggy likely had the same Chicago resident sense of distance. As long as you could get there in a couple hours, you didn't think twice about the drive. Maybe her date wasn't in Justice, but closer to where Peggy lived.

Rae retrieved her street map of the town. She'd walk both sides of the downtown streets and begin canvassing the businesses and maybe get lucky with someone who had had a conversation with Peggy.

From her own observations, the townspeople seemed to tilt toward longer conversations even with strangers than big cities ever did. That would be useful. From the trash Nathan had noted, Peggy had visited the Fine Chocolates Shop, and that was a nearby shop Rae planned to linger at: made-from-scratch chocolates—she'd indulge with pleasure.

{}{} {}{} {}{}

"I understand you want to visit where Joe Prescott lived," Nathan said.

Rae started, nearly dropping the folder with Peggy's photo she had been showing at shops and the small bag of chocolate pieces she had tucked under her arm. She turned to find Nathan at her elbow. "You're going to give me a heart attack with that kind of surprise arrival."

"You were thinking so hard you didn't hear me. And I don't think it was about preordering Valentine's Day flowers."

Rae realized she had stopped in front of the flower shop. "No, I wasn't thinking about flowers." She turned her attention back to the Justice street map she was attempting to refold, the streets marked with small notations recording where she had stopped today. "I can't find Peggy's notebook. If she was working on a story, she had to have notes."

"Makes sense."

He looked good despite the windblown hair and a streak of mud drying on his left sleeve and pant leg. It didn't look like it had been a quiet day for him. She just felt windblown and uncoordinated and a bit caught off guard for what to say.

"I'm heading out east of town to check on a broken-in barn. Would you like to ride along? I can show you the Prescott land," Nathan offered.

She appreciated the unexpected invitation. "I'm due to meet Bruce in twenty minutes. Can I take a rain check for tomorrow?"

"Of course."

"I got you something, not as nice as the roses, but something." Rae dug out the bag of cough drops from her pocket.

Nathan smiled as he accepted them. "They're a godsend. Thanks."

"The strike has kept you busy today?"

"A couple scuffles and one of the management negotiators received a broken car window, but it has stayed contained." Nathan glanced around to see who was nearby. "It may get pretty tense around here later this week; don't take what people say against them, okay? A strike tends to brings out the worst as well as the best in people."

"I rarely let first impressions of someone be my long-term opinion." She offered the bag of chocolates to share her best find of the day—the chocolates were near perfection. "You've heard news that has you worried?"

"I hear lots of rumors, most of which I'm glad don't come true," Nathan replied, accepting a chocolate piece. "Enough work. If you're free tomorrow night, say nine, do you want to join me at Sir Arthur's for a game of pool?"

"If I'm free, I'll be there."

"Good. Thanks." Nathan walked back to his squad car. "I'll see you around, Rae."

She lifted a hand in farewell as his car pulled away.

14

"Charred enough for you?" Bruce asked.

"Perfectly burnt," Rae replied happily, working through the hamburger. Steaks she liked bloody; hamburgers she preferred burnt. She reached over into the picnic basket to retrieve the milk shake she had balanced against the container of cold pasta. "This is not exactly what I expected."

"Think of it as the one hazard of this new job, the constant changing of the best-laid plans."

"I think you mean you forgot to pick up your dirty socks and changed your mind about showing me your place tonight."

Bruce grinned. "Now she figures it out. Try the strawberries; I requested them especially for you."

She selected one from the container. Their plans for dinner at Bruce's home had changed with the reality that Bruce was still working as she got ready to wrap up her day. He'd shown his connections in this town with the ability to get food delivered to him, even while on a stakeout.

Rae gestured out the car window. "He's not cheating on his wife."

"I know that. You know that. His wife still isn't ready to believe that. And I lost my best chance of getting fired by her yesterday. I watched Bob slip out to spend the afternoon with Nathan's grandfather."

"Then what are we doing sitting here?" They had been watching the back door of the union hall for the last hour.

"Paying the rent. Getting reacquainted." He flashed her a smile. "Convincing you to go out with me again, not just come by my place for dinner."

"If you're waiting on that, I may test your patience a bit." She shifted in the seat and pushed off her shoes. She'd walked so many streets of Justice today showing Peggy's photo she suspected she'd raised a blister.

She'd love to date again: the care and thought and time a guy put into a relationship made her feel like a princess. Bruce seemed more relaxed about life now and maybe that extended to what he thought about God, about having a family, about what he wanted for his future. She had plenty of time to figure out the changes, to figure out her own heart and life troubles. She wasn't going to hurry it. The last thing she wanted to do was mess up the one bright spot in her life right now.

She focused on dinner, realizing she had forgotten lunch during the course of the day.

"There's Bob," Rae said, spotting their quarry.

Heather's husband left the union hall and bypassed his car in the lot to walk down to the sidewalk and head north.

Bruce started his car. "Now where is he going?"

Bruce drove past Bob and turned onto the next block. He pulled over to the curb, using the rearview mirror to keep track of the man. "Okay, we need to know who lives at 426 Kline Street."

Rae turned to better see the house. "The red brick with a porch?"

"Yes."

She reached around to the backseat and picked up the street-marketing directory, one of Bruce's expensive luxuries that made his work easier. She found Kline Street and scanned house numbers. "Peter and Ellen Tucker."

"Tucker . . . isn't he the one who owns the farm-equipment dealership and rents out heavy-construction equipment?"

Rae reached for the phone book to see if the yellow pages had an ad.

"It's faster just to call Margaret and ask," Bruce said, picking up the phone to call his office manager at home. Bruce asked Margaret the question and then gestured for a pen. He scrawled down several names beginning with *Peter Tucker* and put arrows between them. "Thanks, Margaret." He hung up the phone. "Peter Tucker owns the business and he's a distant cousin to Bob Teal."

"So Bob's now visiting family."

"Yep."

Rae leaned her head back against the seat. "If every private case is like this one . . ."

Bruce laughed. "This is one of the worst; I just thought I'd start you out at the bottom so when cases got more interesting you'd appreciate it."

"Thanks."

Rae watched Bruce. His gaze was patiently focused on the rearview mirror waiting for Bob Teal to reappear. He had never been this patient in days past.

"Close your eyes and catch a catnap. I've got this covered."

"I'm along to keep you company."

Bruce smiled. "You are."

"I'm not wimping out and sleeping on a stakeout." She reached into the picnic basket for another soda. "I'm just still on East Coast time."

"Humm."

She slapped his leg. "Lay off; it's been a while since I endured this stakeout boredom."

"What did you find out today about those handguns?" Rae broke the silence in the car to ask.

"That I was dealing with someone a lot more interested in my hundred bucks than he was in having a viable lead to give me."

"I'm sorry about that."

Bruce smiled. "I've still got the hundred. One of the gun shops in the area will come through for me eventually with a lead on ammo purchases that match or an attempt to sell one of the guns under the counter. There isn't a shop owner in the area who doesn't want a robber who takes firearms behind bars."

"Where do folks go around here when they want to do some practice shooting?"

"We're wide open around Justice; go out ten or twenty miles and you've got as much privacy as you like. Most tend toward the woods that run along the river; or up around the pavilion at the lake."

Bruce picked up his coffee and finished it, wincing a bit as the heat touched his cut lip. "I heard Kyle got bail set at a hundred thousand this afternoon. That puts him thankfully out of the picture for a while, for there is no way he'll raise that kind of bail money on his own."

"When is Chet and Laura's wedding?"

"Three weeks. I'll introduce you. They make a nice couple."

Fighting sleep as she watched the street, Rae knew she needed a diversion. She reached around for her briefcase. She opened it and pulled out the photos e-mailed by Frank that afternoon.

The Ferrari's crystal red paint job reflected the camera flash, leaving a white spot on the side panel. It was a beautiful eight-year-old car with less than forty thousand miles on the odometer, a gem of a car but for one crucial fact. Blood had run down the inside windows. The owner had put a twenty-two in his mouth and pulled the trigger. She did not relish trying to get dried blood off the leather seats.

"You're serious about cleaning up that car and driving it?"

"Yes."

"You need your head examined, Rae."

"I can't see turning the car into scrap parts, not when it's superficial damage."

"It's got ghosts."

"One ghost, and the man did it to himself. If it had been a murder, then that would be another matter."

"*If it had been a murder* . . . do you ever listen to yourself? It's creepy."

"When you've washed blood off a ceiling fan, knowing its castoff from a knife attack on a kid, it tempers what bothers you. I need another car, I like one that is fast, and this one I can afford." She looked again at the photos and knew she wanted the car. She slid the photos back into the folder. She'd tell Frank to buy it, and then she'd worry about how to get it cleaned up to drive.

Bruce sat up straighter. "There's Bob." He started the car. "I'll let you drive next time."

"Thanks for small favors." Rae jotted down the time on the report. "I'm betting he's returning home."

"I'll take that bet. So what do you think of your first full day as a PI?"

Rae could think of numerous adjectives but she settled for a diplomatic one. "Interesting."

Bruce laughed. "That's my partner."

Bob walked back to the union hall. He disappeared inside again, rather than return to his car. Bruce drummed his hand against the steering wheel. "Well—" He bit off what he was about to say.

Rae laughed.

Bruce parked. "This isn't funny."

She was just tired enough that it was hilarious. "Sure it is."

She was ready to call her first day of work done. She had the police report and coroner report to read over again tonight and a plan to make for her visit to Peggy's home tomorrow. And she would take Nathan up on that offer to visit Joe Prescott's place. But at the moment she couldn't think of anything more priceless than seeing Bruce's expression when Bob walked back into the union hall.

She settled back in her seat and got comfortable, reaching into her pocket for the pack of gum she had bought for just this kind of occasion. If Bob took his time—well, it wasn't the first time she'd caught a catnap in a car, and it wouldn't be the last. Walking over to her own car and leaving Bruce here to continue this on his own wasn't going to happen even if she was ready to call it a day and get some sleep. She liked being back in Bruce's world, and she relished the captive time with him. Over the years, nights like this had led to some of the most interesting conversations she'd ever had with him.

"I bet he's playing a long game or two of chess while he talks."

"Shut up, Rae."

She laughed and unwrapped the gum. She considerately held out the package.

Bruce tugged out two pieces. "I prefer Big Red over Juicy Fruit."

"Tough it out."

"Yeah." He unwrapped the gum and folded it into his mouth. With a sigh he set out to make thin rolls out of the foil wrappers.

15

"Do you like this kind of work?" Rae asked, breaking the comfortable silence in the car.

Bruce turned to look over at her. "How do you mean?"

"The following of leads, the watching of people, the fact that there is nothing particularly life or death in the cases now on your whiteboard?"

"Surprisingly, I do like it. I think it grows on you. I know, you can't imagine this being the adrenaline-addicted Bruce you know and love."

"I'm not exactly the Rae you remember either. And I suppose if I was in Heather Teal's place, wondering if my husband was cheating on me, it would be worth a few dollars to have the question answered."

Bruce tried to stretch out his legs and had to settle for shifting where his knee met the dash. "The case is all in the eyes of the beholder. So we'll sit and watch for another day until I can try again to get myself fired by my client. I'd just quit, but this case has become something of its own making."

Rae thought about that and the man they were watching. She'd studied a lot of people over the years conducting stakeouts but not many like this subject. The man was a civilian in the most pedestrian form of that word, not even showing basic situational awareness as he walked public streets to look around and notice what was around him. Still . . . the man didn't look blind. "Bob knows you are watching him."

Bruce balanced the gum wrappers into a neat triangle on the dash, having borrowed hers to form the base. "He figured that out on about day three," Bruce agreed.

"So he's not going to do anything to tip his hand now even if he was cheating on his wife."

"Very true."

Rae was amused at the fact Bruce knew his cover was blown and didn't seem concerned about it. Life had definitely changed. "So are you charging Heather for this stakeout time?"

Bruce just looked over at her.

Rae laughed. "That's what I thought. You're a softie, Bruce."

"I like the fact I've got your undivided attention for a couple hours. There's no need for Heather to pay for me to hang out with you."

"I'm sitting here yawning on you."

"You have been fighting to keep those eyes open," he agreed. He nodded to the case notes and went back to answer her real question. "I'm not going to lie on the report I hand Heather, saying I was watching Bob when I wasn't. And I'm not going to continue to charge her when I determined on day two that there was no real job here to work. I'm just working out the details of how to get Heather to comfortably trust her husband again.

"Get her annoyed enough with me, she'll blow up at Bob and start talking to him again, which is what she should have done in the first place, and they'll sort out whatever got her wondering about him. All will be fine in Tealville again. A few hours of my time to make that happen is worth it. It's the one thing I really have to offer these days—time."

Rae was startled by his words. "That's your plan?"

"For want of a better one. I don't think anything can make Heather Teal less suspicious and less of a cynic, but I'll make an honest run at it. They've been married thirty-two years; that's got to mean something. Heather can learn to relax and trust Bob again."

Rae felt confusion settle in place of the surprise. Bruce was not only volunteering his time, he was doing it for a noble reason. "You didn't used to be this positive about people's ability to change."

He started to answer her, then just stopped and shrugged. "I got religion somewhere in the last eleven years. The idea that even the worst of people can change their stripes no longer seems naive."

Rae set aside her questions about this particular case, more interested in the first glimpse into the missing years between them. "What happened?"

He studied her, then turned his attention back to the union-hall door. "It's a terribly long and boring story."

She knew the look and the cautioning tone under the words. Bruce placed it as an answer she wasn't ready to hear or would regret having pursued. She hesitated. Over the years she'd learned to trust his judgment about that, to pass when he thought a topic was better left alone for a later time.

His look had been born in those early days of his being an undercover cop, of his wanting a relationship with her that was honest and open, but still protected from what he dealt with. He did it to protect her from knowing what would be hard to forget, rather than to protect himself from the telling.

"I don't mind talking about religion," she finally replied. "And while it might be terrible and long, the story is probably not boring." If he was willing to talk about it, she wanted to know.

He conceded the point with a small nod. "Maybe a story best told in chapters then."

He hesitated and looked back across the street. Her memory of him was more like this, of caution, of weighing details for what he might say, of considering the word picture he'd leave her with before he said the first words.

"I got shot six years ago."

Her breath didn't flow in right. It blossomed like an ache in the center of her chest. She'd expected a lot of things. Not this. "I didn't hear about it," she whispered.

"I didn't want anyone to know."

He gave her a wry smile and a shrug that was anything but casual. An apology, such as she would take it.

She'd take it. She knew part of what was coming now before he ever went on to add substance to those words.

"I'd been undercover for so long, the guys I studied and watched were almost friends. You have to like the guys at some level to be around them seven days a week and be authentic. They were good with repairing cars and following sports and loving their families." He rubbed his breastbone. "Someone gave up my name as being an undercover cop. I took three in the chest in a drive-by."

"You had a vest on."

"Purely by chance. Even so, one round got through as I twisted. Most of the energy in the round had expended, so it didn't splatter my insides all across the block, but it was enough to put me down in a pool of blood. I recovered, but I never went back. I wonder now what happened to those guys I hung with, how their families are doing, who's gotten married, who's had a kid, basic stuff like who's still alive. It's strange the way you still wonder about the chapter of life that is over."

"The cops don't know who shot you."

"I could have named a dozen names, all as probable as the other. I told my boss not to push, to protect the informants I'd built up, and use my believed passing to get another undercover cop working up the ladder. They were smart enough to take my advice. That many years undercover, there weren't many wholesale dealers on the south side whose organizations I hadn't penetrated on one level or another. The fact I'd made it as long as I had was the surprise.

"I'd be dead if my face appeared in the neighborhood again—that's understood. But I still miss those guys in the middle layer. They preferred to talk about the latest baseball scores than how to move more product on the street. Drugs were the business they knew from grade school, the easy career path. But some of the guys were better than that life. Some of them left it. And those were the stories that kept me going.

"I'm not softening it; I hated drugs more by the time my career was ending than I did in those first years—and I was pretty intense about it back when you knew me. I put away more dealers and confiscated more product than any other cop to work that side of the city.

"Those last couple years, they were having to spread the public credit for my busts around the districts to keep from having a bounty go down on the guy who happened to be given the job of taking the microphone and claiming credit in order to keep my existence buried from the press. Those last days were heady, and I suppose I should have read the writing on the wall. That kind of run historically ends with a bullet."

Rae absorbed that and felt a deep regret inside. "I wish I had known; I wish I'd been there for you. I wondered why you weren't working undercover anymore. I'd heard that news through the grapevine, but I wasn't in a position I could call."

"Undercover yourself?"

She nodded.

"The physical recovery was reasonably quick. My boss tried to transition me back inside, but I wasn't cut out for a desk job or a supervisor's shield. It was easier to retire and settle on something new."

Bruce smiled. "But you know me, Rae. I never do something the easy way if I can do it the hard way. After about six months of retirement I was close to being both a drunk and a bum, and I had already picked a couple fights only a fool would pick."

"I noticed the broken nose."

Bruce rubbed it. "Makes me look young and stupid, doesn't it? That was one of my wilder fights. I put on weight, I got mad at the world, and basically I wasn't much fun to be around."

"You were decompressing."

He nodded as he sighed. "I know that now: decompressing hard and fast and in the roughest way a guy can do it. Then I was just looking at the newspaper each morning and seeing more drugs killing more kids, and I decided that the finger I stuck in the dyke for the best years of my life hadn't done a bit of good."

His expression turned distant and she could understand part of what he was saying, the realization that he felt like he had wasted the best part of his life on something that had made no difference.

Bruce glanced over at her. "I think I flipped from the anger to depression to emptiness in one particularly ugly weekend. Life just hurt."

"I'm sorry." There weren't words for this hurt, and she didn't try to find any.

"So am I."

He looked across the street, thinking, then nodded to himself and went on. "I ended up sitting in church one day. A Wednesday, I think it was. I'd followed some good-looking lady inside. Don't ask me what I was thinking or what I was wearing or what I thought I'd say to her if I caught up with her. Turns out a guy we both know was there. Remember old man Cayger? The guy that used to sell those blistering hot polish sausages from that street cart?"

"Sure. He was a fixture in the neighborhood."

"There was some kind of weeknight prayer service happening. Anyway, we got to talking. And I got to deciding it was okay to think there was a God in charge of this world and of making things right, and it wasn't Bruce."

"You always knew that."

"After so many years of Catholic school, I should have. But it started to mean something again that night, religion. You know what I mean?"

"Yeah, I do." Faith could be set aside as a passing piece in life, but eventually it moved up in importance relative to everything else in life. Family, career, health, possessions—they all crashed as the years passed by—and at some point religion started to look like the one stable thing left in life.

"I bumped back into religion again. I didn't go looking for it, but I was at least smart enough to see what it was I'd rediscovered. Substance, in the person of Jesus." Bruce shifted in his seat, looking marginally embarrassed at the emotion in the history he was telling. He glanced over at her. "You know Jesus?"

"Not as well as I need to," she replied, not minding the turn he'd taken in the conversation. She had a feeling if she didn't hear the details tonight, he'd tuck the matter back into his past and she'd just be left with her questions.

"Same boat here—I'm learning." Bruce sighed. "I don't know if I can explain it, Rae. All that stuff in the Bible that Jesus said and did—it always ended with Jesus saying 'Follow Me.' As if that was the answer to the rest of the questions and decisions and confusion in life.

"That Wednesday night—I was a man seeing life as something to be endured, who suddenly encountered in Jesus someone who said life is special and there's something more to be found—so follow me. And I did. I made the choice to say yes and mean it.

"I was too old to make it the partial kind of decision, the check-it-out-and-see-what-I-think-of-this, kind of toe-in-the-water approach. I'd had a lifetime messing up my life and I just wanted that whole swamp turned over to someone else to fix. I started going to church again, that prayer meeting gathering, and a Sunday service. I found an old copy of the Bible my cousin had left around and started reading it.

"I'm not sure God was particularly thrilled to get me in the sad shape I was in, but I'm walking around proof that people can change. You wouldn't have liked me back then, Rae, in the months after I left the force. You've got a good heart, you're kind, you were always willing to take a lot of grief from me after bad days on the job and never give it back—but even you would have walked away from me back then and had cause. It took about a year of God going after my insides before the anger of the past broke. It healed slowly, that hurt, that sense of having failed to make a difference, but the past finally started to go to rest.

"From there, in a very long roundabout way, I ended up here, in Justice, with a storefront detective agency, an old restored car, a big old house becoming a place that feels like home, and something to do with my days that occasionally feels useful again."

His words ended and he rubbed the back of his neck before looking over at her. "A long story and not particularly interesting to someone other than me. I don't expect you to understand the religion thing or the passion and relief I'm describing in what I found. I know what I got rescued from. I was in a pretty deep black hole and Jesus pulled me out of it. But it's my own journey. I told you mainly because you'll be brushing up against that past when you hang out with me and I don't want you feeling surprised by it."

She thought about what he had said. "I appreciate the fact you told me. The job and the career don't last; we both know that. Religion is the one thing that does last. Personally, I'm no longer willing to say it's a small part of my life either." She thought about her last eleven years and her smile was sad as she shook her head. "Besides, I've got a few chapters in my own life much like yours."

Bruce studied her. "I figured you might."

She waited for his question, but Bruce didn't take the opening. "Not going to ask?"

Bruce shook his head. "No need. You keep secrets, Rae, but never about the important things. When you've figured out the words in those chapters of yours, when you're ready, you'll share what's been happening."

"It's going to be a while, maybe a long while."

Bruce smiled. "Time is the one thing we have going for this relationship. There's nothing you're going to say that will particularly surprise me, Rae. In the job I did, I literally saw it all."

She thought in a way he was right. Hearing what had happened with Mark Rivers—Bruce would have already guessed part of it. He knew what a defensive knife wound looked like, he'd seen her house, and she wouldn't attribute to him being unobservant. He'd put together the majority of the physical facts she would be describing—but the why—he wasn't ready for the why. Some things no one should have to hear, and especially not a fellow cop.

She looked across the street. She thought about letting the conversation flow back toward less intense topics, of letting it rest for now, the weight of those chapters just shared. But when this topic closed, Rae didn't think she'd have the courage to reopen it for some time, and questions stirred below the surface that she wished she could have answered. It was rare for Bruce to be so open about what she knew had to be an intensely private part of his life.

She risked the question she had; she risked trying to process what she had heard from him aloud and with him, knowing he would hear in her questions her own heart's struggle with God. "Do you think it was part of some plan, that you got shot so you would end up in that church and rediscover religion?"

Bruce shook his head. "I got shot because someone was willing to exchange the name of an undercover cop for a lot of cash. Ending up in church—God was just kind enough to make something good come out of the disaster that hit my life."

She flexed the sides of the soda can she held. "Do you think God always brings good out of the disasters in our lives?"

"I think He's willing to if we'll let Him." Bruce smiled. "Isn't it strange,

Rae, how hard we struggle to believe that God loves us, that God will do the right thing? The Bible says God is good. It's His personality, His nature. It's impossible for Him to do bad; it's outside His very character. And yet when we start to think about religion, about God, we spend most of our time trying to gather up the courage to trust and believe that God is actually going to be good to us and be willing to help us."

"I know." She risked an observation in return that he might think simplistic. "But maybe it's expected. We live in a messy, painful, fallen world. We live surrounded by good people who turn out to be liars, by people we trust betraying us—we live in a place where evil continually shows up and destroys what is good. And from that past we're supposed to look at God, and despite everything we've lived through, we're supposed to not attribute to Him any of the failings that beset everyone else we know."

She turned the soda can in her hands and could feel the remaining liquid in the bottom had long since warmed to undrinkable. She didn't bare her heart easily, even with the one guy she trusted more than any other in her life, but she wanted someone she could be that honest with, and Bruce was listening and hearing her. She risked saying the rest of it. "I think trusting that God is good is one of the hardest steps there is to take. We get conditioned to expect to be let down. We get conditioned to not trust, because we trusted and we get burned. We get conditioned to be reserved and not take things at face value because we've learned nothing is ever at face value in life.

"We have no relationships that come close to the relationship we are called on to have with God. With God, one side is perfect. The other side, our side, is clinging on by a prayer, asking 'forgive me; please let grace cover my sins.' We can hold that relationship with God only because He's reaching over and holding us up to His level, not because we can ever reach to His level."

Bruce nodded. "Jesus pointed at the Father and said that's life, to know that God who is absolutely perfect and good and loving; and it's an abundant life to trust and obey Him. Jesus knew the Father was the one person we could have a relationship with who wouldn't let us down. And that is the key thing necessary for having a good life: a relationship with Jesus and with God the Father."

Rae thought about her own desperate search to find some peace again, to be content with life and settled again, and she ended up shaking her head. She wanted that relationship with God to work and it seemed she was just always reaching and never quite there. She was still sorting out the hurts of the last year to the point she didn't know what to think even about God Himself anymore. "Is it this hard for everyone, Bruce? I seem to know and understand less about God the older I get. Do you think someone like Nathan ever walks this kind of path with religion? Wrestling with the basics of the relationship?"

Bruce thought about it. "For those who got the luxury of hearing the Good News early in their life, who accepted it when they were young—maybe the questions are just different for them. Once you're an adult—it's hard to believe any relationship, no matter how long it has lasted so far, isn't going to sometime in the future fail. It is always a struggle to trust and not hold something back. It's easy to doubt, and it's hard to trust. But I need to trust, which is why I keep coming back to it. I need to trust that God is good, and from that, find hope again that life can be good."

Rae knew there was wisdom in that. "We used to talk philosophy and about being cops back in the days we were dating. Now we talk religion. I can't say I mind the change."

Bruce smiled. "We've had these stakeout conversations before, Rae. We both end up saying more than we thought we would or go into corners with subjects we didn't plan, because the topics flow around in eddies on us."

"I am glad you told me about what happened. I know it's not easy to peel back layers and relive the history of being shot again. But hearing the story does help me to understand. You have changed, Bruce. And I like the new you."

"I'm beginning to like this new me too."

She shifted around on the seat to find a more comfortable place. "Was there any particular reason you chose Justice as the place to open the agency? A dart tossed at the map? Something more definite?"

"I'd met Nathan's dad at one point in the past and liked him. I'd been through the area before and remembered it. It wasn't anything more than that. The town is close enough to Chicago I figured if I changed my mind about being in a small town, I could always take an apartment back in the city and commute occasionally to the place here for my vacations. But I got here, and I settled remarkably easy.

"Like any small town, there is a variety of stories regarding who I am and how I ended up opening a detective agency in this town of all places. Some have me as still doing deep undercover work for the county narcotics task force, others have me escaping disciplinary action by resigning, others think I'm just another one of the out-of-towners who want to shift assets from big city to small town so I can take huge tax write-offs with the business while not doing any particular work."

Rae smiled. "I'm sure that habit of yours of never explaining has led to a few of those rumors starting."

"I'm sure it did."

"This town has been a good fit for you, I think. I'm glad you invited me to come join you."

"I'm glad you came. You'll find it grows on you too, Rae, and starts to feel like home."

"I hope it does. That would be nice, Bruce, to feel settled again."

16

Rae shifted her jacket to create a better headrest. She was drifting on Bruce, and that wasn't a good thing. He was patiently watching for Bob Teal to reappear. She reached for a new soda and opened it. "Talk to me some more, about anything. I want to stay awake a bit longer."

Bruce smiled, but he complied. He gestured toward the union hall. "Did you realize this case is something of a milestone? My fiftieth case as a private investigator. Sam thought I'd fold up shop after the first half dozen."

"What was the first case?"

He didn't answer her. She looked over and thought this might be interesting. He was trying not to look entirely embarrassed. "What? Give. I can see it's a good story."

"A lost dog," he said so quietly she barely heard him.

She choked on her soda. "You're kidding me, right?"

He looked over at her and his embarrassment shifted toward remembered amusement. "Rae, I swear. Cross my heart and hope to die, absolute truth. My first case was a lost dog."

"Give. I want the story. And don't leave out any details."

"It was a Pekinese. The lady was traveling to a dog show; she'd stopped overnight at the Hilton Hotel and they let her have her dog in her room. She gets up in the morning, gets ready to go down to breakfast, goes to put him back in his travel cage, and her precious dog is gone. I thought Tony was an actual person for the first couple minutes of the phone call. I'd said yes, I had time to help her that day, before I realized she was talking about a dog."

"Give me a napkin. I've got to wipe my eyes here. Bruce Chapel, detective extraordinaire, looking for a little mutt."

"Please, it was a purebred dog, not a mutt."

"Hands and knees looking under the cars? Showing the photo around? Getting flyers ready to put out?"

Bruce just nodded.

Her laughter hurt her ribs. It got to the point she stopped trying to talk, because every new thought triggered another peal of laughter. "Where did you find him?" she finally got enough composure to ask. "You did find him, didn't you?"

"Of course I did. He'd snuck out when the maid brought in more towels. I found him in the hotel sauna hiding under the bench, very well steamed. I hate to think what germs were under there. He sneezed the entire time I carried him back to his owner." Bruce laughed at the memory. "Man, he was very well steamed."

"This is priceless. Did you also keep the first dollar you made as a private detective?"

He shifted on the seat to tug his wallet from his back pocket. He moved the flap to get to the inside pocket. "Still crisp too."

She took the bill he handed her. "I like Benjamin Franklin. His face looks so sweet, and he was so mercenary when it came to money."

"Keep it."

"No way." She took the wallet out of his hand and slid the bill back into its protective place under the flap. "This is like a treasured timepiece." She fanned out two photos he had in the wallet. "Those are timepieces too. I was young." She hadn't expected to see herself, and she could feel her heart tumbling a bit at the reality Bruce had been carrying her photo for so many years.

"We looked good together," Bruce pointed out.

She smiled, feeling like she was stepping on a bit of quicksand. "You always could make me laugh. Where was this, the county fair?"

Bruce nodded. "Just after you got your badge."

Rae pushed the photos back into the wallet and handed it back to him. "You need a more current picture. Folks will think you are robbing the cradle."

Bruce put away his wallet, then reached over and gently traced her chin with a finger even as he smiled. "I figure I'll find an excuse to get a new one of you one of these days."

She could handle talking religion easier than she could handle the rather terrifying thought of talking about their relationship as it had been in the past. So much joy, laughter, love, and just plain emotion roiled back there, deliberately left in the past when she had wisely accepted his push that it was a good thing that she go to the FBI rather than stay with him in Chicago.

She looked away from Bruce, not wanting to duck the conversation with a trivial remark, but knowing this topic had to be set aside. She started. "Bob. He just unlocked his car."

Bruce turned to look and hurriedly shifted to start the car. "Good catch. Had he pulled out and we missed it, you would have been telling this stakeout story on me for the next fifty years."

Rae breathed a sigh of relief for more personal reasons. "It would have been another priceless story to tell," she agreed lightly. "He's going home; he has to be at this time of night."

"We'll see."

Bruce stayed well back, using the taillights of the car to keep Bob in sight. They followed him safely home.

"Want dessert somewhere?"

Rae paused in her search through the picnic basket for anything she had missed earlier. A wise answer would be to ask Bruce to take her back to her car and give her an escort to the hotel. But she looked at him, at the man she'd given her heart to long ago and still thought to call when her life crashed to pieces, and didn't want to walk away just yet from the fact that she had someone to really talk with tonight. That was too good a thing to end quickly. "Pie. I would love a really good piece of pie right now."

Bruce changed directions from heading toward the hotel to heading downtown. "Pie I can do."

"Would this constitute a date?"

Bruce glanced over. "Do you want it to?" he asked, curious.

"I'm just sorting out the *this-is-work–time-and-this-is-not* time," she offered cautiously.

Bruce thought about it and smiled. "Okay. Call it a predate, so I can relearn the things you like best and the things you avoid, before I have to get them right during an actual date."

"I like that." Rae found her shoes and wrestled to slip them back on. "For the record, I like dates that last to midnight, but kind of end then. I need more beauty sleep these days."

"I'll remember. Was this a nice night, Rae?"

She looked over at him, curious about the question. "I think so. You can't figure out the future until you've talked about the past. We both know that. We've been down that road before."

"Then we'll talk about the past a little more when you come over and see my house, and I'll tell you about some of the better chapters of the last eleven years. There have been a few good ones."

"I'd like that a lot."

Bruce pulled into a parking spot near the M&T Diner. He came around to open the car door for her. "Still partial to chocolate-cream pie?"

"A perfect idea."

She let him hold the restaurant door for her. Bruce was trying, in very big ways, to bridge the past eleven years and make it possible for her to be comfortable with him again. She was determined to start matching his courage with her own and to meet him halfway. The best thing she had in her life right now was also the oldest, closest friendship she had ever had. Reviving it would go a long way toward helping her sink stable roots here in Justice. She wanted that, that reality of belonging again, of having a place. If that turned out to be with Bruce and forever, it would close a circle begun years before.

"I seem to remember our first date was also over a slice of pie," Bruce mentioned.

She smiled at the memory he offered as he retrieved menus for them both. That night in their past had been a nice night too. "Some things in life should never change." She followed him to a private table in the back.

17

Rae scanned house numbers as she drove through the Westwood subdivision Wednesday morning, following Peggy's parents' directions. She passed Peggy's home before she saw the number. Rae slowed and found a parking place along the side of the street.

Peggy had a single home on a road with a number of duplexes. The trees were still young and the landscaping needed years of growth on the bushes to fill out the blank areas.

Rae walked to the house, looking around for signs of neighbors who were still home. Duplexes meant lots of neighbors, but not many looked like they were home with small children, the best kind of neighbors for noticing who came and went.

Rae shifted keys in the ring Mr. Worth had given her. She'd suggested they might want to be here, but Mrs. Worth had not felt able to face it. Rae checked the mailbox and found it empty.

She opened the screen door and checked the door, expecting to find it locked. It turned under her hand.

Rae tensed.

She had signed the handgun-carry-permit application but it was still in process, and she hadn't thought this morning warranted breaking the law to carry her weapon. The wise thing to do was to walk back to the car, call the cops, and watch for anyone who left before the officers arrived.

Rae stepped over to cautiously peer into the window. The blinds were lowered but she could see a slice of the room; sunlight from the other windows cut across the carpet and what looked like the arm of a sofa. There were no signs of movement.

Rae reached into her purse and retrieved the small can of Mace inside. She flipped off the tab. Spreading the keys between her fingers, she clenched her fist around the ring. She didn't want to wait for someone else to tell her the house had been ransacked.

She pushed open the front door slowly and looked around, seeing only a large empty living room. She took one step inside and held the screen door so it closed quietly behind her.

A large living room, what looked like the kitchen to the back of the house, to her right a staircase that went upstairs. She could hear steps above her.

The worst place to confront someone was on the stairs where they had the tactical advantage of being higher than her. One person or two? She listened to the sounds, wishing the rooms were hardwood floors rather than carpeted.

No car in the driveway, no obvious way to take items being taken out the back door to a van behind the house. It was possible they had opened the garage door and pulled inside so they could load the vehicle at their leisure.

She moved toward the steps and spotted movement just a fraction before she was seen as well.

"Police! Hold it right there," she ordered, sliding two steps back and toward the front door. "You want to tell me why you're in Peggy Worth's home?"

The man froze at the top of the stairs. "Easy." He lifted his hands away from his body and opened his right hand to dangle a key ring. "She's a friend; I let myself in with keys she gave me."

He looked Bruce's age, his hair turning prematurely gray, the tan dress slacks hanging loose on him, the blue suit jacket unbuttoned. "Your name?"

"Gage Collier."

Rae vaguely remembered the name from Peggy's address book. "Why are you here?"

"We had a date. She didn't show."

"Saturday night?"

"Monday evening. She had a date the night she died?" he asked sharply.

"Come down the stairs, Mr. Collier. Slowly. Let me see some identification."

He slid out his wallet, using his left hand to reduce the threat of the movement. "I don't remember Chicago cops carrying Mace and keys when checking out a potential burglary."

She smiled, the same hard smile she had given her FBI training officer. "You really don't want to find out what they teach at the academy. Set it there on the table and step back."

Gage set the wallet on the table and stepped into the living room. "A friend of Peggy's? I don't remember her mentioning a cop recently, and she would have known I would be interested."

Rae ignored his comment and opened the wallet to read the license under the plastic window while she kept enough focus on him to make sure he stayed where he was at, out of reach of anything he could throw at her.

"I don't claim its accuracy, only that's it's a bad photo of me."

She turned the flap and read his press badge. "What are you doing in Peggy Worth's home?"

He opened his suit jacket, his movements still slow, and reached into the inside pocket to tug out a small notepad. "She mailed me a full notebook with a scrawled Post-it note stuck on top saying I was to take her to dinner Monday where she would explain her shorthand.

"Typical Peg, dangle a story and make me wait. I was hoping she had typed her notes into that BlackBerry she carries everywhere so I could figure out what she was doing down in Justice this last weekend, getting herself killed."

Rae's gaze sharpened. "Killed?"

"I know what the coroner says. But Peggy attracted trouble every day I knew her, and I can't imagine her dying in contradiction of how she lived, the coroner report notwithstanding." He held out his hands. "May I sit down now? I'd rather not stand here debating how my friend died."

Rae capped the Mace and slipped the canister into her pocket. "The coroner and the police department are satisfied it's natural causes."

"So I'm in denial; it feels better than accepting Peggy died in her sleep. She was too young."

Rae agreed with him on that. "I'm Rae Gabriella: ten years with the FBI, currently private and working for Peggy's parents to figure out what Peggy was doing this last weekend." She held up keys. "With keys and permission to be here."

"Touché." Gage sat down on the couch and tossed the notebook on the coffee table. "I can't read it. And no, her parents don't know I'm here. I doubt they knew I had keys."

"You two were close?"

"Not in the way you mean. I'm comfortably dating a nice lady who has two adorable boys. Peggy and I were professional colleagues. I liked her, although I'm a cut above her league in who I write for and how I write, and I don't mean that in a condescending way. She was young, eager, and learning.

"I brought in her mail, fed her cat, and forwarded e-mail while she was in LA, and in return she shared gossip she heard that might apply to a book I've been working on. She's got a knack for getting ladies to talk more than they would normally do about the guys in their life."

Rae thought the story sounded authentic. She chose a seat across from him. "What do you think she was doing in Justice?"

"Following a story, which is what she lived to do. I'm a Pulitzer prize ahead of her and she wanted to find herself a story that would win herself one."

Rae opened the notepad and found it had been filled to the last page with a shorthand she couldn't read either. "Did you find the notes you were searching for?"

He lifted one eyebrow. "I was interrupted. There was nothing useful on her laptop, which is where I expected her to have uploaded any files. The password is vanilla-rich; she tends to file by the date she writes notes, that way she can correlate to the date at the top of a notebook page. I scanned the last month and beyond a few Chicago council nuggets didn't see anything that fit."

"She was trying to locate Joe Prescott."

Gage whistled. "The Prescott kid's death?"

"I'm from out of town, humor me and fill me in."

"Where are you from?"

"Washington, D.C."

"A place with more than a few stories waiting to be dug up." Gage rubbed his chin. "Joe Prescott—it starts with a millennium New Year's Eve rave party. A batch of bad designer drugs kills twelve teenagers, one of them Joe's grandson.

"The dealer was determined to be one of the dead. The cops busted the man who was his supplier and he got a few years for an unrelated coke sale. They never found the cook that made the designer drugs, or anyone who would point to where they had originated."

"It was a big story around here."

"The saga dominated Chicago news for months while the investigation wore on. There weren't any year 2K calamity stories to write and the media had to report on something. Peggy's got a thick file on it in her office; I figured it was old reference material since she had done a couple human-interest stories on the topic last year."

"Would she have been working on another follow-up story?"

"Maybe, but Joe Prescott? He's been dead for months."

"And you would have reason to know that because . . . ?"

"My phone number was in his wallet; they called me when they pulled his body out of the wreck just to double-check when I had last spoken with him and what kind of mood he was in. I published one of his letters on the ravaging attack of reporters running in wolf packs; we got along great for a man that couldn't stand a reporter."

"Peggy didn't know he was dead?"

"Prescott died a few months ago, and I never had reason to mention it. I had no idea she was working on a story that touched on the deaths."

Rae got up and paced over to the window. Peggy went down to Justice to get answers to some questions and she thought Joe Prescott was the person to ask. The source of the designer drug that had killed his grandson? It remained the one intriguing unanswered question in the story she had just heard. "Has Peggy ever shared a story with you in the midst of researching it?"

"No. Which is why I cleared my schedule Monday night, and when she didn't show, went looking for her. I learned about her death from her boss Tuesday morning. I've seen the paperwork: the coroner has a good reputation, but just because something doesn't show up on a medical test doesn't mean nothing happened."

"You're a skeptic."

"She was a friend. It's hard to accept she just went to sleep and never woke." Gage got to his feet and walked over to join her. "I would like to pick up the story she was writing and finish it if only as a tribute to her, but I haven't found what she was after yet."

"She had a late-night date Saturday; she mentioned she was going to see the movie *Holiday Park.* No one seems to know who she was going out with or if she went on that date."

"Stan Bartlett would be my best guess. He'd been asking her out with regularity. She probably finally said yes. He's a sportswriter, and not someone you'd need to worry about."

Rae wrote down the name to track down.

"I don't mean to cut this off, Miss Gabriella, but Mr. and Mrs. Worth are having a memorial at 2 p.m. I need to stop and get flowers on the way, and I need a few minutes with Mr. Worth before the others arrive. Could we talk again another day?"

She held out an agency card. "Yes."

Gage pocketed the card with a smile. "I'm glad they hired you; I think you'll stick until you get answers."

"So far I was the last one to see her alive."

"That would be motivation. I'll let myself out."

Rae locked the door behind him and stood for a moment absorbing the last half hour. She walked over to the couch and took a seat. She started writing verbatim notes as fast as she could scrawl the words of her conversation with Gage Collier.

She had to talk to Nathan about that carry permit, so that next time she wouldn't be holding off a guy with a can of Mace. And knowing her luck, she'd find herself appearing in Gage's story when he wrote that tribute to his friend.

She retrieved her phone and dialed. "Bruce, I need some information as fast as you can retrieve it. Address and basic bio for a Stan Bartlett, all I've got is the fact he's a sportswriter. And I need a read on a reporter, a Gage Collier."

"You found yourself a story."

"Maybe. Call me back."

"Give me a few minutes."

Rae closed the phone and began her own search of Peggy's home. *So where are the rest of your notes, Peggy? Where's that BlackBerry? If no one was with you that night when you died, then they have to be where you left them. The hotel room, the rental car . . . I need a thread to pull.* She took what seemed to be the most current or useful from the office, looked around the rest of the house, didn't find a diary or second address book, and decided she'd come back again if necessary. She headed to her car with what she had collected.

18

Rae shuffled papers on the passenger seat, wishing she had these pages spread across a big work desk. She drank more of the milk shake and glanced at her watch. She was halfway back to Justice and Bruce had told her to stop, find a restaurant, and wait for him.

Peggy was beginning to feel three-dimensional to her. The lady had a snappy sense of humor, wrote mostly people pieces on the movers and shakers in business and entertainment, and had begun in the last year doing more breaking-news articles.

Rae shifted files in the box; she'd tried to take anything at Peggy's that seemed likely to explain a trip to Justice.

The rave deaths were a thick file of press clippings, the tragedy, the trial, even recent clippings on the release of the supplier who had served enough of his sentence to be released on parole. The file was chronological and looked to be what Gage had assumed: background reference material. It was more information than Rae could absorb in a day.

Bruce pulled in beside her in the parking lot.

Rae touched a button to lower the window. "You have an address for Bartlett?"

"I do. Pack the essential stuff; you can ride with me."

She picked up the most critical files and locked up her car to join him. She handed over a milk shake she had bought for him.

"Thanks."

"My pleasure." She relaxed in the front seat of his car, glad to have someone else handling the driving. She'd been fighting the maps while watching for exit signs.

Bruce headed east on the highway. "You missed some excitement back in Justice this morning."

"I've only been gone a few hours."

"Word got out the tile plant is planning to bring in strikebreakers. Someone responded by lobbing a Molotov cocktail into the plant manager's home. By the time the fire department got it suppressed, the living room had taken a lot of smoke damage and fire had pierced the ceiling."

"Is everyone okay?"

"A few smoke-inhalation injuries and some bruises from the fistfight that broke out at the scene. Nathan ended up arresting two union guys."

"A small police department with a volatile strike entering its third week— I don't know how Nathan handles it, Bruce."

"Nathan's looking very tired. I don't know how he keeps his patience in the midst of all of this."

"What are the odds my game of pool with Nathan later tonight is going to happen?"

"Slim to none, I'm afraid."

"That's what I thought. Tell me about Bartlett."

"He's twenty-six, a sportswriter for the *Daily Herald*. He just got back in town this morning from covering a game in Milwaukee."

Rae watched Stan Bartlett walk around the island in his kitchen, shutting down the heat under skillets and pausing his dinner preparations. He was fixing a seafood stir-fry.

"Peggy's the one who cancelled the date. She said she had someone to go see, that it was important to her story, and that she was sorry, but she had to go."

"Did she say who she was meeting?" Bruce asked.

"No. You're telling me she passed away in her sleep Saturday night?"

"Yes," Rae replied.

"Man, that's unexpected. I've been so out of the loop; I haven't even checked messages yet. My brother met me at the Milwaukee game and we headed out to his place for a couple days."

"When did you make arrangements to take Peggy out, to go to the movie?" Bruce asked.

"Tuesday night. I caught her at home about six and she said yes, as long as we could go see *Holiday Park*; she'd been wanting to see it. We arranged to meet at the steak house near the Brighton Theater Complex. I would have picked her up but she wanted to have her own transportation."

"When did she call it off?"

"Saturday about eight, I was just getting ready to walk out the door. She was driving; I could tell that from the background sounds."

"What did you do after that?" Rae asked.

"Besides get annoyed? I was hungry. I went to Kregel's down the street and had myself a steak, then watched the basketball game on the big screen at the sport's emporium.

"My boss paged me about eleven to ask if I wanted to fill in at the Milwaukee game for a reporter stuck out at Denver's airport, and I said sure. I packed and left about eight the next morning, so I could get there and interview the new coach."

"Who could verify that?"

"The waitress at the restaurant will remember me; I talked her into joining me for a drink when she got off work. My boss probably remembers the page, for he put through expense traveling money for me shortly after we spoke.

"Between then and when I left here and got to Milwaukee—I was on-line for a good couple hours pulling current rosters and stats, you can check the computer file times if you like, I was saving most of the pages to print after I got off-line."

"Do you know what story Peggy was working on?" Rae asked.

"No. Last month she was working on a personal profile, some guy who got out of prison that committed suicide. She'd interviewed him last fall for a story and she found his actions—*inconsistent*—was the word she used. At least that was the story she was using as her excuse to say no when I asked her to join me at a game down at the center."

"Why did she say yes this time?"

He smiled. "She appreciated persistence. Listen, I've got guests coming at six. Is there anything else I can help you with later by phone? I really need to get back to this."

"We're done," Bruce said. "Thanks for your time."

Rae waited until they were outside before drawing her conclusion. "He wasn't involved."

"Probably not. Is it worth tracking down that profile she was working on last month?"

Rae opened the passenger door. "Let's look first at the calls she received and made Saturday night. Sometime around 8 p.m. she got the lead she was pursuing. Peggy was back at the hotel by 1 a.m. We find out where she went, we'll know the story that brought her to Justice, and this case will be done. I'll have what I need to present to her parents."

"You're comfortable Peggy's death was natural causes?"

"I've read the coroner's report. I'm comfortable with it. Drop me at my car, and I'll follow you back to Justice."

Rae didn't have a desk yet, and the office still smelled of drying paint, but the bookshelves were in if not yet painted, and the open floor space worked fine for the work surface. She spread all the documents she had collected that day around her on the floor and looked for the final thread of what Peggy Worth had been doing the weekend she died.

"It's not here. Peggy received a local call at the hotel and left to meet someone. There's not going to be a record of it," Bruce concluded.

Rae retrieved another Chinese pot sticker. "She was new to the town of Justice. If she were going to meet someone, she had to write down the directions or else she was going somewhere so obvious she couldn't miss it."

She looked through the box of things she had picked up from Peggy's parents and found the map Peggy had stored in her rental car glove box. The map had been folded back on itself in the past. Rae studied the folds and tried to figure out how Peggy had last held it. "Maybe the lake pavilion? This looks like she was looking east of town."

Bruce took the map and handed her a slip of paper. "What do you think of this? It was in the book she was reading, marking her page."

"Jason? She doodled over the name." Rae reached over for Peggy's address book. "Bruce, we're missing something simple."

"I hate puzzles, Rae."

"You can go on home; there's no need to stay and watch me read papers."

He looked at his watch. "Hand me that research folder you brought from her home. I'll stick around awhile longer."

Rae handed it over. "The boring work is a bit more fun when it's my case."

Bruce smiled. "The next case we'll have to make *ours*."

☗ ☗ ☗

He was hunting a ghost. Nathan turned his powerful torchlight to the steep banks of the ditch beside the road, looking for footprints in the snow or dropped debris, something to show what had been through here was human. He'd heard the screech this time, and Jack was right. It sounded like something dying. It didn't fit any animal he had heard before.

Nathan walked farther down the road toward his squad car. The two-lane road was empty of traffic, the only signs of life the occasional bright eyes of a possum or a stray cat looking back at him. Whatever was in these woods, it would take a group of guys doing a sweep to have a chance of spotting it.

He clicked off his light and the dark night surrounded him. Nathan took a long breath of the cold air and knew a deep exhaustion. The violence he feared had erupted today, a skirmish of what was coming on Friday when strikebreakers tried to enter the tile plant.

He didn't have enough men if things got truly out of hand; first thing tomorrow morning he would need to talk with the surrounding police departments and warn them he might need their assistance. *Lord, there are days I don't want to be sheriff.* The scattered violence today would become coordinated violence if Adam wasn't able to keep control of the union men.

"Did you hear it?"

Nathan turned on his torchlight to illuminate the man coming his way through the pasture. "I heard it, Jack. Have you seen any dead animals or bones, any indication we acquired a fox or a bobcat in this area?"

"I've had the hunting dogs out through this stretch of woods a couple times and they didn't alert."

"Maybe a screech owl killing its prey, I suppose there are a few that could make that cry."

"It sends shivers up my back and I've heard a lot of ugly things. What are you doing down this way?"

"One of Mom's dogs got out, the old sheepdog that belonged to the O'Keefes'. I figure he might head back toward their old house again; that's where he turned up last time."

The dog was a favorite of his mom and Nathan would go the extra mile to help her find it. Neither one of them wanted to see the dog get lost.

"I'll keep an eye out for him."

"I'd appreciate that."

Nathan cast one more sweep of light across the tree trunks and clicked it off. He didn't have the heavy coat and leggings needed to be wading back into that heavy brush. Maybe this weekend he'd bring his own dogs along and hike into the woods. If it was a human sound, he'd find the traces.

The county task force suspected there was a clandestine meth lab operating somewhere in his area. He supposed a pressure kettle cooking over could make that noise although he could smell nothing on the breeze.

Strange unexplained sounds at odd times of day—it raised his hackles. One county over, they'd found a field where a gypsy group had been burying their dead. They'd died of natural causes, but the mere idea of a field of buried bodies was enough to make a man think twice about the woods around here.

"I'll be back when I've got more time to try and figure out what exactly it is." He lifted a hand in farewell as his radio cracked and faintly gave tones.

Nathan took one last look at the woods and walked toward his squad car. This stretch of land adjoined his grandfather's farm and in the back of his mind he wondered what his grandfather might be doing. That mystery he wasn't eager to investigate.

He depressed the transmit button on the radio and asked for clarification of the garbled message. "55-J, 10-9."

"55-J, Possible 10-54. York Hotel."

A possible dead body at the York Hotel. Nathan stopped, not wanting to believe the words. "10-4, ETA four minutes."

A false report? Copycat calls came in regularly after a crime made the front page of the newspaper. He hoped it was a false report, either that or a man in his nineties who had already lived more days than his doctor told him he had left.

Nathan turned on the lights and pushed the speed, but in deference to the hour and those asleep, he left the sirens off.

19

"This is troubling," Nathan said, trying not to let the icy fear that wanted to take over get a foothold. He stepped into the hotel room, careful not to disturb the newspaper pages scattered on the floor by the door. He stopped beside the bed.

A twentysomething brunette lay on her stomach with her right hand lax against the pillow and the other tucked in a fist under her chin. Death was clear in the absence of breath, the way her mouth slacked, and a fly walked across her chin.

Detective Sillman, kneeling near the bed, turned. "A young lady dead in her sleep, with no apparent cause of death. No blood that I can see, no sign of violence, no prescription bottle or liquor bottle. No signs she was ill, suffered food poisoning, got bit by a deadly spider."

"That last one is probably a reach," Nathan remarked, understanding Sillman's frustration. He knelt to study the lady. "There's no sign of a seizure this time."

"Not that I see," Sillman agreed.

Nathan looked around the room. The lady's glasses rested on the bedside table beside a folded-open television guide. Money rested on the dresser, very nice luggage by the door, an expensive coat over the chair. "Not a robbery."

"Can we have two natural deaths within four days?" Sillman asked as he stood.

"Yes, but it's the equivalent of lightning striking in the same place twice." Nathan accepted reality because it was staring at him. "Either we have two natural deaths, we have one natural death and someone just copycatted what they read in the newspaper to try to cover up a murder, or we have two murders. Wake up, Will, we need him on this. And send a patrol officer to pick up the coroner; minutes are going to matter. Who found her?"

"She was traveling with a cousin who came down to deliver a message from their aunt. She's the one who dropped the newspaper. The blood splatter on the edge of the door is hers; she came close to breaking her nose when she rushed out to get help."

"At least we got early word this time. It might help the coroner find a trace of whatever this is," Nathan said.

"She never struggled, never even lifted her hands by the appearance of this. What is it that a coroner would miss after several hours of death? A gas maybe?" Sillman asked. "She breathes something that kills her and the traces fade quickly?"

"Toxicology was clean with Peggy, but maybe there's something more sensitive they can test for."

"I take back what I thought of Miss Gabriella meddling on the Worth case; I hope she has found out more about where Peggy went and who she saw Saturday night. We need to know if these two ladies ever crossed paths or what they might have in common."

"I'm going to guess the only common link we find between them besides female, twenties, and staying at a Justice hotel is the killer they have in common." Nathan didn't like the close timeline between the deaths. "We need to track down Bruce and Rae tonight and reopen the Worth case."

Gray nodded. "If they can tell us anything more about Peggy, it will give us a leg up on this. I don't want to shift officers away from the strike patrol to run down the questions they have already spent time working. We are way too shorthanded to be chasing threads they've already pulled."

"I'll leave Will with you to handle this scene, while I work with Rae and Bruce to see what I can turn up at that end. I figure we get half a day to decide if this is a murder or not before we have to make some very tough resource calls."

Nathan dialed, and while it rang, he found the lady's purse in the closet and opened the billfold. "Karen Reese, twenty-nine, from Lefton, Georgia." Nathan found a business card. "She's an associate CPA."

The phone was answered. "Bruce, hey, buddy, wake up. It's Nathan." Nathan stepped into the hotel room bathroom and scanned the countertop. "I'm at York Hotel, room 167, and we're dealing with another young lady apparently dead in her sleep. You awake now?"

"You're not kidding."

"No."

"I'm up; my feet are on the floor. What do you need?"

"Answers. Where are things with Peggy Worth?"

"She cancelled her date Saturday night in order to meet with someone about a story she was writing. We don't know who she met or what the story was about, but we think it was related to the Prescott kid's death. Rae was still working on that puzzle when I left the agency about ten."

"Find her."

"We'll be with you in twenty minutes."

⚭   ⚭   ⚭

Rae covered a yawn as she leaned against Bruce's car. The hotel had too many cops crowding the first floor and the beginnings of a spectator crowd to want to wade through them to find Nathan. He knew she was here; he'd find her as soon as he got a free moment.

"You need gloves."

Rae glanced over her shoulder to see Bruce heading her direction across the parking lot. "The cold keeps me awake. What's happening in back?"

"The coroner has arrived."

"This looks the same as Peggy?" Rae asked.

"A young lady dead in her sleep, with no indication of violence or cause," Bruce confirmed.

"They've got to be related despite that natural-causes ruling for Peggy. And it's got to be something the coroner wouldn't pick up on standard toxicology screens."

Bruce reached in the car to store his flashlight. "Nathan is working under that assumption, which is why they are putting a rush on this case since she may have died within the last two hours. It's something not leaving much of a trace."

"What do you think, Bruce? We may not know the story Peggy was trying to write, but the general topic that brought her to Justice seems clear—that rave party and the designer drug deaths of several teenagers. Maybe a bad lot of drugs is killing them?"

"I doubt Peggy would voluntarily take something, and this lady was apparently passing through town with her cousin. I'm thinking something they ate or drank."

"Really?"

"Hotels have a few things in common—vending machines for one. Nathan's got an officer clearing the contents of the machines on that floor."

"If it's something being put in a food or drink, this could just as easily be twenty deaths instead of two," Rae said.

"A scary thought, isn't it?"

"I'm trying to remember what I last got from the vending machine on my floor at the hotel. I would have used the same one Peggy did."

"Please, I don't need nightmare ideas like that one. Why don't you avoid the hotel food for a while?"

"It could be something absorbed through the skin, put in something like a shampoo bottle or the soap, randomly placed for whoever happens to check in to the hotel room," Rae offered. "Although the odds of picking off two single young women at two different hotels being purely at random—that suggests the victims were chosen."

"You fit the victim profile: young, single, pretty, staying at a Justice hotel," Bruce pointed out.

Rae smiled. "If someone wanted to target me they'd probably shoot me in the back."

"What are you two talking about?"

Rae turned, as did Bruce, to see Nathan walking over to join them.

"The odds Rae becomes the next victim of the ghost killer," Bruce replied.

"Please, that name will stick. And I don't want to think about a third victim."

"Is this victim number two? Or is this a coincidence?" Rae asked.

"I would love to know that answer. The coroner stands by the autopsy re-sults for Peggy Worth, and this death doesn't show the same early signs of a seizure. Maybe this is natural too, but for now we're assuming it isn't. We're reopening Peggy Worth's case to see what we can find as common. Tell me about the progress you've made. I understand you ruled out her date."

"Stan Bartlett. He's not part of this," she confirmed. "Peggy cancelled the date to meet someone involved in the story she was working on."

Rae wished she had worked it another hour before calling it a day. "Peggy was asking about Joe Prescott. That's where she began, and where we'll prob-ably find a thread to tug. My best guess—it was a local call to her at the hotel that arranged the meeting Saturday night, and the first name for who she met may be Jason. It does appear she went somewhere she didn't need to write down directions."

"At first light, we'll go out to Prescott's old place and talk with the neigh-bors," Nathan decided. "We'll see if it was one of them who Peggy went to see that night."

"That isn't likely to connect Peggy to this lady."

"I know. Hopefully by the time we finish figuring out Peggy's movements, we'll have Karen's full itinerary. Her cousin is already taking an officer through step-by-step who they saw and where they went; he'll have that account con-firmed by midmorning. The coroner should have early answers by then too. I've got just over twenty-four hours before strikebreakers start entering the tile plant. I need to know if I'm calling in the state police to help us also track down a serial murderer, or if this town is just having a string of very bad luck."

༄༅ ༄༅ ༄༅

She'd died. He shoved his briefcase into his car, annoyed with the outcome. No seizure this time, just stopped breathing. Either two milligrams was still too much, or the formula was a fractional amount too high in the sedative.

It was such a finely balanced designer drug, beautifully conceived, but in practice hard to perfect. Maybe if he extended the base and slowed the release down . . . the instant high was important to sales, but it triggered an equally fast fall off of the drug. That change was the next logical tweak to make.

He looked at his watch and the date in the corner. Nine days, he didn't want to move the meeting with his backer again. Devon's patience had limits. If he recalculated the mix and got the next batch prepped and drying by tomorrow afternoon, and if his partners could do the forming and wrapping tomorrow evening . . .

They'd have to consider moving beyond Justice to test it, and that would complicate things. Maybe if they split up the testing to be done, they could get the final checks done before his meeting with Devon. He started his car.

He passed the hotel and squad cars in the parking lot, ignoring the officers swarming over the crime scene. There was nothing there for them to find. He'd been seen at the hotel, he was likely already in their to-be-interviewed lists, and no one would think anything of it. They'd call or be around to ask him questions tomorrow. He made a mental note to stay in town until they came by. He wouldn't want to delay their investigation.

20

Nathan turned off the two-lane country road onto a private rock drive that was broken up in several places where rain had washed away segments of the ground. "Andrew Kirk is Prescott's closest neighbor."

Rae leaned forward to see the house up ahead. In the early morning light, it was clear the once white two-story farmhouse was in need of a new coat of paint. The land they had passed did not look actively farmed; the brush was high and the one fence she had seen needed repair work. There were two large metal-sided buildings beyond the house. "Does he have a family? Has he lived here long?"

"I went to high school with him. Andy's been divorced about four years." Nathan pulled to a stop before the larger of the two storage buildings; the huge doors swung open. A semi and trailer were pulled inside and music blared into the countryside.

"Andy, do you have a minute?"

The man stepped down from the semi cab, a black trash bag in his hand. "Hi, Nate. Sure."

"How was the run?"

"Not one of the best for turning a profit. I lost a tire in the middle of the night on a road to nowhere. A rock struck the window and began a splintering crack. Gas prices were obscene heading east."

"Not exactly what you hope for."

"That's for sure." Andy dumped the trash bag in a metal can and secured the lid. He walked out of the garage toward them, snapping his finger at his dogs racing from the backyard to join them.

"When did you get back?"

"Saturday evening. I'm heading out this afternoon to ship some wire spools from Chicago down to Indianapolis."

"I'd like you to meet Rae Gabriella; she's new in town and working with Bruce Chapel."

Andy touched his cap. "A pleasure, Ma'am."

"We're looking for a lady who might have been asking about Joe Prescott." Nathan offered the photo he held.

"Sure, she was by. She left a note tucked in the front door. I called when I got back."

"She was out here Saturday night?"

"Around nine, I guess. Nice-looking lady, overdressed for standing around a garage while I unloaded gear. She brought an offering of beer; I answered all the questions she had."

"What was she asking about?"

"Prescott, and where his place was. She seemed stunned to hear the old man was dead. This town doesn't like reporters much, if it took finding me to get that answer."

"Did she say what story she was working on?"

"She asked about Prescott's grandson, who he hung around with, what rumors I heard around town about who he was buying stuff from, did I remember much about anyone who left town back then who had recently moved back here. She seemed to have the impression that designer drugs were being readily sold around here. A bunch of big-city jive if you ask me."

"I appreciate the vote of confidence."

"Well, it gets troubling, all them drug assumptions and not a trace of evidence behind them. She was asking about Prescott's land, who owns it now, if I saw strangers coming and going at odd times. As if I would and not give you a call on the radio first thing."

BEFORE I WAKE 159

"I know you would; you have in the past. Did she mention any names? ask about any other people?"

"She read off some names from this bright orange-covered notepad she carried but no one sounded familiar. You know me, Nathan. I'd been pushing hard for the drive, half a beer and I was not remembering names or dates that well. I suggested she talk with Nella down the road. If there's gossip in town worth knowing, Nella would have the details."

"What time did she leave here?"

"Before ten, I guess. She drew herself a map for Prescott's place. I half expected to see her back out here this week."

"She passed away Sunday morning, Andy."

"She what?" The man's voice broke higher and he held up his hands. "She left here, Nathan, driving that fancy rental car and talking about seeing Nella and the river. You know I don't take the town paper; this is the first I'm hearing of this."

"Relax, I'm not looking at you, Andy. We're just trying to figure out where she went and what she was doing, who she saw."

The man relaxed but only a bit. "I don't want pulled into this, Nathan. I've got a business such as it is and I don't want my name showing up in newspapers and having a bunch of reporters out here bugging me."

"It's not going to happen. We'll chat with Nella and see if Peggy stopped by there Saturday night."

"Nella's place was dark when I drove in that night; I figured she was out with Walter, it being a Saturday evening."

Nathan closed his notebook. "What's on your schedule after you haul the wire?"

"I've got a load of generators to haul back from Tennessee for a Chicago boatyard. I figure I'm back here long enough to read the mail and pay bills in between."

"I hope these runs are more profitable."

Andy leaned down to quiet one of his dogs. "I hope so. I'm no farmer. I figure I get some of this land sold and that will take one of those bigger tax bills off my plate and let me fix up the truck to run more than patched together. I'd hate to see moving away from this place entirely to work for one of those outfits who pay a salary but want a ton of paperwork and have you on a vacation schedule."

"I hear you," Nathan agreed. "I'd miss having you around during quail-hunting season. If I don't see you again before you head out, take care on that drive."

"Appreciate it, Nathan." Andy turned back to finish cleaning his truck.

Nathan unlocked the squad car. He tore off the fax that had been sent while they spoke with Andy, scanned it, and passed it over to Rae. "Read while I drive."

"Where are we heading next?"

"Prescott's place. It's on the way to Nella's."

Rae drank her coffee and scanned the sheet of paper. "Karen Reese and her cousin's itinerary since they arrived in Justice. They ate east of town at the steak house around 5 p.m., checked into the hotel before six, and spent a couple hours chatting at the poolside. Karen called it an evening first and went up to watch some TV. The cousin got a late-night call from her aunt; she went to tell Karen their O'Hare flight times were going to have to change and she found Karen dead in bed."

"They never left the hotel."

"They barely had time to be here. Vending machines, something she drank or ate, you're not talking many options if it's something other than a natural death."

"I don't like coincidences."

"Neither do I, but I know from firsthand experience they do happen. You can assume she talked to other hotel guests and a few of the local townsfolk's who work at the restaurant or the hotel, beyond that—it's going to be hard to spot overlaps with Peggy. Different hotels and different restaurants as far as I can tell."

Rae folded the sheet of paper and slid it in Nathan's logbook. She covered a yawn. "When will the coroner have preliminary results?"

"Midmorning. Let's hope they are definitive one way or another." Nathan turned left onto another country road. "I appreciate the time, Rae. I know I cut your night pretty short."

"I'm glad you let me come along. It will let me wrap up the case for Peggy's parents. Once they find out someone else died in their sleep, I'll have a hard time convincing them Peggy's was a natural death unless this one is locked down tighter than a steel drum."

Nathan slowed. "Here we are."

"That's Prescott's land."

"Yes." Nathan parked on the side of the road where the two country roads met and a stop sign gave the right-of-way to the north-south road.

"His land starts here and runs half a mile east and a mile and a half west. You can see the old church steeple there on the horizon; that's the edge of the property. Prescott's house is down by the river.

"The bridge you cross to reach it gave way late in the fall to an old chestnut tree that came down and since no one else lives back that way it's not been repaired yet. They'll need to drive steel beams to come up to code and that's a lot easier in the summer. You can get close through this pasture or from the other direction you can hike through woods to the house."

"Why hasn't the land been sold?"

"I think probate is just finishing up; it's been slow to move along. The bank owns this property now and they'll find a buyer eventually. Joe's brother out east has a small parcel of property pretty much right in the middle of this land and the bank was hoping to work out an exchange so the section they put up for sale is contiguous."

Rae stepped out of the squad car. The land was snow covered in spots and melting and the ground covered with scraggly grass. "If she had his old address, Peggy would have come down here, probably getting into the brambles trying to walk back on that road."

Rae walked down the fence line to the gate entering the section of land. "The rust on the latch was recently broken away; you can still see the flakes on top of the snow."

"Open the gate up; we'll drive back there a bit."

Rae worked the latch and swung open the gate. "Did he keep cattle in this pasture?"

"Yep. I'd watch where you are stepping."

"Now you tell me." She waited for him to pull through and then closed the gate behind them. She got back into the car. "I bet this is a pretty place in the summer."

"Secluded, and the woods fill out nicely." Nathan drove them along the worn path of a road and toward the river. They came upon it suddenly, the banks high and dropping swiftly down to the water.

He parked. Rae stepped from the car to walk closer through the underbrush. The water ran at a steady pace, clouded with picked-up dirt. "You're right; there's not much to see."

"Just a river. In the spring this river comes close to overflowing the banks. It's why there are cattle here and not a field of corn."

"The bridge is down there?" She pointed toward the curve.

"Yes. And the house just past it."

"I can see why Peggy got lost." Rae walked back to the car, rubbing her forearm. "Do you have a drug problem in town, Nathan?"

He shrugged, more resigned than bothered by the question. "It's available. Mostly marijuana and small quantities of the harder drugs. We get a lead on meth production around here every few months. Most of it is coming around the town bound for bigger markets around Chicago. Better prices."

"Peggy's questions make me suspect she thought that producer of those rave designer drugs was around here."

"The kid who sold the stuff at the party, and the guy they think sold the stuff to him, neither was from around here." Nathan touched his radio transmitter. "55-J, 10-9."

The message was repeated. "55-J, 10-21 to Larry Sikes."

"10-4." He opened the squad-car door. "There's enough abandoned land and fallow acres around here that a clandestine lab is not going to surprise me. I'd like to know the names Peggy had in that orange-covered notebook of hers."

"I'd just like to find her notebook," Rae replied. "You need to go?"

"A return call request to Larry Sikes, the union's number two—I'm betting things are about to take an unpleasant turn in town. We'll need to stop and see Nella later."

"It's no problem. I'll go back through Peggy's things and over to the hotel to check her room, see if that orange notebook is somewhere and I just missed it."

"Peggy's rental car is still at the police lot; it's getting picked up this evening. Check with my assistant; she can get you to the right person who can unlock it for you to search it again as well."

"This is going to turn out to be a coincidence, Nathan. I don't see what the two ladies could have in common. They were never even on the same side of town. If these two are murders, they are like nothing I have ever seen before."

Nathan picked up the car radio, acknowledged a 10-87, meet officer request, at city hall. "It's been a while since I worked a murder case. I've been hoping to keep it that way."

"Coincidences do happen. Trust me on that. These two deaths could both be natural causes."

21

Nathan leaned back in his desk chair until it rocked onto two rollers and he could feel the fatigue taking over. "I'm reading through a fog, Will." He dropped the fax back on his desk and looked at his deputy chief. "Give me the highlights."

"Twenty-nine strikebreakers being bused in from the north from a hotel outside Waukegan. They'll come in at 6 a.m.; plant security will open the gate for the bus and lock the gates behind them."

"Which if the union guys have their act together means the plant staff will have to be prepared with a blowtorch to cut off chains from the gate. Officers are sitting in front of both front and back gates to prevent that?"

"One at each gate and a third on foot patrol around the plant grounds keeping an eye on the plant security guards so they don't get pelted with bottles or the like. I've got the officers on six-hour rotations throughout the night so we keep fresh eyes and ears out there."

Nathan thought about the size of the plant, tucked as it was abutting up to a residential neighborhood, and figured the manpower was stationed about as well as they could do it. The east side of the plant was facing undeveloped land still heavy with trees and underbrush, while the back of the plant was a road that hadn't been paved in so long the trucks in and out by that direction threatened to break an axle. The union lines had pretty much kept to the front of the plant and the main gate where the road was traveled regularly by townsfolk. "Has the tile plant deployed free-roaming guard dogs as they threatened to do within the fenced grounds?"

"No, and I think we have Chet to thank for that. He talked some sense into the security chief out there, about what would be happening to his own men if trouble erupted and they ended up facing down their own guard dogs while trying to respond."

"I'll take any small favor we can get; I didn't relish hearing our guys were having to watch for not only people but animals out there. What's the mood like?"

"The union picket lines have been thinning out; men are caucusing this evening about the strikebreakers coming in. It sounds like a pretty intense debate on what to do is already under way, but at least it's bought us a couple hours of quiet."

Nathan nodded. "I got a message from Larry and a request from him for a couple more officers to keep things under control at the union hall. Chet's going over this evening, along with two officers from the patrol group."

Nathan rubbed his eyes, thinking through options. "I need a list in hand for who we call in first if trouble breaks out. Let's avoid the guys with anniversaries and birthdays and significant events happening tomorrow if we can. But it may have to be a pretty deep list of names."

"I'll have it for you within the hour," Will promised.

"Thanks."

Will headed out.

Nathan glanced at his watch. In about twelve hours he would have strikebreakers entering the tile plant. The hours of Thursday were rushing by and he could feel it inside. After he'd dropped Rae back off at her hotel to get some sleep, he'd come back to the office to see what else was heating up on him.

The only thing he was certain about was the fact that tomorrow would unfold on them before they were really ready for it. At least he had good men working the problems. There were a few guys among the union membership he might wish he could proactively arrest and remove from the equation, but at this point all he could do was hope for the best and be prepared to react if trouble started.

Nathan waved in the detective heading toward his office. "Come on in, Sillman. What's the latest on Karen?"

It was obvious from the way he was working on the coffee he held, that he was dragging for energy right now. Sillman had spent a long night at the hotel. He stopped inside the office and leaned against the wall. "You're going to love this, Nathan. The coroner finished the autopsy half an hour ago and says death is consistent with a heart attack."

Gray set down his coffee on the bookshelf to free up his hand. He turned pages in his notes. "The preliminary blood work has faint traces of a painkiller, consistent with two over-the-counter tablets and a sedative, also in levels that fit over-the-counter medication.

"The hotel confirms Karen stopped by the front desk to request," he read his notes, "an ironing board, two more towels, a packet of aspirins, and a Band-Aid for a torn hangnail. The night receptionist remembers the details because Walter was over at the hotel having dinner with his dad, and he restocked the medical-supply box for them before he left the hotel."

"So it's natural causes."

"I'm no doctor, Nathan. I've got a coroner telling me nothing so far looks off but he'll keep checking, a cousin who can account for practically every minute of Karen's time before she died, no sign of any kind suggesting foul play, and no witness to anyone coming or going from the room other than the cousin. And that lady is still in shock; there's no way she killed Karen."

"Where are we at with testing on the items found at the scene?"

"Karen was snacking heavily while watching TV. I've got everything from candy wrappers to potato chips to fruit-filled pies from the vending machine. All of it is now at the lab being tested, along with what we pulled from the vending machines. They are about half done with the initial tests; so far nothing looks off."

Nathan felt like he was having to play God, for justice was balancing on this resource decision. "Is there any sign someone else at either hotel was also getting sick? Reports of upset stomachs, headaches, flu—anything at all being reported by the other guests?"

Sillman picked up his coffee and finished it, looking over at the coffeemaker

Nathan kept on his credenza to see about a refill. "I thought of that while I watched the coroner move her body. I've asked managers at both hotels and there is no other guest feeling ill they can identify in the days before or since these deaths. I think we've got what we got—a lady who died in her sleep."

Nathan wished someone else was sitting in this chair having to make these decisions. "Okay. Push hard on the case until the coroner gets his final test results in. If you can't find anything off at the hotel and the coroner is prepared to sign off on this as natural causes, then we close it. I need you backtracking those stolen handguns before some union guy decides to go buy one of them on the street and use it. Are you okay with that?"

"As much as I don't want to say natural causes, yes, I think we've got no choice but to go with the coroner's verdict. I'm not finding anything at the scene so far to suggest it isn't that. And I'm tired enough after chasing down even the dust bunnies under the bed to be pretty confident nothing in that hotel room was missed. There was no pill bottle, nor stray pill she dropped when she took a handful of something that killed her."

Sillman regretfully threw away his empty coffee cup. "Did you discover anything else about Peggy's itinerary? Was there any overlap between the two ladies at all? Is there anything else we can work with?"

"There's nothing so far. Peggy went to see Andy Kirk Saturday night, asking questions that suggest she thought someone in this area had a hand in those designer drugs that killed Prescott's grandson. She probably went to see Nella after that, and given how Nella can talk, that probably explains the time Peggy arrived back at the hotel. Nothing so far suggests Peggy ran into foul play or the like the night she died; she was just out asking questions. When is Noland Reed starting with the county narcotics task force?"

Sillman had to look at the calendar to figure out what day it was today. "Two weeks, I think. He's already got his desk cleared out and his shoes shined; eager doesn't describe his interest."

Nathan smiled. "I remember days we were both so young a new assignment looked like that to us as well. I'm so glad we got that slot. At best we can tell so far, this reporter heard a rumor about the designer drugs that killed Prescott's grandson and came to ask questions. Odds are good the task force has heard the same rumors. Tell Noland to look at anything they have, even the most unlikely rumors, about who's been manufacturing some of the more exotic stuff hitting the market around here."

"Do her notes suggest what it was she heard?"

"Her own brand of shorthand isn't readable, making the one notebook we have worthless. The other notebook she was seen carrying on Saturday night hasn't turned up yet. Rae's looking for it."

Nathan shook his head. "So far these two ladies have absolutely nothing in common but the fact they both died in one of our hotels, apparently of natural causes. Even if Peggy had a rumor to chase about designer drugs, all we've proven so far is how little she learned while she was in town. She didn't even know Joe Prescott had died until late Saturday night. I just don't see how she got herself in so much trouble after learning that news that she got herself killed that night. If the coroner says natural causes for both ladies, I've got to admit I can't see evidence that says he's wrong."

Sillman nodded. "I don't like it, but that's the way this is breaking."

Nathan waved in his assistant and accepted the stack of phone-call slips. "I'll talk with the coroner again to see if there's any way we've got a new designer drug going around that his tests can't pick up, but the last conversation I had with him on the topic said it was 'theoretically possible' but highly unlikely.

"I'll also work the Peggy angle through the end of the day to see if I can nail down anything more about the story she was writing. But if you don't find anything from the scene of Karen's death which suggests foul play and the coroner is ready to sign off as natural causes, we'll move on. We've got no choice."

"Will do."

Nathan flipped through the call slips and slid the lot into his pocket. "Track me down if you need me. I'll be somewhere in town."

"I'll keep you posted."

Nathan hated the county coroner's office. Nice furnishings and comfortable guest chairs notwithstanding, it was an unpleasant place to visit. He knew what was inside those manila folders piled up on the desk and shoved into the file cabinets. Franklin didn't seem bothered by it, but Nathan was. "Could the blood tests be missing something?"

"It's not likely."

"But it is possible."

"Anything is possible, Nathan, you know that. But possible and probable are vastly different things." Franklin tugged off his glasses. His white coat worn in the lab was still crisply pressed and clean; it didn't fit with the fact he'd paused an autopsy to take a coffee break when Nathan arrived.

"I'm casting a very wide net looking for something triggering the seizure and heart attack I found in Peggy and the heart attack I found in Karen. I don't like seeing young people die of natural causes—their age itself suggests a contributing factor. But I've found no signs of a systemic allergic reaction, of a poison, or of a known drug in their system, legal or otherwise, in a quantity that concerns me."

"What about a new designer drug? That's what I'm worried about most," Nathan clarified.

"Most designer drugs are derivates of existing drugs on the market. The tests might not be able to identify the precise substance, but they should still be picking up traces of the common elements that are present."

Nathan was at the edge of his medical knowledge to figure out what question to ask, but he had to leave this office comfortable with the conclusions being reached. "This situation just feels wrong, accepting these two deaths are both natural causes. Hypothetically, assuming these two cases are murders—can you give me anything that might suggest this is a substance, either man-made or natural toxin, causing the deaths?"

Franklin rocked back in his chair as he thought about it; then he nodded. "Okay, hypothetically. It's killing fast with a seizure, a heart attack. Something they ingest that quickly metabolizes and affects their heart—a liquid maybe. Or it could be something that is affecting the brain directly. Something they might inhale."

"Something they inhale. A perfume."

"It doesn't have to be that elaborate. Like smelling chlorine in a pool or broccoli steaming—the concentrations wouldn't have to be that high to do damage if the toxin is powerful enough."

"That's helpful. Anything else?"

"Theoretically, and I'm really reaching here—it could be a new class of substances that we just don't expect—kind of like how aspirin and Tylenol are both painkillers but are very different at their molecular level. Designer drugs run in those kinds of unique classes too.

"Get something so designer it's not even expected to have a narcotic effect, and that changes this equation. Once a decade some new category appears—meth exploded into the market, ecstasy, PCP—something that changes the look of the entire narcotics landscape. But those massive sea shifts in drug designs tend to appear on the coasts and work inland, not originate in small-town mainland USA."

"You're talking a first-rate chemist for creating a new drug category," Nathan clarified.

"More than that," Franklin replied. "You're talking about very expensive precursor chemicals. You're talking about control of formulations, repeatability, scientific focus. The homegrown meth cook looking to make a more potent batch so he's tinkering a bit as he heats his pot isn't going to be this kind of cook. It's basic things like writing information down. Otherwise it's just a new batch of something the cook tries on himself and you find him dead next to his hot plate. It might have been a fascinating new drug, but it will never get made again—the cook didn't write down what he did differently this time, and he just killed himself."

"I see your point. The drug that killed those kids at the millennium rave party years ago—you'd be able to spot it?"

"In the formulation that was used then, or any reasonably close similarity to it—I'd see it," Franklin promised. "Nathan—science of the kind I do can never be perfect. There are too many variables that change between the time of death and when the body is found. But let me offer a reassurance. If I'm right that these two deaths are natural causes, then statistically there should be no more unexplained deaths within the Justice area for some time. If they have a cause—you'll be learning about death number three soon enough and

I'll be asking nationwide for help to figure this out. I'll take the media hit for declaring these natural-cause deaths."

"You know it's more than that."

"I know. But in this situation, we either leave the cases open, pending more information that we don't know where it will come from or we close them as natural causes. The honest thing to do is to close them as natural causes, and if I'm wrong, admit that publicly. We both have to flow with what is before us as facts and work from there. I'll call if there is anything that shows up in blood tests still being run on Karen. But if they're clean, I'll be ready to sign off on her death as natural causes by tomorrow morning."

Nathan wished he felt better about that answer, but at least they were answers. "That's good to know. Thanks for your time, Franklin."

"I wish it was an easier answer to accept."

Nathan got to his feet, relieved to be leaving the office. "It's what you have. That matters. It will have to do."

Nathan stretched out on Bruce's couch and closed his eyes. It felt very good to fade into oblivion for a minute. If he had returned to the office he would have to start returning calls on the phone slips still shoved into his pocket, and the day had just been too long to want to deal with the inevitable tussles of people in this town that were not life-and-death situations but needed a sheriff's touch to mediate and resolve. He didn't have it in him this particular hour.

He was beyond tired right now. He shook off that desire to cut and run and told himself to suck it in. He'd known days like this would be part of the job when he'd put his name on the ballot and asked townsfolk to trust him. "Where's Rae?" he asked, stopping the circling thoughts running around in his head.

"At the hotel catching a nap," Bruce answered.

The idea of a bed sounded so much more appealing than this couch. "We got preempted earlier on a trip out to Nella's. You want to come along?" That stop was the last one Nathan could think of that might give him an answer on the details of the story Peggy had been working on at the time of her death. After that he was going home to let his dogs out and crash for a few hours of sleep.

"I'll pass. That lady doesn't particularly like me."

"Why am I not surprised?" Nathan sighed. "This is typing as a second accidental death and that is freaky."

"I don't know what you could do besides what you're already doing. If it is murder there has to be something that says murder."

"I know. And I'm no doctor. The coroner is the best we have in the county, and I would have said he is as good as any in the state."

"Then let him do his job and trust his judgment. It's the best you can do."

"Yeah. I got a science lesson today that convinced me I'm definitely not on ground I understand particularly well."

If there was a link between these two cases, it circled back to the story Peggy was working on, it meant a designer drug, and that meant a cook somewhere in his area willing to kill people—the thought of that was more than just depressing, it left him chilled. Who?

Nathan swung himself back to sitting up. "I need some dinner before I probably end up out at the tile plant for the night. Let's get Rae, go find that thick steak I owe you, and then I'll take her out to meet Nella and we'll try and wrap up the Peggy Worth questions tonight."

"It sounds like a good plan." Bruce closed the file he had been working on. "You'll get through this, Nathan. Peggy and Karen really will be natural-caused deaths, the tile-plant strike will end, and this town will get back to normal. You'll get back to dealing with the occasional vandalisms and the domestic fights and your grandfather speeding."

Nathan smiled, appreciating the encouragement. "Answer me one thing first. You met folks in your career who would cook up stuff like what killed Prescott's grandson. What were they like, the cooks who did that kind of thing?" Bruce might have been retired for years, the drugs might have changed, but the people didn't.

Bruce rocked back in his chair and thought about it. "Not flashy, not out in front. Dispassionate about people, cold, the better ones enjoying their craft just like an arsonist would enjoy striking a match to watch it burn."

Bruce looked over, his eyes colder now from the memories. "Greed drove them, rather than power. They wanted the cash that came from their new product but rarely wanted to work to be the power broker in an area, the one holding the most territory. Cooks were the face in the background, rarely seen, avoiding connections to the dealer crowd. Very tough men to catch. I always thought of them as assassins at heart."

"You caught a few."

"Not as many as I knew were out there working against me. Some were artists, labeling their products with initials and fancy names; others were clinical about it, their products merely hitting the streets with a number. One guy, I always knew his stuff was six-nine-something. After I caught him I realized sixty-nine was his street address." Bruce winced at the memory. "That arrogance was more rare than common. Most just wanted to stay in the background and get rich. And most eventually ended up spending the money in ways that gave themselves away."

Bruce shrugged. "I once had a kid boast how he had burned up a million dollars' worth of cocaine swiped from his dealer brother as he figured out how to make cocaine-laced lollipops. That kind of cost structure—you will find financial backers for cooks occasionally, but it is rare. There is so much money to be made in known drug formulas that there is not much investment interest in creating more."

Nathan listened and he realized it was the most he had gotten Bruce to say about his former job in all the years he had known him. Bruce had forgotten more about the subject of drugs and dealers than Nathan had personally ever known. If there was something here to see, Bruce would have already spotted it.

Nathan pushed his hands through his hair and had to laugh. "Up until a couple years ago my biggest headache around here was worrying about the kids who were splitting open fireworks to use the gunpowder to make their homemade rockets go higher. Please just give me back those days."

"They'll be back," Bruce promised, amused. "If there really is a local connection to the Prescott kid's death, it's just a couple people, Nathan. Justice is too small a town to have its own population of drug dealers and players living here. They need big cities and plentiful customers nearby. Two or three guys who will eventually either get busted by you for a crime or who will move on, because everyone moves on in this mobile society, and they will become some other town's problem."

"You know how cynical that is, hoping that any bad guys that happen to be in the area just move away?"

Bruce shrugged. "You take whatever works. And if they are good enough to not get caught—let them move and become someone else's problem."

Bruce got up from his desk chair. "Population growth in Justice being what it is it's major news having five more births in a year than deaths of elderly residents. Face it, Nathan, Justice is a small town that will always be a small town. That's one of the reasons I moved here. It's hard to have a long-term serious crime rate when criminals consider the town boring to live in."

Nathan smiled as he got to his feet. "Before you cheer me up too much more, let's go get that steak."

Bruce grinned. "I did the math before I moved here, you know. A 2 percent criminal population—which you don't have—gives you two hundred fifty people to worry about, and only one or two of those are capable of being trouble with a capital *T*. You've got twenty-some officers. You should be able to take them eventually."

Nathan pushed his friend in the doorpost as he went by. "Eventually indeed. You really did the math?"

"Insulting, isn't it?"

"I want a raise. I can count two hundred fifty troublemakers that show up at the city council meetings alone."

22

By the time he was headed out to Nella's, Nathan felt like he had relaxed for the first time in days. Bruce was the kind of guy that had that influence on him, and listening over dinner to Rae and Bruce talk about their former days together at the Chicago PD brought back good memories of his own first days as a beat cop.

Traffic was light, and the snow in the air was holding off to only an occasional skiff. Nathan glanced over at Rae. She sat beside him now, quietly looking through her notes for what she might want to ask Nella. He liked that quiet focus she brought to her work.

He'd suggested she ride with him rather than have her drive separately, figuring it was better to know what she was finding as she worked for Peggy's parents than not. He skirted the line of having a civilian along for police business by accepting the technically true fact that Peggy's case was no longer a police matter, for they still didn't have enough to override the coroner's ruling and formally reopen her death. Truth was, he didn't want Rae to find out something sinister without a cop at her side.

Andy had suggested Peggy talk to Nella, and the reporter had been persistent enough on this story that she would have taken that suggestion and stopped by Nella's on Saturday night after leaving Andy's. Nella had probably told her an earful of news.

And knowing Nella, she would likely have more questions for them now about Peggy's death than they had for her about Peggy's visit. Nella was the kind of lady whose life revolved around what she heard as news and what she could pass on as news. Nathan liked Nella well enough, for she meant no harm in the gossip. Single and without family in the area, being a part of the town grapevine helped give her purpose in life.

Nathan turned into Nella's long driveway, slowing to avoid the depressions and sinkholes taking over the crushed rock. The hardware-store owner might know someone willing to dump a load of rock for Nella free of charge. It wasn't something she would think about dealing with until it tore up her car's undercarriage, and she was perennially short of funds for things like home repairs.

Nathan parked near the front of her house rather than pull around to the detached garage. The trees in front of the house cast shadows that just brushed the front porch. Enough snow had melted through the day that he could see patches of grass peeking through.

Nathan picked up his notebook. "Rae, you'll want to let me do the introductions and handle the conversation for the first bit, or you will have Nella asking enough questions to get your entire life history before she answers a single one of our questions about Peggy. She will want to end up with the scoop on the new town resident or she'll feel shortchanged in this exchange."

Rae smiled as she pushed open her door. "Got it."

Nathan could hear dogs barking inside as he walked up the steps to the porch. Nella had a couple mixed-breed dogs, leaning toward the aggressive breeds. He opened the screen door and knocked on the door.

Newspapers were by the door, buried behind the planter box she still had set out, and a dozen letters were in the mailbox. The newspapers looked soggy.

Not hearing Nella coming, he pushed the doorbell and heard chimes echo inside. The dogs intensified their barking. She was normally home of an evening and quick to come to the door when she heard a car arrive.

She hadn't been at the diner eating dinner in town, and her car hadn't been parked on one of the streets downtown; he would have remembered that red station wagon she drove. He rang the doorbell again.

He walked down the porch and glanced through the window but could see only the living room, glasses on the kitchen counter, and more mail on the counter. They'd made a wasted trip; he should have called first. "I'm sorry, Rae. She's not home."

"Want me to leave her a note?"

"Leave her your hotel number. Knowing Nella, she'll call you as soon as she gets home."

While Rae dug out paper and a pen to write the note, Nathan walked back to the driveway. It really did need a load of rock to smooth it out. He estimated the width and walked toward the garage to check the length and estimate the volume she'd need. As he rounded the back corner of the house he smelled it. Garbage going bad, but worse.

"Rae."

She came around the house.

She stopped when she got a first whiff of the odor. He could see it in her face, as her expression went still, that she recognized it too. "What kind of car does she drive?"

"A station wagon."

Rae walked to the garage and found a window. "Her car is here."

Nathan went to get his flashlight.

He walked the house circumference, opening the backyard gate and checking windows and doors as he went. Nothing obvious looked out of place, but the smell grew stronger.

He shone his light on the window at the east end of the house. The window screen had flies congregating on it and even a line of ants around the sill. He leaned against the house and shone his light inside, but the curtains were heavy and he could see nothing inside. The smell made his eyes water.

"We need in the house, without the dogs attacking us."

Rae looked around. "We can force the back door and let them into the fenced backyard. If you pull over the picnic table and stand on it there should be decent protection from them going at you."

"Which just leaves me stuck on the picnic table watching them go for my toes. I don't want to have to shoot the dogs."

"We can't exactly wait around until animal control gets out here. Assuming they can find the place."

"The roads have street signs even out this far, Rae. It's not Siberia. What did you have left from dinner in your carryout bag? Food will distract them while I get inside."

"A couple dinner rolls and some of the chicken. You'll get maybe ten seconds while they woof them down."

"It will be enough."

She went to get the carryout bag. He pulled the picnic table over near the door to provide him a perch of last resort. The dogs were not in a good mood, and breaking in would just intensify the sense of threat they already felt.

There was no screen door to contend with and the doorframe didn't look like it had been updated since the house was built sixty or seventy years ago. It would pop with the right kind of impact.

Rae came back with the sack and he pointed. "Stand over there, where the dogs can see you as the door opens. Throw the food toward them as soon as they lock onto seeing you and then swing that gate closed to protect yourself. That should give me enough time to get inside the house and push this back door closed behind me."

"Okay."

"On three."

She nodded.

He judged his footing. He started counting.

"One."

"Two."

"Three."

He slammed his boot into the door just below the doorknob. The wood in the frame splintered back. The locks snapped free. The door crashed inward.

Snarling dogs came through so fast they were one moving body. He flattened against the house siding.

"Here, boys!"

The fence gate slammed closed. Nathan darted inside as the dogs attacked the food and shoved the back door closed behind him.

The linoleum in the utility room area bore the marks of dogs trying to dig their way outside. The smell overpowered now, of decay and of dog urine, the heat oppressive in the still air. Flies buzzed around him. Glad he was wearing boots, he walked through the quiet house. He didn't bother to call Nella's name.

He walked down the hall. He pushed open the door. She was still in bed. He forced himself to look, to see what could be seen from the doorway that might suggest cause of death, and then he backed away. The decay had already made her nearly unrecognizable.

Nothing appeared disturbed in the living room, the kitchen. He noted that orderliness as he moved through the rooms. He flipped the lock open on the front door and turned the knob.

Nathan stepped outside, waved off Rae, and moved several feet down the porch. He put his hand against the porch column and looked at the grass poking through the melting snow. He took half a dozen deep breaths and then shook his head. He looked up. Rae was watching him. "She's dead."

"I know."

"It looks like she went to sleep and never woke up. Blankets are still over the body." He shook his head again trying to dislodge that image of the blankets that had moved because of the crawling maggots on the body but it sat there in his mind like a picture he couldn't look away from.

Her hand touched his left one. "Open your hand, let go."

The keys he'd held in his hand as a possible defensive weapon against the dogs had left an impression in his palm. "Yeah. Thanks."

"The newspapers here on her porch, the mail in the box—she never took Saturday's mail inside. Time of death is Friday night, early Saturday morning?" Rae asked.

"I'm not an expert on scenes like this, but that fits with the body, I think."

"This wasn't a shooting, a knife attack? She lives out in the middle of nowhere."

"No signs of blood on the walls, on the bed, no signs of struggle. The rooms don't look disturbed and doors were locked."

"If it's another death in her sleep, that puts you at three since I arrived in town."

"Not to mention a strike about to turn violent. What's happening to my town, Rae? It used to be such a quiet place." The town was coming apart around him and he couldn't figure out how to stop it or even what to fight.

He felt sick, and he stopped looking for his phone to just take a few more breaths and shake it off some more. Some things a man needed to expect to see, and that scene was outside anything he had expected. He had known he would find a body but hadn't prepared for the blankets moving.

"I saw my first body when I was seventeen, and cleaned up my first murder scene at twenty. The images don't settle well."

He thought her quiet words worth a halfhearted smile. "I've been walking into hard things since my first year on highway patrol, but the bugs—you never quite get used to the bugs that come with an undiscovered death."

"It's the dreams afterwards that I hate. They are always three-dimensional, and the dead people have a habit of getting up and walking around."

He did smile at that comment. "Thanks a lot for that image; it rivals this one. I'm going to find excuses not to sleep tonight, I think."

Rae let him have a few more moments with his own thoughts; then she nodded toward the house. "Peggy, Karen, Nella—even if it is not foul play with a person behind it, maybe there is a trigger. Something in the water, something they eat, something."

Her eyes narrowed as she studied the front door. "As awful as this is, maybe this is a break in this mystery too. The calendar at least suggests it might be. Nella may have been the first death. Then Peggy, then Karen. Maybe the source of all the trouble originates right here."

Nathan took that thought to its conclusion and nodded, appreciating how it did help. "We need a source, a cause. Nella's at least a resident, and someone local. Peggy and Karen were both just passing through town.

"If Nella did die on Friday night, and then Peggy came to this house on Saturday night, maybe the contagion traveled with Peggy back to her hotel. That doesn't explain Karen, but it's a start. We link someone from Peggy's hotel room to Karen's hotel room—maybe a housekeeper who works both hotels—and the chain is built to a common source."

He thought about it some more and winced. "And if that's the case, we've had law enforcement trampling through both hotel rooms and spreading whatever this is all over town without realizing we were doing so."

"If it is environmental or a toxin, catching it at three deaths is going to seem like a minor miracle—most of these situations are dozens of deaths before a common source is discovered."

Nathan picked up the newspapers on the porch and double-checked the dates to give himself a few more moments to think about this situation.

He shook his head. "Time to get a bit back more into reality, I think. This one could be a pure old-fashioned murder—pillow-over-the-face suffocation or hands-around-the neck strangulation—Nella's body is in no condition at first glance to answer that question." He looked at the house. "She doesn't fit the profiles of the others very well. Let's at least hope this is something squarely in that reality part of the spectrum. I've got too many hypothetical questions dancing around."

He looked at Rae. "I'm glad I came out with you. Getting a call from you saying, 'She's not home, and I smell a dead body' would have been even more of a shock than this already is."

"She was a friend."

Nathan nodded. "In the small-town way of knowing everyone who's been here for years."

He opened his phone. "This is going to reverberate around the town tonight. Let me start getting the calls made." He nodded to the keys she still held. "Go start the car and kick the heater on; no sense in you freezing while we wait. It's going to be a long night."

23

Nathan held the door to the pharmacy for Rae Thursday night. Gray Sillman had the scene—whatever it was—crime scene, environmental, toxin—Nathan was no longer sure what he was facing. It just felt so very wrong to say natural causes three times in a row.

By morning they had to know a whole lot more than they did now about Nella's death. He'd changed his mind and decided to keep Rae with him. His officers had their hands full, Rae was a decent sounding board, and the one thing he did not want right now was her out investigating on her own. If someone was out there doing this, Rae's asking questions could end her up in a heap of trouble, and he had had enough victims in this last week. For tonight, he just didn't want her out on her own.

Walter Jr. was working on restocking the cough-syrup selections. "Your dad around, Walter?" It wasn't much of a secret in town that Nella and Walter Sr. went back together quite a ways.

"Sure. In back, checking dates on the refrigerated drugs."

"I'm here. I heard the bell." Walter Sr. came around the counter to meet them. "What can I do for you, Nathan?"

Nathan looked around the store to see how many interested customers he would have for this conversation and thankfully found them in a lull of traffic for the store at the end of the day. The cashier didn't work evenings and was already gone for the day.

"I've got some bad news, Walter, and I'm sorry to have to break it this way. Nella has passed away."

"She's what?" Walter Jr. reacted first, pushing to his feet.

Nathan kept his focus on Walter Sr. There was no mistaking the fact it was a surprise to the man and also a serious shock. He went pale; he started to speak and changed what he wanted to say, then shook his head. "What happened? When?"

"It appears she died in her sleep a few days ago."

"Oh. Oh, my. She's been fine. I fill her prescriptions, and she's been just fine. Oh, I need to sit down."

Walter Jr. pushed the stool he was using over and Walter Sr. collapsed on it. "Dad?"

He tried to smile at his son and wave away the concern. "Sorry. It's just a shock. Nella—" He shook his head.

Nathan pointed and Rae understood the silent request. She walked over to the store entrance and flipped the sign over to closed, then turned the key in the door.

"When did you last see Nella, Walter?"

"Ah . . . Friday, we had dinner together. She fixed pot roast and burned the rolls again. We laughed about it and she promised we'd order pizza next time. She's not much of a cook. Did she have a heart attack or something?"

"The coroner was just arriving at her home and it will be a few days before we know much. We need to talk for a bit. Would it be easier on you to walk over to the house?"

"Yes, sure." He looked at his son. "Can you close up?"

"I'll call Scott to come over and help me. I've got it covered. Do you need to talk to me as well, Nathan?"

"A few questions. Come over to your dad's after you lock up."

"Twenty minutes."

Nathan made himself at home in Walter Sr.'s kitchen, pouring himself, Rae, and Walter lemonade from the pitcher in the refrigerator. He'd sat at this kitchen table many times as a young man, playing checkers with Walter Jr. He'd shared coffee and offered condolences with Walter Sr. at the death of his wife. He'd sat here a few years ago to inform the family Scott had been arrested for lighting fireworks outside the high school cafeteria and starting a small fire on the roof of the building. Tonight was going to be another of those conversations to note in their shared family history.

Walter accepted the glass Nathan offered him. "I've filled nearly every prescription Nella has ever been given. She has allergies and a tendency toward a hoarse voice when she gets a cold and occasionally when her feet were persistently cold her doctor might put her on water pills for a few days to help with her circulation. But that was it. She'd complain about the aches and pains of growing old, but that was just her way. She was in remarkably good health."

"Had she filled any prescriptions recently?"

"No. I can't believe this, Nathan."

"I've got two concerns, Walter. Until the coroner can tell me why she died, I have to treat this as an unknown cause of death. And that means I need to re-create Nella's movements over the last couple weeks, and I need to know about the people in her life. So anything you can tell, however small, will help me."

"Where do you want me to start?"

"Talk to me about Friday."

"We have dinner together almost every Friday night. We ate about six, she talked some about her week at work, and we made plans to go see a movie tomorrow night.

"I'll be honest, Nathan. We've been seeing each other almost six years, and we've been sleeping together about three. She didn't want to get married, and I stopped pushing about it because she might have ended the relationship. Things were good between us.

"Most Friday nights I would have stayed over, but I had a meeting last Saturday morning and she wanted to get some housework done. I left around eight. I stopped over to see my brother and then came on home."

"Had she complained about not feeling well?"

"No."

"Did she eat something you didn't?"

"Maybe some peanuts? She had a dish on the kitchen counter." Walter shook his head. "It was just a normal night."

"Did you speak with her again that night?"

"No. I tried to call her on Sunday afternoon but got her answering machine. I assumed she was at Stella's and I didn't leave a message. I tried her again last night and left a message on her machine."

"You weren't surprised she didn't call back?"

"I was working late, and she doesn't like answering machines. I assumed she called and missed me. Who's handling arrangements? She doesn't have family in town, Nathan."

"It will be a few days before those decisions can be made. Besides you, who else would have normally been out to her house? Does she talk about friends? Anyone else from the past week?"

"Her bridge friends come and go." Walter rubbed the back of his neck then looked over at him. "She could have been seeing someone else, I guess. She liked to go out and I work a lot of evenings at the store. We'd get into semi-arguments about it, but in the last year she hadn't been making a big deal of it. I admit I've wondered. Nella—she's always restless."

"Anything concrete? Someone you saw her with in town? A car in her driveway, a name she mentioned more than usual?"

"Nothing like that. And I'm probably wondering things that were never there. I just never figured why she kept going with me. I could understand her going out with the fine-chocolates guy, Keif, if only as a way to satisfy that sweet tooth of hers; she loved the stuff. But me—I'm too old for her. But she'd just laugh about it and ask me over again. We got comfortable together, I guess."

Nathan saw Rae smile at the summary. Nathan figured it really was those kind of reasons when it came to why Nella did what she did. "Do you know why they broke up, Nella and Keif?"

"That son of Keif's, I think. You know the trouble Isaac gets into. It wore on her after a while."

"Has Nella had problems with anyone lately? Did she have a dispute with anyone? Have an unexpected financial problem? Anything out of the ordinary that she's mentioned?"

"I tune out most of the town-grapevine stuff she hears, about who is seeing who and what so-and-so did now. I'm old enough I don't care. Nella would talk and I'd nod occasionally.

"Lately—Nella was bored, nothing going on in her life, nothing happening at work; it was so slow, the latest refrains were let's take a vacation and go see Nashville, or Chicago—anything to change the scenery of her days. I suggested she take a couple days off work and spend the afternoons going through the antique malls; she enjoyed that kind of thing."

Walter shook his head. "I'm not going to be much help to you, Nathan. Seeing her on Friday nights and occasionally going out on Saturday night if I wasn't working was such routine that we didn't really talk about day-to-day plans much anymore."

There was a tap on the door and Walter Jr. stepped in. "The store is locked up, Dad. I put the cash drawer into the safe and left it for you to balance in the morning. Scott dealt with the ice chest."

"Thanks."

Nathan closed his notebook and got up from the table. "I've got what I need, Walter. I appreciate your help." He looked over at Walter Jr. "Just one last thing. Do either of you remember Nella buying anything at the store recently? Gum? Candy bars? Anything at all?"

"I don't think she's stopped in at the store at all in the last couple weeks. Are you thinking this is something she ate?"

"I have no idea. I'm just trying not to miss anything no matter how remote."

"I can check the receipts for you; she normally used a credit card, even for the small purchases," Walter Jr. offered.

"That would help, thanks. Give me a call if something shows up."

Nathan said his good-byes and ushered Rae out the door.

"You don't want to talk with Walter Jr. about where he was Saturday night and when he last saw Nella?" Rae asked him urgently as they headed back to the car.

Nathan shook his head. "I want to better know time of death first. Nella sleeping with his dad—I could see that being enough to make Walter Jr. have a serious problem with his dad, but he's not the kind of guy to do something rash about it."

"Ruling out the town's two pharmacists when this may be a designer drug is a mistake, Nathan."

"Do you see Walter Sr. making a drug that kills people? Walter Jr.? His son Scott? Their family has been in this town for as many generations as mine. I know them. There are not bad seeds in their family history; there are not financial problems, drinking, drugs, petty theft, getting into fights—they are folks who are what they appear to be. Beyond a bit of mischief with Scott there's no record there. Walter Sr. seeing Nella as he has been is not something I like to hear, but it happens."

"Walter Jr. likes to experiment with creams and with special formulas for specific results. Nathan—"

He stopped her words with a finger across her mouth, aware they were in danger of attracting attention, and leaned in closer to quietly answer her. "I know. But just listen. Be as skeptical as you want to be about what they could do or might do or had cause to do—and weigh that against this fact: Walter Sr. and Walter Jr. have lived in this town all their lives.

"Other than a few years away at school, I can pretty much tell you where both men have been every day of their lives for the last twenty years. During that time how many unexplained homicides have there been in this town? None. In this entire county? Probably two.

"Someone doesn't just start making illegal designer drugs capable of killing people without a reason, and that's a personality willing to take a lot of risks. Focusing on Walter Jr. or Walter Sr. is just going to distract from someone else I need to see."

He sighed. "I'm sorry I'm so intense about it. If we find facts that make something like this fit, I'm ready to listen. But in this rare case I do need facts, not speculation."

"They're friends," Rae replied, putting into words the simple truth.

And it felt like he was having to choose between doing his job and giving his friends the benefit of the doubt—but he was going with his gut and trusting people until he had reason not to. He dug out his car keys. "Yeah. They're friends. And I'm beginning to wonder more and more if it's not a person behind this, but something entirely different. Something in the water, a bug like a mosquito, some disease. We need a trigger that reaches three people, Rae. And I need to know that trigger tonight, not next week. Not after another body shows up."

"I know, Nathan. Where do you want to head next?"

"The diner. A regular player in the bridge group would be Stella Patterson and she's normally working as a waitress there at this time of night."

"Clothes," Stella offered. "Nella was shopping for a lot of clothes lately, and that tells me she was seeing a guy she wanted to impress. After six years, I don't think that was Walter."

"Any ideas who?"

"No, and I've been trying to guess. You have to understand something, Nathan. Nella liked attention. Without suggesting she was unable to commit to a relationship, I know for a fact she was the kind to see more than one guy at a time and not think it was that big a deal. She'd see someone she got to know from work, someone from back in her school days, someone who was a friend of a friend—that kind of socializing. Dinner out, a movie, conversation—not everything was a relationship with a capital *R* for Nella."

"When did you last talk with her?"

"Last Wednesday? It's been a hectic week with my nephew visiting. I didn't think anything about it when I didn't hear from her the last few days. She works her own schedule and she's been talking about taking some vacation time." She looked across to where customers were taking seats. "I need to get a couple orders. Sorry I can't be more helpful."

"This has been a help," Nathan reassured.

"I hate prying through Nella's life like this," Nathan remarked to Rae, leaning back against his car and reviewing the evening notes.

"It's the only way to retrace her steps. Do you want to go back out to the scene?" Rae asked.

"Sillman will call if something unusual shows up. I've got strikebreakers set to arrive at the tile plant at six tomorrow morning, and I need to shift gears here soon and make sure that's in hand."

"You're worried about trouble tomorrow morning with the strike."

He nodded. "There's only so much pressure a man can take before he snaps and does something totally out of character. I've got a whole group of guys now under that kind of pressure. I just want to get through tomorrow without incident and get a weekend here where maybe cooler heads can prevail and this strike can get settled."

"Are you planning to bring in state help?"

"I'm trying not to reach that step. It would add even more tension on the picket lines to have strangers in uniform separating them from their job site. And I don't want to drop the ball on murder investigations by having all the resources tied up with the strike—but I don't know right now that I even have foul play happening.

"I've got a coroner whom I deeply respect, a man who has a solid reputation in his field, telling me Peggy and Karen are natural-caused deaths. Nella—she doesn't fit any common profile with them for age or location. I'm not even sure what I'd ask the state guys to do."

"Bruce and I want to help however we can do so without getting in your way."

Nathan smiled. "It's a small town, Rae. Your focus on Peggy has helped, and Bruce working every hint of a lead on those stolen guns—it's been appreciated. I know how far this strike has pushed my own guys. I'm smart enough to take qualified help when it's available."

He ran his hand through his hair. "I still owe you a carry permit; sorry I forgot about that. The paperwork should be finished by now. Remind me to check for you."

"I'll stop by and talk with your assistant in the morning."

"Please do."

"Why don't you drop me off at the agency and I'll track down Bruce. I'll do some more work on the story Peggy came to town to research."

Nathan unlocked the car. "I'll drop you at the agency, but you should think about calling it a night. Given the last few days, I don't want to speculate on what this weekend is going to be like."

"You take events like this a day at a time and follow where the facts take you," Rae replied, sliding into the car and reaching for her seat belt. "It will get better, Nathan. Everything has an answer. Some are just tougher puzzles than others to solve."

"Isn't that just the truth? This week seems unsolvable right now."

24

The tile plant was surrounded by a layer of ground fog, the temperature having melted enough snow to create an eerie dawn. Nathan stopped beside Chet as the patrol officer ended a radio call. "The bus will be here in ten minutes."

"Who's escorting it?"

"Martin, with Will and Lewis trailing the bus and keeping other cars a safe distance back."

Nathan shoved his hands into his pockets. "I don't like this at all." The picket line was empty; there wasn't a union guy in sight.

"The mayor stopped by last night. Maybe she had some influence."

"My mom can move mountains, but even she doesn't have this kind of influence. Last night they were talking about news media and banks of cameras and having their kids on the picket line to shame the strikebreakers crossing the line—something's happened in the last couple hours to change that thinking. Something that can't be good news. What time did the last picketer leave?"

"They broke the line at ten last night. They normally reform the line at 7 a.m. They know the bus is rolling in before that time today; we've been expecting to see the guys as early as 4 a.m. They normally park at the tire-repair shop and walk down."

"Do me a favor. Get a couple of your guys on the plant roof with binoculars and tell me this area is quiet."

"They won't burn down the place they work, Nathan. Or shoot it up. The union may have decided to simply keep this a normal day—arrive at seven, make their protests as the strikebreakers leave at the end of day, and try to let the media move public opinion their way going into the weekend."

"Maybe. Still, get your guys up there and give me a sweep before that bus arrives. The union's top officers, Adam and Larry, aren't returning my calls this morning, and that's not like either one of them."

Chet nodded and picked up his radio. He assigned two officers to make the check. "Ever since the plant manager's home got hit with that Molotov cocktail, Adam and Larry have been proactive with us. They aren't going to let violence flare up without warning you of trouble. I think we're going to get a break this morning."

Nathan hoped that optimism was right.

He heard an approaching car and turned. His grandfather pulled in behind his squad car. Nathan watched the union's top two officers get out of the car, along with his grandfather.

Nathan walked back to meet them. "Adam. Larry." Nathan shook hands with the men, looking at them, then at his grandfather. "The three of you together starts to explain some of this unexpected morning."

"The union is having a breakfast meeting at the union hall for all members and their families. You're invited to stop by when you are done here," Adam explained.

"I'll be there. Why?"

"Nella. You don't make a public disturbance on the day you mourn a friend's passing," his grandfather replied. "Her dad formed the union, you know."

"I didn't know."

"Zachary and I decided last night that things were just too volatile on both sides," Adam explained. "We were looking for an excuse to avoid this morning's confrontation and we'll take what is provided. We both want a deal. It's in both our interests to keep the situation such that it's possible to get a deal. If this becomes media driven, everyone loses."

Adam pushed his hands into his pockets and looked at the plant. "Besides, I let the guys on the line this morning; I'm looking at not just eggs and tomatoes and toilet paper going airborne, but also rocks and bottles. We've already got longtime friends barely speaking with each other if they are on opposite sides in this dispute. I don't need more of that grief coming down on my watch. And arresting neighbors doesn't do your officers' morale any good."

They all heard the bus approaching. Nathan watched it arrive, escorted by a squad car and trailed by two others. Security guards at the plant swung open the massive gate, and the bus rolled through.

"How many strikebreakers did they send?" Larry asked.

"Twenty-seven. Two scheduled to come decided to honor the picket line and not cross. They stayed put at the hotel."

"The plant won't make tile today. They'll be lucky to get the mixers cleaned with a crew that size," Larry noted, satisfaction in his voice at that reality.

"They'll ship finished product we had in the warehouse and pipeline and not much more," Adam agreed.

"Do I need to worry about the plant trucks, Adam?" Nathan asked. "We've already had graffiti and slashed tires. Someone shooting out their tires as they leave the plant hauling tile wouldn't sit well right now."

"I'm not pretending to have my guys cooled off, Nathan. Today is a kick in the gut seeing strikebreakers take their jobs. At best I just bought everyone through the weekend to try and get this strike resolved."

"Okay. I do sincerely appreciate these hours of quiet."

"How are things going with Nella? Is it true she just died in her sleep?" his grandfather asked.

Nathan nodded. "It looks that way at the moment. Sillman's working the scene for me. I'll be heading out there after I stop by the union hall."

ɛꙮȝ   ɛꙮȝ   ɛꙮȝ

A squad car blocked the road in front of Nella's. Nathan parked as far over to the drainage ditch as the snow would allow and walked the rest of the way up to the house. The driveway had become packed snow to the point it was near sheets of ice. He found his deputy sitting at a card table set up in the garage, squeezed into the space beside her car. "Tell me there is something useful here, Gray."

"Besides the smell?" Sillman offered a grim smile. He waved at the table covered with notes. "I'd rather freeze than not be able to eat again for a few weeks, hence this office. Inside it is still pretty intense."

He moved aside the sketch of the rooms and the notations where evidence had been gathered from and picked up one of the notepads. "There's not much, but I have a few things worth knowing.

"I've got a bathroom toilet seat which is in the raised position. I've got cigarette butts in a dish beside the microwave. I've got two wineglasses in the sink.

"The messages on Nella's answering machine—the first one she had not listened to is from Saturday morning at ten-eighteen. I checked the recorder time, and it's set accurately. Her Saturday mail was still in the box waiting to come in.

"There is no suggestion of robbery that I can find—her purse is still here, loose cash is in the glass canning jar on the kitchen back counter, there are a few nice pieces of jewelry on her bedroom dresser. Her home office looks undisturbed.

"We've got lots of prints. The wineglasses gave solid prints and those are probably the most interesting. The lab is trying to match them now. The cigarette butts are promising for DNA. The brand isn't going to give us much; they are sold in every store around here.

"The coroner hasn't provided an estimate on the time of death yet, but based on everything I have here, I agree with you that time of death is sometime Friday night, early Saturday morning.

"The coroner arrived with just about everyone on his staff, so we should have information back from him in short order. He was not pleased to hear there was a third death."

"I can imagine," Nathan replied, knowing how Franklin would have taken this news.

Sillman set aside the notebook. "Did you have any luck on the people side of this?"

"A bit," Nathan replied. "Walter Sr. was here Friday night for dinner; he says he left about 7 p.m. He doesn't drink, not even wine, and he most certainly doesn't smoke. And he probably would have mentioned smelling cigarette smoke—so assume the smoker was here sometime after that. Stella didn't have much on who else might have been in Nella's life, but she thought there might be another guy."

"Whoever it was, he doesn't seem to have covered his tracks to hide the fact he was here. The cigarettes and the wineglasses left in the kitchen were in the open. We should end up with both prints and DNA for Nella's guest. Based on this—it says someone came by the house after Walter Sr. left, stayed for a bit, he left, she went to bed, and she died in her sleep."

"Or he stayed, she died in her sleep, and he didn't want to be answering awkward questions by calling the cops to say I woke up beside a dead lady," Nathan modified, appreciating Gray's attempt to cast the most favorable light on the facts but accepting reality. Nella had been seeing someone else besides Walter Sr., and they had to identify that person quickly to either eliminate or confirm him as a suspect.

"This could still be a pure old-fashion murder like you said—pillow over the face or hands around the neck—they couldn't answer that question based on the initial look at the body. I'll keep on the coroner to get that answered."

Nathan almost wished for something that obvious. "Two weeks ago, that would have been our assumption going into this scene. What's your gut opinion?"

"Three dead in a week—saying all three are natural causes starts to strain credulity. But Nella doesn't seem to fit any pattern. If the time of death guess is right, she would have been the first of the three to die. Who would want to kill her? She's a gossip but harmless. Nothing here says a stranger showed up on her doorstep to murder her. Nothing says it was something self-inflicted as a suicide. My gut says this is not a murder, neither are Peggy and Karen. This town is just having some very bad luck.

"Face it, Nathan—you put these deaths a mile outside our jurisdiction and there's no reason they would ever be linked. Three ladies died of natural causes. They just happened to die in the same week and in the same geographic area. It happens."

"We're chasing hypotheticals and assumptions," Nathan agreed, "trying to fit something to connect the events because of when and where they happened, when there is absolutely nothing concrete yet saying they are actually related. But three natural-cause deaths in this period of time—it's getting very hard to swallow. Can you finish out this scene with the help you have? I know I've left you shorthanded for this one with so many helping out with the strikebreakers."

"I'll manage. It's just going a bit slower than normal to call the scene done. The coroner wants environmental samples from everything from the filter on the furnace to the food in the refrigerator, so I'll be watching his guys work for a while. End of day, we should be wrapping up here. How is it going over at the tile plant?"

"Quiet. The union decided to let the strikebreakers arrive without a picket line to meet them. I don't know how long it lasts, but I'll take every hour of quiet I can get."

"What time does the bus leave the plant?"

"Five."

"Call if you need us to leave here and help out. Five more cops are at least something if trouble appears."

"I will. What did you decide to do with Nella's dogs?"

"Your father volunteered to take them. A piece of steak got them inside the carry cages. They'll be okay dogs once they get settled down a bit."

"It sounds like a project Dad would take on." Nathan looked at his watch. "If you get anything on those fingerprints for Nella's last guest, track me down. I'm running out of people to interview. Nella didn't tell her friends who she was dating. It's turning out she was good at keeping a secret or two in her life."

"I'll track you down," Sillman promised.

෫෪ඃ ෫෪ඃ ෫෪ඃ

Rae, heading toward the police department, changed directions when she saw Nathan. She sat down beside him on a bench across from the courthouse and offered the paper sack she held. "Hot ham and cheese on sourdough," she explained, glad she had thought to get something hot. "I figured you probably forgot lunch in there somewhere."

He accepted the sack with a smile. "What time is it?"

Rae smiled back. "My question answered. It's about four. How long have you been sitting here?"

He shifted the folder of notes he had been reading to rest on the bench beside him and opened the bag. "Long enough to realize a concrete bench in the winter is cold. I'm meeting one of the union guys; he's running a bit late."

He unwrapped the sandwich. "Thank you. Food hasn't registered on my mind today and that doesn't happen very often."

"You're very welcome. The union showed class this morning, letting the strikebreakers through without incident. They'll do the same as they leave."

"That's my hope." He bit into the sandwich and nearly sighed. "This is great." He reached for the napkin as melted cheese overflowed the bread. "Have plans for your Friday night?"

"Bruce invited me over to see his place; he's been offering all week and it's finally fit the flow of the days for me to go over."

"I like his place; you will too, I bet."

"That's likely." Rae spotted Mark Yates, the union worker who had given her directions to the café her first day in town, coming their direction. She got to her feet. "I won't keep you. I just wanted to say hi."

Nathan had seen Mark coming as well and lifted a hand in greeting. "I'm going to remember this sandwich. Thanks, Rae. You can find me anytime."

"I plan to often; you're going to make my job in this town easier, and food is a great way to earn a favor or two. I took Sillman cheeseburgers and fries— I think if he wasn't already married he would have kissed me."

Nathan laughed. "Sitting out at a crime scene freezing, I'd kiss you."

Rae smiled back at the teasing, wondering how much of that emotion in his eyes was not teasing, and left Nathan to his job.

Rae walked back toward her car. She was trying hard to stay out of Nathan's investigation now. Three deaths had her convinced it was a cop matter and not something she wanted to cross into. Other than confirming that Karen and Nella were deaths unrelated to Peggy's so she could reassure Peggy's parents, she was content to stay out of the way unless there was something specific she could do that would help Nathan out.

Sillman wasn't going to be an easy relationship to develop; he wasn't keen to have a private investigator anywhere near a police case, but she was determined to soften the ground to at least make it friendly territory. Sillman would probably be surprised to find how much she agreed with him. She didn't particularly want to be back in cop business either, not the way the luck of her past ran.

She looked at her watch. She was still early for going over to meet Bruce.

She had been in town a week. Given everything that had happened in that span of time, it felt so much longer. She would never have imagined she would be on a first-name basis with so many people by now. She almost felt comfortable in this town. What would it be like after she had lived in Justice for a month? She began to hope that Bruce was right and that maybe this town would begin to feel like home.

25

Bruce had bought himself a small-town mansion. From the street the house looked like something from another era. Rae let her car coast to a pause at the curb so she could better study the place.

Two stories, square, with big pillars on a porch wrapping around three sides of the house—architecturally she thought it was maybe early 1900s. The home sat on a corner lot, with a spacious yard stretching in all directions, the trees towering above showing off a hundred years of sturdy growth. Big. Built by someone who had money even in that day.

One guy. Bruce must have walked around that much space and just laughed and said I'll buy it. Hardwood floors throughout, she bet, and probably an updated kitchen. She knew Bruce. He wasn't a man for small increments. Retire, get out of cramped one-room undercover apartments, and step up right to this. She smiled. She was glad for him.

Rae pulled into the driveway and parked on the other side of the drive from Bruce's car. Knowing her friend, she figured the garage had already been transformed inside into a comfortable workshop for his reconditioned Jaguar.

She opened the backseat door of her car and retrieved the gift. The walkway had been swept off. She balanced her housewarming gift in her arms as she walked in the dusting of snow toward the back door. Bruce had decorated the porch to make it more like front door number two, with a big wreath and welcome sign.

The door opened before she reached it. Bruce laughed and stepped out onto the porch. "Next time remind me to qualify the invitation to just being one guest."

"You remember George?"

He grinned. "How could I forget?" He reached for her gift, so she could walk up the stairs with a hand free for the railing. "What did you do, go unpack those boxes your movers neatly put into storage just to find him?"

"Just a couple of the biggest boxes. A tall neck, you know."

The giraffe was straining his attempts to get it inside the door. "I think I'm honored. Or speechless. Maybe something in between there. What brought this to mind?"

"Those county-fair pictures. We had to tie him to the roof of the car the night you won it."

"I remember."

Rae stepped inside the house after him and pulled off her gloves. "Never say I forget a promise. I said we'd share him. Since I've had him a decade, I thought he could keep you company. He can be a hat stand or something and be useful."

Bruce draped his arm across the giraffe's body. "No need; he's a conversation starter, and that will do just fine as his purpose in life. Make yourself at home; I'm going to give this guy a place of honor in the main hall."

She looked around the open kitchen they had entered. "Go. I like the idea of exploring."

Bruce disappeared through one of the two doorways. "I picked up all my socks in your honor," he called back. "There's hot cider or hot chocolate. Take a mug with you."

Rae pulled off her coat and hung it next to Bruce's on the coat tree by the door. The kitchen was at least twenty-by-thirty, with tall windows filling the room with natural lighting, and she had to look way up to see the ceiling. When the house was originally built, this must have been where the family spent a lot of time, and while it had been modernized, they'd left in the character.

A fireplace in the far wall had above it a baker's oven, and two big ranges were reproductions of the original cast-iron stoves. Heat would have risen with the high ceilings and left the work areas at least functional back in the days before air-conditioning. The big island in the middle of the room was a new addition, a place for barstools at the counter, while a nice table still held the place of honor by the windows for enjoying the view.

Bruce had their dinner well under way. The two skillets on the stove were simmering, occasionally blowing steam around the covering lids. The cutting board had chopped lettuce in the works, and plastic bags held vegetables yet to wash.

Rae fixed herself a huge mug of hot chocolate from the pot on the stove and carried the mug with her as she went to explore. She knew Bruce was leaving her to the first look on her own for a reason. She'd already seen the first small items she remembered from their past, from the sun catcher on the window to the mug he was using for his own hot cider.

She smiled as she ran her hand through the tassels of the hat hung on the wall leading into the dining room, remembering when he had bought it. She wandered into the dining room and over to his grandmother's hutch to see what new items he had acquired over the years.

She found Bruce working at the kitchen island, grating cheese, a bowl of diced tomatoes already done. Rae wrapped her arm around him and hugged his back, resting her face against the rough fabric of his shirt and closing her eyes for a moment; then she pinched some of the cheese he was grating and moved on. She loved what he had created in his house. "Mexican for dinner?"

"Yes." He looked over his shoulder. He didn't ask. He went back to working on dinner.

He made great Mexican meals. She opened the refrigerator. "What do you think? Hot salsa or mild?"

"Stay mild."

Rae pulled the glass jar from the third shelf. "It's strange, seeing you settled in a house. Don't get me wrong; I love this place, it's just so—" She laughed. "Well, settled. You've even got matching towels in the kitchen."

Bruce turned down the heat under the skillet. "Those I can't take credit for. The lady who sold me the house left me some of her household goods. She was downscaling to a nursing home and I promised to give things away that I didn't personally need. Try the tall cupboard for tortilla chips, either there or the bread drawer next to it."

"Found them." Rae dumped the salsa into a large bowl and opened the bag of chips. She perched on a barstool and watched him work while she started on the salsa and chips. "This kitchen is larger than my first couple apartments."

"I'm learning to appreciate having two dishwashers. The lady loved to entertain."

"Your game room—now that is classy. That pool table looks new."

"Something to keep you entertained. I looked at that old parlor with its high ceilings and hardwood floors and just knew what had to go in there." He added the next round of seasonings to the meat and turned his attention to chopping onions. "We need to get you out of that hotel soon so you can have a settled life again."

"The house out east will hopefully get an acceptable offer this month; then I'll see. I like what I've seen of this neighborhood. It's quiet?"

"Yes. It's mostly families with grown kids. A few newly married couples. Not much in between. The homes are old, but they are obviously spacious. And nicely affordable compared to where you have been living. I could do with a little less yard to mow though."

"I think I'd like something a little more on the edge."

"You'll get into enough trouble with the job. You don't need to be courting trouble with where you live. I meant to ask—did you get the carry permit today?"

"I did. I'm carrying my old Chicago PD backup piece until I get something a little more modern."

"I suppose it won't blow up in your face, but that's about all it's worth."

"I don't intend to ever pull it from its holster. Have you ever needed your weapon since you became a private investigator?"

"Nope. But then I rarely needed it when I was a cop, either."

"True." She turned a chip to rescue a tomato chunk in the salsa. "I'm thinking I might go to town and work on the Ferrari tomorrow if you could give me a lift. A few more hours and I should have it ready to drive home. I got the insurance on it put into effect today."

"I can give you a lift. But do you really think you can get it clean enough to drive?"

"Frank already has the bulk of the cleanup done, and my uncle finished the metal work. The rest is just cleaning the thousands of crevices the blood managed to soak into."

"A very appetizing thought. We'll change the subject until after we eat."

She smiled but agreed. "Talk to me about your day."

"Not the most fascinating topic you could have chosen, but we'll get it out of the way anyway," Bruce replied easily. "I spent the morning handing out my card and trolling for information on the handguns. A reward isn't working nor is a mild threat out on the street. If someone local was the thief, he's wisely letting them cool off before he tries to move them. After that turned into a waste of my time, I made some more progress tracking down Mrs. Elan's half sister. The late afternoon I spent tailing Nathan's grandfather—or trying too. He's been visiting a lot of the guys in the union."

"What's going on with Nathan's grandfather?"

"Over the last year Henry has bought himself a couple new vehicles, both with cash. One of them is a very pricey Porsche and the other a new pickup truck that wasn't cheap either. I've been trying to figure out for Nathan where the cash is coming from. There's no obvious source for the income."

"Can't you just ask him?"

"He's not saying. We're not trying to stop Henry from spending his cash; we're just trying to figure out where the cash is coming from. He was the sheriff of this town before Nathan's dad; he's not a wealthy man. Some things are so obviously in your face that the question has to be asked."

"What have you decided so far?"

"I've ruled out a cashed-in life-insurance policy, sold land, stocks. He's gambling—that's my latest hunch."

"He'd be what, in his eighties?"

"Eighty-four."

"Has he ever gambled before in his life?"

"Not that I can find. But there isn't hidden wealth buried in that family history just waiting to appear."

"Henry's wife?"

"She passed away last year. A schoolteacher from a reasonably middle-class family the next county over. The money isn't coming from her side of the estate."

"So a grown man just suddenly starts gambling at a level that provides cash for expensive cars? Bruce, you know that's not it—you lose more than you win when you gamble. Unless you're telling me he cashed in a winning lotto ticket."

"Not that I've been able to identify. What would you suggest?"

"He found the cash."

Bruce set down the knife he was using to dice the onions. "Found it."

"It makes more sense than won it. Maybe he found a buried coffee can of old gold coins on his land; maybe a former homeowner left behind a letter signed by Abraham Lincoln under the floorboards. People come into things of great value all the time. That's why they are called discoveries."

Rae shrugged. "Maybe it's as simple as the fact the man tossed his change into a barrel all his life and he finally got around to cashing in all that loose change. I heard a guy once cashed in twenty thousand dollars worth of pennies."

"Henry has been hanging out with Bob Teal lately. The man is the former president of the local bank."

"So maybe the man got some good financial advice fifty years ago and took it. Did you ever think Henry might have just turned eighty-four and decided it was time to spend rather than save some of his lifetime earnings? His family doesn't need the cash; his wife has passed away—it's time to live a little."

"I'm all for that answer. I'm just afraid it's not going to be something that neat."

"Unless you think he just became a criminal and the cash came from something illegal." She looked up from the chip and salsa she held and saw his expression. "Bruce. Don't even go there. I can see by the silence you aren't discounting that idea."

"The former sheriff is at home in this community. He knows where every secret is buried."

"The man has Nathan for a grandson; he'll be honest to the point of being squeaky clean. I personally vote for the buckets of change getting cashed in. You want me to ask him?"

"He's already pretty much told both Nathan and me to mind our own business."

"I ask nicer than you do."

"You can have a run at him if you like. It can't hurt."

"He drives a Porsche? He's got a nice eye for a good car."

"You'll have something in common."

"True." Rae accepted the plate Bruce handed across to her.

"Don't wait for me; these are best eaten while the wrap is still warm."

"I don't plan to." The soft tacos were going to be a mess to eat, but she loved them. She found herself extra napkins and moved from the island over to the kitchen table. She pulled out a chair. "What did you hear about Nella?"

"Not much different than this afternoon—Sillman was still searching the house and the coroner was busy with tests."

"Personally, I'm guessing she was murdered by a boyfriend."

"Facts or hunch?"

"Pure hunch," Rae replied. "It just felt like a personal death. She lives out in the middle of nowhere. Someone had to want to go to Nella's house."

"It's not going to be natural causes?"

"Three times in a row?" Rae shook her head. "At least one of these is a murder. And Nella would be the likely fit."

"The rumor at the diner is that she was seeing a much younger guy."

"Any basis for that rumor?"

"Not that I could tell."

Rae smiled. "The blessings of a small town—rumors circulate themselves into becoming facts."

Bruce brought over a plate for himself. "What time do you want to head into the city tomorrow?"

"Early, if you don't mind. Say nine."

"That will work for me. Assuming you get home tonight in a reasonable time to get some sleep."

Rae laughed. "I've missed these Friday nights together. Nothing ever quite replaced them in those years away."

"I'm hoping there are many more of them to come. I even bought a pie for dessert."

"Great planning."

Rae settled into the leather couch in Bruce's living room, extending her sock feet to absorb the heat coming from the fireplace. "This is perfection. Moon out, snow on the ground, a cozy couch to disappear into while you watch some television. You've got a very nice place, Bruce."

"You look good right there." He settled into the big chair at an angle to the couch. "You'd best make it a habit to come over often."

She set her mug of hot chocolate down on the floor rug within easy reach. "I'm good at making myself at home." She leaned her head against the cushioned back and studied the ceiling. She laughed. "I'm so tired it feels like part of the world is spinning in circles."

"It's been an intense week since you drove into town, and I did mention you might want to go easy on those hot peppers."

"I know, but I love them so." She listened to her own heartbeat for a while as her socks warmed up, then found the energy to move again and look over at him. "Where are we going, Bruce? You and I?"

He considered her. "Someplace interesting, I suspect. We know each other, Rae. You want to move slowly; you also just want to be done with this transition and be back on stable ground. So you'll ignore the caution you feel and knock down the historical stuff fast and sort out the pieces of what you find after you see them all."

"You do know me."

"Still like you too." He smiled. "Drink your chocolate; no use letting good stuff go cold."

She reached for the mug. "That's one of the things I missed most about our Friday nights—the hot chocolate and the pie and the conversations that disappeared into the dust corners of unimportant topics, but never seemed to end no matter the hours we'd already talked."

"You still talk more than I do on occasion."

She rolled her head toward him on the back cushion of the couch and smiled. "There are a few years' worth of talking bottled up unsaid. The trivial subjects have got some steam behind them now."

"Why wasn't there someone to talk with?"

She shrugged. "Dallas wasn't so bad; I had lots of friends to hang around with the first year or two on the job. And the years before that at the academy—I was like a duck in water, quite comfortable and not even realizing how much I was missing everything I'd left behind. But Washington, D.C.—you know how hard it can be to work undercover, Bruce, all the things you know or suspect but can never talk about. It turned out to be a place where there weren't safe people to hang around with."

"Talk to me about Washington. Not the ending, just the beginning. Did you want to make the move?"

She had to think about it but then she nodded. "I did. It was a big assignment, the kind of case that gets followed by the director's office and can send an agent up several rungs on the career ladder when it's over. I was at the point in my career where that kind of return for the risk seemed like a good calculation to make."

She looked over at him. "That's hindsight. You get asked to work a substantive case, you jump at it. That's the cop in you. And this was one of those cases. I barely heard the basic details they laid out before I said, 'When do I move?' I regret that now. I regret I didn't take the time to sort out how much was personal ambition and how much was the case that drew me to D.C."

She finished her hot chocolate and studied the bottom of the mug. "They approached me in Dallas with the need for someone with good undercover skills who would be a fresh face in the Washington area. They needed someone who had never done a rotation at headquarters. I wasn't really aware of all the dimensions of the case or all the dynamics going on with it until I arrived in D.C."

"You were investigating another agent," he guessed softly.

"Yes."

She looked over at him. "Cuts doesn't it, the very idea of a bad cop? They didn't know who it was; they just had a list of names and a suspicion the agent they wanted found was on the list."

"A bad cop gave up my name for money and I ended up shot—I understand what it's like to hear the news there is a bad cop in a place of trust."

"Maybe that's one of the reasons I didn't look so closely at the assignment before I said yes. It was a visceral need to get the guy located and out of our midst."

"What was he doing?"

Bruce knew it was classified information; she knew it was classified. But it ate a hole inside her as she tried to sort it out on her own—and if Bruce was going to betray her, no one in the world could be trusted. "This will go to the grave with you."

"I've got so many secrets going with me I'll be lining my coffin with the notes."

She smiled at his attempt to lighten the moment. "There is something scary about just how much ugly information you have tucked away inside that head of yours."

She studied her socks and the frayed edge on the left one. "Someone is selling the names and addresses of people in the witness-protection program." She looked up in time to catch his wince. "Yeah, my thoughts too.

"An internal investigation narrowed it down to nine people on the inside they thought might be the source. They transferred me from the Dallas office to D.C. to get close to one of the agents high on their list."

"It's a bad kind of case to work."

"The worst. And there was an . . . urgency to the case. If enough witnesses die, it doesn't matter if the rogue agent is found and stopped and prosecuted. No one will ever be willing to testify for the government again, when the protection promised them has been publicly turned into a piece of Swiss cheese."

Bruce nodded and she knew he understood the type of pressure she was describing.

"It was the first time I'd met the counterintelligence types, Bruce. They're a different kind of agent, the set of people who were running the investigation. You started to wonder if they believed anything anyone ever said to them."

"Finding spies in their midst—that's a recipe to suspect everyone, and a motto that becomes trust, but verify."

Rae brooded over that. "I wasn't ready for it, no matter what I thought about my undercover skills going into it. It wasn't like undercover work where you knew the guy was guilty, but you were looking for the evidence. I was getting close to a guy that was numerically more likely to be a good cop than the one bad one, and I was trying to figure out if he was the one bad one."

She sighed. "I think I started to get paranoid; that's the only way I can describe how the case affected me. I was trying so hard—knowing the investigators needed me to not miss any detail, knowing the guy that was selling these names was extremely careful and deadly, feeling caught between thinking I knew this guy I was investigating and yet suspecting everything about him—it messed up my head a bit."

He didn't answer her right away and she was glad he wasn't dismissing her words with the suggestion it hadn't been that bad. It had been that bad.

"Rae—when you're undercover in a big case, you're in the midst of a fast-flowing murky river. You're often swimming in the dark, working with incomplete information, seeing only shadows of facts. You depend on your handlers, those spotters standing on the bridge watching everything, to put the details together and keep you swimming in the right direction. It sounds like this is a case where you didn't have that help; your handlers weren't connecting very well with you."

"I always felt like they were assessing me as much as they were assessing the details and evidence I brought them," she agreed. She was grateful he'd worked undercover as long as he had and could articulate what she could only look back on and understand.

"It didn't help that I often used gut instinct to say something was right or wrong and they didn't know me well enough to trust that answer. Since I couldn't rely on it as a reason for what I reported, I was often on the defensive."

She felt the words themselves as a frustration, just remembering. "Then another witness got murdered; the intensity ratcheted up . . ." She let the words trail off as she remembered those last months.

"What?"

She realized tears were washing down her cheeks and she pushed them away. "It ended very bad."

"I saw your house."

She either told him the rest of it or she buried it again. She wanted to bury it, the truth was so raw, but it was never going to ease off. It needed to be said, at least once.

"His name was Mark Rivers. The case looked solid against him. I thought it was him. But as it turns out, he was not the guy selling the names. I accused an innocent man of murder, Bruce."

She couldn't look over at him, didn't want to know his reaction to her words. It was so intensely bad, that ultimate failure. "And I can't even apologize to him. He's dead."

He let her drift in her thoughts, let those words settle before quietly asking, "What happened, Rae?"

She looked up and saw nothing in his expression but the quiet stillness of him listening to her that she had depended on all her life. She tried to hold his gaze but couldn't and looked away, back to the fire, blinking against the tears.

"Mark found one of the hidden microphones. My back was to him, and I didn't realize why he was asking the questions he did until the last moment. I saw the instant it clicked with him that I was suspecting him, that the wire was to capture him—and I think he lost it mentally in that moment. He had wanted to be an agent since he was a kid, and I was literally destroying his life even as I stood there and smiled at him and asked if he wanted pineapple in the stir-fry or not. He put his hand out to grab something and it happened to be the knife that was on the cutting board."

"Your handlers?"

"They were in a house across the street, recording from a distance."

She didn't say more, couldn't. The night was still a living wound inside her. "It became personal, Bruce. And maybe that is where the biggest of the errors was made. I didn't realize just how personal the case had become to me after that witness died."

"Have they caught the agent that is selling the names?"

"No. And I'm sure my dramatic ending gave the guy they wanted to find plenty of time to go deep underground again. There was no way to cover up a dead agent and another injured one, not when the agents on the suspicion list worked in the same basic area of the building."

"I wish you'd called me. I wish I had been there for you in those first days after it came apart."

"I thought about calling you; it's one of the reasons I had dug out your number." She tried to smile. "I'm decompressing, Bruce; I know that, in my own unique way. I'm still trying to find my sense of balance again. I can't figure out how to pace this fall into a new life—it's cautious; no, fast ahead; no, cautious. I fluctuate between nothing and everything."

"I don't mind."

She brooded over her empty mug. She did. "Tomorrow morning I'm going to hate the fact I told you."

"You're already regretting it. But that's why I've got such notoriously forgetful hearing. We can wait to talk about this again for six months if you want." Bruce got to his feet and took the mug from her hand. "Hot chocolate or hot cider?"

"Cider this time."

He ruffled her hair. "Welcome to the land of recovering cops."

She smiled but still caught his hand for one last serious question. "Tell me it gets better," she whispered.

His hand tightened on hers. "It gets better."

"How?"

He thought for a moment, then ran his knuckles along her jaw. "Hang out with Nathan some more, and remember what 99 percent of cop work really is about. You loved this job, Rae. You still can. There's just a couple nasty detours that have to be sorted out and left behind first. Don't throw out the first love just because life kicked you in the gut."

"Easier said than done."

"So hang out with me too; I'm reforming slowly."

She smiled back. "Got to love a man that went from a cubbyhole of an apartment to a private hotel of a house."

Amusement lit his eyes. "Oh, that's good. I'm going to have to remember the private hotel answer. Maybe add a couple signs to the front yard. Folks in the neighborhood would get a kick out of that."

"What did you say when people asked why you wanted this big old place for yourself?"

"I mentioned I had a lot of ghosts coming with me."

She blinked. "Oh, that's good too."

He smiled. "I thought so. Find us a movie; I want to listen to you snore before I send you home."

"I'm not falling asleep watching a movie on you, Bruce."

"Yes you will. Find something John Wayneish. Or *Midway*. I always like watching *Midway*."

"We're going to town early tomorrow to pick up my car."

"I remember. We're still going. Just after you watch a movie with me. You can't break a Friday night tradition the first Friday night you happen to come over."

"True." Who was she kidding, she wanted to stay. "Where do you keep the movies?"

Bruce gestured with the mug. "Third shelf of the cabinet."

"You're getting something more on the line of *March of the Penguins*."

He laughed. "All those animals; you never change. Hot cider coming up. If you're good, I'll find the popcorn too."

26

Nathan leaned against the window in his office Saturday morning and watched the snow fall outside. It was finally coming down at a rate that would please the kids and make this day an adventure for drivers. He hoped it eased off soon. As stretched as this town budget was for finances, snow removal was always hoped to be an overfunded line item in the budget come April. He sighed and turned back to his desk. While he scanned papers, he picked up the phone and called his deputy chief to confirm the most pressing item of the morning was handled. "Will, are you sure the negotiating teams are tucked away in a private enough place?"

The strikebreakers may have been able to leave the plant without incident on Friday, but if they appeared again on Monday Nathan didn't expect that quiet to be repeated. He needed the strike to be history this weekend.

"Your dad and I got them out of their homes while it was still dark and snuck them out to the lake pavilion," Will confirmed. "No one knows they've assembled. They're using Ford's lakefront home as the meeting site. It was as far as I could get them out of town while leaving them in the city limits."

"We need a deal today."

"Both Adam and Zachary are more serious than I've ever seen them. They know what Monday is going to bring if they don't get a deal done this weekend. I promised we would bring them out dinner around five unless they call us earlier. They'll decide over dinner if it makes sense to do another round through the night or break for the day. Your dad is staying out there to facilitate anything the group needs."

"Have Dad call me if there's any word from Adam and Zachary on progress. I'll plan to go out to meet them when they are ready to break for the night."

"Will do, Boss."

Nathan hung up the phone. Losing the tile plant would kill this town. They had to get a deal this weekend. And there wasn't much he could do to help make that happen. It was awful sitting on the sidelines waiting for news.

"You okay, Boss?"

Nathan looked toward the doorway. Sillman looked like the week had worn on him as much as it had on his boss. "Pending bad news on the tile-plant front. Come on in, Gray." Nathan started looking again for the file on the stolen handguns. He was personally going to go talk to the top candidates on his list for having done the robbery. Even if he couldn't get the guns to mysteriously turn themselves back in, maybe he could put the fear of life and limb into people that the guns should never be allowed to reach the street and be sold.

"You want the interesting news of the day first?"

"Hit me with it; I'm as braced as I'll ever be."

"Nella shows no sign of dying by murder in the traditional way—no knife wounds, gunshots, broken neck. The coroner thinks she may have died of cancer."

Nathan stopped his search. "You're kidding me."

"Franklin found bone cancer, pretty advanced. It was at a stage it would have begun spreading to her organs. Given the time lapse in finding the body, he may never be able to rule out other contributing factors to her death, but his opinion leans toward natural causes."

"Nella had no idea she had cancer."

"The aches and pains she complained about she probably wrote off to her age. She never got it checked out. If you've got to die of cancer, I guess not knowing you have it would be one of the better ways to go."

"How sure is Franklin that this killed her?"

"The cancer is there; enough to kill her, but he said he'll have to go by absence of other factors at the scene to rule on this one."

"You're right. This would constitute interesting news. You've got more?"

Sillman nodded. "The final toxicology reports are back on Karen Reese. They are clean. Franklin is ready to rule her case natural causes. Everything he has seen points to a heart attack. He was on the scene within an hour or two of her death and still nothing showed up in the toxicology. We'll have the results of the last vending-machine-food tests today, but I doubt we find something. All the food tests so far are clean too."

Nathan squeezed the bridge of his nose. "Close the door."

Sillman moved aside the box fan and closed the door.

"What are the odds someone in the county's own forensic lab is in on the designer-drug production, and these blood-test results are being intentionally messed up?"

His deputy chewed on the coffee stir stick he held and thought about it, then looked over at him. "You really want to go there, Boss?"

Nathan knew what he was suggesting and the fallout that would come if his suspicions got out. "Just ask a couple quiet questions, okay? See if the tests are being run by the same shift. Ask the coroner if it's possible to use another lab to rerun the most critical of the test results. I'll pick up the cost to get it done."

"I'll ask."

"Anything on the fingerprints you found on the wineglasses at Nella's place?"

"We've got unknown prints. DNA from the cigarettes may still give us something, but it will be a day or two more at the lab."

"That fits our luck with this case." Nathan shook his head. "Three dead by natural causes? I just don't buy it, Gray."

Sillman leaned back against the door. "Assume the reporter is murdered to stop her story investigation, assume Nella is murdered because she knows something; that still leaves Karen out there as a strange anomaly. There's no way Karen could learn something dangerous about this community in the few hours she was passing through town. If you start saying this one is natural causes and this one isn't, it needs something to hang its hat on. We just don't have it, Nathan, that one tangible fact that says murder."

"I know we don't. Keep on the environmental samples. Let's try and rule out anything at Nella's being a toxin that Peggy picked up." Nathan looked at his officer. "Nella dies of cancer, two young ladies die of natural causes in Justice hotels—what are we going to be saying when the fourth body shows up?"

"I hear you, Boss."

୧୬ଽ   ୧୬ଽ   ୧୬ଽ

Bruce eased his car into a void in the alley, creating a parking place for the Caprice between an overflowing Dumpster and a discarded mattress.

"This is where you think the handguns are at?" Rae questioned, looking around the area before she considered opening her door. She didn't mind the extra stop in their morning to pursue a lead, but normally Bruce had better information to work from than this. They were far enough outside of Justice that the Dumpster had a county address on it for the responsible collection company.

"The kid did see one of the stolen guns; he remembered the last three digits of the serial number and they were right. But he was a nine year old going on thirty-nine. He negotiated forty bucks out of my pocket just for those numbers."

"You should have negotiated for the name of the friend who showed him the gun."

"He wanted an even hundred for that; I didn't feel like being that generous given the phone call woke me up."

Rae laughed as she pushed open her door. "You were better able to haggle in the past. So what are we looking for again?"

"His friend who was showing off the gun shares a bedroom at home, so anything he considered important he never takes home; he leaves it stashed in his secret place. My nine-year-old hustler says that secret place is somewhere in this alley. Precisely where, he doesn't know."

"You would have been better off spending the hundred so we could just go talk to the friend."

"If I have to. The store was robbed by a guy in his late forties or fifties so we're still a ways away from the final name we need to find. This gun may simply be a discard, and forty bucks is enough for that."

Rae scanned the depth of the alley and the stacked trash. "At least I dressed appropriately for the occasion."

"You look cute in overalls."

"I look like the trash man that never visits here. I'll take the right; you take the left?"

Bruce held out a pair of work gloves. "Find it, and I'll give you the hundred."

"For a hundred, I might even show some competitive spirit in this search."

"This is promising," Bruce said.

Rae set aside a rumpled army jacket to look over at Bruce. Twenty minutes of searching had left her with a profound appreciation for neat people who threw their trash away properly.

Bruce pried the lid off a steel drum and looked inside. He nodded. "One secret stash site, nicely protected against rain, wind, snow, and less-persistent searchers." He glanced over at Rae and smiled. "The kid had a box of dog doo sitting on top of the barrel."

"That would be a good deterrent."

Bruce set aside the lid and began lifting out items, starting with a layer of folded clothes. "Baseball glove, autographed ball, jacket with stitched name—*Stephen*—schoolbooks, school ID, bus pass—the kid's life is in here."

Rae opened one of the schoolbooks. "Stephen Foster. It matches the school ID. Sophomore? Junior maybe? I don't remember the course work well enough to tell. I'm guessing from this that his home is somewhere he stays as little as possible."

"Sadly probably true. It's odd that a nine-year-old kid would have such an older kid as a close friend."

"I don't know; street friends are a breed of their own," Rae guessed.

"One box. Heavy." Bruce lifted it out and passed it over.

Rae opened the top and found several layers of fabric. She unwrapped the first piece of cloth in the box. "Handgun." She read off the serial number.

"That's one of them," Bruce agreed.

Rae checked the box. "Six handguns, safely stored away. Do you have a full list of the serial numbers?"

Bruce tugged it from his pocket and she started checking each gun against the list. "Anything else from the robbery in that barrel?"

Bruce continued searching. "Not that I can see." He returned items to the barrel in the same order he'd removed them. "The guns got too hot to hold or sell, got discarded, and our Stephen was enterprising enough to find them?"

"It works for me. Leave the kid the hundred bucks," Rae replied.

"What?"

"Leave him the hundred bucks, your card, and a note that says there's another hundred if he tells us where he found the box."

Bruce dug out his wallet. "You're awful generous with the company's money."

"Nathan is going to be able to get prints off this box or the guns. But I want to gift wrap it for him with names and everything."

"And everything is right. For this price, we'll end up losing money on the case."

"Think of it as charity for street kids."

"I prefer the tax-deductible kind," Bruce replied, amused, but he wrote the note.

27

Nathan could not remember the last time the M&T Diner was standing room only. Folks were spilling over to Sir Arthur's for seating and carrying over lunch. He listened to the talk around him and tried to sort out those who were only gossiping from those who sounded overly stressed. The strike was hitting families hard. He could hear it in the voices around him.

"Is this chair for me?"

Nathan smiled at his mom as she squeezed into the nook. He pushed over the coffee he had ordered for her. "Mabel wants to know if you would like peach or apple pie," he mentioned, guessing the question he'd just been asked in pantomime by the lady behind the counter.

"Peach."

Nathan pointed to the left plate Mabel was holding up. "Ready for the council meeting?"

"Never, but that's beside the point," his mom replied, cheerful as always. "The agenda should have us talking until dinnertime just to get through the public inquiries. I did get you the extra cash you need to deal with the building's furnace. The fire chief was feeling generous this morning and gifted you part of his capital funds."

"Truly? When can I spend it?" He was hoping that answer was tomorrow.

She laughed. "I already called Peter and told him to deal with the problem. You'll hear metal slamming around and guys fussing over that old beast on Monday." She leaned over and tapped her cheek. "You owe me a kiss."

He obliged.

Mabel brought over the pie for his mom.

"She's fixing my furnace, Mabel. I'm thinking bumper stickers in her honor. *Linda Justice—Mayor for Life.* What do you think?"

"Who else is ever going to want the job?"

Linda laughed. "How very true. You do know he's telling you about it just to make sure I can't back out of the commitment."

"You raised a resourceful son. Would you like more coffee, Sheriff?"

"Keep it coming," Nathan replied, knowing he would need every bit of the caffeine before the day was over. He sliced into his pie. He'd start working his mom for funds to deal with the roof next.

His mom poured cream into her coffee. "I met Rae Gabriella briefly this morning. She seems like a nice lady."

"She's a very nice lady," Nathan agreed, amused at her opening conversation subject.

"Private."

"Very."

"Good sense of humor."

"Trying to make sure I noticed what I already noticed, Mom?"

"Just doing some basic checking."

Nathan was accustomed to the trespassing into his personal life and didn't mind it on the whole. He liked to know what his mom thought about people. "I'm interested, but then so is Bruce."

"It crossed my mind that that might be the case. She blushes quite easily, Miss Gabriella, when the subject of the ring she wears comes up. It's not so clear from my conversation with her who it is from."

"I always assumed Bruce. They dated seriously eleven years ago." The pearl ring Rae wore on her right hand didn't fit as a friendship ring, and the setting was too new in style to suggest it was a family heirloom; he'd noticed it because his life went better when he did.

"She strikes me as not the kind of lady to give her affections or friendship lightly."

The photos set out on the dresser of her hotel room had convinced him of the same thing, but Rae was not a subject he was ready to discuss with his mom. "Let's leave that thought for another time."

"Have you introduced her to Henry yet?"

He smiled. "She'll meet him on her own soon enough, I think."

"Sheriff, you and I need to talk."

Nathan turned to find the coroner at his elbow. It didn't look like it was going to be a pleasant conversation. "Mom, may I abandon you for a few minutes?"

"Go. I need to get to the council meeting early anyway. I'll catch up with you later tonight."

"Thanks."

"Thank you, Ma'am." Franklin touched a gloved hand to his hat.

Nathan left cash on the table for both his and his mom's coffee and pie and pointed to the door. He followed Franklin outside.

"You suspect someone in the lab is fixing the blood-test results."

Nathan shook his head and kept walking, determined to have this conversation without being overheard. "I've got three deaths, two of which are being ruled natural causes, and the third possibly being cancer. I'm thinking about what I do when I'm looking at death number four. There's nothing that is pointing to the lab beyond the fact it could theoretically be an explanation. I'm just trying to rule out the long-shot possibilities now, before I'm having to do it with the media looking over my shoulder."

"Well, I don't like the suggestion."

Nathan accepted that. "I've got to do something, Franklin. Right now what I can do is to check out intentional errors by those doing the investigation. I'm not just asking the hard questions about your people; I'm asking them of mine too. If death number four appears and I can't figure something out, I'm going to be inclined to turn in my badge and resign the job. Not doing something right now isn't an option."

Franklin shoved his hands into the pockets of his coat and sighed, then nodded. "I'll have the blood tests rerun by another lab. We can request help out of Chicago to look again at the food items from the scenes."

"Thank you."

"I understand the worry, Nathan. I signed my name on those death certificates, and with that my reputation. But I'm telling you, everything says natural causes with Peggy and Karen, and Nella did have an advanced case of cancer."

"I understand that, Franklin. I'm just stepping back and seeing the bigger picture. The tile-plant strike is an economic blow to this community that may get much worse. If the tourism business starts to drop off because coincidences start to be too much for people to accept as coincidences—this town just can't survive that kind of second hit.

"I need facts I can tell the newspaper reporter for Monday's edition to keep this tamped down. I'm already having to convince the editor not to run the photos of Peggy, Karen, and Nella across the top of the front page with a bold reference to the town's 'ghost killer.' He's seeing a chance to finally get his paper's circulation numbers to improve with some sensational headlines."

Franklin winced. "He'd do it too. Tell the reporter to call me directly."

"I appreciate it. I just need time. I'll take any straw I can grasp to give me that."

"I'll call as soon as I get any of the lab tests back," Franklin promised.

⚜ ⚜ ⚜

Rae dropped her cleaning rag into a ten-gallon bucket and blew a strand of hair off her face. She leaned back on her heels studying her work, pleased with the progress so far. The red paint of the car gleamed and the rich leather seats were starting to look closer to their original factory-installed condition.

She felt a bit guilty for working on her car rather than pitching in to help her uncle and cousin around the warehouse, but her uncle had just laughed and told her to go play with her new toy. He understood why the car had the attraction it did for her. Style was part of it, speed, but also the fact that in the car she was in her own world. Not much of life felt that way anymore, totally hers.

"I think you ought to reconsider this, Rae," Bruce said, settling onto a stool beside her next to the cart of cleaning supplies. "You really want to drive this car?"

She patted the side panel of the car. "Hey, be nice." She pointed out the progress. "The bullet hole in the roof is patched; the blood is mostly soaked out. The leather isn't entirely stain free, but it's merely a shadow now, and it's too expensive to replace the seats. If someone didn't know this was where a guy had died, there is nothing here to indicate it."

"I think the smell might."

"Pulling the odor out will take weeks," she conceded, "but it will eventually clear up. I think the car cleaned up remarkably well."

Bruce leaned in to study the interior. "It's relative, I suppose. In the meantime you're going to step out of that car with your clothes and hair smelling like a dead guy—not exactly the funnest company I've been around."

She smiled. "I'll park it with the windows open for the next month; it would take a brave car thief to want to climb in. What did you hear from Nathan?"

Bruce looked at the phone in his hand. "The disturbing kind of news. Nella most likely died of bone cancer."

"Cancer."

Bruce nodded. "That makes three natural-caused deaths in no time at all. I told him to stop by our office tonight and we'll let him talk himself in a circle one more time. He's convinced he's missing something, but I'm at a loss for what to suggest."

"I meet with Peggy's parents on Monday. It would be nice to have something to tell them other than the fact her daughter was one of three natural-cause deaths in Justice, Illinois, in a matter of a week."

"It does seem less than ideal as an answer."

She returned to work, washing the car windows for a final time. "Did you tell him about the handguns?"

Bruce shook his head. "Since Foster called wanting his second hundred, I just told Nathan I had a solid lead and I hoped to have something for him this evening. I'll meet this kid on the way back to town and then check out the area where he found the box and see if there are any other robbery items which got tossed. I'll take the guns over to the station and turn them in after that."

"Nathan is going to be relieved."

"I'm going to enjoy marking that particular case off the board," Bruce agreed. "The cops will eventually get the robbery solved, but I'm betting it wasn't a local who did it."

He leaned into the car to gather up the rags she had used to wipe down the dashboard. "Who owned this car? Do you know?"

"A guy named Danforth. He did a stretch of time for dealing drugs. He got out and a few weeks later shot himself. The car sat in the police evidence lot and then the alley of the guy's sister until it was sold off."

"The expense of the car suggested he'd had money stashed on the outside just waiting for him to get out. Why kill himself then? If he was suicidal, you figure he would have committed suicide in jail and saved himself the hard time. Once he was out—it doesn't make sense. You figure a dealer might go by an overdose while celebrating his freedom, not from a bullet to the brain."

"It's a puzzle," Rae agreed. "But then my life is full of puzzles right now."

She moved around to finish up work on the back window. "I've been thinking some more about what I'll have for Peggy's parents. We know Peggy had the orange notebook when she talked with Andy. She likely went from his place to Nella's home, and then there's a time gap before she returned to the hotel. That orange cover notebook is not in her hotel room or her car. I think she went to Joe Prescott's place late that Saturday night and managed to lose her notebook. I'd like to check."

"You think so?"

"I've run every other idea I can think of into the ground for where it might be."

"We can look. Why don't you plan to stop back at the hotel and grab a shower and clean up while I stop off and talk with this kid, then we'll go out to Prescott's place?"

"Thanks." She stripped off her gloves and stretched to take a crick out of her back. "Did I tell you I got a call from the Realtor out east?"

"No."

"She's got an older couple who are moving from Atlanta who are interested in the house. It's a decent offer. I'm thinking about taking it."

"Try for a short close date as part of the deal. In thirty days I can show you a bunch of great houses around here to buy with that cash."

She sorted out bottles of cleaning fluid and put them back on the cart. "You could show me a double-wide trailer and it would look fine at this point. Houses are a lot of upkeep and yard work."

"Houses are permanence and roots."

"You're going to enjoy house hunting with me, aren't you?"

"Absolutely."

"At least it will be an experience. I'll call the Realtor back tonight." Selling the house at a fair price would suit her just fine right now. She wanted D.C. wrapped up and no longer a part of her life; she wanted the last threads to that painful past to be cut for good.

"It's going to sell. That chapter in life will close."

She looked over to see Bruce watching her. She smiled. "You know me too well." She dug keys out of her pocket and her mood lightened. "Have you heard this baby purr yet?"

"I'll go lift the warehouse door and let you back it outside. I want a nice highway ride in it a few months from now, after the smell has at least become less than a skunk hit."

She laughed and walked around to the driver's-side door. She was going to enjoy teasing him about this car the next couple weeks. The smell wasn't that bad.

Rae glanced into the rearview mirror and confirmed Bruce was behind her. The drive to Justice seemed faster now, but she looked at the dash and saw her speed was safely just below the speed limit. It just felt faster in this car.

She would enjoy house hunting with Bruce. He wanted her around and settled, and she wondered again about the intensity she picked up from him about that. She reached down and turned the radio on, then started scanning for interesting stations and presetting them into the entertainment system.

The car handled like a dream, but the smell really was rough, even under the layer of deodorizer that dominated right now.

She pondered the events of the last week as the road raced by, sorting out what felt like fact and what felt like theory.

Three deaths, all in their sleep. Peggy died in a hotel room. Karen died in a hotel room. Nella died in her home. Peggy and Karen the coroner said were natural causes. Nella—he thought it was cancer.

Had Karen died one town over, they would not be trying to connect hers to the other deaths. Had Peggy gone home and died, it would not be connected to this town at all.

Coincidence.

Three coincidences.

That conclusion, supported by all the facts now in evidence, weighed itself against a theory that had been in front of them since this started—the deaths were caused by a new designer drug and Peggy had been researching a story on it, maybe triggering the deaths to begin by the questions she was asking.

That idea of a trigger for the deaths to start resonated, and Rae realized she'd never asked that question before. Peggy came to town on a Thursday, and Nella died Friday evening. Saturday night Peggy died.

Nathan was right—in all the years around Justice there had never been unexplained deaths like this. They suddenly started. That suggested a trigger. Peggy's arrival in town, a reporter digging and asking questions—that could be a trigger for murder. Karen was then killed to create a diversion? to test the drug?

None of the victims was into taking recreational drugs. That meant they were taking it without being aware of it. Something they drank? ate? breathed? absorbed through their skin?

Rae could feel herself going in circles, talking herself into a source for the murders and a motive. Pushing suspicions together into something that could sound logical. Was it really there?

Finding something that wasn't there to find—she'd proved it was entirely possible to do that when she had falsely accused Mark Rivers. If she wasn't careful, she'd end up pushing this case so hard she did the same thing. They could be looking at two natural-caused deaths and one case of advanced cancer—and that was it. But the idea of a trigger starting this—that resonated as very interesting.

Where was that orange notebook Peggy had with her Saturday night at Andy's? That was the last truly open clue as to what had happened here. If Peggy had learned something, she had written it down. Rae needed to find that notebook. She needed to explain why it hadn't been in that hotel room the night Peggy died.

Bruce flashed his lights, and Rae touched her brakes to acknowledge him. He turned off the highway to go meet with Stephen Foster. Rae hoped there was enough information to say who had initially stolen the handguns by the time Bruce was done tonight. It would be good to completely wrap up that problem for Nathan. The man had so many worries on his shoulders right now; she wanted to know they had been able to remove at least this troubling one for him.

Bruce opened the gate to Joe Prescott's land and waved Rae through. They had driven separately so Bruce could go from here to the police department and turn the guns in. Rae parked where the path widened, partway down to the river. Bruce drove in and parked beside her.

Bruce got out of his car. "What are we looking for again?"

"That orange-colored notebook of Peggy's and her BlackBerry. Andy said Peggy drew a map to Joe Prescott's place. Peggy is out here at night; she's probably got a flashlight, but who knows how good it is. She has a rough idea of where Joe's house is located on the property. She may or may not know the river bridge is out. She's carrying her notebook with her, and she trips or gets spooked—she drops it somewhere and doesn't feel like sticking around to recover it, or maybe it fell down the riverbank far enough she doesn't want to retrieve it in the dark. Only she doesn't get a tomorrow to come back out here and retrieve it in the daylight; she dies that night."

"Okay. It's a long shot but possible."

"If Peggy didn't lose that notebook, it means someone most likely took it from her hotel room and that says foul play. I need to find and explain the notebooks location if only to prove there wasn't foul play involved."

Bruce looked from the gate to where they had parked to where the path such as it was went to the river. "Why don't you head toward the riverbank, and I'll walk back toward the gate. Just stay in sight—no wandering down into the trees on a hunch."

"Not a problem." Rae tugged her gloves on tighter and set off to walk toward the river.

The water rushed by even in the winter, icy edges along the flow. Rae looked down at the water but made no attempt to get closer. She wished she had thought to check out here days ago when it might have been possible to see any lingering footprints in the snow. Peggy would have been walking toward the water and heard it long before she came to the steep drop off of the riverbank. The notebook was not going to be down there.

Rae looked carefully through the brush around where the path ended. The only man-made items she found were a couple smashed soda cans littering the side of the riverbank. Nothing orange.

She clapped her hands together to warm them and started back up toward the gate. Cars had dug into the mud as they turned around and the ground had become rough and torn up and frozen into odd angles. Rae felt her ankle turn for the second time. Next time she got a hunch, she hoped it was about a building so she could at least search in warmth.

She nearly stepped on the notebook. The orange was nearly brown with the mud on it, but the spiral caught her eye. She dug it out of the depression it was in. "Bruce!"

Rae waved her hand and held up what she had found. Melting snow and a week outside in the weather had done the notebook's condition no good, but it was still intact. "As orange as an orange can be," she called, getting down to what was visible after she wiped it off on her jeans.

Bruce walked down to meet her. "How's the writing?"

Rae took off her gloves and then carefully opened the notebook. "Ink is running, but it is still basically legible. We need a heater to set this on; the pages are going to tear just being touched they are so soggy."

"We'll go back to the hotel—your room heater will do the job."

"It will bake us out at the same time," Rae guessed, remembering the fight to find a comfortable temperature for her hotel room. "Peggy was also carrying a BlackBerry organizer."

Bruce started circling out from where she stood, brushing over shrubs with his boots to see what might be hidden. "Finding one of the two items is better than nothing. It's not in shorthand is it, like the other notebook?"

"A mixture. This one looks pretty readable."

Bruce stopped his walk around. "Let's see what the notebook can tell us, then have Nathan come out tomorrow with some guys and we'll look for the BlackBerry. Enough bodies, it's an hour to do the job right. We stay out here, and we're just going to freeze in this wind and still probably not find it."

Rae agreed with him. "Care to order a pizza that you can pick up after you drop off those guns at the police department?"

"I'll feed you," Bruce replied with a smile. "Want everything on it?"

"Definitely."

They walked back to the cars. Rae opened the trunk of her car and set the wet notebook into the pail of cleaning rags she had brought with her to finish polishing the car. "You want to be the one to call Nathan?"

"And spoil your treasure-hunt news?" Bruce asked. "Call him. Make nice. Tell him I'm bringing in the guns and that you found the notebook. Ask him to meet us at the hotel and join us for pizza while we decipher it."

Rae laughed. "Make nice?"

"The man needs cheering up. He's had a killer week, no pun intended."

"I get your point. I'll call and invite him to join us. Recovered handguns and a found notebook—at least it's a good-news call for a change."

"Let's just hope that notebook is the gold mine of information we've been hoping to find."

28

Nathan turned over notebook pages on top of the heater, the paper curling as it dried. The blue ink was running and faded out in many places, but he could piece together enough to read it. "The list of names she was asking about is interesting."

Rae wiped pizza sauce off her fingers and turned her focus back to carefully separating more pages of the notebook to dry; the pages clung together and the job took tweezers at times to coax the pages apart without tearing. "How so?"

Nathan looked over at her from his seat on the floor and thought she looked cute as she bit the tip of her tongue as she did the fine-level work. "Someone told Peggy a bit about this town to put together this list," he explained. "It's mostly the high school crowd that would have hung around with Joe Prescott's grandson. Vernon Hill is on the list; the chocolate maker's son, Isaac Keif; Walter's boy, Scott. Most of these guys would be in their early twenties now, and only a few still live here. Some are away at college; others have already left to pursue job opportunities away from Justice."

She paused to consider that. "Drug involvement, maybe?"

"Maybe Isaac with a little marijuana, but this isn't the drug crowd as I would know to list it. Just friends of Prescott's grandson."

"Maybe Peggy thought a friend of Joe's grandson knew who made the designer drug?"

He thought that might be closer to what this list represented. "Maybe. But the dealer who sold the drug at the party was among the dead, and the dealer who supplied him went to jail on an unrelated drug charge—neither was from around here."

He leaned over to the table and picked up another piece of the pizza. The room was crowded for this work, but the wall heater was getting the job done as Bruce had hoped.

With his free hand Nathan moved pages on the heater to fit one more in and turned over two of the drier pages. He picked up one of them and studied another smaller list of names he didn't recognize. "I admit I can read these notes, but I don't understand yet what they mean. Who's the reporter friend of Peggy's who got mailed the first notebook?"

"Gage Collier," Rae replied. "I gave him a call and told him what we had found. He was very interested. He's coming down Monday morning to see if he can help us put together the pieces that are here."

"Good."

"I've got something that may be part of the initial tip that brought Peggy to Justice," Bruce offered.

Nathan turned to look at his friend. Bruce was stretched out on the second bed, using the bedspread as a place to lay the dried pages Nathan was moving off the heater, as well as serve as a table for his piled plate of food.

"This page is dated the Wednesday before Peggy checked into the hotel here. As best I can read it, '*Message from H.S.R./Justice. He'll confirm notebook found. Unique delivery system rumor is true? Pulitzer???*' The rest of the page is a list of phone numbers for Justice hotels, like she switched over to planning her trip here."

"H.S.R.? Who has initials H.S.R.?" Rae reached over for what she had of Peggy's address book.

"Henry Raines? He's a dentist," Nathan offered. "Hank Rolmer? He's a car salesman."

"Neither of which sound like candidates for Peggy to call."

"The message itself doesn't make much sense," Bruce added. "*He'll confirm notebook found.* Was the notebook some kind of evidence? The people that reporters tend to call to confirm things are law-enforcement types or court-house clerks."

"There's nothing that I know of related to the Prescott kid's death that went through the police department here or the county courthouse," Nathan said, equally puzzled. "Is there anything in Peggy's address book that fits H.S.R.?"

Rae shook her head as she turned pages, looking. "Not that I see. You know, H.S.R./Justice could mean someone who works with the department of justice, not this town," she pointed out.

"Justice as it's written here could mean the justice department," Bruce agreed. "Maybe DEA would make sense."

"Okay. Forget the caller for a moment," Nathan said. "Peggy heard a rumor about a notebook that had been found and she called someone, probably an investigator who was involved with the case, to confirm that notebook existed. He said it did. That same day she's making plans to come to Justice. We know she's looking for Joe Prescott."

"After hearing a notebook exists, the next step is clear: she's going to want to know what it says," Bruce offered. "She's got confirmation a notebook exists that could be important to her story, but that's all she knows about it."

Rae set aside her drink. "So Peggy thought Joe could tell her what the note-book said? Or maybe Joe was the one who found the notebook and turned it in? Or Joe was the one who still had the notebook? Maybe it was the notebook found among his grandson's things?"

"I think you're in the right ballpark," Nathan agreed. "Maybe Joe's grand-son wrote down who he was meeting at the party, or maybe he had written down a phone number of someone he was to meet at the party? That would be a reasonable fit. Investigators would check out that kind of thing if it were found in one of the victim's possessions."

"Joe could have gotten the notebook back as part of his grandson's personal effects, which was why Peggy came looking for Joe," Bruce offered.

"I like this general idea," Nathan said. "But still—it looks to me like Peggy heard the rumor about the notebook, confirmed it existed, came to Justice looking for more information—and that's as far as she got. She never talked to Joe, who she thought could tell her something about it. It's still a dead end."

Nathan thought about what he had just said and sighed. "We now know what brought Peggy to Justice, we have a timeline resolving the last night of her life, and nothing in this suggests something which contributed to her death. It's still natural causes." Nathan rubbed at his headache. "Rae, you just found one of the very last missing pieces to Peggy's time here and it confirms what we already have."

"Basically," Rae replied, disappointed too.

"This is really giving me a headache."

"Chocolate. It always works for me." She dug her hand into the sack of chocolates from the Fine Chocolates Shop for a couple more pieces, then passed the sack over to him.

"Death by chocolate—I picked up a pound and a half this morning to have in the car with me. This stuff is simply too good, and the strike has unfortunately been driving Keif's business into the ground. Okay. Does all this tell us anything else useful?"

"We know this H.S.R. called her back, so she must have called him originally. I'll check her home-phone record again. There has to be a way to put a name to that note. We did get a lead to a living person at least."

The last of the garlic-butter sauce disappeared with Bruce's pizza crust. Nathan collapsed the empty pizza box and slid it into the trash. "A very nice dinner. I may not move again for hours."

"I'll agree with that."

Nathan looked over at Rae. "I saw your new car in the lot; it's hard to miss. Interesting choice. I think you'll have the only one like it in the county."

She beamed and sat up straighter in the chair. "It drives like a dream."

"Smells bad, though," Bruce pointed out. "Like crossing a skunk and old trash."

"Only for a while," Rae replied. "I can't wait for warmer weather and a chance to really test it out on a long drive." She paused to squint at the last notebook page she was trying to tease apart with tweezers. The final pages in the notebook were in particularly bad shape. "Here's another note that is interesting. '*Unique-delivery-system rumor strong on street. EE?*' At least that's what I think it says."

"EE?" Nathan asked

Rae studied the page again and nodded. "That's what it looks like."

"Maybe a homemade brand stamped on the drugs if they're being put into pill form," Bruce guessed.

"That's the third or fourth time she's used the phrase *unique delivery system*," Rae noted. "You're the drug expert, Bruce. What's it mean?"

Bruce shrugged. "It could be anything from how the drug appears to how it is shipped to the customer. Black tar started showing up in small red balloons, which I would consider a unique delivery system. Any more names appearing that we can at least reinterview?"

"No. But these pages need to dry some more before I can decipher the fainter stuff. We may end up needing a document expert to get some of the most washed-out text recovered."

Rae stretched sore shoulder muscles from having hunched over so long working on the wet pages. "You know, this notebook, coupled with the file of articles Peggy had on her desk, suggests this is a story she would hear rumors about, work on for a while, and then set aside again when it went cold.

"I don't think this notebook is a coherent set of research with one interview leading to another one, as much as it is a set of rumors and phone-call notes and what-ifs. This wasn't a story coming together, it was a collecting pot of ideas that might one day relate together. She was in town not working on a particular story, she was just poking around to see what she could find."

"Good point. If she was writing a story, it doesn't look like she was very far along," Nathan agreed. "Keep deciphering, Rae. Once pages dry out we'll photograph every page and take another look. Maybe a good filter light on the camera can bring out the contrast for us and raise a few more words."

Nathan began to repack his briefcase, pleased with the course of the evening. "Handguns found, notebook found, I don't suppose you two want to go out with me to see the negotiators and nudge the strike along to a settlement would you?" He'd pushed off his visit out that direction to see Adam and Zachary when he heard the news of what Rae and Bruce had found, but it was time to get out there and see for himself how the discussions were going.

Rae smiled. "Only a few supersized things can get done in one day. Maybe tomorrow." She glanced at the clock. "Or rather maybe in an hour from now when it is tomorrow."

"I'm going to head out that way and check in on their progress in the negotiations, then head home. Seriously, thanks for finding those handguns." He looked over at Bruce. "I'll repay you the cash you laid out to find them."

"This one is on us. Rae said we had to gift wrap at least one case for you," Bruce replied.

"Did she?" Nathan looked over at Rae to see her starting to blush. He smiled. "I'll take gift wrapped cases anytime."

Bruce stacked together the pages they had dried out to this point into a somewhat neat pile on the bedspread, and then looked at Rae. "Promise me you won't work until all hours on this."

"Just a little longer. I think there is more to tease out of the notes than it first appears. Peggy was orderly in her own way. I've just got to figure out how to think like her."

"I'll come by the hotel and pick you up for church in the morning if you like," Bruce offered. "We could do lunch afterwards and you can show me what you've figured out."

"I'd like that."

She walked with them to the hotel-room door. "Good night, guys."

Nathan heard Rae's room door shut as he walked with Bruce down to the elevators. "The notebook is an interesting twist."

"Very. At least Rae will have something to show Peggy's parents on Monday. This closes down the last of the missing time window for Peggy's Saturday evening."

Nathan nodded. "Peggy went from Andy's, to Nella's, then out to Joe Prescott's place. She walked around a bit, probably twisted an ankle on that rough ground, lost her notebook, and came back to the hotel. She died."

"It's the died part I don't like."

Nathan grimaced. "I hear you. Listen, do you mind if I ride to church with you and Rae in the morning? I'm doing some back-door shuttling with this strike situation and I need to speak with Larry. I'd rather have an excuse, however lame, as my reason for being at your church in the morning rather than mine, given I'm going to have to hand off my Sunday school class of boys again."

"Come by and get me about seven. We'll stop and pick up Rae and get breakfast together before services. Knowing Rae, she'll have that notebook transcribed to a pad of paper by then."

"Thanks, Bruce. Seriously—I think you saved some lives today, locating those handguns. I owe you a big favor in return."

"I'll find a reason to collect one day," Bruce promised.

29

Snow was beginning to fall as Nathan pulled into the drive at Ford's lakefront house late Saturday night. All the lights were on in the lower level of the house, spilling out to touch the snow-covered ground. He pulled on his coat and gloves as his breath crystallized in the cold air.

His father walked down the porch steps to meet him. "How's it going out here, Dad?"

"They're breaking up to catch a few hours of sleep, to let folks take their families to church in the morning, and they'll reconvene at noon. Go on in. I think it will do them good to have a fresh face to talk with."

"From that quiet answer, I take it the day has been tough."

"The mood inside is still constructive. They broke for dinner and then went back into session to keep working. But there's no deal and until there is, they all carry that weight."

"Can you run interference for another meeting out here tomorrow, or should I look at someplace in town for the guys to meet?" Nathan asked.

"We'll try to reassemble here again if we can avoid the reporters spotting where the negotiators are going. I hear Bruce found the handguns."

"All six," Nathan confirmed. "They got dumped outside Harristown behind a bowling alley and an enterprising kid who is there every weekend found the box."

"That's very good news."

"Beyond anything I could have hoped for," Nathan agreed. He left his dad to the task of sweeping snow off the porch and he opened the door to step inside. Warmth met him and the smell of coffee. A dozen men were working around two long tables brought in and set up in the dining room. From the discarded pages across the tables it was obvious they had spent the last hours drafting and redrafting language.

"I brought more food."

"Always welcome, Nathan. I think we've about died on Cheetos this last hour."

Adam, the chief union boss, got up from the table to come shake hands. "All quiet in town?"

"We're good," Nathan reassured.

"We're going to pause discussions where they are for tonight. We'll let guys go sleep a few hours, catch a shower, take their families to church. It will be easier to get the details right when we're not quite so sleep deprived. We've made progress."

"Very good progress," Zachary agreed on behalf of the management team. "I don't suppose you snuck donuts into one of those sacks, did you? My wife is never going to allow them in the house again and it's the one thing that I've been craving tonight."

Nathan smiled. "Dad mentioned it. Powder-sugar-coated as well as glazed donut holes. I remember what these sessions get to be like." He set down the sacks to locate the boxes.

"Good man, your dad."

"Who has draft five on overtime?"

"Here it is."

The men around the table were sorting out layers of papers to make sure they had the working copies together.

"Send the working copies with your guy Adam, if you think you can get a copier to collate sets for us to work from tomorrow," Zachary suggested.

"Rich?"

"I can get sets made," he confirmed. "Do you want the Post-it notes duplicated? I can slap them on pieces of paper to get them to copy."

"Sure, if you can figure out a way to safely mess with them."

Rich began taking the Post-it notes down from the dining-room wall.

Zachary tugged on his coat and then picked up a handful of the donut holes. "I need some air. Step outside with me, Nathan. Tell me more about what's been going on in town today."

Nathan got the silent message; he followed his friend out through the patio doors.

Nathan settled at the table on the back patio, watching as the guys walked around inside to stretch and find something to eat. There hadn't been signs of anger in the group, or of shouting matches creating splits, or of any of the other group dynamics that could so easily flare under this kind of pressure. He looked over at his friend, aware the upbeat words by both Adam and Zachary in front of the group hadn't matched the quiet look of the two men between themselves.

"Talk to me, Zachary. What's going on?"

His friend looked beat-up exhausted after the marathon day of talks. "We're not going to get a deal."

It was said so simply and directly that Nathan took a moment to absorb the quiet words. "You can't not get a deal, Zach."

His friend slipped off his glasses and rubbed his eyes. "It's not Adam. He and I have hammered out good solid ideas to bridge where we are at on the contract language. He's even offered some concessions we hadn't thought about that will improve the overall training costs for new hires. We're probably another afternoon away from having working language hammered out on all the points still open."

"But—"

"I'm working in a vacuum of dead air and Adam knows that. The tile plant is a good business. But it's just like every other manufacturing business in the world; it has to keep shifting under the currents of what is going on worldwide. Tile prices are falling year after year. The business is also capital intensive, and we don't compete well against divisions which are more paper driven and less raw materials. Corporate may simply see the write downs for closing the plant as worth the loss of the small profit line in future years."

"There's nothing you can do?"

"I'm flying to headquarters on Monday to make sure they really understand just how good a deal has been structured with this contract, and to lay out again the profit projections for the plant through the life of this deal. The thing is, even if the plant went to no health-care costs at all—it's not the health-care issue that will make or break this decision. I can't even tell if it's more than a passing factor when it really comes down to it."

"What is?"

"Does corporate want to be a bread-and-butter company that makes things, or does it want to be a nonmanufacturing enterprise? That's where we are at."

Zachary sighed. "Maybe it's tired pessimism talking right now. Monday may well bring a presentation that corporate looks at and says good, we like that predictable profit number, and no, we don't envision investing much capital in plant expansion, so stretch your budget to cover the capital needs. That kind of answer management can deal with. It's what we got three years ago when the last union contract was negotiated. We've just not been getting the same clear answers this time. If corporate says no to this draft contract, it won't be because of language in one or two paragraphs; it will be because they don't want to be in the tile business."

"Worst case. Are we talking a shutdown decision this week?"

"By Wednesday we should have a blessing to do this deal and the plant opens again with union employees, or we'll have found out the strikebreakers are turning into the teardown crew that is going to gut the plant. I wish I knew what to tell you to prepare for. I wish I knew what Adam could tell his guys that would help with the pain of waiting. This is hurting friends, Nathan. But as lead negotiator for management I can't tell you tonight if the plant is open or closed a week from now. I honestly don't know which way this is going to break at the end."

"I appreciate the candor."

"Would you do me a favor and look again at the home-security situation for Adam's guys and mine? This pressure point isn't going to remain quiet for much longer."

"We'll do everything we can to keep tempers in the range of words and not violence," Nathan promised. "I've already talked to Luke Granger over in Brentwood about having some of his men come help us out if needed."

"I appreciate that. I hope it doesn't become necessary, but I worry."

"You're not alone in that."

Nathan left the lakeside home shortly after midnight. The ground was shifting under him and this town.

Jesus, does a prayer for work count? This town needs jobs to survive so guys can support their families. I don't know how else to ask this. This town needs a deal; I need a deal.

A week ago this had been a strike with a disagreement around particular points proposed in the new contract. In a week it had changed to become the fate of the tile plant. Nathan didn't know how to grasp how fast life had moved under him.

A car passed him in the opposite lane, doing well over the speed limit. A red car. A Porsche.

Nathan reversed directions, punched on lights, and gave pursuit, anger pushing his foot down on the gas.

He pushed up his speed and eventually caught up. He settled in behind his grandfather and when the lights didn't do the job, touched the sirens for a brief warning.

His grandfather touched his breaks and slowed, then turned on blinkers and eventually pulled off onto a side road and stopped.

Nathan got out of the squad car and looked up at the sky. His patience was exhausted. He dug out the ticket book and his flashlight and slammed the squad-car door closed. He walked toward the Porsche.

Henry lowered the driver's-side window.

Nathan shone his flashlight into the car, half expecting to see someone with his grandfather. He exploded. "Open liquor in the car? Are you crazy, Henry?"

His grandfather opened the car door so abruptly it hit Nathan in the gut. "Back up, boy. And it's not liquor."

Backing up was necessary to keep from falling; any other civilian pulling that move and Nathan would have already put them on the ground.

Clear voice, steady movements, nothing on his grandfather's breath catching his attention—most definitely not a man who was drunk. It didn't change the anger Nathan felt at the man for speeding at midnight. "Henry, you'll explain this or I'm arresting you."

"If you're like this with every stop you make, you're going to be getting yourself fired."

"Answers, Henry. Now." Nathan shifted the flashlight to the side to not be in his grandfather's eyes even as he repeated the warning. "What's in the open bottle?"

"Soda."

"No label?"

"My own brand," Henry retorted. His grandfather scowled at him. "You want a taste to believe me then?"

Nathan shifted on his feet. "No. And I apologize for the assumption it was liquor. But you will explain what is going on. This speeding tonight. The cash to buy this car. I'm tired of spending my time worrying about you when I've got other things to be worrying me more."

"And if I said it was none of your business, or any business of that Bruce Chapel fellow you've got following me all over the place?"

Nathan refused to go there. "We're past that point. Either you start talking, or I'm going to arrest you for speeding every time you so much as go a mile over the limit, and then I'm going to start working on getting that license revoked. I've had it with the mysteries around this town."

"You don't have to get testy about it."

"Henry—"

"Things aren't going well out at the negotiations."

"No. They are not."

"I was taking a batch of the sodas out to the guys to sample. This batch is pretty decent."

Nathan tried to shift gears and listen to what his grandfather was saying, even as he dodged the questions Nathan wanted to hear answered. "You sure you're not just going to poison them with another experimental brew?"

Henry leaned back against his car and crossed his arms across his chest. He smiled. "You have to admit, the lemonade wasn't so bad until it gave folks the runs."

"Everyone who sampled it spent the next day groaning about the lemon pits growing in their guts. Soda this time?"

"It's not such a far-out notion. Big Joe's Soda—it's got a pretty good kick without much sugar in it."

Big Joe's Soda—Joe Prescott and his grandfather had been involved in something if this was how Henry was honoring his friend after death. Nathan sighed and leaned against the car beside his grandfather. "I'm declaring myself off duty. It's been a month out of a horror novel, Henry. I don't need more of it coming from family right now. Please, explain it all. What are you up to? And where's the money coming from?"

"We're working on some new business ideas, Bob Teal and I. This town needs something better than the tile plant to depend on. Your grandmother thought it was a foolish notion, but soda's got potential."

"You're going into the beverage business?"

"We worked on a glue formulation first, but it didn't pan out. We tried a formulation of mud—you know the kind major league baseball rubs on the balls before games—there was some interest among the T-ball leagues to come up to professional standards with their baseball preparations, but it didn't fly. Now we're experimenting a bit with soft drinks. There is low overhead costs in soft drinks—just soda water and some flavorings. It's more the bottling and shipping costs that make a business profitable or not."

"That's what you've been working on out at your place, causing all those odd sounds late at night from the woods?"

Henry frowned at him. "Don't go claiming it's a big secret that I've got a workshop back there in the timber. You helped haul the ceiling joists out there with your dad. Your grandmother refused to let me pour concrete on good tillable land, and she wasn't going to have a metal-sided building larger than the house sitting up near the road being an eyesore."

"I was under the impression you were still using that building to store farm equipment."

"You know I haven't driven a tractor in close to a decade. The land's been tenant farmed for years. All I do is hassle Jim about how many weeds he's got growing in the beans."

Nathan had indeed heard a few of those friendly debates between the two men over the last years.

"Bob's been doing the reading and the studying, and I've been doing the experimenting and the trying out of his ideas. Joe was helping us out, back in the days he was around. His idea of making fishing lures turned out to be a mighty nice idea. He had the old wood-press equipment from his father still around his place, and we modified it a bit. They made some real fast-moving bass shimmies. If the treble hook piece of it wasn't so hard for old hands to tie off, we would have done more with that business than we did. We handed that business idea over to Vernon and he's been making a nice side business out of the lures, selling them at the hardware store."

"You've been busy. I didn't know."

Henry shrugged. "I'm old enough I'm bored, and this town needs workable ideas. There's no reason I can't be trying to come up with solutions."

"I'm not disagreeing. But where's the funding for this experimenting coming from?"

"Now don't go disapproving on me. I don't approve of what Joe did, killing himself. But he left a chunk of cash for Bob and me to use for the town's good and we're doing it the best we know how. He didn't have a grandson to leave it to any longer."

"You could have said something."

"And listen to the townsfolk comment on every new idea Bob and I decide to explore? Or have to put up with the outrage of folks about Joe being so deliberate about what he did in preparations before he killed himself?

"I'm too old to put up with what this entire town thinks. Joe didn't give us any hint of what he was planning; you know we would have sat on him to knock that stupid idea out of his head, but we aren't disrespecting his memory and his final wishes."

"I thought you were mixed up in something illegal."

"Me?" Henry snorted. "Your grandmother would come out of the grave and drag me down with her. About the only law I've broken lately is speed limits and that's just a heavy foot in a very nice car."

"Or something."

"Well, I've got some living to make up for. We never had a new car, your grandmother and me. Always used. Always well broke in. I've been thinking red Porsche since before you were born. I'm going to enjoy spinning its wheels a bit in my last years of driving.

"Besides—the car is leverage. Bankers haven't changed. We'll invest cash with this old guy since he's got more cash than he needs to begin with. He just bought himself a Porsche for cash. We'll give him a loan to make some fishing lures."

"You bought that car because you love to drive fast."

"Mainly that. But seriously, the fishing lures and a few of the other ideas—they did make quite a bit of money. There just wasn't any way I was telling that to your grandmother while she was talking up a storm about going to see Alaska on a cruise. Her health wouldn't have made it, and the only reason she was carrying on so much about it was the fact she knew we couldn't afford to go. It gave her something to safely hassle me about and I quietly let the money accumulate in the bank. When she passed away—well, I should have taken her to see Alaska. So I spent the money on a car instead and I hear her hassling me about it every time I turn on the ignition."

"Henry—spend the money any way you like and enjoy every penny of it. But know that when your health gets so bad you can only talk about cruising around in that car, I'm taking your license away and you can just safely hassle me."

"I'll drink to that." He opened the car door and reached in for two of the soda bottles in the case. "Icy cold, the absolute best soda there could be."

Nathan popped the top on his and sampled with a bit of caution. "Nice."

"This batch turned out particularly well."

They drank the sodas, watching the snow fall. Nathan thought it nice they weren't arguing for a change. And the soda was pretty good.

Nathan handed back his empty bottle. "Drive more carefully, Henry. There's no need to smack up a particularly nice expensive car." He looked at the car. "Your grandson wants to inherit that car one day."

Henry laughed. "Absolutely right you do. Now that's more what I expect from you." He stored the empty bottles back in the case.

Nathan picked up the keys his grandfather had dropped. His flashlight reflected off the medallion on it that Henry's wife had given him. H.SR. *Henry Senior.* Nathan wondered if he was so tired he didn't connect even obvious facts together anymore. "Were you the one who called Peggy Worth and confirmed a notebook was found?" he asked, handing back the keys. "A week ago Wednesday?"

Henry looked puzzled. "I called and left a message; that was Peggy Worth? It never registered that I heard a name." He frowned. "I got handed a slip of paper by one of my old cop buddies with a question and a phone number and asked if I could answer it. Not that the answer was material to anything. Still, I would have mentioned it to you if I'd realized that was the reporter who died in town."

"I need details, Henry. It might be important."

Henry shrugged. "Not much to tell. Some reporter called one of the investigators on the Prescott case a couple weeks ago looking for confirmation there had been a school notebook found among Joe's grandson's things and what had it said. He had no idea what she was talking about, and the note got bounced around and eventually the question got passed to me.

"Prescott found the notebook among his grandson's things when he was getting ready for the boy's funeral. Nothing suspicious in it. Kids that were going to the party, the time they were going to meet up, a couple scrawled names Joe didn't recognize. The investigators back then looked into the details on it and returned the notebook to Joe. There wasn't anything particularly useful about the information. I couldn't figure out why the reporter even cared about it."

"Where's the notebook now?"

"I've no idea. Joe kept a lot of his grandson's stuff, but he wasn't the kind of guy to neatly file items. About the only thing we cleaned up was stuff related to the will and the land. The rest is still sitting out there."

"Thank you. It answers a puzzle for me."

"I'm sorry I didn't know to mention it earlier. I don't mind annoying you, Nathan, but making the job harder—that I never intended."

"That distinction is appreciated. Drive carefully, Henry. You want those sodas drinkable when you arrive out at the lakehouse."

Nathan watched his grandfather leave and then he let himself rub his eyes. He'd send an officer out to Joe's place tomorrow to try and find the school notebook. But from the sound of it, Peggy really was a wrapped-up case now with not much left to even pursue.

The death was natural causes. It didn't sit well, but it was what the evidence said. At least Rae had pulled a first case that looked like it was going to close itself for lack of questions to answer. He just hoped they were seeing everything they should.

Jesus, I need a quiet day tomorrow, a settled strike, and for this town to slide back to normal. I'm looking forward to church in the morning and a chance to leave aside the job for a few hours. I need that break so badly. I'm tired, God. Deeply tired inside where hope tries to live. If You wouldn't mind, please send some energy to get me through the next week.

He started his car and clicked on the interior light. He stored his clipboard. He wondered what was going to interrupt that hope for quiet. The dispatcher had at least been quiet tonight. It was past time to go see his dogs and find some real sleep. He glanced at his watch. Tomorrow was already here.

30

The Sunburst Hotel had few guests coming and going Sunday morning. The parking lot was half empty. Bruce wondered at that and what it meant for this town as he walked with Nathan toward the front entrance. "This hasn't been good for business."

"It will blow over."

Bruce glanced over, the near dead sound in Nathan's voice telling him the man was struggling this morning to even be interested in how much business the hotel was doing, something he would normally care an enormous amount about. "You should have stayed in bed another hour and met up with Larry after services. You're beat."

"The alarm about got thrown across the room. Let's do breakfast somewhere they'll leave the pitcher of coffee on the table."

"I like that idea." Bruce held the door for them to step inside the lobby. "Seriously, Nathan. Take a few hours off. You can't work every day of the month and still care about what happens to lost dogs and upset grandmothers."

The words got his friend to at least smile. Bruce figured something had to give today or his friend was going to end up with his friendly sheriff reputation getting tarnished when he snapped at the next problem that came across his pager. The town needed a sheriff who at least got some sleep occasionally.

Nathan punched the elevator button for the third floor. "I'm planning to hibernate for a long weekend out at my country place when this strike is over."

"You should make it at least a full week," Bruce suggested. "Thanks for making it possible for Rae to keep working on this case, rather than shift it all to Sillman. I know we've been stepping on his toes a bit this last week."

Nathan shrugged. "I don't have enough evidence to override the coroner and formally reopen the matter, but you're welcome anyway. I've appreciated the way Rae has tackled it. Peggy's parents were right to hire her to get their questions answered. She does a solid job. And Sillman kind of likes her, you know. They'll work out an understanding."

"Rae's going to have the notebook transcribed and have a list of questions for us to answer over breakfast," Bruce guessed.

Nathan laughed. "I'm betting she does too."

They walked the hallway toward Rae's room.

"We need to find her somewhere other than a hotel to live once this settles down," Bruce noted, thinking again about his conversation with Rae the other night. Rae would be the kind to move into a rougher neighborhood if he or Nathan couldn't talk her out of it. "I don't want her having an excuse to move farther north into the city. Her family's crime-scene cleanup business will suck her in if it gets the chance. Having her walk into scenes like Nella's to be the one cleaning it up just doesn't sit well with me."

"You won't get a disagreement on that from me."

Bruce knocked on her hotel-room door. "Rae, it's Bruce and Nathan. Ready for breakfast?"

There wasn't an answer.

Bruce knocked again and checked the doorknob out of habit. "The door's hot."

"What?"

"The door is hot. Look the other way."

"She's here?"

Bruce felt a desperate fear in his gut as the heat reminded him of past cases. "If she's not I'll have some explaining to do. Look the other way." He put his foot into the door lock and popped it. The door crashed back against the wall.

Heat met them, heavy in the room with the room heater still running, pouring it out. Rae was stretched out on the far bed, sprawled facedown across open folders and notepads of paper, a stack of drying pages from the notebook half slid to the floor beside her. She didn't move. Bruce felt his heart stop.

Nathan moved through the room to shove off the heater unit and push open the window. He threw back the drapes to let in as much light as he could.

Bruce headed to Rae and shook her still form. "Rae, wake up. Come on, honey. Wake up." He shook her harder, but she was limp, his hand feeling the heat in her through the shirt she wore. "You're not doing this, Rae." She didn't look blue from lack of oxygen or that sickening red of carbon-monoxide poisoning he'd seen before. But she wasn't responding at all.

Nathan placed an urgent call to the dispatcher for an ambulance.

Bruce held his hand just above her nose and mouth. "She's barely breathing. Get me ice, cold rags, anything that will cool her down."

Nathan was already dumping the little that was left from the melted ice bucket into a towel. "Whatever it is, she likely ingested it." He passed over the cold bundle, scanning the room fast. "I'm seeing a drinking glass on the end table, a soda can in the trash. Candy-bar wrappers, aspirin packets, a box of wheat crackers, one tube of them open and half gone. We ate the same dinner she did; it's not the pizza."

"We try to get her to toss her stomach, and she's going to aspirate it and choke to death." Bruce used the towel to try to wipe down Rae's face and neck. Her hair was already damp from the heat inside her and her very stillness made him worry at how she was slipping away even as he watched.

Nathan hurried into the restroom and turned on the sink taps. He drenched three more towels in cold water and brought them back with him. "She's got to fight whatever is taking her under this hard. Why did she shove on the heat to full?"

"You're assuming she did it." Bruce buried her in the cold towels, draping them behind her neck, across her arms, along her face.

"The chain was on the door you just kicked open; it's possible someone went through the connecting door to the next room, but that lock is on this side and it's closed. She was alone whenever this hit."

"The rate she's sweating, she hasn't been cold for some time. She's still dressed in what she wore yesterday. Assume best case based on when we left her, she would have turned in by three at the latest if she were coherent enough to crawl into bed. At a minimum it's been four hours of this already."

Nathan felt for a pulse at her neck under the towel and shook his head. "It's taking her under like a rock. Get her up, Bruce. We're walking her, same as a sedative overdose."

Bruce surged to his feet and reached down. He lifted her from the bed and to her feet. Nathan got her arm across his shoulder while Bruce took her other side. "Walk, Rae. Move your feet," Bruce ordered. Between them they walked her, even as Rae's legs barely stirred.

"She didn't know it was coming. Whatever this stuff is, not one of the victims appeared to realize they were in trouble until it was too late."

"Something just hits them hard enough to crash them," Bruce agreed. She had never felt fragile to him before or this close to being lost to him. It was haunting, the fact she simply wasn't waking up.

"Walking her isn't working." Nathan reached again for one of the cold towels. "Come on, Rae. Fight this thing." He wiped at the sweat on her face.

"Get her down. Hurry! Get her down. She stopped breathing."

Nathan shoved back the bed to give them more room.

Bruce struggled to start mouth to mouth. "Come on, Rae. Come on," he pleaded between breaths.

Paramedics streamed in through the door.

"What took you so long?" Nathan demanded, letting them past him to get to Rae.

"Someone tried to plow a backhoe into a truck; the fire department was cutting people out."

The lead paramedic took over for Bruce. "I've got a thready pulse."

"What did she take?"

"The same bloody unknown thing that killed the last three ladies," Bruce replied, wiping his mouth, his hand trembling. "Seizure, heart attack, something abrupt just shuts their system down."

"Let's get a strip running and set up to handle a cardiac crash and then get her out of here. Pushing her onto life support may be the only way to manage it if the toxin is building in her system like it appears to be doing."

"What about airlifting her out of here? Should she be heading to a trauma unit?" Nathan asked.

"Being near the right equipment is going to matter more than the number of doctors around. We get her through the respiratory collapse, then the doctors can caucus."

The paramedic set aside the air bag. "I'm getting some shallow breaths on her own. The way she's laboring even for the shallow breaths makes me suspect it's got a paralyzing agent in the mix."

Bruce looked at Nathan. "Find the coroner. He's got the most experience with whatever this is as any doctor at the hospital. Something has got to transfer for how to treat it in the living." It was the only hope Bruce could find, the fact this wasn't the first case the man would have seen. Nathan nodded.

"Let's get moving. I don't want to be treating a seizure while we're on the elevator." They shifted her to the stretcher.

Nathan pulled out his keys. "I'm giving you an escort."

The paramedics got the gurney through the door.

"I need to call her next of kin," Bruce said grimly.

"It's not going to go that far. We found her in time."

"Four hours, Nathan. At a minimum we were four hours too late."

Bruce felt a rush of warm air as they crossed the threshold of the ER. The paramedics were moving fast. The coroner and the hospital's top two doctors were waiting for her. "Take her to area four."

The lead paramedic called out vital signs even as she was moved and lifted into a new bed. Leads clipped on and monitors flipped on around the bed, reading out oxygen and heartbeats and blood pressure.

"Let's get this stuff out of her system as best we can. Lungs, blood, bowels. Tell toxicology I want blood panels run against every poison, chemical, and prescription they've got on file; keep those blood vials flowing until they say they've got enough. I also want a white-blood-cell count as fast as they can give it." The chief looked at the coroner. "If we transfuse two pints?"

"Make it three." He was studying her pupils. "We keep the lungs and heart from crashing, it has time to become a stage-two poison and no one has lived long enough to show those symptoms. I'm guessing kidney and liver get a huge poison-load factor."

"Transfuse and then straight on dialysis overnight?"

"Yes. And get me a good eye doctor down here. I don't like the look of this."

The head nurse blocked their view. "She's in good hands, Nathan. Let them work."

"We're staying, Crystal."

"Not here, the waiting room is twenty feet away."

Bruce lifted her hand from Nathan's arm. "We're staying within sight, so point out where we will be the least in the way. It's not negotiable, Crystal. And while he may have the badge and gun, I've got the emotion. So where do you want us?"

She took a half step back, lips pursed, then nodded and pointed. "Station three, until we need it. You can leave the curtain pushed back."

"Thank you."

Bruce watched the doctors work and the sickness inside him turned into a tight fist. "Someone got to her. Somehow, someone got to her."

"We'll find out who," Nathan said quietly.

Bruce glanced over at him. He wasn't sure what to make of Nathan's expression, but he got enough of the gist to understand the impact this was having on his friend. He'd never seen Nathan look this way before.

"I'm going to go find the hospital chapel. It's that, or put my fist into a wall," Bruce muttered, not able to watch another tube get stuck into Rae. She was alive, and God was likely the only one who could keep her alive right now. The doctors could do their best, but they were working in the dark for what to treat.

"Pray for Rae. Pray for yourself. And pray for me. Right now I'd murder the guy who did this if I had a name."

"I know the feeling. I'll get Rae's family on the way here."

"Thanks."

Bruce squeezed Nathan's shoulder and left the sheriff there.

Bruce knew Nathan would find him if there was a change—good or bad. And he knew Rae would understand why he had to step away right now. Nothing hit harder on a cop than standing in the emergency room waiting to find out if a friend lived or died. He wasn't having this be his last memory of his friend. He wasn't going to do that to the two of them.

31

Nathan watched Rae through the ICU glass Sunday afternoon. She was holding her own, had been for the three hours since they had moved her here. He watched her breathe and would be content to watch that steady rise and fall of her chest for a long time to come. He forced himself to turn his attention to the coroner. "Why is she alive and the others dead?"

"The dose she got is the most likely reason. She got a borderline lethal dose, not enough to trigger a heart attack or seizure. She got hot, and heat is one of the body's defense mechanisms. It's possible her body was able to sweat some of it out of her system before it got hold. Fast transfusions, hydration, help for her lungs—we got lucky with something, enough to help her body win."

Nathan looked back at her and at the awful stillness as she lay there, monitored, but on her own now to fight this off. He worried about how much of that fight she had already lost in the last hours. "How long before we know the damage?"

"She'll be stirring by morning; there's no indication of coma. It's fast acting which gives us some help on the recovery side—it's fast to decay out of her system too. We'll know a lot more in forty-eight hours." Franklin rubbed the back of his neck. "I'm sorry, Nathan. I didn't see this coming."

"You've been giving me 100 percent and then some on this mystery. At this point we've just got to find it."

"I've got blood work going to every expert I can think to ask for help."

"Rae may give us the best clues for where to look. We need to talk with her just as soon as she begins to stir. If she can talk to us."

"MRI and CAT scans were both promising. We're hoping for the best. Don't fear the worst until we know something. The staff can find you some relatively comfortable chairs for the room. There's no reason you and Bruce can't stay with her even through this ICU stretch. All the signs are she's returning to a normal sleep."

"I appreciate it."

Nathan flipped through the photos Gray Sillman had brought him. The officer had walked through Rae's hotel room taking detailed pictures of everything in the room to start giving them something to work with for the search. "You've bagged everything."

"Tried to. We know it's a drug, Nathan. We know it's something they breathe in or eat or by some means get into their system. But you and Bruce are walking around, so it's got to be something that she encountered between when you left and the early hours of Sunday morning."

"You said she left her hotel room."

"Three times. Twice briefly for about two minutes each time: we walked it; that suggests a trip to the ice machine and vending area on her floor. I've closed both vending and the ice machines for that floor as a precaution."

"We used the last of the ice trying to cool her off, so if it was something in that ice she used with her drink, we destroyed what evidence might be left."

"I bagged the towels you used; all may not be lost there. The third time she left the room was for about eighteen minutes. I think she went downstairs to use the business-center copy machine—we found photocopies for ten curled notebook pages and I don't think she made those while you and Bruce were there. Rae had jotted notes on the copies, deciphering faint phone numbers."

"She hadn't made them before Bruce and I left her. So she was downstairs in the hotel. That widens the scope of this considerably."

"Management is cooperating. I've got guys trying to photograph and bag

BEFORE I WAKE   265

anything from the business center that she could have touched or anything she might have eaten—the complimentary welcome table is in the hall between the elevator and the business center. Coffee, cookies, nuts, chocolate squares—it's all being removed to be tested."

Bruce joined them. "Her family is here."

Nathan nodded at Bruce's quiet words. "Tina told me. We'll give them some privacy for a while. What do you think?" he offered the stack of photos.

Bruce looked through the stack, flipping several to the top. "All the obvious things to check, the drinking glass she used, the empty soda can, the food— but we're looking for something not obvious at this point. I don't know."

He turned one of the photos. "The pillow she was using as she stretched out on the bed. Was it something on the pillowcase that she breathed in? It's something that hits at night. Every lady so far—they've been pillow people."

"Yes," Nathan agreed. "It's that kind of thinking we need more of. Gray, when the next batch of photographs come in from the business center and what's between her room and that center, get some of the clerical staff to just brainstorm what-ifs. We need a list of those pillowcase-type ideas. We've got to check everything."

"I'll get it to happen." He slid the photos back into his folder. "Will wants to know if you want to call in the state guys."

"Are your guys tripping over themselves at the hotel?"

"Pretty much."

"You can handle the evidence collection. Franklin has already brought in drug experts to help him with the toxicology on the blood. The strike is another matter—we may need to borrow Brentwood guys if the negotiations collapse." Nathan looked at his watch. "Give me an update every two hours for how it's going at the hotel. I'd like to just get us through tonight if possible and see where we are at in the morning before we go for outside help."

"Will do."

"Nathan."

Nathan opened his eyes and raised his head to turn and see his chief deputy in the doorway. "It's okay, Will." A day of no change wore on a man in ways nothing else ever could. He glanced at the wall clock and realized it was after midnight. Nathan stepped out of the ICU room to join his deputy.

"The negotiators have a draft contract in place."

"They got it done." Nathan breathed out a sigh of relief. "That's good."

"Yeah, I thought so. I just left the lakefront house, Zachary is catching a plane to walk corporate through it and to fight to get it blessed. Adam is heading out for a few hours of sleep."

"What's the mood?"

"Fifty-fifty, which seems to be better than it was a few hours ago. If corporate will sign off, Adam expects the union will vote to ratify it. No one will be happy, but it's a fair deal on both sides."

"Strikebreakers will be at the plant this morning?"

"Yes. Zachary couldn't get that decision reversed. We'll escort the bus in the same as we did Friday. The union line will be heavy, we think, so we're going to have Chet bring in several of his patrol officers to create a cordon in and see if we can't defuse anything from getting started that way."

"Do you need me out there?"

Will looked toward the ICU bed where Rae rested. "We need to know who's killing people in this town. Stay put. As bad as the strike is, this is much worse. You can be at the plant in five minutes if it starts to go bad. Adam and I will stay tight, and I'll have your dad and grandfather serving as intermediaries with the union rank and file."

"Remind me to talk you into running for sheriff next election. You deserve a pay raise."

Will smiled. "And deal with the media? You know I've got the better job of the two of us." Will nodded toward the ICU room. "I hope she comes out of it soon."

"The docs are optimistic. Stay in touch."

"We'll get through this Monday," Will reassured. He headed back to the elevators.

Nathan walked back into the ICU room and moved over to the bedside to study Rae. He thought she was breathing just a little easier. He'd been grasping at straws all day for any signs of change. He looked again at the clock.

Almost twenty-two hours since they thought she had collapsed in that hotel room. "It's time to open your eyes, Rae," he whispered. "Time to smile at your guys. We're worried about you."

He moved her relaxed hand on the blanket to change her position a small bit, wondering if in her sleep she could feel the movement. Her family had visited for several hours, and finally had been talked into going to a nearby hotel to get some sleep.

"She's going to wake up eventually."

Nathan looked over at Bruce, the man so rumpled and tired and with a heavy shadow of a beard coming in that he looked like a grizzly stirring from hibernation.

"She will, if only to keep you on the straight and narrow," Nathan replied.

Bruce smiled at the whispered words. "Yeah." He sighed. "Hard to imagine her not in my life, you know? We've been friends back as far as my memory goes."

Nathan settled back into the chair beside his friend. Bruce was slipping Rae's pearl ring that the hospital had removed earlier in the day on and off his little finger, holding it for her so it wouldn't be lost. Nathan couldn't imagine what this day had to be like for his friend. They had spent a good three hours on the edge of losing her before the doctors began to show their first signs of relaxing and expecting her to make a recovery. "She'll pull out of this none the worse for wear."

"Has to." Bruce sighed. "I nearly asked her to marry me eleven years ago, had the ring bought and everything. Not smart, not asking her then. She's been carrying around a ring won at a county fair instead."

Bruce rubbed a hand across his face. "I'm going to go get more coffee. I hate waiting. It's a whole lot easier to be the one in the bed than to be sitting here waiting."

"I know."

Bruce got to his feet. "It means a lot to me that you stayed. Just in case I don't tell you that later."

Nathan glanced at the bed. "There's nowhere else I'd rather be."

"Hey, lady."

Nathan nudged Bruce, waking his friend. The long night was ending for all of them. Dawn was peeking in the window, so that he could watch her stir without a side light on. He'd been seeing the early signs for a few minutes now but hadn't dared hope he'd see those eyes open until they finally did.

"Nathan," Rae whispered. He watched her assimilate where she was at. She lifted a hand and rubbed at her forehead. "Talk about a killer headache." He moved with Bruce to the bedside. She lowered her hand, glanced at the taped-down needles in the back of her wrist, and gave him a tired smile. "I won't ask where am I; it's not the first time medical staff have stuck me full of tubes and assumed it was for a good cause. Almost victim four?"

"Way too close. We couldn't get you to answer the hotel-room door. Bruce kicked it down." She looked much more coherent than he had expected, and her voice was softer than normal but clear. He could feel the relief settling inside at those realizations.

She smiled over Nathan's shoulder at her friend. "Thanks."

"What happened?" Bruce asked softly.

"I don't know—I was working. I was pleasantly punch-drunk from lack of sleep. My notes were turning into gibberish. I turned down the temperature and stretched out to close my eyes for a minute before I crawled into bed."

"It was close to ninety-five in your room. You turned the heat on full blast."

"Really?" That puzzled her but she shook her head. "I don't remember feeling ill; if anything I was feeling pleasantly good. But the dreams were bad, too real to be dreams."

"Do you remember them?"

"Floating images of ghosts, blood smears, someone asking about flowers." She gave a fading smile. "Not exactly workable facts."

"Did anyone stop by your hotel room?" Nathan asked, hating to push for answers but needing them urgently. "A room-service order? A fax? A delivery of any kind?"

"No. I had all the Peggy files and notes in the file box I've been carrying with me; I spread them on the bed and started working through them, comparing them to the drying pages from the notebook, looking for common names, dates—just working."

"You had several things to eat and drink in your wastebasket. Did you get them from the vending machine at the hotel?" Bruce asked her.

"I've avoided the vending machine since Karen's death. I had picked several items up at the pharmacy and the corner store. I had the sacks next to the dresser; I set them off on the floor when we opened the pizza box."

"Did anything taste odd? smell odd?"

"Not that I noticed."

Nathan moved over to the side table and poured her a glass of ice water. He held it and the straw for her. She sipped at it and gratefully nodded her thanks.

"Talk to Walter about his itch cream," she whispered. "It was the one new thing I've used. I started my second jar of it yesterday. That, and the shampoo was a new brand for me."

"Do you have any of the itch cream at the hotel room?"

"My purse, in a small tin."

She closed her eyes, sighed. "Sorry, guys. Nausea is bad. We'll have to do this later."

"The doctor is on his way in," Nathan reassured.

She tiredly smiled. "More poking and prodding. Just what a girl needs to make her morning." She caught his hand. "Seriously. Thanks," she whispered. "Both of you."

"You're welcome."

"You're going to be fine, Rae. You'll be walking out of here in another couple days or I'll be breaking you out," Bruce promised.

She smiled at her friend. "You need a shave. They'll declare you a walking danger zone soon."

"Like it?" He rubbed the beard.

"Bet it still feels like a porcupine kissing you. Go away. I want to rag on the doctor in private about how much I hate needles. I just realized how many IV lines they have stuck in me."

"Yeah." Bruce smiled and tweaked the blankets covering her feet, then stepped back to let the doctor through. "I thought that might be high on your list of first comments too. We'll be back."

32

Franklin tugged off his glasses and rubbed his eyes. Nathan understood that reality of little sleep since Rae had been found in the hotel room twenty-four hours ago.

"The cream matches Walter's recipe, all over-the-counter items in the specific proportions he quotes. There's nothing showing as an unknown substance."

"The aspirin? At least two of the three had used aspirin."

"The tablet remaining in the packet Rae opened tests as pure aspirin. If it was poured in their drink, there would be a residual trace in the liquid remaining in the glass or can. There isn't. If it was mixed in something they ate, then they ate the entire thing it was mixed with."

"Maybe something we haven't thought to look at—toothpaste, deodorant," Nathan offered. "Maybe it's slowly being absorbed over time then overwhelming the system like a snake venom does."

"Rae's observation that rather than feel bad she had the sensation of feeling unusually good—that suggests an opiate reaction. A synthetic drug, mimicking that kind of pleasant high."

"But this drug kills. That's not a profitable designer drug."

"It didn't kill Rae," the coroner pointed out. "The drug is getting more refined. Peggy was a seizure then a heart attack. Karen was just a heart attack. Rae, as best we can tell, was a pleasant high that went toward paralysis—had the sedative otherwise been tempered a bit more she might have woke with a headache, memories of weird dreams, but otherwise remembering a night of feeling very good. This drug is being perfected, whatever it is. At some point it's going to stop killing, and start being an expensive and nasty drug on the street. Probably highly addictive."

"How long do I have to find it and the person doing this?"

"At the rate we're seeing the tests—he'll have his formula ready for the market inside two weeks. After that—the only limiting factor on this guy will be how much of it he can make."

Nathan closed his eyes, then opened them and faced reality. "Have any idea what we're dealing with, Franklin?"

"If we're looking at a new drug class and I'm afraid we are—it's a month of several labs working just to isolate the substance in Rae's blood, assuming we even have enough of a level in her blood to test, another month to figure out the chemical compound. If it's truly new—current laws won't even classify the compound as a controlled substance, so technically, it won't be illegal to possess the final product, even if it is illegal to possess all the precursor chemicals being used to manufacture it. Having a recommended way to treat overdoses, developing a blood test that can recognize it, training doctors—"

"I get the picture. It's not good."

"If manufacturing of this drug can happen in quantities, we just became the epicenter of a new storm."

33

Nathan left Bruce with Rae at the hospital late Monday afternoon and drove through town, turning his attention to his other growing crisis of the day. The entry into the plant this morning by the strikebreakers bus hadn't gone smoothly, but at least it had gone by without injury. Getting the bus safely out—it was looking to be an open question.

Nathan parked down the road from the plant. He got out of his car and just stood absorbing the scene. A day of shouted words, of watching someone else take their jobs, of swirling rumors of the plant closing, had turned the strike line from righteous anger to deep-seated anger. He didn't like the feel of the situation. He wondered how many on the line knew the decision on the plant's fate was less than seventy-two hours away. His officers on the scene had done a remarkably good job managing the situation through the afternoon.

Nathan walked over to join Adam and offered his hand. "It's been a long weekend, friend."

"Very. How's Miss Gabriella?"

"Coming out of it well, I'm thankful to say. Sillman is trying to get a handle around what is happening." Nathan nodded to the two management negotiators talking with his father. "Zachary got safely away this morning?"

"His flight left at 5 a.m."

"He'll get them to see reason."

"I've got my fingers crossed. We made it a three-year deal just to buy us some more time before we would have to do this again. I give it a fifty-fifty shot, Nathan."

"You haven't told your guys?"

"The word we've put out on the line is that negotiations reconvene after Zachary consults with corporate folks. Not that several of the guys don't have nearly as good an idea as I do of what is happening. This town is a hot sieve for news."

Nathan nodded to the plant. "I heard it was a tense but doable arrival this morning."

"No one swung a punch at the plant security guards when the gates opened for the bus; I considered that a success. And there were a couple surprises. One of our guys crossed the picket line today. Isaac Keif."

"Really? I'm surprised at the name." The son of the owner of the Fine Chocolates Shop was a fairly new union member but known to be a vocal one about the importance of the strike.

"He works part-time in the tile-plant warehouse moving raw materials and finished product around. It's not that deep of a secret that he took this job three years ago to help support his dad's business. And the Fine Chocolates Shop has taken at least a 70 percent hit in its business since this strike began. Isaac figured they couldn't lose both incomes."

"How did the other union guys take it?"

"Not happy about it, but Larry got them to cool down. They'll cut Isaac a bit of slack." Adam nodded to his line of guys. "There's talk of blocking the bus at the hotel tomorrow to prevent it from even leaving; we're discouraging it, but you should know it's floating around."

"I'm just surprised it wasn't tried this morning. Thanks, Adam. One day at a time. We'll see if we can't get this evening to end quietly. Please spread the word it's going to be zero tolerance for violence when the gates open for the bus to leave. My guys are as tired as yours. And we're too shorthanded to let trouble get a foothold. We'll have to be responding pretty tight. It's going to be courteous, but it's going to be tighter than everyone is comfortable with."

"Understood. I'll pass the word," Adam promised.

Nathan joined his officers assembling by the van from the patrol department. "Where do you need me, Will?"

"We're shorthanded for the gate. The union guys managed to get creative this morning and roll trash Dumpsters in the way of the bus just as it would have entered the plant, and having the bus get stopped across from the union lines was a bad experience. The cordon will have to be tighter around the gate as the bus leaves."

"I'll join in there," Nathan agreed. "Sillman will be here in a couple minutes, and he can add some more weight to that buffer."

"Good." Will looked around to see if he had most of his officers assembled. "Okay, guys, listen up. We're escorting the bus all the way to the hotel tonight. When we get there, the bus is going to pull to the building entrance and the guys are going to walk from the bus into the hotel. There will be security supplied by the company already at the hotel waiting for our arrival."

Will nodded down the street. Pickup trucks and cars were already rumbling in the parking lot at the end of the block, more than a few of the strikers planning an escort of their own. "We need to separate these guys from that bus and make sure that separation sticks. None of these cars are going into that hotel parking lot. That's the chief job tonight.

"I want you to pull over and arrest any driver who speeds, even if the vehicle owner is going just a mile over the limit. Any vehicle being driven in an unsafe fashion in traffic—pull it over and arrest the owner on suspicion of being intoxicated. We'll have state guys joining the highway stretch of this drive just to give us more vehicles in the mix. We control the small stuff, and we hopefully end up with no one getting hurt tonight. Questions?"

There were none.

"Okay. Let's get it done. And let's hope this is the last time we need to do this balancing act."

The officers moved to their assigned locations.

Nathan walked down to the main gate. The time wore by as Nathan talked casually with the plant security guard. He heard the bus start. Nathan moved into the street to make sure no one wanted to interfere with the unlocking of the plant gate.

The plant security guards swung the heavy fence gate open and Nathan stepped aside as the bus rolled through.

Nathan saw bottles going airborne. Glass smashed, and a window on his side of the bus dented in, covered in a cobweb of fine splinters. He touched his radio and passed on to Chet the name to arrest. He could only hope that the thinning out of the guys willing to throw a bottle would also stop those willing to throw a fist.

The bus made the end of the block and slowed for the first turn.

Will blocked the road with his squad car, boxing in a couple of the union vehicles and taking his time clearing through the stop sign. A second squad car made a similar slowing move.

The union line began to disperse in groups of twos and threes.

Nathan waited at the plant gate until it was securely padlocked again, lifted a hand to the officers assigned to walk the perimeter, and headed back toward this car. Will and Chet would get the bus safely delivered, and this town would get another few hours of breathing room.

Nathan got cornered in the hospital lobby by the town's newspaper editor, and it was close to 8 p.m. and the end of visiting hours when he made it upstairs to the ICU. The nurse nodded toward Rae's room as she held out a cup of coffee for him to take in. "Bruce is staggering; get him to get some sleep. We'll even find an empty bed for him if necessary."

"I'll try," Nathan promised.

Nathan paused at the door, not seen yet, watching Bruce near the bedside having an earnest quiet conversation with Rae, a pad of paper and pen in his hands. They talked in the shorthand of old friends and shared memories; the longer Nathan was around them the more that realization settled inside. He tapped on the door and smiled as he stepped into the room. "Hey, lady. Bruce been picking your brain clean?"

Rae smiled over at him. "Trying to get me to laugh and agree to be hypnotized. He thinks I'm missing things."

Nathan settled his hand across hers, saying a gentle hello. "I think he just wants to get you to answer questions like where your car keys are at to that Ferrari so he can take it for a spin."

She looked flushed, like she was running a bit of a fever. Nathan glanced over at Bruce and saw the worry on his friend's face. He regretted the fact he'd been gone as long as he had. "The coffee is for you," he told Bruce. "The nurse volunteered you needed it."

"Thanks."

Nathan accepted the pad of paper Bruce held out, and they traded items.

"Every second of my life last Saturday night—fascinating how boring someone's life can be when it's looked at minute by minute," Rae whispered.

"Oh, yeah. Real boring," Nathan teased back, as he kept reading. Bruce had nearly a minute-by-minute look at her life after they left her Saturday night. Something here would pop as the way the drug had reached her. It had to.

Nathan looked at Rae, relieved she had been able to give them this, wishing he was looking into clear blue eyes rather than ones fogged by fever. "You did good, Rae. This will break the case open, I hope."

"I tried."

Nathan could tell she desperately needed more rest. "Bruce, why don't you go get some shut-eye now. The nurse offered to find you an empty bed. I'll stay and watch her snore."

"I don't snore."

Nathan glanced at Bruce and saw the small amused smile on the guy's face. "Rae, you snore," Nathan replied, figuring it was not information she hadn't heard before.

Bruce rubbed the back of her hand. "I think I will go catch some sleep. You need some rest."

"You need that shave even more. I don't want to be blamed for a new beard."

"I'll see what I can do."

Nathan thought there was a more silent message being shared between the two of them under those teasing words.

Bruce looked over at him. "See if you can coax her into eating some more pudding. The doctors want something in her stomach with all these medications, and she's fighting the idea of even Jell-O and Cool Whip."

"I want some of that coffee."

"Food, not caffeine."

"I'll figure out something," Nathan promised, watching Rae. He wondered if Bruce realized she was scared to eat. Probably so, his friend wasn't slow at picking up the subtle notes with Rae. Scared to eat because as much as she had given them of her history Saturday night, Rae didn't know herself how she had been attacked. Just that someone had tried to kill her and almost succeeded. Nathan could empathize, but they had to figure out something.

"I'll be back first thing in the morning, if not before," Bruce promised. He leaned down and gently kissed her. "Be good, lady."

"You do the same," she whispered. "Bye, Bruce."

Nathan pulled over a chair and checked out the dish of pudding on the table, giving her some privacy to get back her composure, feeling very much an unwanted third at the moment as Bruce left.

Rae pushed away the hospital tray to adjust her position in the bed and raise her head a bit.

Nathan looked back at her and smiled. "Feel like a sick peanut at the moment, don't you?"

She laughed at his choice of words and wiped tears off her face. "Fourth loop on a roller coaster. I hate it when he's gone, and I don't even know why it bothers me like this."

Nathan did. "Your security blanket. Bruce makes a good one. And at the moment that kind of company matters." He pushed the pudding cup with one finger. "They really expect you to like vanilla?"

"It's not a favorite," she admitted.

"You do need to try and eat a bite more. Sealed, canned, pressed—how do you want the thing packaged?"

"Lock and key would do." She rubbed at her stomach. "Nothing sounds like it will stay down right now. I don't know, Nathan."

He resolved to solve this for her. "I'll be back in two minutes then, with something that should work magic."

"What's that?"

"Peach pie."

She looked marginally interested.

"They had it listed as the cafeteria special today. They'll open back up for me to make a late-night purchase." He got to his feet, and his smile faded. "Just dive back in and trust the fact this guy we're after missed you; however he got the drug to you, he missed. We'll have him before he can try for you again."

"Thank you," she whispered.

"What are friends for?" He nodded to the television. "Run channels while I am gone and find a distraction. We'll make this night pass for you."

"I'm going to owe you a favor or two when this is over."

"Consider this one thanks for that ham and cheese the other day. It was surprising how hungry I was that day."

She smiled. "Subtle push noted. Go get that pie."

He rested a hand on hers, smiled, and then headed out of the room to see what he could find that they could share. At least he'd have an excuse to eat half the pie before he handed the plate with the rest of it to her.

34

Rae could hear Bruce and Nathan talking in the hospital hallway. The words were faint, but from the conversation she could make out, they were talking about Peggy. The guys were coming toward her; she was pretty sure of that.

She gripped the side rails on the bed and shifted herself up to take the pressure off her hip. The headache had been gone when she woke, and the fever. She almost felt normal on this Tuesday morning. She was glad she had been moved into a general-floor room where nurses didn't bustle in every five minutes and most of the needles were gone.

She wished she had a hairbrush and could do something about the hospital gown she was stuck wearing. She tugged the blanket better around her and thought she'd kill for a shower today.

"What do you think of this?" Nathan asked, his words in the hallway to Bruce faint but clear. "Will found it in a box in Joe's bedroom."

"It's the notebook Peggy was asking about?" Bruce asked.

"Has to be. It was still in the evidence bag returned by the investigators. They looked into the details on it and returned the notebook to Joe. Henry was right; I don't see much in it that would cause excitement. Kids that were going to the party, the time they were going to meet up, a couple scrawled names Joe didn't recognize."

"It feels ugly, figuring Peggy died just for asking around to find out more about this notebook."

"If we've got a cook in the area doing this, he's not waiting for people to actually find information that might lead to him. He's killing people just for asking questions. Rae was asking questions just like Peggy did, and the guy focused on her."

"It's beginning to feel that way."

"I'm awake, guys. Get in here," Rae called out. "I hate having to eavesdrop to find out what's going on."

Bruce, followed by Nathan, entered her room.

She grinned at Bruce. "Hey, you shaved."

"About cut my throat trying to get the layers off," Bruce replied, rubbing the still slightly abraded skin. "The things I do for you."

"Admit it, you never liked having a beard."

"That's true." Bruce perched on the edge of her bed. "No need to ask if you're feeling better. They said they had moved you because you were being a pain in the—"

She slapped his leg as she laughed. "Can I help it if I don't like hospitals? I'm better. They wanted the ICU bed for someone who was staying sick."

"You do look better," Nathan agreed. "It has to be the pie. It works every time."

She smiled back at him. "So—" she looked between the two of them— "when do I get out of here? This morning is fine with me."

"It's Tuesday. You're not going anywhere yet," Bruce answered.

"I'm tired of being cooped up in this bed getting poked at. They've drawn blood until I feel like a stuck turnip. Besides, this is personal; I'm the one he came after. And I'm well enough now to be mad about that fact. I want to go back to work."

She watched the two guys share a look. She was about to get handled and smothered for what they thought was her own good. Her odds of being able to work on the case were diminishing rapidly. It wasn't a pleasant realization. She really did feel fine, and she wanted to get back to work.

"We'll see what your doctor says tomorrow," Bruce compromised.

"You haven't tried to sleep in one of these beds." She pouted.

"Having slept in the chair, I guarantee it was worse." Bruce grinned at her. "I like having you back in a bad mood. You are definitely feeling better."

"Don't placate me; I hate that too." She sighed. "What's going on around town? What's happening with the strike? I've lost two days, guys. At least give me an update on the news."

"The union and management have a draft contract finished. We're waiting for word from Zachary if that contract is going to get blessed by corporate or not. We should know that answer in the next twenty-four hours," Nathan told her.

"That's soon. Are you ready for that? And what happens if it falls apart?"

"We'll have to be."

"And on the deaths. There haven't been any more suspicious deaths or illnesses around town while I've been lying here?"

"Nothing you don't already know," Nathan promised. "You're our biggest new information source to work. We're going through your timeline step by step and testing everything we can locate."

"Let me see the notebook you two were talking about."

"You don't need to be working from a hospital bed, Rae," Bruce replied. "Tomorrow afternoon, maybe."

"This is personal; he about killed me. I'm going to work on it even if I have to do it on my own. And I'm bored silly just laying here. So let me see."

Nathan looked at Bruce.

"Let her see it. What can she do about the information here but get on the phone and ask people more questions? That should at least be relatively safe for her to meddle in."

Nathan smiled. "True." He opened his briefcase and retrieved the school notebook. He turned to a page in the back. "Here's the more interesting page."

Rae looked over the page from Prescott's school notebook. "Well, guys, I hate to tell you something you don't know given how you two just made a big deal out of this . . ." She looked between the two of them and just smiled.

"What?" Bruce finally asked.

She tapped the page. "I recognize this name at the bottom of the page. I'm driving the guy's car."

Nathan blinked. "You're kidding."

"Brad Danforth. He was convicted of dealing drugs, did time, got out of jail, and shot himself in his car. I bought the Ferrari, bullet hole and all." She looked at the page and the faded penned item. "That's a B Danfo . . h and something that might be a time. Danforth was involved in the rave-party deaths?"

Nathan pulled over a chair and sat down. He didn't answer immediately, and she wondered if he would. He looked back over at her and nodded. She was glad he'd correctly decided that she had a right to know what he could tell her.

"They suspected Danforth was the one who passed the drugs to the dealer who was among those dead at the party. They couldn't prove it, so they got Danforth off the streets on an unrelated cocaine charge."

"Okay. So he goes to jail on an unrelated crime, gets out, finds out the same cook is preparing to bring another batch onto the market—Danforth kills himself before the drug hits the market, before he gets swept up in another investigation and he's now facing time on death row for his role in the death of twelve kids."

"It was odd the guy waited to get out of jail before he committed suicide," Bruce agreed. "It made more sense that he'd kill himself in jail to stop from serving the hard time, than kill himself after he got his freedom back. But this does help explain it. He shot himself because he knew something was coming back onto the street that would snag him into a death-penalty-type case. He didn't want to face it."

"We can check that idea out a bit more," Nathan agreed. "But does it help us identify who is creating these drugs? The investigator's suspicion that Danforth was the one who passed them to a dealer at the party is more than likely true, given Danforth's actions now. But he's dead. He won't be telling us who the cook was. And they searched hard to link Danforth to that person years ago."

"I agree it doesn't tell us much," Rae said. "But maybe Danforth saw someone after he got out of jail that will be a useful name to check out? He must have confirmed that kind of suspicion about the cook being back in business before he took the extraordinary step of killing himself."

"I wish he had killed the drug designer instead, if he knew who that guy was," Bruce remarked.

She looked between the two of them. "Please, guys. I want out of here tomorrow so I can help check this out. I'll be careful, I promise. But I know enough about this overall case to be helpful. You've got to at least let me try."

"If your doctor says you're ready to go, I'll get you out of here," Bruce reluctantly agreed.

"The same hotel, the same room."

"Be reasonable," Bruce protested.

"They gave the room Peggy died in to a nice couple traveling through from Florida and nothing happened to them. The hotel room is not the source of whatever this is. Being back at the scene of the crime may remind me of something I missed. Besides, all my stuff is there." She looked at Nathan. "All my stuff is still there, isn't it?"

"We'll have to buy you more toothpaste and the basics. But yes, your personal stuff is being cared for," he said and changed the subject. "Have you had lunch yet? They might let you go down to the cafeteria with us."

She looked at Bruce. "You brought me a change of clothes?"

He nodded to the sack he had set down. "I found the jeans and sweatshirt you described."

"Then go find a nurse for me and ask if I can go to the cafeteria, and I promise in return I'll be good about being stuck here for another day."

Bruce grinned and went to comply.

Rae handed the school notebook she still held back to Nathan. "Sit and talk about the hotel review while he's searching for a nurse. I want to know everything you've ruled out so far as the cause of this. I was an idiot to walk into it, and I want to know what I did."

"I don't think we know," Nathan replied. "And I don't think you could have avoided it, Rae. He knew how to get to you. But we're interested in the pillowcase and some of the odder possibilities now. He's creative, whoever this guy is. You were already on guard enough not to be using the vending machines."

"Pillowcases. That's an interesting idea."

"He knows he can put the drug in place and be a fair distance away before it is encountered or before it takes effect. That at least suggests it's not an aerosol that disperses or something that decays swiftly on its own. He's found something to use that we aren't expecting. We'll just have to get creative for where to search."

"Maybe not so creative," she suggested. "If these are test trials of the drug, he's not going to have much of the drug available to use. And if his quantities are very small, he can't afford to have any of it wasted. That suggests something we drink or we eat or something that we hold and it is absorbed through the skin. But whatever it is, we're using all of it that is there."

"Which suggests Sillman is wasting his time trying to find any of it left at the scene," Nathan agreed. "But we'll look anyway. Had the deaths been later in the morning, we'd be interested in shampoos and face creams and things absorbed by the skin. You don't know you encountered the drug; that itself is our strongest clue for where it is hiding. It's tasteless, odorless, and not obvious in its amount."

"Lipstick. All of us used lipstick."

"Believe it or not, I called Sillman this morning to ask that very question. The tubes are at the lab being tested."

"Most of my stuff is at that lab being tested right now?"

Nathan smiled. "Sorry. Everything we could think of is. We'll replace it for you."

"At least I'm the one alive to care about it. How long do we have to find this guy, Nathan? He nearly perfected the drug with his test on me."

"Assuming he wasn't trying to kill you."

"True."

"Franklin thinks a couple weeks," Nathan replied. "After that, large quantities start appearing somewhere on the street—probably a richer market for that kind of thing than Justice."

"The fact he's testing the drug here is precisely because it is a small town;

with easy access to people, he can come and go without it catching a big police department's attention—and when he's done what he needs to do, he moves on with his new product."

"That's what we are afraid of."

Rae offered a sympathy smile. "My first case was not so pedestrian after all."

"Let's hope you spend the rest of your career totally bored."

Rae laughed at that.

Bruce returned. "You're on for a trip downstairs; you just have to take a wheelchair."

Rae groaned. "Great. Then you're not 'helping' push me. You'll drive the chair into a wall."

She pushed back blankets. "Go away, you two. I'll be changed in five minutes. And I'm hungry for a burnt cheeseburger if they can fix such a thing."

35

Rae pulled on tennis shoes and took her time knotting the laces so they wouldn't come undone. She ordered herself not to look again at her watch. Wednesday had arrived and she was getting out of this hospital room for good today. Bruce would be on time this morning; he knew how badly she wanted to be out of here.

She pulled over the paperwork the nurse had gone over with her and folded it into thirds, then found a place for it in the sack of odds and ends the guys had brought in for her. The plastic band on her wrist itched, and she scratched under it. She couldn't wait until she had a pair of scissors to remove it.

"What time did you tell Sillman we would be over?"

Rae looked up as she heard Nathan's voice in the hall.

"Ten," Bruce replied. "So are you going to tell her or am I?"

Rae looked over at the reporter in the chair across the room and held a finger to her lips to urge him to stay quiet. He grinned back at her.

"You lost the coin flip in the parking lot. You're telling her."

There was a tap on the door, and Bruce entered first, followed by Nathan. The two men stopped.

Rae smiled. "Guys, you remember Gage Collier?"

"The reporter who offered to help us sort out Peggy's notes," Bruce replied first. "Sure." He walked over to shake hands.

Rae wondered if the reporter was being oversensitive when he winced at the handshake. "He's not only offered to help us sort out Peggy's notes; he knows a great deal of interesting information regarding my former car owner."

Nathan leaned against the wall of cabinets inside the doorway, studying the reporter. "Really?"

"Brad Danforth was a known dealer on the south side; he took over Peter Jirinski's territory," Gage replied, focusing on Bruce as he said it.

"I know the man."

"Your cover name is on one of his arrest warrants; I figured you did," Gage replied. "Brad Danforth also had someone above him who thought he was worth protecting. That stretch of time in jail—no one moved in to acquire the turf in his absence, and when that happens on the street that says patron."

"Agreed. I never got a lead on him; that would have been after my under-cover time. Any ideas?"

"No. But they suspected Danforth of being the source of the exotic stuff at the rave party for a reason. He's got a reputation of being first on the street to supply the new thing."

"Which means he knows a guy with some connections—probably the same patron protecting his territory while he was in jail."

Gage nodded.

"So this tells us what about the case now?" Nathan asked, looking between the two men. Bruce was the one with the most expertise in the room.

"Our designer drug maker—he's got business connections north of here, so maybe he lives north of here too. That's harder to say. It's at least the lab he's using to make the stuff which must be near this town. He's testing the drugs around here, because he doesn't want to transport them yet. And he doesn't want any bad outcome casualties showing up in the market where the drug will eventually be sold."

"In an ugly way, that makes sense. The rave-party deaths taught them to keep the product out of their own area until it was fully ready to mass pro-duce and sell."

Bruce nodded. "What this does confirm is the fact Danforth is a solid lead to work. Who he talked with after he got out of jail would be useful information. At least that's a lead we can ask the guys in Chicago to pursue for us. Find the patron, and he should be able to give us a name of the guy who is designing this stuff and testing it around here."

"It's definitely worth a shot," Nathan agreed. "You're not going to be writing about any of this," he cautioned the reporter.

Gage smiled. "Tell part of the story, when I can instead get a Pulitzer by writing the full story? I promised Peggy I would write the story she was working on as a tribute to her. I'll wait until I have the names to expose. I haven't been around this business so short of a time that I haven't learned the value of patience." He looked back at Bruce. "For that patience, you'll keep me informed."

"You'll hear from us," Bruce promised. "And we'll want to know back anything you are finding through other sources."

"Fair enough."

Rae looked between the three guys, relieved there seemed to be both an understanding as well as a bit of useful news being passed around. This case really was coming down to tracking names and relationships, and that was the work Bruce had spent his career perfecting how to do. It was a drug case, but it would still be solved by one person leading to another person, who could give them the name of their drug designer.

She figured a change of subject about now would help. She looked at Bruce. "So what were you two flipping a coin about to decide who would tell me?"

Bruce looked at Nathan and then crossed his arms across his chest and looked back at her. "We moved you to a different hotel, under a different name."

"You did what?"

"Don't protest; you're not going to win this debate. Be an idiot on your own time; but you're not going back to the same hotel when we haven't figured out how you got slipped the drug in the first place."

"This guy has demonstrated access to two hotels in town; you're telling me he doesn't also have access to this third one?"

"So humor me. It's closer to where I live."

"It's got to be something I ate or drank, and that is not something where I sleep is going to influence."

"I would stuff you in a locked room if you would let me; I'll settle for moving you."

She knew she had lost the discussion before it even began. Rae pushed herself to her feet. "Fine. Just as long as we are leaving this place in the next ten minutes." She looked over at the reporter. "Thanks, Gage. I enjoyed the company this morning."

"Anytime."

"You'll be back to look at the notebook pages later?"

"Whenever you call," he promised. He looked at Bruce, then Nathan. "You really might want to think about finding her something to do. She's going to drive you crazy until you do."

Nathan grinned. "Absolutely right she will. It's a pleasure to have her back doing it too."

Rae laughed. She headed to the door. "You all are awful. Bruce, I want to drive."

He tailed behind her. "Forget it."

଼ଃ ଼ଃ ଼ଃ

"Lift your feet up; let me get your shoes off."

Rae opened one eye and wished the room would stop spinning counterclockwise. She had the energy of a drowned mouse right about now. "I can get them." She sighed and sat up on the hotel-room bed. "The mattress is too hard."

She had laid down for a few minutes while the guys carried in her suitcases and got her hanging clothes put away. She felt like a wiped-out baby just from the walks from the hospital to the car, and from the car to her new hotel room. This was not good. She pushed off her tennis shoes.

"The bed will feel softer the more tired you get," Bruce promised. "You'll be okay here?"

She looked around the room. It was more expensive than the last hotel room, bigger, and there was even a full recliner next to a reading table. "I'll be fine. I'm just complaining to complain."

He smiled. "You're allowed."

"I've got a headache and right now I want a few hours of sleep; but after dinner I'm going to be fine again and I'll want to go to the office. I don't want to spend the rest of the day in this room."

She expected a fight in reply to the words and was ready to insist. It was a pretty room. Nathan had replaced her roses with fresh ones and added two pretty pots of daisies. It was still a hotel room. And she wasn't staying here the rest of the day.

"You could come over to my place," Bruce offered instead.

She looked at him and let the emotion inside her show in her eyes. "I need to work."

He reached over and squeezed her hand. "Then set your alarm for six. I'll be back at half past and we'll go to the office and eat while you read files."

"Thanks. That's a good plan." She staggered a bit as she got to her feet and then she looked past Bruce to Nathan. "Thank you. For all of this. The flowers are lovely."

"You're welcome. Rest, Rae; give yourself time to get better. You've got the painkillers the doctor prescribed for that headache?"

She patted her pocket and the thin vial. "They aren't going out of my sight."

"Good."

She walked with them to the door.

"I've got myself a second key card just in case I get so worried about you I'm thinking about kicking in the door again," Bruce mentioned.

She hugged him. "That's appreciated. Now go away. Get a nap or something before six. You two look worse than I do and that's saying something."

Nathan laughed. "Or something."

"I shaved," Bruce protested good-naturedly.

"The shirt is a couple days ripe though," Nathan pointed out. He lifted a hand in a silent farewell to Rae and pushed his friend toward the hallway and the elevator.

Rae watched them go, then stepped back and locked the hotel-room door and pushed the chain in place.

Jesus, now I lay me down to sleep . . . the last time about killed me. I can't do that again. I can't.

She pushed back the cover on the bed to tug out the pillows and pile them up. She collapsed facedown with her arm wrapped around one of them. She was scared to close her eyes, to reach for a drink without pausing, to eat without feeling like she was going to choke on the food. It was no way to live.

If I should die before I wake . . . please don't let Bruce and Nathan be the ones to find me next time. Don't let that be their last memories of me. Don't do that to them again.

She was going to find the guy who had come after her. Somewhere in her memories of that Saturday was the answer to who it was doing this.

She knew the guy. That was the one thing she was absolutely certain of—this drug designer or whoever he had used to slip her the drug was someone she had met since she came to this town.

She just needed some rest before she began that work. She closed her eyes and took a deep breath. Tired didn't come close to describing how exhausting just getting out of the hospital could be. She felt sleep coming and welcomed it.

֍ ֍ ֍

Rae smiled as she entered the Chapel Detective Agency, relieved to be back on familiar territory.

Bruce set down the box he'd brought in. "Margaret said to tell you most towns-folk don't know your full name or address yet, so they took to dropping off their get-well cards here. There's a basket of them waiting for you in your office."

"That's sweet."

"Let's hope you still think so after you write out all those thank-you notes." Bruce locked the front door behind them and then led the way down the hall toward her office. "Did you remember your keys?"

She shook her head. She wasn't even sure where she had put her purse. He dug out his and unlocked her office for her. He reached in and turned on the lights.

Her move into her office stopped before she crossed the threshold. "Oh. Oh, my furniture arrived." She turned to beam at him.

He rubbed her shoulder. "This afternoon. Nathan and I thought you would like a place to sit down. Sillman helped us with that desk—I swear it's the heaviest piece of furniture ever made."

"It's all so gorgeous." She entered the room, her smile growing. She walked around gleaming polished furniture. She ran her hand across the vast desktop and took a seat in the black leather desk chair. She swiveled, loving the feel of it. "Mahogany?"

"Yes. And every other piece too, including the floor lamp columns. You said you liked the scrollwork finishing, so I took you at your word."

It was richly done pieces of wood, beautiful and yet subtle with the carvings tucked around to accent the flow of the wood. "I was thinking a nice table or two to complement your basic functional desk. You spent some cash."

"I bet it outlasts your career as a private investigator," Bruce predicted comfortably. "Besides, I had to be able to enjoy sitting in here. You're going to be hollering for me to come down to your office for us to talk about cases." He took a seat in the leather chair opposite her desk to make his point and gestured around the room. "We left room for you to bring in your own couch if you like. And the files are negotiable. They would look fine in the front office if you would prefer that wall to stay open."

"I'm liking everything I see right where it is. A few more plants, a couple more table lamps, my pretty knickknacks on the shelves and photos on the wall—" She laughed. "This is really great. Thank you, Bruce. Seriously. I appreciate this more than you can know."

"You're welcome."

She sat looking at him for a moment. He'd meant to touch her heart, he had, and she'd remember that in his lasting favor every time she turned on the lights in this room and sank into this seat behind her elegant spacious desk.

"So—" She opened the file drawer behind her desk to find it empty. "The only problem is no case files to work. Let's fix that. You've got my box of Peggy Worth materials?"

"In my office. I'll get them after we figure out what we are ordering in for dinner."

"Chinese? I would love that taste right now."

He looked relieved she was suggesting something substantial. "Let me go make a call."

"I'll find new file folders I can label as we sort out paper. I'm going to be officially an office person again."

Bruce laughed as he got to his feet. "I knew this was something you were going to take to like a duck takes to water."

She shooed him out the door to go call in their dinner order.

"Now this is what an office should look like."

Rae looked up from the papers she was sorting out to see Nathan standing in the doorway of her office. She waved him in with a grin. "I hear you were part of this magic transformation."

"Bruce just asked for muscles. Sillman and I took one look in the back of that truck and said, 'You want us to do what?'"

Rae laughed. "Well, it's very much appreciated. That sack you're carrying wouldn't be what I think it is, would it?"

"Dinner. Bruce said take a break and join us, he was buying. He just didn't mention I'd be the one picking it up. You want to eat in here or set this up in the break room?"

"Here, definitely. Let's get this office officially broken in. Food is the best office-warming gift there is."

"You're getting your appetite back."

"Doing my best to take your advice and just ignore what happened. I happen to love Chinese."

"I'll remember that." Nathan set down the sack on a discarded newspaper and went to get them plates and drinks.

"Hey, buddy. I think she liked the furniture."

"Ye of little faith," Bruce replied, laughing as he headed down the hall. "Find me something with caffeine and bring me a spoon—you know how miserable it is to eat fried rice with a fork. I'll be with you two in a minute. A call's come in from Chicago."

36

"Talk to me, Rae." Nathan gestured to the folders on her desk with his fork.

She set aside the fried-rice container she was working her way through down toward the bottom. "Wouldn't you rather have Sillman join us for this?"

"I sent him home to get some sleep. I don't think he's paused since we found you at the hotel."

"I like that about him, the fact he wants the guy that tried for me as badly as I do."

"There's a reason he's my top guy on investigations. Bruce will be back whenever he can get off that phone call, but he's heard most of this already, so just start somewhere. He can catch up when he shows up."

"If he's talking to his Chicago cop buddies, we may see him a century from now. I noticed he piled his plate pretty high before he went to make that call."

"Good point." Nathan pointed to the whiteboard she'd confiscated from the break room. "Start with the highlights about Peggy. Let's make sure we're not stepping past a piece of information that would make a difference in how we proceed with this case."

Rae found a Magic Marker from the mug of pens she had added to her desk. "It's very simple at its core." She used the board to track the timeline of events and began marking down dates.

"Peggy was chasing a rumor that a new designer drug is coming on the market very soon, something with a unique delivery system. I can vouch for the unique delivery system. I never saw how I got hit with the drug. The initials *EE* she mentions in her notes may stand for Extra Ecstasy; that's a guess based on a washed-out page in her notebook.

"Peggy came to town Thursday, started asking questions, and Nella died Friday night. That remains our strongest tangible link to the cook that we have found. Nella was shut up before she could talk to a reporter, and that says she knew something, either about the cook, or where he was working.

"Saturday night the reporter Peggy dies. We've found her orange-covered notebook, but not her BlackBerry. It may still be lost out on Prescott's land, since we never got back there to finish that search.

"Karen dies next. She's passing through town and seems to be truly just a test of the drug. Based on how she died, it was a more refined version of the drug than what killed Peggy.

"Saturday I found Peggy's notebook. That same night, I somehow got taken out. The fact the notebook pages were not removed from the hotel room after I was hit—maybe it was just the fact I was out running around asking questions that was considered the threat. We know this guy is close to having his drug perfected; he just needs to keep people off his trail for maybe a couple weeks and he's done and gone."

Nathan nodded. "He's stopping the people asking a lot of questions. He's not worried about the investigations of the deaths easily leading back to him." He grimaced. "He knows we don't have much of a path from the scenes back to him."

"The pattern in the cases will show up eventually," Rae reassured. "It's there. But figuring out who it is crossing all of our paths isn't an obvious name."

"It's a good summary." Nathan studied her notes on the board. "What else do we know? Or know that we don't know?"

"Good distinction." Rae thought a moment. "Three things. We don't know where this drug is being made. We don't know how many more tests of the drug have been done that didn't result in a death. We don't know if this is the same cook that was involved in the millennium rave-party deaths. Danforth's suicide strongly suggests it might be the same guy coming back on the scene with another drug."

Nathan added an observation of his own. "We know from Franklin's work that it's likely a new class of designer drugs. The tests should have picked up on variations."

"Another indicator it might be the same guy. The cook had to lay low after the kids' deaths; he's been using that time to create something new," Rae suggested.

"And while that cook may not live around here, he at least has a place to work around here that probably goes back a few years." Nathan shook his head. "I'm not hopeful we find that lab. It could still be a spot in the woods, and probably is given the sounds and smells to be covered up, but it's tucked someplace it's not attracting attention."

"A mobile home on a remote corner of a property, maybe," Rae offered. "Someplace able to be used for a number of years in all kinds of weather. But I doubt it would be a home or an address where a postman would be delivering mail."

"A warehouse, hog barn, hunting cabin, abandoned house. You'll find protected places against the weather dotting this county."

"He's being careful to not get connected to his product. I think that extends to how he treats where he's making it. He'll try to stay a step away from being easily identified to the location."

"I won't find an electric bill for the lab in his name," Nathan said with a rueful smile.

"Probably not."

"Okay. So does any of this change how we're working this? It still says our focus here is on the timeline of your Saturday night and lots of lab tests. Tracking down Danforth's contacts to see if we can find a patron to squeeze to get a cook's name—that's weeks if not months of work for the guys up north."

"He's got to have some raw-chemical ingredients to work with and he can't just be out buying that stuff in this town. So where is he shopping? Maybe we can work on that a bit."

"We can try." Nathan studied the list she had jotted down. "We're already doing all we can."

"I think so."

"And we're waiting for victim five to show up." Nathan hated that reality but knew he was stuck at that point.

"I'm sorry."

"So am I. The source is still here in Justice. Somewhere. We've just got to find the person before he moves on."

He thought about it and sighed. He nodded. "Thanks, Rae. I needed to see this laid out one more time. I'm planning to head over and talk with Franklin this evening and see what he's thinking now." He got to his feet and started collecting food cartons. "Bruce took all the egg rolls with him?"

"I bet he did."

"Then I'm taking the last of the spicy shrimp. You sure you don't want to finish up this beef and broccoli?"

"I'll pass." She dug a fortune cookie out of the sack. "Has there been any word on the union contract?"

"Zachary thinks maybe he gets the final decision tomorrow. Corporate has been taking apart the profit numbers and asking a lot of questions but hasn't been tipping their hand much one way or the other. If they decide to close the plant, they say that to Zachary and then lean across the table and say, 'Sorry, we think you've done a great job, but your position is being eliminated and you're being laid off too.'"

"I hadn't thought about that."

Nathan shrugged. "Zachary has. If it weren't for what that would mean for this town, I think he'd actually be relieved to be done with these people at this point. Anyway—maybe the final word one way or the other comes tomorrow."

"Can I do anything for you? Bake you cookies? Walk your dogs? Toss snowballs at you? Just generally be a distraction?"

Nathan grinned. "I'll be okay. I'm one of the few that knows what may be coming. I've been absorbing this for a few days now. I'm ready for whatever it is we get handed. But thanks for the offer. It was novel."

She smiled. "Anything I can do, please, Nathan, ask. I prefer to be useful."

"You know I will."

He stepped out of her office to dump the trash and find Bruce.

ԑ⍥ʒ   ԑ⍥ʒ   ԑ⍥ʒ

When he wanted to kill a lady, he managed to miss. He stewed about that as he measured liquid into an oversized measuring cup. He'd wanted to kill the lady but also not give them enough of the drug to test after the fact to figure out what his formulation was. He'd guessed wrong on the amount to use. That was his mistake.

He added the liquid slowly to the kettle on the old stove, letting it mix into the warm water at a steady flow. He thought about trying again but decided he'd better pass on that idea. Three deaths and one attempt had occurred without even a close call for being discovered. A fifth might be pressing his luck.

The formula was right. They'd tried ten more samples across other area towns without any adverse reactions, just the pleasant euphoric high promised to their willing testers. Free drugs did find willing partakers, he reflected cynically. The only open question now was how many doses over what period of time made a user fully addicted to the product. If his assumptions were correct, it was so highly addictive that three to five users would be enough to create a craving which could be filled in no other way. The money to be made was always in the addiction.

He looked at his watch and the date in the corner. The formula was figured out. Now he was just in a race against time to get enough prepared before his meeting with Devon to meet his backer's expectations for enough to do an initial marketing trial. If Devon liked the feedback he got, they would be in business. The manufacturing would be small scale at first, and he'd handle that himself to ensure the quality control until the product was established on the street and the price was rising. After that—the formula itself would be worth a serious seven-figure purchase price, and Devon could own it outright. His backer was in a much better position to deal with the bulk manufacturing problems. He'd get out of this business a wealthy man, which was what he had always planned.

He listened to the kettle begin to boil inside and turned down the heat to no more than steam the core ingredients together. He turned to begin work on the second-stage powder.

He saw the kid working on the packaging reach for a brown bottle. "No! Not that one. The flask of yellow liquid next to it." The forming agent wasn't particularly dangerous unless you dumped in a flask with some hydrochloric acid, and then the angels took over and you got to explain why your body was in bits and pieces. "Why don't you just not touch anything."

"But you said—"

"I know what I said. You also said you'd had some chemistry courses."

"If you had some of this labeled or in proper containers . . ." The young man let his words fade away.

How his partners had thought bringing in this kid to help with the packaging would be a help rather than a hindrance, he did not know. The extra hands out here were needed, and he understood why his partners were not free to help tonight given the alibis they had to maintain—but still, this was an unworkable reality. The kid might be their meth production helper, but it wasn't the same as doing this kind of work.

He turned down the burner heat under the ten gallon soup pot. "Come over here and take this pot, set it outside in the snow to cool down."

The young man picked up pot pads and carried the smelly pot outside.

He moved to the dried powder bench and began the laborious job of adding the suspension liquid so the drug would have enough volume it could be measured into controllable doses as it was formed.

By the time he measured components, heated them together, cooled it, dried it, pounded it to powder, and then resuspended the product in its suspension medium to be able to measure it into the final product, this job became so laborious that there was a reason few cooks could be found willing to do the work.

BEFORE I WAKE   303

The young man didn't return.

When shouts for him didn't get an answer, he angrily tugged off his gloves and face mask and went toward the cabin door. The kid wasn't going to try to walk miles home from here. He was probably out there pouting.

The young man had walked out of the cabin with the pot, managed to take about eight steps, collapsed to one knee and set down the pot, and then went down hard.

It chilled him for a moment to see the way the kid had just fallen, but then the anger came. Touching the body would just leave more evidence to find. He picked up the cooling pot, thankful it hadn't tipped, and he moved it to a thicker snow drift to keep cooling.

The list of bad breaks on this job just kept growing. He'd told the kid to wear a mask for a reason.

He had enough components cooked that he could do the final forming and wrapping at his home. There was more than enough counter space there, and quiet. But he'd have to rush it, get the packaging done, and get himself out of this county entirely in twenty-four hours. Devon would understand the need for setting up at another location; as good as this one was, it had still lasted years longer than most labs ever had.

He stepped around the body and ignored the melting snow around it. He went back to finish his work for the night.

He could blow up the cabin easily enough, but that would just make its existence easier to discover, and there was no need to attract the attention. It would likely be days before the kid was reported missing and many more after that before someone happened onto this place. He'd be long gone by then. Long gone.

By the time the kettle was ready to pour he had his plans made for the night. The notebooks were outdated, and most of the chemicals stored here were unused since the millennium disaster. His prints were nowhere to be found for he never came here without gloves. If his partners' prints were around to find—well, someone had to be connected to this place or the cops would keep looking. Their carelessness wasn't his concern.

If they were caught—they knew well what would happen if they tried to exchange his name for a lesser deal with authorities. Devon would deal with that for him.

The cops would eventually match him to be Nella's guest, for he hadn't tried to remove the fact he had been at her home, but his alibi for the time of her death would withstand the scrutiny. He worried about his move away from the town being the red flag that gave him away as the man they hunted, but he'd been setting down markers for his departure for long enough now; he thought it would be accepted as the natural course of things.

He finished his work for the night. He loaded his truck. He took the cooled pot with him on the last trip. It felt odd carrying a pot of powder that would translate into more money than he had ever seen in his life. He'd been dreaming about this payday for years.

He started his truck and kicked up the heater. He studied the cabin in the light cast by the truck headlights. It looked like less now than when he had first seen it years before. But it still felt a bit sad parting with what he had built here. A season of his life was ending this next week.

He backed out on the long narrow road and headed home.

37

"You can't play music aimed at the tile plant at that decibel, even as free speech," Nathan stressed for the third time Thursday morning, trying to make his point to the grandson of Mark Yates. Families of the union members were on the strike line today, and the teenagers were getting creative.

"This is arbitrary harassment," the teen protested. "So I can't play it at twelve, then I'll play it at seven."

Nathan put his hand on the volume control. "You'll play it at three, if you play it at all." He had never felt less like a diplomat than he did today. "Give it a rest, Greg. You've made your point. As interesting a protest as this is, they can't even hear it inside the tile plant when the mixers are running."

More strikebreakers had been sent in today. The tile-plant guys were getting a few trucks in and out of the back gate, hauling finished shipments. Product was being made today, and product was being shipped. It was taking Nathan sixteen officers just to keep the two sides separated so the trucks were able to go out without slashed tires or smashed windows. He didn't need this noise adding to the stress.

His pager went off.

"Leave it low, or I'll be pulling the plug permanently. Understood?"

Greg didn't answer him, but at least he didn't flagrantly flip the volume dial back up as Nathan stepped away.

Nathan walked away from the union line, read off the number on the urgent page, and called back on a secure channel. "Go ahead, Will."

He heard the sound that was someone throwing up.

"Will?"

"Sorry. Can't believe what I just walked into. I was trailing a bleeding deer Taylor clipped on the highway and got more than I bargained for."

He coughed again and then his voice came back stronger. "It looks like I found our clandestine drug lab, Nathan. There's a kid out there, dead in the snow, about ten feet from the front door of the cabin."

"Where?"

"Peterson's former place, that hunting shack he built when he got out of the service. We'll need the HazMat team out here. This kid made a mistake and got himself killed. No telling what is left half made inside."

"A young kid—a meth lab or something more upscale?"

"I'm guessing he's sixteen. But he's probably not working this place alone. I've got lots of vehicle tracks in and out of here since the snow began to pack on the ground last month. A glance through the cabin door confirmed no more bodies, and that's as far as I went. It's a lot more than a hot plate inside. I've backed off."

"I'm on the way. I'll bring the guys we need to work the scene. Keep it quiet, Will. We need to use whatever we can find at that scene to our advantage before word gets out we found it."

"Agreed."

⟨⟩   ⟨⟩   ⟨⟩

Nathan felt a bit sick at the turn this day had taken. He'd been waiting for a break in the case, but he had never wanted this. Not a dead kid. He watched the best trained HazMat person the county had suit up in protective gear. The former cop now worked full-time with the fire department.

"Let's get a good half mile around this place cordoned off so we don't get downwind deaths. Whatever this concoction is, we know it kills fast and easy," Charles said.

"We've already got roads blocked," Nathan assured him. "We're calling it a gas truck accident scene on an icy road. That will work for a couple hours."

"Good. You think this might be your designer drug guy's place?"

"It's probably just the meth lab the county task force has been hearing rumors about, but I want to know if it looks like more than that inside. If this is our guy, he was probably here when this accident happened, he's already running, and we've got to get on his trail in the next couple hours if we are going to have any hope of catching him."

"I can understand the need for speed." Charles checked his breathing apparatus. He wouldn't be breathing the air inside that cabin until he knew what was floating around.

"You and Will, get suited up. The van has more protective suits. If it looks safe enough I can point you where to stand and what to touch; I'll get you a look inside before we start neutralizing the place."

"Thank you."

"How do you want to handle the body?"

Nathan hated this part of the job. "It doesn't make sense to put guys in danger documenting the scene and preparing the body to be moved until the cabin is dealt with. If you can clear Will and I to come up to the cabin, we'll bring a tarp with us to cover the body. If it's not safe to move him until tomorrow, that's the reality we live with. If we can find any ID on him or take his fingerprints, we'll let that be enough for now."

"As awful as that is on the deceased, it's the right answer. The danger is going to come not only from what he was working with and left half created in there, but the cleanup we try to do. If we pick up the wrong bottle or make the wrong assumption about what is in a pot, the place could explode around us. I'd rather not have cops working a few feet from the cabin door if something like that goes wrong."

"You don't work a simple job."

Charles gave a grimace. "Some of the stuff you find in these labs—it's a wonder more don't explode under their own fumes."

He finished his preparations, put the digital camera he would use into his front pocket, and then tested his radio. "Find somewhere comfortable to sit. I'll be a while."

Nathan watched as the man began the long walk toward the cabin down the snowy path of a road, a solitary man in a gray body suit, the breathing mask being slid on a good fifty yards before he reached the cabin.

"This way, officers." Charles's chief assistant pointed them toward the van.

"Will, are you up for this?" Nathan asked.

"I've done my throwing up for this case. I'm good for this. Besides, who else do you want to volunteer for it?"

"True. Noland would say yes."

"He needs some more real-life training in caution first. You get blown up as sheriff, I end up being promoted into your job. Given that thought, I'd rather be beside you when the tragedy happens."

Nathan smiled but understood. "I appreciate you watching my back. I always have."

"Someone's got to. This is going to be our guy, Nathan. I can feel it in my bones."

"I hope you're right. We're going to get the guy one way or another. Doing it today would be particularly sweet."

The suit was hot and uncomfortable and Nathan figured out after the first quarter hour that the only comfortable way to survive in one was to lean against the van and let the weight of the suit sag into his boots. He patiently waited, hearing a few occasional words over the radio from Charles to his assistant about neutralizing agents he needed assembled from the stock in the van.

Several officers on the perimeter of this, more officers sitting on the tile plant, and Nathan knew he was now totally at capacity. The next shoe that dropped anywhere in Justice and he was calling Luke to send his officers and the state guys to send theirs. They were finally at the line it was no long something to consider, but something he would have to do.

He wondered how long it would be before Bruce or Rae heard the news about this lab. Not long, he thought. Rae had about been victim four. She had a right to know this place had been found.

Charles reappeared through the cabin door and walked down the road toward them, removing his breathing apparatus as he walked. He chief assistant moved to take the air canister the man carried.

Nathan moved to meet him, and Will joined them. "Charles?"

"It's no meth lab I've ever seen. There's some serious chemical work going on in there."

"How dangerous?"

"No active heat sources, no open chemicals exposed to the air. Someone else was with the kid and shut this place down."

"He cleared out stuff?"

"I don't think so. There's no obvious places on the tables or shelves where things look missing. They just shut down explosive sources and walked way from the body hoping the place would probably sit out here undiscovered for a few weeks."

"It probably would have, if it weren't for a bleeding deer," Will remarked.

"Did you ever find it to put it down?" Charles asked.

"No."

"It's a shame about that." Charles used a towel to wipe sweat off his face. "Let's the three of us take that tarp and go up to the cabin. I'll get you a look inside. It's safe enough we can go inside without the air masks. But based on what I've seen, we're going to be lucky to get the chemicals moved out of that place by nightfall. There's no way the coroner can be up there today."

"Would it help to have other HazMat teams come in to assist?"

"It's tight in there to walk around. One guy inside, one at the doorway, and three guys walking stuff back and forth to the disposal van is about the max we want to try. Slow means safe; no use hurrying our way into trouble.

"We'll be able to move the van in to about that old oak tree, but it's still going to be a lot of careful carrying. And for many of the liquids I saw, we'll have to stop and do a complete contained burn in the chamber before we move on to the next item. The more I think about it, the more I wonder if it can even safely be cleared in a couple days."

Nathan looked around the place they were currently parked. "We can create a staging site right here, and get set up for a couple days stay."

"Good." Charles gestured to the path he had walked in the snow. "Let's go see if we can find something you can use to identify your guy."

Will found a wallet on the boy and opened it, then nodded to Nathan. They had an ID to work with. They set the tarp across the body and used some fallen branches to create a weight against any wind gusts. It wouldn't protect from bugs and small animals but it was what was possible.

Charles used the broom he had carried with him to gently clear the steps he had walked earlier. "I don't need to tell you to watch your footing. Stay behind me and in the same path I walk. I'm going to circle the room and point out some things I've noticed as well as give you time to study the room. We'll go slow.

"Note what you want collected, and let me be the only one reaching for items. Sometimes perspectives are different looking at something from the side versus direct on. I don't want wires, items leaning against something, or other unintended surprises catching us off guard. Only one of us reaching for items ensures at least two of us are studying what is going to be moved before it is touched. I know you'll need items handled to not disturb print recovery."

"Understood," Nathan said.

Will nodded.

Charles laid down the broom so it couldn't fall, slowly pushed open the cabin door, and led the way inside.

૬૭૩   ૬૭૩   ૬૭૩

Bruce parked behind Nathan's squad car. "Rae, stay in the car. You don't have the energy yet to be traipsing out in the woods in the snow getting yourself frozen. The entire area is cordoned off; you won't get a look at the lab even if you tried to get back there."

She pushed her coat around and retrieved her earmuffs from a pocket. "You're beginning to sound less like a partner and more like a mother. I'm coming along to at least talk with the cop that just got transferred over to the county's narcotics task force, Noland Reed. He hasn't started work there yet, but he has been interested in this case and asking me questions about Peggy so he had to look into the matter more once he's over there. Besides, Bruce, I'm going to be so bundled up I'll be sweating anyway."

"He's not going to be able to tell us anything useful." Bruce waited for her to come around the car. "I should have just not called you."

"Right. And you would be missing one partner if you had gotten news like this and not called me." She slid her hand comfortably under his arm. "I'm good."

They headed past vehicles toward the cops ahead.

"Sillman." Rae tugged Bruce's arm and pointed. "Let's go talk to Sillman first."

"You sure?"

She nodded.

Bruce changed directions.

"Is it our guy?" Rae asked as they got close enough to be comfortably heard.

Sillman smiled. "I figured you would be taking it pretty personal about now. Nathan and Will went up to the cabin with the lead HazMat guy about twenty minutes ago. There's no word yet on what they've found."

"I hope this is the place."

"Don't get your hopes up too high. It's probably just the meth lab we've been looking for. But Nathan did look hopeful."

"We'd like to stay."

Sillman shrugged. "Suit yourself. We're going to be staging from here. Food and warmth and hot coffee for the guys are at the top of my work list right now. But if you stay and talk to a reporter, I'll make your life miserable for the next year."

Rae smiled. "I do like you more all the time, Sillman. There's a Gage Collier likely to show up when this hits the rumor mill in town."

"As reporters go, he's tolerable. He's in town?"

Rae nodded.

"Figures." Sillman looked around and pointed. "You might want to move the car back that direction and park so you're facing back to town. We'll be crowded here soon."

Bruce pulled out his keys. "Thanks."

"If you weren't here where I could see you, I'd just be wondering where you were and what you were getting into. And it's too bloody cold today to be wondering about much of anything."

Bruce laughed. "I hear you." He pointed at Rae. "Watch her for me. She's being particularly pushy today."

"My pleasure." Sillman pointed to a truck. "That one is mine; you'll find a coffee thermos in the backseat if you're interested. Once it goes cold, no one is going to want to touch it, so help yourself."

"Thanks." Rae headed toward it.

ʃʟʃ   ʃʟʃ   ʃʟʃ

Nathan felt more claustrophobic than he had expected as he tried to walk in the cabin in the confining protective suit without brushing against anything. It was a crowded cabin with only a narrow walkway around the table in the center of the room; the walls had been filled in with built-in workbenches and counters and shelves. What had once been room for furniture had been gutted out and made a work area.

"There's a notebook open on the table." Will pointed.

"I see it. And more notebooks on the shelf." Nathan counted and saw eight composition books.

"You want them?" Charles asked.

There was only so much they would be able to carry out of here on what might be their only trip inside for a while—Nathan nodded and Charles carefully took the books off the shelf and handed them back to be slid into plastic sleeves.

Nathan tried to absorb what he was seeing. The number of jars, bottles, canisters, and small bowls across the tables bothered him. The stove top had been well used, pans stacked on the counter beside it. The sink had a brownish stain going deep into the porcelain. He was surprised there was no obvious smell.

"There, on the counter under that window. There's a BlackBerry—it looks out of place with the rest of this. Peggy Worth's BlackBerry maybe?"

"That would fit." Nathan pointed it out for Charles to retrieve for them.

"The lack of electronics is probably deliberate—even a power source warming up in a PC would be enough to explode some of the more volatile fumes if they were not careful about how they ventilated this place. Beside the fact you wouldn't want the sound of a radio or computer game traveling on cold night air and advertising your presence," Charles noted. "I'm seeing only the most rudimentary safety precautions have been taken in here. There's not even a fume hood. Our guy looks to have some chemistry sophistication but not much in basic laboratory work."

"Two or three people were working in here," Nathan guessed.

Charles nodded. "Probably one person supervising a couple of others. I'm seeing a lot of transition type work—heating, cooling, crushing, sifting—and it's getting down to some pretty precise measurements. That digital scale—you're talking precision on small weights to a thousandths of a milligram—it's an unwelcome accuracy in all but the most pristine environments. In this place it's way out of place.

"He spent five figures on the scale and didn't spend fifty dollars on some PVC pipe and a sheet of aluminum pounded into a fume hood. He cares about being very precise, but he's also very narrowly focused. This is probably not a guy that got his hands dirty in shop class."

"Any idea what the final product was?"

"About the only thing I can tell you is it likely left here in powder form. If it were leaving as a liquid, I think I'd be seeing a box of new vials to transport it in—something equally as pristine as he was trying for in his weighing. And I don't see the press I would expect to see for a tablet or pill final staging work."

"A powder is the most versatile."

Will carefully knelt where he stood to look under the table. "These are tile-plant cans, Nathan." He pointed under the workbench. "And those are tile-plant boxes. Someone who works for the tile plant is our cook?"

Without touching it, Nathan studied the contents of the one open can near him, careful to not lean over it and peer down, but look in at an angle. He read the label on the can. "Definitely not gravel, pea-size grade. Do these look like precursor chemicals to you?"

Charles looked. He nodded. "The coffee filters being used to stack the powder—that's common for the more pure stuff being sold by weight. Whatever is in that particular can probably has a street price of five figures or more."

"They were using the tile plant to get the raw ingredients they needed shipped in and out," Will speculated.

"Or the discarded cans in the plant's Dumpster came in handy as they needed storage," Nathan replied. "You're not going to go to the hardware store in town and buy twelve empty paint cans without getting questions asked about what the cans are for."

"They could be innocently here or not."

Nathan nodded. He looked at the number of cans and boxes with tile-plant labels on them. "Let's write down the lot numbers from these cans and run them back through the plant paperwork. If they are old lot numbers, I lean to discards being reused. If they are new lot numbers, someone working for the plant has been using their shipping department as his own private transit point. I just don't want to think we caught a break when what we really caught was a Dumpster behind the plant being used for supplies."

Will began to write down lot numbers, awkwardly holding his pen with the protective gloves still on. "Do you want to hold off entering the tile plant to check until we know more about this place?"

"Whoever was working here knows the kid is dead. They already know they need to get out of town. It's best to chase every lead we can as swiftly as we can."

Nathan looked at Charles. "What else here is worth noting?"

"Over here, on the side table. You'll want to see this too."

38

Rae perched on the tailgate of Sillman's truck, holding a cup of coffee to keep her hands warm. Bruce walked over with Nathan to join her.

"Nathan?" She looked at him, hopeful.

"You're already in far enough on this case I'm going to bend every rule of the game I know and talk to you two. Will, Sillman, come join us."

Will walked over, still wiping disinfectant rags across his jacket sleeves.

"You think this is the lab he's been using?"

Will nodded. "We're certain of it. Peggy's BlackBerry was discovered inside. This is our guy."

"Her BlackBerry—that makes sense. He wanted to know what she had found out about him."

"I turned it on. It's password protected for the notepad section. You can see her address and phone numbers, but I doubt he got to the rest of it."

"I think the password is vanilla-rich; it's worth a try at least."

"Thanks, that will help."

Rae looked at Nathan. "What else?"

"We've got composition notebooks that look like formula books. Eight of them, and some date quite a few years back. Nothing in them looks particularly recent, but it's something Franklin can explore."

"He took the current one with him."

"Looks like it."

"Did he leave any leads for who this guy is or how the drug is being given without our knowing it's happening?"

"All we saw in the cabin were powders and liquids, nothing that looked wrapped or packaged or prepared like pills. For all I can tell he may be changing the delivery method every time—one of you got it in a drink, one in something you ate, another through something you touched—it's impossible to know if it requires a particular form to be effective or if it's just the amount of it you get that matters."

"I hadn't thought of that. You're right. It could be different in every case, based on what was available to put it in," Rae replied, surprised she hadn't realized that before.

"There are also both paint-sized cans and boxes from the tile plant. What's inside them doesn't match the label on the outside," Will told them.

Bruce straightened from leaning against the truck. "The tile plant—that's a big deal."

"Maybe it's an innocent connection and someone is reusing their cast-off materials," Nathan said. "Or maybe the tile plant is being used as a cover for incoming raw source materials and later shipment of the drug powder out. If that's the case, then either the cook or someone he is working with works at the tile plant."

"You're heading there now?"

"As soon as the warrants come through," Nathan confirmed. "I don't know what we're looking for yet, but we'll start by tracing the lot numbers on these cans and figure out if they are something that was already tossed in the Dumpster, or if the lot of materials had just arrived at the plant and these cans were recently smuggled out with their contraband contents."

"That's got to be it, Nathan. We were trying to figure out where he was shopping for his raw materials. He was having them shipped into him."

"Maybe."

"The boy. Do you know who it is who died?"

Sillman looked at Nathan.

Nathan shrugged. "Go ahead and tell them, Gray. I doubt the name means any more to them than it did to us, but I've been wrong before."

"His name is Tim Pliner, a high school kid from the next town over. He cuts school regularly, and his mom didn't pursue it after she got the call from the school yesterday. When he didn't come home last night—she sounded like she really thought he had run away and that would have been a good thing."

"Ouch."

"Does his identity help us out?" Bruce asked.

"Not much, I'm afraid," Sillman guessed. "We'll push his friends hard to get what names we can, but he was probably trying to keep this job his secret. Talk to friends about this place; they know they can hit him up for cash or drugs. But maybe a friend saw Tim with someone and we can get a description to work with."

"Could we go back and see the cabin?" Rae asked.

Nathan shook his head. "It's as hazardous as anything I've ever seen before. It will be a while before we can start even the normal process of dusting for prints and looking at papers. My suggestion is you go back to town."

Rae smiled.

Nathan smiled back. "My second suggestion is you find someone willing to keep you supplied in that coffee and you stick around out here to see what might change as the day wears on. I don't mind you providing good ideas."

"You'll continue to share enough info we might be able to be helpful?"

"Almost victim four means I think you have a right to know some of this as we learn it. That's as far as I'm going until I know more about what happened back there or where the tile-plant connection might lead us."

"Deal." She even held out her hand to make it official.

ॐ ॐ ॐ

Nathan walked over to join Rae. "I'm heading into town."

"Your warrants have come through?" From her perch on Sillman's truck tailgate, she leaned back and caught a bag of supplies. She offered him a dry pair of gloves.

He gratefully swapped them out. "Will is walking around the papers now. He'll have what we need by the time I get there. I want to hear what you and Sillman have been thinking up before I leave. You've been thick as thieves over here."

"We're just comparing notes."

"Hold still." He lifted her foot and set her boot against his coat. He retied her dragging laces. "So start at the top and give me the highlights. I like highlights."

"Do the other one too, please."

He obliged.

"A reasonable guess: one or two boxes or cans, specially marked, hidden in a warehouse of stuff coming and going isn't going to surprise me. Those tile-plant trucks go all over the state—it's a perfect distribution point for some drug ring to have developed for just their traditional drug shipments, not just this."

"Agreed."

"That means someone involved in this works at the plant, at least enough to smuggle out those cans for cash. I lean toward them not knowing what they are actually moving, or thinking it's something like meth production that they may have been involved with before."

"So I'm not searching for a chemist working at the tile plant, but someone who probably unloads the trucks and moves around pallets of materials. What else?"

"The kid who died—he's from another town. That suggests they intentionally didn't want someone local helping them. And they wouldn't use someone totally green at this level of a place. You'll probably find a history of the kid working at a meth lab or some other drug connection which is how he got selected to be here."

"You're saying *they* rather than *he*."

"There might be one guy in charge, but there are partners in this, Nathan. Sillman is the one that pointed that out. Every time we get a lead to tug on, it points to more people. A single cook working on his own doesn't bring in someone this young to be his first helper. The tile-plant connection—our cook is not working out here, keeping a full-time job at the plant and testing the drug. Just the fact we haven't been able to identify a common person or way the drugs got to the victims—it was probably more than one person involved with Nella, Peggy, Karen, and I rather than one person getting to all of us. We didn't spot a common pattern because the group behind this is the pattern, not an individual."

"You're convincing me. It's reasonable."

Rae rubbed her arms. "You've got to look at the pharmacists again, Walter Jr., his son Scott, and Walter Sr. Those notebooks were the precise notes of someone reformulating and tweaking his product."

"I already am," Nathan assured quietly. "But I know at least Walter Jr.'s handwriting by sight, and I didn't recognize what was in those composition books. What else?"

"If there is someone at the tile plant, he would have been working there at least a couple years to know the system well enough to safely smuggle those shipments through. I doubt it is something which started in the last few months. It's probably been going on for years."

Nathan felt his phone vibrate in his inside pocket where he'd tucked it to keep warm. He pulled it out, looked at the incoming number, and took the call. "Yes, Will. You've got the warrants?"

"In my hand. But there's other trouble here. Word just came from Zachary. Corporate rejected the contract deal. The tile plant is being shut down effective Friday night, midnight."

Nathan felt like someone had just kicked his heart out of him. "Say that again."

"Tomorrow, Nathan. It never reopens. Zachary gave us as much of a heads-up as he could, but he's got to call Adam now. Word is going to move fast."

"Head to the plant; you're in charge until I get there. Arrest people if you have to, disperse the union line, anything that seems warranted to keep the situation under control. I'm on my way with lots of backup."

Nathan hung up on Will. "Gray!" He waved over Sillman.

Rae slid off the truck tailgate and put her hand on his arm.

Nathan looked at her, not knowing what to say but to just say it. "The draft contract was rejected; the tile plant is closing."

320 BEFORE I WAKE

"Oh, no."

"Get Bruce. I need a favor."

Rae nodded and headed toward the officers by the warming tent to find him.

Nathan pulled a number out of his pocket and called the Brentwood chief of police.

39

News of the plant closing surged through the union lines. People were streaming into the area from around the town, not all of them directly tied to union members, but coming to show their support. The crowd was well past the hundred mark in size and looked on its way to several hundred.

Nathan pushed through the crowd that surrounded his car and got through to the van where his chief deputy had set up station.

Will muted his handset and leaned over to be heard. "We'll never get that bus safely out of there tonight. The back gate looks like another smaller version of this crowd."

"Tell the guys inside the plant to just sit tight until further notice. I don't want any movement through that gate right now."

Will relayed the order to the security chief inside.

"He says they've voted to extend their workday another hour of overtime rather than just sit idle and wait, but he wants to talk with you on an exit plan."

Nathan nodded. He scanned the street. "We disperse that line and we end up with clusters of men around this town to worry about. For now it's better to keep the union guys gathering in an area where we know where they are. We'll take the strikebreakers out of here in squad cars later if we have to. Let's just keep the sides apart and let people vent."

"I like that idea better than trying to wade into that crowd to ask them politely to leave the area. We've had guys trying to climb the fence and get into the plant grounds, but otherwise the lines are staying apart."

"Where's Adam?"

"I last saw him down by the main gate. You'll hear him on a bullhorn occasionally. He's been repeating the news as Zachary gave it to him, trying to dispel rumors that wash through this crowd with every new group of people who arrive.

"Adam said it's not all bad news. Zachary got a severance plan approved that covers all employees. That's the two-sentence summary Adam had time to convey before they started shoving his car around. I'm hoping there are enough details it can temper a bit of this initial shock. But guys are taking this hard, Nathan. I saw some of the twenty-plus-year guys start to cry when word first passed along the line. This gets worse tonight before it ever gets better."

Nathan agreed with that prediction. "Brentwood is sending over a dozen officers. I'm reassigning all but six of Chet's guys to you here; I'll have the others pair up with some of the Brentwood guys and handle patrols in town for the night. State will take the highways for us as well as all nonemergency calls we'd normally assist on."

"Good. Every extra hand is going to help."

"Let's start making it uncomfortable for more people to reach here. We'll start with closing the side streets. We can at least discourage the spectator crowd. It's cold and high stress—so let's also get some hospital people down here just in case they are needed."

Sillman joined them in time to overhear the last part. "Let's use the cold to our advantage and get the community center open. People are looking for information; let's try and oblige. We'll advertise a community meeting to begin at the top of the hour. The mayor can work some magic on holding people over there rather than here on the street. Adam can talk after the mayor does, and we can make some rapid announcements on assistance plans. Anything to keep people together and talking, rather than acting rashly."

"Great idea. Find the mayor and make that happen."

Sillman nodded and disappeared back into the crowd.

"What about the warrants for the tile plant?" Will tugged them from his inside jacket pocket.

Nathan hesitated but then looked at the plant. "We've got no choice but to serve them today. Who knows what those strikebreakers have been told their job assignments are for this last twenty-four hours. It's a hard close down of the plant. They may be planning to literally empty the warehouse into trucks or clear all the office paperwork to be shipped out. The last thing we need is our evidence disappearing on us or being so corrupted by handling, the defense team walks right over us and gets it tossed out of court."

"Do you want to hand it off to Brentwood officers?"

"No. As soon as the Brentwood guys get here, you and I are handling the warrants. Chet and Sillman are tough enough on crowd control to manage this while we're inside. Find five guys you think are good at working under this kind of pressure and get them ready to go in.

"I'm going to find Adam and Larry and privately alert them to what we found today. I think we'll be okay for controlling this if we can split part of the group away to the community center, and the rest that stay here see cops heading into the plant in numbers. I won't discourage the rumor that we're serving a warrant. If they speculate we're seizing financial documents from the plant, we won't correct it until we're done with the search."

Will nodded. "I'm fine with that."

Nathan found himself admitted to the union crowd but not welcomed. It was the first time he'd seen anger in the faces of townsfolk directed at him. He bore the stares and the abrupt words cut off when he arrived and made his way through toward Adam and Larry.

The union chief came to meet him with an outstretched hand. "Nathan."

"How are you holding up, Adam?"

"I'm sick to my gut. I knew it was coming, but I didn't want to believe it would ever happen."

Nathan put his arm around the man and pointed to the porch of a nearby house. He knew the home belonged to one of the union's rank and file. "Come on. Let's talk."

Adam walked with him, and the crowd parted to let them step away.

"There's been threats to Zachary's home, the plant itself, talk of lawsuits against the corporation," Adam said heavily, taking a seat on the porch chair.

"I already anticipated that. There are officers doing what they can to protect both property and family members. Will you speak at a community meeting if we get it arranged for the top of the hour?"

"Yes. That's a good idea."

"I'm sorry for all of this."

"So am I." Adam struggled to find words and then just shook his head. "It's a blow."

"We'll get through this one day at a time. It won't be the first time the town has rallied from trouble; it won't be the last."

"Larry and I, we'll do what we can to help."

"The guys have never needed your leadership more; I'm glad you're there for them, Adam. It's going to make a difference."

"I hope so. You've got other news. I knew when I first saw Will that he was only half hearing me."

"We found a drug lab and a dead teenager."

Adam closed his eyes and rubbed them. "It does put this in perspective. It's just a job, despite all the emotion we invest in it."

"It's a livelihood. A different weight than life or death, but still as important."

"This lab explains the deaths in town? The ladies at the hotels?"

"I'm hoping it does once we sort it out."

"Why did you tell me?"

"I'm serving warrants on the tile plant in a few minutes. We're looking for some contraband that may have shipped through using the tile company trucks and been smuggled out of the warehouse once it arrived."

Adam looked at him, devastated. "One of my guys?"

"I don't know. I won't catch you with a second surprise today, Adam. I'm looking first to see where the lot numbers we found fit into the timeline at the plant. Then I'll look for who might have had a hand in those cans leaving the plant."

"The warehouse guys—they turn over more often than any other group at the plant. Most are newcomers, with less than two years at the plant. They move on whenever they spot a less physically demanding job elsewhere."

"Okay. That kind of information will help." Nathan looked at the crowd on the street. "Do you want me to do anything particular in regards to how we handle this tonight?"

"We need to take this in the opposite direction from what it is heading now. Pizza, hot dogs, soft drinks—let's push so much food and conversation at folks they end up wanting to go home, because they've been taken care of today with someone just willing to offer an arm around their shoulders and a recognition they just got badly hurt. The town is in this together—that's got to be the message right now."

Relief made Nathan smile. "A very good idea. And I know just the guy to help make that happen fast. Henry."

"Yes. That's perfect. Henry and your dad—folks will see them as the town's elder statesmen and it will mean something coming from them."

"Spread the word about a community meeting at the top of the hour. By the time you get that message out, Henry will have food and drinks arriving, both here and at the community center."

Nathan walked with Adam back to the union gathering, and then he headed back to the police staging point, on the phone to his grandfather as he walked.

40

Once Nathan was satisfied the Brentwood officers were paired into assignments with his officers and that Chet and Sillman were on top of the crowd management plan, he rejoined Will. "Are we ready to go on the warrants?"

Will nodded to the officers with him. "Yes. These are the guys."

"How many people are inside the plant?"

"Counting security guards, thirty-eight total. How do you want to handle this?"

"Let's move people out of the office area and out of the warehouse area and assemble everyone in the cafeteria. The people inside the plant that are of the most concern to us are not the strikebreakers, but those who normally work here—people in management, the security guards, and there was one union guy that crossed, Isaac Keif. Let's make sure we quickly account for every one of those people. The last thing we need is someone inside destroying evidence on us."

Will looked around at the assembled officers. "Noland, you and Tom take the warehouse area. Ben and Dan, you've got the offices. Jim, round up the security guards and bring them inside. There are enough cops on the fence perimeter to handle that outside security. I want thirty-eight people in the cafeteria five minutes after we cross through that gate. I don't expect trouble, but I want you to all go in prepared for it. Assignments clear?"

At the nods around the group, Nathan stepped away and headed toward the locked plant gate. He could feel the union focus on his back as they tried to decide if he was arranging to bring that idling bus through with strikebreakers aboard. He felt like a target. It wasn't a comfortable feeling.

The security guard opened the gate for him. Nathan cleared his five officers in and followed Will toward the plant.

"This is crazy, Nathan. Search warrants?"

"Just read them and stand aside, Logan. They were signed by the judge this afternoon." The temporary plant manager was more than just flustered and Nathan didn't want to deal with him. Even under the best of circumstances he had a hard time getting along with the guy.

"But what are you looking for? This doesn't make sense."

"Exactly what it says. Inventory records and warehouse materials."

Will came to rejoin them. Nathan was grateful for a chance to step away from the conversation he didn't want to have.

"We've got people assembled in the cafeteria. Everyone is accounted for on my list except for the union guy, Isaac Keif."

"Did he cross the line this morning?"

"The warehouse supervisor says yes. But there's a good chance Isaac just walked out as word spread the contract was rejected and the plant was closing. No one remembers seeing him in the last hour."

"Adam may know if he just left the plant. Let me check with him before we focus in on Isaac as our plant employee of interest. He works in the warehouse, but I would have put him low on my list of names to wonder about."

"Tom is stationed at the cafeteria door. I've got Noland focusing on the office paperwork and the others working the warehouse. Twenty minutes, Nathan. They keep the warehouse shipments housed in sequential lot order. We'll know quickly if our lot numbers are from a recent shipment."

"Good. I'll have an answer on Isaac by then. Are you okay in here if I step out?"

"Yes. I'll just escort Logan to the cafeteria now, then go back to supervising."

Nathan shared a private smile with Will and then headed back out of the building to find Adam.

Isaac might have crossed the strike line, but he wasn't going to stay inside the plant after he heard the news the plant was closing. And he wouldn't be on the strike line now near union folks he had betrayed. But maybe Adam could find out if someone had seen him leave the plant. If not, Nathan would send an officer he couldn't spare to check Isaac's apartment and see if he had returned there. It wasn't the first name he thought he'd have to track down before the day was over. He just hoped there weren't too many false trails to follow before he found the one he was hunting to find.

Bruce and Rae were helping his grandfather. Nathan spotted them down the street on the far side, passing out what looked like soda cans to folks. A makeshift tent, blue canopy fluttering in the mild breeze, was now open in the center of the street, and he was seeing the first signs of people carrying plates with them. The first of the food was beginning to flow.

He spotted Adam and changed course to meet up with him. "Adam, I'm looking for Isaac Keif. Do you have any ideas where he might be?"

"He wouldn't be staying around this crowd, not after having crossed the line."

"Did he leave the plant earlier today? That's what I'm most interested in knowing."

"Larry—ask around, see if anyone saw Isaac leave the plant grounds as word spread the plant was closing."

"I'll check. But he must have, Nathan. I didn't see his car down at the lot and it was there this morning. I worried about it enough I wanted to make sure he didn't come back to find himself missing four tires or something else rash on the part of the other union guys."

"Good to know. I just need confirmation that someone saw him leave the plant."

Larry nodded and began to make his way through the clusters of people to see who had useful information.

"Have you found anything concerning you inside the plant?" Adam asked quietly.

Nathan shook his head. "We're just beginning the search. But if we do find something and need to locate any more suspicious material remaining in the plant, how much are we looking at having to open and inspect to answer that question?"

"They aren't going to leave the one can they are trying to hide sitting out as the top can in the pallet. You'll spend most of the time with a forklift moving items around to reach what you want to inspect. It would take half a dozen guys a week to do the job if you wanted to open and look at everything."

"That's what I feared."

A rifle retort cracked. Nathan flinched. Concrete slapped beside them.

"Get down!" He pushed Adam to the ground and shoved him toward the protection of a nearby car.

A second shot slammed into the concrete beside them, sending up a puff of white powder and stinging bits of broken concrete.

People screamed. Scattered. Some tried to drop and crawl for cover.

Two more shots in a rapid beat slammed into the squad car down from him and popped window glass like it was a piece of ice.

"Inside! The shots are coming from inside the plant."

Nathan jerked around at the shouted words and saw an officer waving frantically and pointed to the southwest corner of the plant building.

"The first two weren't from inside the plant! Those were incoming from north of here," he yelled back. Should he force Adam to move? Which side gave better cover for this?

Another shot slapped into the concrete and that one Nathan tracked. "That originated inside the plant! Two shooters. We've definitely got two shooters!"

He scrambled to push Adam back toward safer protection. "Clear this street, however you have to do it. Move!"

There were civilians all over the line of fire.

Nathan ran toward the first exposed group, as officers along the street realized the danger and began to rise and scramble toward those near them.

Nathan's heart sang with stress as he put his body between where he thought the south shooter was and the lady he reached first. "Let's go, Ma'am. The house porch. Head to the house porch and just keep going right on inside. Don't even think of pausing to knock."

The man beside her was already rising and grabbing her hand. They paired up and were moving. Nathan pulled a child past them into his grasp and handed her off to another officer to carry.

People on the street began to rise and run toward safer hiding places. Nathan kept waiting for the first civilian to fall with blood on them. As he ran he counted numbers and knew they were going to lose someone. They had a good sixty people exposed to the shooting angles.

The bus within the tile plant began to move.

Nathan realized what was happening a moment before the bus began to roll toward the gate and he darted for the swinging gate now unlocked to throw it open before the bus had to ram it to get through. Metal scraped paint as the bus cornered and struck the post.

Bruce was driving the bus.

Nathan didn't ask how he'd gotten inside the plant or if he knew how to even drive something this size. He ran for the first group of people to his right. "Use the bus for cover! Get behind it and clear the street."

He felt a ray of hope that they would get this done. A shot picked up his left arm at the elbow and slammed it forward into the side of a van.

41

"Stay still. The bus is covering us."

Sillman had something in his mouth muffling his order and Nathan realized it was the tie Sillman wore but liked to complain about. "Stay with me, Sheriff. That's an order." Sillman wrenched the fabric tight as a tourniquet. Nathan refused to scream, but it came close.

"Will. Answer me!" Sillman ordered over the radio.

"We don't have him. We're sweeping the place, but we don't have him."

"Nathan's down."

"Bad?"

"Bad enough. The bullet went through his arm, and the elbow is at best dislocated. Any ideas on the rifle?"

"Has to be a team. One inside, one outside. Chet's going to silence that rifle one way or another."

"Get me up," Nathan found the breath to order. "Get me on that bus. They need you running this, not handling me now."

"You sure?"

"You've got to get manpower in there sufficient to sweep that tile plant. Find the inside shooter, and he'll tell you who the outside shooter is."

Sillman nodded. "We'll get it done. On three, Boss. This is going to hurt something awful."

"A fitting end for this day. Who else is bleeding now?"

"They just started with the sheriff."

"It's nice to be popular. On three." Nathan tried to position his good hand to help.

Sillman counted it down and then ignored the cry of hurt and got Nathan standing.

Walking those steps into the bus wasn't going to be as easy as he had hoped. Ten seconds later Bruce had hold of his belt and Sillman had his back and he was being lifted aboard.

Rae was driving now, but from a seat on the floor, her head barely visible over the dash when she raised up to see where she was going.

Nathan hung on to the pole behind the driver's seat and collapsed his body into the closest seats.

"Idle it," Sillman ordered Rae. "Let me get officers moved up, then slow roll back into the plant and take us right to the door. We're flushing that shooter inside the plant; at the same time we're covering strikebreakers to get them out of there and onto this bus. Good?"

"Good," Rae guaranteed.

Nathan watched her strain to see around Bruce and see how badly he was hurt. "I'll be fine. All this fussing," he whispered.

Bruce just pushed him lower than the windows and grabbed his watch to time the tourniquet. It had to loosen every minute so blood flow to his hand would survive this even as they tried to stop him from bleeding out.

"The shot went straight through the back of my arm and tossed it forward. It's dislocated, not shattered," he repeated with grim certainty what he hoped, not willing to look and know it was worse than that.

"The doctors will tell us that soon."

Nathan fought the reality he was going to throw up. The pain wasn't in this stratosphere for being controllable. "We have to get more help to Chet, trying to find that shooter with the rifle."

"You've got good men working the problems. Let them work," Bruce replied. He leaned over and changed the pressure of the tie.

Nathan shivered with his coat now partly off and the bus even idling not able to keep it more than about mid-fifties in here.

"Go," Sillman ordered through the open bus door.

The bus lurched forward. "Sorry!" Rae shifted her foot on the gas pedal and the bus began to roll more smoothly.

"The street sign—" Bruce warned. She rolled the bus over it. "Never mind."

She flinched as a bullet struck a back window and the bus scraped the fence gate on the driver's side.

Sillman managed to step up into the rolling bus, crouching on the floor below the window line. "Good. Good. Stay right; put it right into that brick entry."

The officers using the bus for cover slapped the side.

"Stop it now."

Rae shoved on the brake and threw the gears into park.

"Three teams, sweep this building! Stay on the radios and call it out. I've got the center hall and stairs," Sillman ordered.

Will was ready and waiting. They surged people on the bus, cops pushing men across the six feet from the plant door and onto the bus stairs. "Stay low. Get to the back."

Will stepped aboard after his last officers. "That's thirty-eight less Isaac Keif. Back it out of here."

Gunshots erupted inside the plant. Rae threw the bus in reverse and drove without caring about what she hit on the way back out.

"Right there, Rae. Good. Pull the keys." Bruce swung himself off the bus as it came to a stop. Nathan forced himself up to his feet, determined to join him. Will grabbed his good side. "This isn't a good idea."

"None of this is."

Will grimly smiled at that terse reply but half carried him down the steps of the bus.

Adam ran to join them. "We're running headcounts via shouts between houses and cell-phone calls. I can put my hands on all my men except Isaac Keif. Management is down to searching for four names besides the guys on the bus."

Nathan got his good hand on his radio and fought to focus. *Five minutes, Jesus, that's all I need. Five minutes of focus; please. My guys need me.* He sucked in a breath and depressed the button. "Chet? What are you finding?"

"Our rifleman is rapidly losing places to hide. Flush the one inside; we'll corner this one."

"Sillman?"

"Good to hear your voice. We've exchanged gunfire with this guy twice; he's getting pushed toward the back side of the plant. Five shots at us didn't hit anyone, but I don't think we got lucky enough to hit him either. "

The county bomb squad van rolled past them, one of their officers with the driver directing him. It would be enough armor protection for the cops searching the plant to get safely back out if necessary.

"Don't take chances. There's more help moving up to join you, and safe transportation out of there is coming in now." Nathan watched the van enter the plant grounds and stop by the same door they had used.

"I hear you," Sillman agreed. "We'll get this guy."

Nathan nodded and looked at his deputy chief. "Will, we need to get the people on this bus to the courthouse, where we can keep them together under the safety of security and get the interviews of what happened in the plant. But I need this bus staying here to help us shield folks. Find us other transportation?"

Will nodded and called into the dispatcher.

Nathan struggled to sort out next steps after pinning the shooters. Isaac Keif, that was one of the missing. He looked to the union chief. "Adam, you said four were unaccounted for on the management side. Do you have those names?"

A piercing alarm from the plant shattered the afternoon. The circling sound vibrated the bus windows as it passed over.

"Fire! We've got fire in the plant."

Nathan managed three steps toward the front of the bus, leaning his good hand against it for balance, to see for himself. White smoke circled up into the air above the south side of the plant. Even as he watched, it thickened and began to puff up in small mushroom bursts. The warehouse area was burning.

"Whatever evidence is in there, it's going up in smoke," Will said quietly beside him. "Which is exactly what they wanted with all this shooting. Time to destroy the evidence."

Nathan watched the rising smoke and felt personally numb. "We were close, Will. We were ever so close to having the proof."

"One inside the plant and one outside. Two names, and we still have them. Destroying evidence doesn't end this."

The fire chief scrambled forward, running low along the line of cars to reach them.

"If we can get those shooters stopped, can you contain the fire?" Nathan asked urgently.

"Automatic building fire suppression is going to dump and smother in the next minute; that's the warning alarm sounding now. If it doesn't do the job—there are too many chemical vats in there for us to stop the explosions once they start. Ten minutes, Nathan. We'll know if we're going to lose the entire plant or not in about ten minutes."

Sillman appeared near the bomb squad van, not bothering to try and be heard on the radio over this piercing alarm. He signaled hands down. They didn't have the shooter. He started slapping shoulders, counting men, as he pulled his guys out.

"Hurry, buddy," Nathan whispered, watching them.

He looked at Will. "Assume the worst and we're going to lose it; how many blocks have to evacuate with a fire?"

"Two upwind, four downwind on this side. The high school can receive."

"Put every officer on it except for those Chet has working to pin down the rifleman. Nothing else is higher priority. Get this place evacuated."

Nathan swayed and Will grabbed his good shoulder. "I'll handle the pull-out. You're going down for medical attention right now."

The ground was beginning to turn on him. Nathan knew he didn't have a choice in the matter. "Sorry, Will. I'm leaving you a mess."

"Good thing I'm prepared to clean it up then."

Nathan could see paramedics and one of the emergency-room doctors rushing up the street to join them. He'd be poked and prodded and stuck before long. He favored living with the pain a few more minutes. He staggered without a choice and Bruce moved him to sit down on the snowy ground. Nathan sat and looked at the blood dripping off his hand.

His arm was a mess.

When the paramedics took scissors to the sleeve two minutes later he saw just how bad a mess. He tried to joke about it with the lead paramedic but didn't even rate a smile from the guy at the humor. Nathan looked away from their work.

Rae was sitting on the bus steps, watching him be an idiot.

He tried his smile out on her, but she just rested her chin on her hands and watched the paramedics work. She didn't have a coat on anymore. She had to be cold.

"Where's your coat?"

"Don't know."

She didn't sound like she cared.

"How did you and Bruce get into the tile plant to reach the bus?"

"Picked the lock."

"Picked the lock, while under fire."

She just nodded. "Sometimes I'm an idiot too."

He laughed. He tried to find a reply to that and realized there wasn't a good enough one available.

He watched the doctor try to deal with a dislocated elbow and a bullet hole and thought about what it would be like to have the sheriff pass out on the town street during treatment. He could mentally feel himself losing focus, rather fascinated by the sensation, as he realized he was heading toward passing out.

"We need to get you to the hospital to deal with this."

"No. You can have me all you want tomorrow to fix it, but today I stay put. So just do what you can."

"It's a clean dislocation, and I can deal with it here. But I strongly advise against this. It's going to *really* hurt," the doctor warned.

Nathan just closed his eyes and nodded.

The doctor put his elbow back in place.

Nathan threw up.

He thought it was the pain exploding at first, the noise that reverberated through his head as he retched; then he heard the second blast. The tile plant began to shower pieces of metal down on the street.

42

Nathan shifted soda cans around on the ground to find one still unopened. The number of dropped cans in the snow as people darted for cover had left him with several very cold ones to choose from. He selected an orange one and opened it with one hand. His head felt clearer and he was finally beginning to feel like he was getting his bearings back, even if he'd never been out of the loop for more than twenty minutes since this crisis began.

"We've got the second shooter's perch," Chet radioed in. "He was on the rise firing down into the street. We've got casings."

"Any witnesses? Anyone see the guy come or go?"

"Not so far. We're still canvassing."

"It's still a great find. Get dogs up there; let's use anything we can to track where he went."

"Gladly."

The wind changed and thick dark smoke puffed down to street level again. Nathan used his temporary sling to breathe through the fabric until the wind shifted again and clean, cold air reappeared.

What was still standing of the tile plant was a smoldering mess. They still had no idea who their inside shooter was, or if he had gotten out of the building in time. The shootings had stopped rather than been stopped.

He pushed through the pain in his arm, bandaged enough to get him through to probable surgery later tomorrow, and he kept up his walk along the road, stopping to talk with people he passed. He joined the fire chief at the back of the smaller of the town's three engines. "What are you thinking as a plan for the night?"

"We'll maintain a perimeter to make sure we stay on top of any embers flowing out in this wind and kicking up secondary fires. I've got crews sorting out assignments and areas now. But we basically wait it out."

"Do you think Isaac is dead in there?"

"I'm hoping you'll be able to tell me that before the search begins tomorrow. It will be morning before I want investigators walking those grounds. But we already know what they are going to find. Arson. The fire started in the warehouse area by a guy who knew what to light up to get a fast blaze.

"I don't think whoever set it realized what that siren meant. I wouldn't have wanted to be near that place when the suppression foam tried to grab the fire and choke it out. For what it's worth, I didn't hear any reports saying there was someone spotted going out the back of the plant."

Nathan didn't know what to think about that observation. He hoped the fact Isaac's car was missing from the lot said he had indeed left the plant earlier in the day as word spread about the closing. Too many officers had been too busy to sort that out yet. He nodded his thanks to the fire chief and moved on to the police staging area.

"Thanks for the help, Luke." Brentwood's chief of police had joined them, along with a second group of his officers, just about the time Nathan was losing what there was left of his breakfast into the snow.

"I'll be glad to have my guys stay on another day."

Nathan considered it and smiled. "I'll appreciate the highway help, but the rest I think we're actually getting back in hand. The plant is gone; the union folks have very little left to fight to save. And my drug problem and unsolved deaths appear to have turned into a manhunt."

"What do you know for certain at this point?" Luke asked.

"I've got a drug lab, with one kid dead out there. I've got cans from this tile plant in that lab. I've got a shooter outside the plant, and another one inside who also likely set the plant fire. I know I'm looking for at least two people and maybe a third who was working at the cabin with the kid. It's a busted-up group now and those guys are running. I doubt they remain in Justice, waiting to be found."

"Whoever has unexpectedly disappeared in the last twenty-four hours is a pretty good place to start the search."

"I've already got one possible name on that list. I'll find the others."

"For what it's worth—I can't remember the last time a town got shot up like this in broad daylight, or when a business closing reverberated so seriously, and I have never even seen a four-alarm fire with explosions going off like clockwork every few minutes. Put all that together in a period of one day—property damage and the one significant injury being the sheriff—that speaks of both a lot of providence and great training among your men."

"It was their finest hour," Nathan agreed, pleased at his friend's observation.

Nathan gestured to the mostly empty street. "It's going to take some time to debrief my guys and figure out everything that happened, but if you wouldn't mind sitting through the summaries, I'd like you and Philip to walk it back through with me and help me figure out what I can learn for next time."

Luke smiled. "'Don't get shot' should sit high on the list." He nodded. I'll be glad to help however I can. But I can give you my initial assessment right here. Your department handled this extraordinarily well. Justice is a peaceful town. Let's get it back that way for you."

"I think the way your thinking." Nathan held out his good hand and shook on it.

"Hey, Rae." Nathan sat down on the porch steps beside her. She'd found her coat sometime in the last couple hours. Or Bruce had found it for her. Her earmuffs were back on and gloves. She looked exhausted. Given she'd been out of the hospital all of a day, it was a wonder she wasn't needing to be re-admitted.

She smiled at him rather than answer.

Adam had set up base in this house, one of his men offering his home for a gathering place, and among the union men was no longer an unwelcoming place for cops to mingle. Shots being fired had changed that equation fast.

Nathan nodded toward the front door. "Bruce inside?"

"Making calls."

"You should go home."

"I'm not interested in a hotel room and watching this on television. The television reporters are all from out of town; they basically don't even know what they are talking about."

He smiled. "I doubt they get many street names right; but importing media does fit the amount of excitement around here today. The town will be talking about today for as many years as it has left in its history."

"The town will survive the plant closing. It has to."

"I hope so."

She looked at his arm. "Do you understand God? Why He allowed this to happen?"

Surprised by the question, Nathan studied her, then eased his good hand around hers and gently squeezed. "Don't worry so much about it. Sometimes life is just awful, and that's the way it is. It doesn't have to reflect so much on God, as just be noted as this is what man is willing to do to his fellow man. It doesn't mean God is like this too."

Rae thought about that and nodded but still looked at him with a question haunting her eyes. "I still don't understand why God lets evil like this exist. It hurts. How can God let us get so hurt if He loves us?"

Nathan felt sick that he didn't have a good answer for her. He was so rarely asked this depth of question and he heard this one and knew it was deeply important to her. "I tell my boys in Sunday school that asking why is like a line that never ends; there is never a point you will have all the answers you need. But if you ask instead who, it gives you a tight circle. A lot of the picture still isn't clear, but it is complete.

"God is good, Rae. Men have free will and often do evil. God has freewill and constantly chooses to do good. That's the difference between us. God is good. Men have a bent toward evil that won't change unless we appeal to God to take us in hand and make us good again. And since only a small fraction of men ever think it worth laying down their will to ask for God's goodness instead, we end up with days like this."

"God not stopping something like this is God being good?"

He so understood the emotion behind that question. He saw violence every day on the job and yet went to church on Sunday to worship God and proclaim Him as good and perfect and loving.

"God is passionate about good happening in this world, not evil. I'm convinced of that. God hates what happened here, Rae, the same way He hates divorce, and He hates injustice. But He won't destroy people to proactively prevent them from doing evil things, nor will He destroy them today after they have done evil things. Not until His great patience has extended to them every chance and opportunity there is to change and become good again."

"I may buy that in my head, Nathan. But it still feels so incredibly cold to the rest of us. He says He loves us, and yet He lets our lives get destroyed by others and seems to do nothing about it. I don't understand God."

Nathan smiled at the depth of that emotion in her voice. "Yeah. I appreciate that level of emotion too. When love your enemies to us sounds impossible, and to God it sounds like the obvious thing to do—it should be obvious how deep is the gulf between man and God. Only someone who is fully good can understand a being who is perfectly good by His very nature.

"It's not a lack of love, God's vast patience. It's not an eternity of this, Rae. He knows days like this badly hurt the innocent, and there will be a day He'll say for the sake of the innocent, 'My patience is eternally over.' Evil around us may last a lifetime, but it won't last past that final judgment. And in the vastness of eternity, these few decades of life will eventually be seen as just the blink of an eye. Evil will cease to be a part of our lives in heaven. Think about that future, and don't worry so much about this one. This life you just live one day at a time and trust God to take you through it.

"God showed up in person in Jesus to say 'I get it; I really do know what is happening here. I feel your pain having lived through it Myself. But trust Me. Eternal life is very different than this.'"

She thought about it and eventually just nodded. "Thanks. I don't necessarily think that solves my problem with today, but at least it wasn't a cardboard answer."

Nathan smiled. "I'm not good at answering adult questions; it's why I stick to ten-year-old boys. They prefer to talk about King David and how he used a sling and a rock to kill Goliath or how he dealt with the lion and bear coming for his sheep."

Rae smiled. "They've got a teacher who is a good role model."

"Let's hope I can be. Sometimes I wonder."

Nathan considered the last of the orange soda and poured it out.

"Where are you heading now?"

He tried to put together a plan. At the moment he was interested in just sitting here. "Will is getting warrants for Isaac Keif's apartment. I've got to find an Andrew Grayson that works for the management side—he hasn't been accounted for yet. The coroner thinks he has some information teased out of those notebooks from the lab that I should hear."

"And tomorrow they operate on your arm."

Nathan grimaced. "I sincerely hope not. But yes, I work tonight, because tomorrow afternoon someone in a white coat is going to be ordering me around and dictating my life."

"I saw Sillman a few minutes ago. He sounds pretty certain the shooters can be found and this can be wrapped up by this weekend."

Nathan smiled. "I pay him to be optimistic." He pushed snow with his boot toe and found another layer of reserve energy. " I've got to go. Anything I can do for you before I disappear?"

"I don't like it when you bleed on me."

"Sorry about that. I don't think I can promise I won't ever do it again."

"I know." She leaned over and kissed his cheek. "Go back to work."

Nathan sat there for a moment considering that. "Okay."

He pushed to his feet, adjusted the sling, and headed back to work. He glanced back when he reached his car and saw her smiling at him. "Okay," he whispered to himself.

43

Will drove them to Isaac's apartment. Nathan scanned the warrant paperwork one last time, then pushed it into his jacket pocket. It would cover the searching of any e-mail or files they could locate as well as personal belongings.

"Isaac was listed in Peggy's notebook," Will pointed out. "He was a friend of Prescott's grandson. He's involved. Why else cross the picket line and risk the wrath of friends, except to get access to a shipment? A day's wages isn't enough to explain his actions. He's most likely our inside shooter."

"I'm leaning that way," Nathan agreed. "But he may have left the plant earlier in the day when news of the closure came down, and that means he might be the outside shooter, or he may simply be the guy picking up a few bucks to move a can out of the building occasionally."

"Are you sure you want it being just the two of us knocking on his door?"

"With vests on and caution, but yes, just the two of us. I'm not having another officer get shot at today. If Isaac is our guy, he'll have split town entirely by now. Who are you thinking for the second shooter?"

Will crossed through downtown and turned into the block where houses had been divided into duplexes and most turned into rental property. "Isaac hasn't been hanging around with anyone in particular that I am aware of; he's either at the tile plant or the chocolate shop or working on his car. It doesn't fit that it is Andrew Grayson—I think the guy just picked up his wife and got away from the trouble for the day, probably went to see family. And if the shooter was involved only because of the drug tie-in and not the strike, then maybe it is someone who doesn't even live in this town." Will parked behind the house they were interested in.

"We just walk up? His entrance is that west door," Will pointed out.

"We just walk up." Nathan confirmed his vest was tight. He pushed open his car door. "Did your wife have words for you about today?"

"Not many. She wanted to know why I hadn't called to tell her I would be missing dinner."

Nathan looked over the roof of the car. "Truly?"

Will smiled. "A standing question with her. When she doesn't mention the fact I missed a meal with her, I'll start to worry about the marriage. She's fine. I don't think she ever thought I was in much danger."

They walked together up the path toward the door.

"She got so many details at the café for what happened; she was telling me facts about who did what that I didn't even know myself. She just said, 'I heard the sheriff got shot' and went on from there to talk about how Mrs. Vernham suddenly had twenty-two people bursting in her front door to take cover and how much excitement that was in her day."

"One of us probably needs to apologize to Mrs. Vernham in the next day or so."

"You got elected," Will pointed out.

"I keep wishing I could forget that," Nathan replied. He turned serious, studying the house they were approaching. He moved into position to the side of the door, waited for Will to get into position, and he reached over and knocked.

They got no answer.

Nathan knocked again. "This is the police. We have a warrant to search these premises."

A neighbor appeared to see what the shouting was about and Nathan pointed him back into his house.

"Kick it in."

Will stepped back and obliged. The door had decent locks but a poor frame, and the wood splintered.

Nathan moved left to sweep the rooms, and Will went right.

"Clear."

"Clear."

"He was back here, at least briefly," Will decided.

"I agree." Nathan could still see the snow tracks that glistened with water leading from the kitchen back to the back bedroom. The signs of someone frantically opening drawers and cupboards were everywhere.

"Clothes are cleared out. The chest is open; the underwear drawer is empty."

"Think he grabbed his bag and got out as fast as he could?"

"I don't see much care taken in the leaving."

Nathan put in a call for Sillman to join them. They would need to sort out anything they could find for where Isaac was heading. A few hours too late, but at least they knew one person they were after.

"What's this?" Will leaned over the beat-up sofa in the living room and then shoved aside the piece of furniture. A sledgehammer rested on the floor, and the wall had a nice hole in it, about knee high. "Stash site."

"I'd say."

Will got down to check out the busted wall with his flashlight. "Cash. More than I've ever seen in one place before." He reached up into the wall and pulled a plastic wrapped bundle out from between the studs. He reached in and found another one.

Nathan walked over to watch. "How much is in there?"

Will tried to get a look into the wall. "Possibly several more bundles. I can't reach that high."

Nathan picked up the one near him and tore through the plastic wrapping. He held one of the dollars up to the light. "Real bills. Security stripe, watermark, and all look like used bills, not new. Isaac must have taken what he could carry and left the rest. Or he took the twenties and left the smaller denominations. This package looks like ones and fives."

"Same with these."

Will picked up the sledgehammer. "What do you think?"

"I'm not planning to leave this kind of thing around for just any officer to watch over. Break it out."

Will put a hole in the wall higher up.

Bundles of money tumbled out to the floor. Nathan got his first real look at the wall as a chunk of drywall flapped out. "Bundles between every stud? What did he do, drywall over a million dollars?"

Will poked his fingers into a gap and tugged more drywall free. "Don't laugh. Inches per bundle times the number of stud openings in a standard wall this length—it's probably more like two million."

"He never spent it around this town."

"I knew the kid was disciplined, helping his dad with the shop as he was and working the part-time job at the plant, but disciplined enough to do this kind of job and just sit on it?"

"Ambitious is more like it. He wanted to make it big by the time he was thirty and the only way not to give himself away in a small town was to be very careful about it."

"He left a lot of money behind."

"I'm betting it's not personally his money. Remember those tile-plant boxes? They fit for holding a couple of these bundles. Isaac was probably receiving in money, storing it, and sending it on for someone else. A money mule."

"Okay. That makes sense. Which means the bundles he took with him might not be his own money, and someone out there is going to be very upset with him when they realize we have this house."

"I'm leaning that way," Nathan agreed. "Let's get a statewide APB out on him."

"Where's he likely to run?" Will asked, tugging more money bundles out of the wall to stack up on the couch.

"I suppose it depends if he's just trying to hide, or if he's trying to leave and get out of the country. His family is mostly around here."

"Do you think his father is involved? The senior Keif?"

"He loves chocolate and that shop. There's never been a suspicion the man was anything but aboveboard. Maybe a bit of this money is keeping the business afloat, but I can't see its source being something known to the father."

"This isn't a new designer drug we're seeing here Nathan. This is an established drug business transit point—cash, drugs, not a small vial of something new they are testing. That may be almost a minor side business of what was really going on here."

"I agree."

Sillman joined them and stepped into the living room. "If you told me about it, I wouldn't have believed it. What is this, his private bank?"

"Sure looks it. I need you to handle this scene, Gray, so Will and I can chase down where this guy is heading."

"I can take it. But you'd better get someone from the DA's office sitting here with me and someone from the bank able to open their vault tonight. This money is real; it's not counterfeit?"

"It's genuine US currency," Will confirmed. "I want to know how he was managing to move this kind of cash around without someone hearing rumors of its existence."

"He was working at a tile plant part-time, he was working for his father at the chocolate shop part-time, and he had a growing large scale drug business forming. This is one enterprising young man," Sillman agreed.

"This kind of cash says he's had a long-term operation going on under our noses. Or at least he's been working for someone else for a long time."

Will put another hole in the wall, then stopped to nod at the money piles. "You have to admit, stopping by restaurants and hotels frequently to refill free chocolate sample baskets is an awful good cover for also meeting customers who are buying drugs from you. Cash transactions, public parking lots, stopping to chat with someone he knows just looking like a chance encounter and social exchange. He was all over this town and no one would question seeing him."

Sillman thought about that. "And working at the tile plant—he could raise the volume of product he could handle just by being able to ship in a case of contraband occasionally instead of just a can or two. Why be involved in a new designer drug? From the look of this he's got a large business already under way."

Nathan pulled down window shades, aware they had residents of the block now beginning to be spectators wondering what was going on at this Keif place. "What do you think? Isaac is the second guy we're after, the facilitator?

For cash he'll move product via the tile plant warehouse; he'll handle the distribution of product to buyers for a cut of the profits. He'll store and ship money around. He's a utility fielder, not someone using his own product. A designer drug isn't his game, but maybe it is someone else's who's in the area and Isaac's just willing to be of help for a price."

"The shots at the tile plant—maybe they were protecting something related to this designer drug. Or maybe it was just to protect a few pounds of pure cocaine still stored in the warehouse."

Nathan knew they could talk it in circles all night, but he had enough to make some judgment calls. "Sillman, let's take apart this place and learn as much as you can about Isaac Keif in the next few hours.

"Will, I need you to talk to the HazMat guys and see how the cabin cleanup is going. See if there is anything which points us more toward who the cook is. What we have so far seems to be just Isaac and the distribution side of this. I'm going to meet up with the coroner and see what he can tell us about this designer drug itself, based on the chemicals being used to make it. As diverting as the tile plant has been today and this find, we need to get focused back on locating this drug designer and stopping him before we get a call about another death. This is cleanup; that designer drug is an imminent threat."

"Give me an hour, and I'll tell you if there is anything like a paper stash in this place that might give you names or dates of who Isaac was working with," Sillman agreed.

Nathan pulled out his keys and hoped he was up to driving. He looked around the living room one more time. "Let's hope the state boys don't want to claim all of this seized cash for their task force. I could fix the department roof with one of those bundles."

Will smiled. "What do you say I stick with Sillman until the DA guy arrives? I'll call for another car to pick me up."

"Very good thinking. I'd hate to have one officer run over by townsfolk hearing there is two million bucks in this apartment. Put high on the list coming up with a way to block that busted front door too."

Sillman laughed but nodded.

Nathan left them to sort it out.

Nathan let himself into the Chapel Detective Agency. Bruce was pushing around papers on Margaret's desk, muttering to himself. Nathan smiled. "I got your call, Bruce. It sounded urgent."

"Rae has something you need to see." He looked up and paused to take a second look. "Man, you look awful."

"I feel worse."

"She's back in her office. I'll join you if I can ever find this phone number."

Nathan remembered carrying in Rae's new desk. He didn't think he could lift so much as her lamp right now, but he did appreciate the fact her office furniture was beautiful and new. With blood dried on his jeans, a borrowed shirt from someone, and who knew what staining his shoes, he didn't plan to cross the threshold. "I'll stand here, I think."

"Get in here, Nathan. Chairs clean, I'm tracking around who knows what too, and the carpets will clean. I'm sorry to make the call so urgent, but I thought you might want to hear this in person. But your news can come first, if you don't mind."

Nathan took a seat and nearly sighed with the comfort of it. "I love these chairs. Isaac appears to be alive and well and to have skipped town while the plant burned. He's the inside guy at the plant. He was the one handling shipping product in and out. And he had about two million plus in used bills stuffed into the walls of his apartment."

"You're kidding me." She paused as she thought about it. "They were moving currency with the tile-plant boxes, shipping it around?"

"I think so. This wasn't a new designer-drug operation, Rae. Isaac has been active for quite a while with more traditional products. The designer drug looks to be just a small sideline of what Isaac was doing."

"I was about to tell you the same thing, but with a different twist. I think you're going to find Isaac was a lot more involved than just shipping product around. Remember Peggy's notes about a rumor on the street—a drug with a unique delivery system. Chocolate. Our guys figured out how to deliver their drug in a piece of chocolate."

Nathan rocked forward in the chair and nearly put his hurt elbow down on his knee before he caught himself. "You're serious? You can prove it?"

Rae started to smile. "Yeah. I think I can. Franklin sent over some of the notebook pages from that cabin for me to compare handwriting samples with this file of items Peggy had collected, thinking she might have had a better lead on this cook than we realized. I haven't found anything on that yet, but I did start to make sense of what was on the formula pages, and that's what got me thinking chocolate in the first place. It fits, to a few things in Peggy's notes, and some of the unusual items being retrieved from the cabin tonight. We've found out how the drug was being delivered.

"The heat of melted chocolate would destroy most drugs; that's why you rarely see drugs mixed with other things. They must have figured out a solution to that problem. And a guy who had been around making chocolates all his life would bring that expertise to the table. Talk about a clean way to put a drug on the market and sell it to the masses. They could form the chocolates into foil-wrapped chocolate kisses and sell them for twenty bucks a piece. No cop is going to be able to tell a piece of chocolate with a drug mixed in it from a piece that didn't have it."

Nathan began to comprehend the scope of what it meant overall. "The beauty is in the packaging and delivery of the drug. The drug mix might be popular for what it is, but the real genius is making it safe for Middle America to try it."

"Exactly. Profitable. Easily shipped. With no way to detect it from millions of pounds of good chocolate in the retail world, and a way to made addicts out of a huge new slice of the public who would never think they would buy drugs."

"Can we prove that, that they got it to work? That these drug tests were getting delivered in the chocolate pieces?"

"We know Peggy stopped at the Fine Chocolates Shop. We found the bag in her trash can. Karen may have tried one of the free samples at either the hotel check-in desk or at the restaurant checkout counter. Nella was known to love the chocolate and even dated the senior Keif. I've eaten the free chocolate samples and visited the store."

Rae moved around papers. "It's very possible some of the deaths were a failure in the delivery system, the way the drug was formulated into the chocolate.

Either the interactions under heat were not well understood, or the concentrations were going higher than they expected in the samples. This isn't the kind of thing they would try on themselves to see how it worked, not those first pieces of chocolate. We'll find some samples, Nathan, eventually there will be some found to test. At least we know the likely place to now look."

"I like the fact it fits, Rae. I like the fact it starts to remove open questions, rather than just create more."

"You still need to find out where they were mixing the drug into the chocolate. I don't think they were doing it at the cabin; there weren't basic things like butter and the rest of the ingredients for making chocolate out there, and nothing like the flat trays or wax paper or spatulas I think you would find. And I don't think it's being done at the chocolate shop—Isaac wouldn't want his dad stumbling into something, assuming he wasn't involved in this."

"We'll find the place. I'll check out the older Keif, but given it appears Isaac has been involved in this drug business for years, and the older Keif has already spent a lifetime building his chocolate shop and hasn't eased off that pace in the last couple years—I think the son just decided to find a way to make an easier, faster living. The older Keif has put too much sweat equity into that business to risk throwing it away on something this illegal at this age of his life."

Rae nodded, agreeing with him. "Isaac Keif is half the equation. He's the unique delivery system expert, the one who can take the drug and package it in chocolate in a way that can hold its properties. We're still missing at least one more guy. There has to still be another cook out there who is making the drug powder itself. Isaac was too busy with his own business to spend hours poring over test tubes and textbooks. Whoever is making the designer-drug powder has to have a good solid knowledge of pharmacology and patience."

Nathan thought she was right. "The notebook found at the cabin, the formula notes, if this guy gets away, he's still carrying his last notebook and the knowledge of his drug with him. He'll just set up to manufacture it somewhere else."

"I know you don't like the option, but maybe one of the town pharmacists?"

"I personally had the handwriting in the notebooks checked against what we knew the men had signed. It's not Walter Sr. or Walter Jr., and I've already got officers checking on Walter's son Scott. His alibi for the last two days when the kid died looks tight. And I can prove he wasn't one of our two shooters at the plant." Nathan shook his head. "I don't know; I'll keep pushing that angle until I'm more comfortable they are off the list."

"Talk to the coroner. Maybe the drug they were trying to make will tell you something about who was trying to make it."

"I was on my way over there when Bruce called. You want to come along?"

She hesitated.

"Exhausted?"

"As much as I so badly want to come, the idea of getting out of this chair right now is beyond me. I think I'll sleep on Bruce's couch tonight."

Nathan smiled. "Watch out for that support spring that likes to dig into your shoulder if you lay with your head toward the office door."

"It's still there?"

"Oh, yeah."

Rae changed her mind and got to her feet to walk with him through the agency as he headed out. "You'll call if there is something interesting the coroner has found?"

"I will. If I don't see you yet tonight, have a good rest."

"You're at the hospital for your arm tomorrow afternoon?"

"The white coats have me at 1 p.m. Let's hope this is all wrapped up before then and they can just put me to sleep a happy man and I'll stay sleeping for a couple weeks."

She smiled. "I just hope the surgeon is good."

"Please. They will x-ray it and tell me to take two aspirins and call them if it turns more swollen than it is. The elbow hurts, but it's not that painful anymore. And the gunshot—at least he was a lousy shot and didn't hit any bone."

She was starting to pale on him. "And since just listening to it is making you queasy, I'm going to forget about it for a while now." Nathan smiled and nodded to Bruce. "Tell him to bring you in a sundae or something tonight. Start blocking out today."

"I will. Drive careful, Nathan."

"You want some company tonight, Nathan? I'm going to be done here in an hour. I can drive you around if nothing else," Bruce offered.

"Let me talk to the coroner and see what he has; then I may take you up on that. If I'm heading out to the cabin tonight, I'd like someone along who can push the car out of a snowed-in ditch if necessary. I'm sure that road has turned into a sheet of ice by now."

"I'll be around. Just call, and I'll come pick you up."

"Thanks, Bruce." Nathan nodded a final good-bye to Rae and headed out.

ༀ   ༀ   ༀ

Nathan settled gingerly into the chair in Franklin's office, wondering and hoping this was the last visit he would be paying the coroner this year. At least Franklin hadn't said to come on back to the morgue and talk while he worked.

Franklin finished up the call he was on. "It's good to see you walking around, Nathan. I heard it was bad."

"I hope to not repeat the experience," Nathan replied, appreciating the doctor's words. He wondered how many times he would be asked how he was doing or asked to tell the story of how he got shot over the next month. He lived in a curious town.

He changed the subject before Franklin could ask. "I know you're just getting started looking over the notebooks found at the cabin. Can you tell me anything at this point about the designer drug they were trying to create?"

"Nothing here tells us much about the new drug. It does tell me this cook was the one who designed the rave-party drug that killed the twelve kids. But we don't have the current notebook he's using, and that leaves a big gap."

"Anything you can tell me based on the precursor chemicals that were out in the cabin?"

"That gets a bit more interesting. There was a legal prescription drug used to treat Parkinson's disease found in bulk powder, like prescription tablets had been crushed. It's the same drug that causes a very small percentage of its patients to become gambling addicts overnight. It gives a very nice high. I think that is a key component to this new drug. We found prescription sedatives, a smaller amount, but also in a crushed powder form. And one thing very strange." Franklin pulled out the lab report in his in-box.

"He's using something called Vytribit, a man-made synthetic drug taken straight out of the rattlesnake venom family. It is used in the drug-manufacturing world like salt is used to preserve meat. You see it in the more sophisticated meth production batches out east. He probably picked up the technique there and was trying to cross-promote it here. It turns out, even in low doses, to have paralyzing properties to it when improperly heated. I doubt he intended that side effect."

"He's figuring this formulation out fast if he's down to tweaking those factors."

Franklin nodded. "He has a working designer-drug recipe that is close to being perfected, and if Rae is right about the chocolate, a very difficult delivery system to beat. If you can't find this guy—Nathan, he can open a Web-based chocolate store and ship product around the country and look totally legit."

Nathan rubbed his face. "Franklin, the drug could be mailing now for all we know. At best we may have found the cabin after he was finishing his last test batch. The kid who died—he was the extra hands helping with a larger production batch. The first time something like this expands in higher quantities and volumes is always the most dangerous. Something went wrong and the kid got a face full of the product without realizing it."

"I don't have toxicology yet, but I'm hoping the boy died of enough of the drug, was in a deep freeze of snow for the night, that his body is going to still have measurable quantities available. I'm going to know that in about twenty-four hours." Franklin smiled and nodded. "About the time they are working on properly dealing with that arm."

Nathan laughed and pushed himself to his feet. "That's the problem with too small of a town—all the doctors have to compare notes. Do you want to be there when they patch this up properly?"

"I was hoping you would ask. I specialized in gunshot wounds. And dead people are not the only people I know how to doctor."

"I want an X-ray and a new bandage and to be sent home to recuperate for a week."

"What you want in life is rarely what you get."

"True. I'll see you tomorrow, if I don't talk to you again before then."

Nathan headed out. Home would have to be soon, but the office was his next stop. He still hadn't thanked his guys for the heroic job they had done at the tile plant today. He planned to shake hands with every man on the force before the night was over.

"Will, tell me we've got some word from the APB on Isaac Keif."

"Not even a good false sighting. I fed his photo to reporters a few minutes ago, and let one even tape a brief clip of us loading money bundles into the armored car the bank sent over. We're going to literally put the armored car into evidence, I figure it's safer than trying to keep the cash loose in the evidence room. The reporters will find Isaac Keif for us or at least start the tips rolling in for where he might have gone."

"How high a reward do you want to put out?" Nathan asked him.

"I was thinking two hundred thousand had a nice sound to it."

"Good. Do it." He thought a second moment and called Will back. "Who do you have answering the phones?"

Will laughed. "Don't worry about it. The state crime stoppers program said they would handle it for us and feed us the information. Sillman said he's bored enough he can do the first review of what looks interesting."

"Good. I'll be back at the office for a few minutes if you need me. Then Bruce and I are going out to the cabin to check in on the HazMat team's progress."

"I'll find you if anything breaks here," Will promised.

44

It felt like his last meal. Nathan took a seat at the hospital cafeteria table. Rae reached across to sample one of his fries.

"These are good." Rae looked at Bruce. "You mentioned they had cheese sauce available for nachos? Think they'll sell it for fries?"

"You might get lucky."

Rae stuffed dollar bills in her pocket. "I'm going to go check. I'm starved."

Nathan watched her leave. "She's looking better."

"You're looking worse."

"They were pushing around the arm to get the X-rays they wanted. Then they frowned at the pictures and said come back in an hour."

"Sounds about right." Bruce pushed aside his tray and shifted the chair so he could use the adjoining chair as a footrest. "We thought we would come keep you company after they get done with you, commiserate with the misery or something."

"What are the odds they are going to let me go home tonight?"

"Slim to none."

"Yeah. That's what I figured." Nathan dumped catsup in an open corner of his plate. The thought was depressing. His family was threatening to visit en mass too.

"They let you eat?"

"They said I could eat. They apparently plan locals for what they are doing this afternoon. I can't say that idea went over real well."

Rae returned with a second tray to stack on the one she already had. A basket of fries smothered in cheese sauce threatened to slide over. She gingerly pulled one out.

"So I gather you two have been checking in around town this morning?" Nathan asked, working on where to pick up his sandwich.

"Just listening to gossip, talking with Adam at the union hall, comparing a few notes with your grandfather on cars. He saw mine this morning."

Nathan smiled. "I'll hear from Henry about your car soon, I'm sure. Any interesting rumors going around?"

"I think most people are just sharing news back and forth, kind of shocked with everything. No one seems to have realized what Isaac was doing. Did you have any better luck?"

"Sillman and Will ran me down what has been found at the tile plant, at Isaac's place, and out at the cabin, but it's precious little that we didn't know twenty-four hours ago. That's a bad sign. Finding these guys is growing cold on us fast."

"We know the guy that committed suicide in my car was in the transportation side of things for that millennium rave party. Based on the notebooks found at the cabin, this cook was also involved before. Isaac—his enterprise had enough depth to it he could have been involved back then too. That leaves what, the second shooter? The financial backer probably behind this?"

"The chemicals found in that cabin were not cheap. And while Isaac was holding a bunch of cash, if some of that was being diverted to this effort, the decision was likely being done by someone higher up the food chain than Isaac. He was moving cans around a tile plant part of the day, pouring chocolates on weekends for his dad, acting as a delivery person for cash—that says he was still a utility player with a novel delivery system idea for the new drug, but still not the guy ultimately running this show."

Rae pulled another cheese fry from the basket. "Finding Isaac is your best lead to this drug designer. It's going to take a while to get at him via the financial backer. Isaac has worked with him and will more easily give up a name."

Nathan nodded. "We know this cook exists, but that's about it. We've got his handwriting in the notebooks, but the prints in the cabin aren't turning up anything useful about him. And he's the one guy we have to find. We don't find Isaac—well, we already have all his money and the tile plant is no longer a drug transit point. Isaac can't do much more damage. But this cook—he's either got that last notebook with him or enough information in his head to recreate it where he is at."

"Has anyone else in town split like Isaac did? Just up and left their life?" Bruce asked.

"Not that I've been able to find, and by this point I think I'd be hearing about it."

"Isaac didn't plan to run," Rae pointed out. "He may have some things planned, but I doubt he planned to just be gone for good at a drop of the hat. Have you tapped his father's phones?"

"Yes. The man practically pushed the idea himself not more than two minutes into our initial conversation." Nathan shook his head at the memory. "I swear Isaac was being disinherited in six different languages. He told me to burn his son's things from the apartment, that he didn't want them back. He even insisted I have his mail checked before he saw it. He swears he knew nothing and will do whatever it takes to prove it to us. I lean toward believing him, but we'll be doing a lot of checking."

"It's going to hurt his business."

Nathan looked over at Rae at that comment. "Are you kidding? There were more townsfolk lined up to buy chocolates and talk with him today than I have ever seen in his store before. He's the good parent with a really bad son; everyone has to rally now, both to support him and gossip about who caused Isaac to go bad."

"Really?" She shook her head. "It's going to take me a while to get used to a small town."

"It will start to make sense eventually. You see Peggy's parents tomorrow?"

She nodded. "I'm going by Peggy's place first to return items I took from her home office, and then I'm going to her parents' home to give them my report. I wish I had more definite news to tell them."

"This will keep unfolding for a while. But Peggy was the trigger that uncovered all this. That has to mean something. And confirming Peggy was murdered—I'd say you went far beyond where this case initially looked like it could go."

"Sheriff."

Nathan turned in his chair. The nurse coming toward him was not someone he wanted to see.

"The doctors are ready for you."

"Already?" Nathan pushed back his chair and got to his feet.

"I'll take care of your tray," Rae offered as he reached for it.

"Thanks." He straightened his sling. "Franklin was coming over too. This is going to be fun."

"Smile, Nathan. And just remember it will be over in a few hours."

"Make sure I get something better than Jell-O with Cool Whip or that vanilla pudding tonight."

She laughed. "Promise."

He shared a final smile. He turned and followed the nurse. He felt like he was walking into his own worst nightmare. At least when he got shot, he hadn't known it was coming.

45

"Thank you, Mrs. Worth." Rae accepted the china cup offered her and settled gingerly into the seat the lady indicated, the delicacy of the chair suggesting it was old, French, and not made for this kind of casual use.

"I appreciate you coming to visit me here, Miss Gabriella. After watching the violent happenings in Justice the last few days on television, I wasn't up to visiting the town again and seeing it up close."

"I only wish I had been able to keep our originally scheduled appointment or to bring better news with me when I came." Rae had hoped to bring complete news and a wrapped-up case in her final report, but that wasn't possible. Hopefully what she had was enough to set their minds to rest about their daughter and begin to help Mrs. Worth find the closure she had sought.

Mr. Worth took a seat in a more substantial chair across from them. "Our daughter was working on a real story."

"A very substantial one. Peggy's arrival in Justice, her questions, have led to the breaking up of a very large-scale drug enterprise. I'm so very sorry she isn't here to be able to see the results of her work."

"I believe she knows."

Rae opened her portfolio and retrieved two copies of her final report. She handed Lucy and Richard each a copy. "The reporter I believe you have met, Gage Collier, is working on completing the story Peggy was writing as a tribute to her. His story in a week or so will be better able to give you a much fuller picture of what occurred. Too much of the matter is still fluid to have answers to some of the questions yet. As you have no doubt seen on the news, every day has brought new significant developments."

Richard smiled. "I would say you have more than successfully handled our case. You've answered the core questions we asked. Our daughter was murdered, and we know the story she was working on. And to get those answers, you nearly became a victim too. That effort has been far beyond anything we could have hoped for."

Mrs. Worth nodded. "The coroner called this morning to personally apologize for his initial findings, and he's asked for and received permission to exhume Peggy's body if it's discovered there is a way to test for this new designer drug. We might never be able to get a court conviction if all they can prove is the man had Peggy's BlackBerry, but even so, we'll now know the truth. That is what I most wanted and needed. To know the truth."

"I'm glad it has come to this point where much is known."

Rae nodded to her report. "Regarding the men involved: all the police have right now is a strong lead for the identity of one of the men. A man named Isaac Keif. You'll have seen the reward being offered and his photo on television."

"We have."

"It's believed there are one or two others directly involved. Arresting Isaac Keif is the most direct way to learn who those people are. The investigation is proceeding, but it is slower now that the people they seek appear to have dispersed and left the Justice area."

"I'm certain the reward will eventually lead to finding Isaac Keif," Mr. Worth agreed. "Tell us more about the story, Miss Gabriella. Tell us about what Peggy was so passionate about during the last days of her life."

"The lead that took her to Justice involved a school notebook. It belonged to Joe Prescott's grandson and was recovered from the boy's belongings after his death. The young man was one of twelve who died at a millennium rave party from a bad designer drug. Peggy thought the notebook could give her a lead on the man who designed the drug. Having now seen that notebook, she was on the right track.

BEFORE I WAKE   367
will be

"Isaac Keif, or one of the other men who were involved in this, gave your daughter a lethal dose of the drug, either intending to kill her or with the expectation she'd grow ill enough to leave town. She probably received it within a piece of chocolate among a batch that was simply pure chocolate. I believe that same method was used to test the drug on a Karen Reese, another lady who died in a way similar to your daughter, as well as how they were able to drug me without my being aware of the danger."

"Are there plans to make some kind of public warning about that possibility?" Richard asked.

"I'm sorry; I wish I could say I knew what kind of final decision will be made by law enforcement as this unfolds. It is possible, by breaking up the group now, that it has eliminated the chances this drug will ever reach the public in a large-scale way. The actions now, triggered by Peggy's questions, may have delayed this threat from ever reaching the public."

"I don't suppose bulletins warning *death by chocolate* would be viewed kindly by the confectioner's industry," Lucy remarked.

Rae smiled. "That is why there are good reporters like your daughter pursuing stories like this, to keep the public fully informed. Gage Collier will do that now with his tribute to your daughter."

Rae opened her purse and retrieved the set of keys to Peggy's home. She offered them to Lucy. "I have returned the files I had removed from your daughter's home office and the items you were able to share with me—her address book, her phone—I left on the desk in her office. The police have both her BlackBerry and the last notebook we recovered. They'll be returned with time."

Mrs. Worth nodded. She gripped the key ring. "Do you think it awful when I say I'm glad this is over?"

Rae offered a sympathetic smile in reply. "It's closure, Mrs. Worth. After a loss of this magnitude, it's a very necessary and good thing to find."

She rose to her feet and shook hands with Mr. Worth, then with his wife. "You have my number. Please don't hesitate to call if I can answer any further questions you have."

"Thank you. For everything."

Rae nodded her good-byes. "I'll let myself out."

❦   ❦   ❦

"How did it go with Peggy's parents?" Bruce asked.

Rae looked up from the files on her desk she was sorting and packing away. Her partner was leaning against the doorway and looked remarkably nice in a suit and tie and polished boots.

"It went well. They hoped for more answers as to who had done this I think, but they seemed pleased to at least now know what happened to their daughter." She added a square label marked *Gabriella Worth* and the date to the side of the white banker box. "You look particularly dressed up. Have a meeting?"

"Just one with you."

She looked over.

"You got dressed up for your meeting; I figured we would do lunch somewhere a step above cheeseburgers and fries and paper napkins."

She smiled. "I'd like that."

Bruce settled into the chair across from her desk. He smiled and gestured to the box she was packing. "As a first case, you have to admit, it beats a lost Pekinese. You're a seasoned private investigator now."

"Seasoned is right. Let's hope this was my one and only case that tries to kill me."

Bruce turned serious. "Are you still comfortable with the idea of being a private investigator?"

"This job can grow on you," she admitted.

"You'll stay?"

"Were you really worried that I might not?"

Bruce relaxed, studying her. "I wondered, if only for a brief moment."

"I rarely quit on anything," she replied seriously.

"I'm glad. For numerous reasons."

She smiled and pushed to her feet, knowing if she didn't shift this conversation, she'd be having one way too deep and personal and more emotional than she wanted to have right now. "Store this box for me, Bruce, and let's go find one very expensive place to have lunch. We need a few new traditions in our lives, and this sounds like a very good one to have."

He walked with her through the building, paused to put her case box into storage, and then found his car keys. "When I close my next big case, we go fishing."

"Please. Anything but time in a boat with you. I still remember the last drenching," she pointed out. But she smiled.

46

Nathan pulled in behind the squad cars blocking traffic from one lane of the highway early Sunday morning and shut off his car headlights. Dawn was just breaking. He awkwardly turned to get out of the car without banging his aching arm. The doctors may have fixed things, but his arm hurt a whole lot more after they had done their work than it did before.

He joined Will and the two patrol officers who had called the scene in and looked down the steep embankment to the river. The railroad bridge supports had taken another nearly catastrophic hit, this time by a Jeep. "What was he doing, about 70 mph when he hit that pillar? That engine block is barely recognizable."

"At least that."

The breeze had driven the fog from the river this morning and they could make out from here what had happened. Sometimes all that was visible on mornings like this was the glow of a car fire to indicate the wreck was down there. At least this time there didn't appear to have been a fire.

Nathan picked his way down the steep embankment to join Sillman at the wreck site.

"Sorry to call you with this kind of news, Nathan."

"I'm getting used to the unpleasant surprises."

The driver was twisted behind the wheel and shoved around in the front seat wreckage. Nathan leaned over the wrecked engine block to get a look at what remained of the man's face. "That's Isaac—or was," he agreed.

"Two bullets to the head. A tire may have been shot out to force his vehicle off the road, or maybe it was simply rammed off. But the death is not such a puzzle—two bullets to the back of the head. They weren't going to chance that he survived the crash, and they came down to finish the job."

"Overkill I'd say. He was dead before he got shot. What do you think? One shooter? Two?"

"Probably two guys. One handles the high-speed chase; the other handles the gun. They have to get down here to finish the job and then get back up that embankment and be gone before someone can respond to reports of shots being fired. No reports came in overnight," Sillman added before Nathan could ask.

"Isaac has been missing a few days. Let's figure out where he has been hiding if possible. Maybe there's a hotel receipt in there somewhere or a cell phone and we can learn who he's been talking with recently."

"If it's still here, I'll find it," Sillman agreed.

Nathan looked around the scene and then accepted what Sillman handed him. He turned pages and sighed. "Thanks. Collect them all."

"I will."

"Can I help you with anything in particular?" Nathan offered.

"You can get some sleep. This is two hours to document the scene and collect evidence, at least four before we can get to the slugs that killed him. I need you fresh about 3 p.m. when I hand this to you and say I'm not thinking anymore. It's a department of overworked, underpaid, and sleep-deprived cops right now. Let's see the top guy start setting a good example. Besides—" Gray nodded to his arm—"you still look like death warmed over."

"I feel about like it to. What's it been, three weeks since Peggy was found?"

"And add two weeks before that, for when the strike happened. This department hasn't stopped to breathe since this started. I'd like to start fixing that by telling you to go get some sleep and set a good example for the rest of us."

Gray smiled. "Seriously, Nathan. You'll be in my way for about the next six hours; then it's just working lots of details through the system and seeing what pops out. Right now you need to worry about telling Isaac's dad his son has been killed, and the rest we can handle."

Nathan appreciated it and nodded. "He's traveling this weekend, Isaac's dad. To see family he said, and to get away from the reporters constantly asking questions."

"I can't blame him for ducking the reporters."

"I'll take care of getting him notified. Call me if there is anything you need out here. I'll be back at noon otherwise."

"I will."

⟷ ⟷ ⟷

Rae was perched on the railing beside the highway, looking down at the investigators working around the car. Nathan climbed back up the steep slope to join her.

"Isaac is dead. Two shots to the head, although the crash probably killed him first."

"Will told me it was him. I figured it was bad news when the tones kept rolling this morning."

"You're becoming a police-scanner junky."

"When it goes back to just being lost dogs, I'll quit listening in."

Nathan smiled. He held up what he carried. "It gets worse. We've got similar bound notebooks to what was found at the cabin tossed about in that vehicle, with two of them down the riverbanks and touching the water. They were being pulled out of the car."

"Do you think they got that final formula book we've been after?"

Nathan perched on the rail beside her. "It's hard to tell. These notebooks have earlier dates then the ones we found at the cabin. Same handwriting, I think, so it's the same cook. I don't know; maybe Isaac knew where the notebooks were stored and had come back to try and clean out some evidence."

He rubbed his sore shoulder that still ached. "I have the reasonable hunch that when we dig those bullets out and compare them in the records, they will turn out to be guns stolen ten years ago in California, and they are now somewhere at the bottom of Lake Michigan."

"True." Rae nodded to the wreck. "Someone knew about the Jeep Isaac was driving and knew he was coming back to Justice in the middle of the night. Someone sent these guys who killed him."

"Any ideas?"

"I suppose the cook could be killing people who knows who he is. The cook sent Isaac back to town on an errand—maybe he told Isaac one of these notebooks was the real formula—and then the cook kills Isaac or has Isaac killed. There's only one highway in and out of town and that Jeep is recognizable."

Nathan thought about it and decided it made a lot of sense. "Isaac was the only one who apparently lived in town—kill him and this group can more easily disperse. There are no more ties to the town for us to pursue. And Isaac is expendable. The tile plant is gone, we have his money, and the cabin is shut down. His usefulness has disappeared, and he's a liability. Killing him makes sense in an awful kind of way."

"Isaac is still an active lead. Who he called, where he traveled, who he saw in the days and weeks before today. It's slow work, but it's there. The same with the guy who killed himself in my car, Brad Danforth. He had a patron, and it may be the same man who was bankrolling this work. We have a cook whose handwriting we know. Eventually one of those threads starts to give answers you can work."

"Eventually isn't a very good answer, not when there is a designer drug out there now."

"It's addictive, illegal, and easy to distribute," Rae agreed. "But if it is out there now, then it just became like a lot of the illegal drugs cops have to fight. You have to find the production labs, find the chemical sources, find the dealers, track back the money, and shut the labs down. We at least know a lot more about this drug than we do about most new products hitting the streets."

Rae pushed herself off the railing and stood to dig out her car keys from her pocket. "Maybe we got lucky, Nathan. Maybe the cook is dead too. The financial guy behind all this decided to clean up a mess that could trail back to him and he shot the guy, just like Isaac got shot. It's a shame to lose a cook's expertise but in the big picture of things—there are always more chemists and this one failed twice now and has a string of bodies that can be traced to him. That's a guy who is very much a liability. I don't think he stays alive long, regardless of how much money is in what he can design."

"I can hope that is true, but it's a bit like Bruce hoping the bad guys just move out of town and became someone else's problem."

"Then let me offer one more possibility—they may have the drug, but do you really think they have the delivery system?" Rae nodded toward the wreck. "Isaac was not a guy to write things down. If he was the one tasked with getting the drug powder to form into chocolates without the heat destroying it—I guarantee not many people will solve that problem. Isaac likely went to the grave with the distribution system in his head. And tracking white powder—this designer drug will be no different than the cocaine or the meth you already fight. Produced in clandestine labs by people hoping to sell it for cash. The drug may change, but the people don't. Police work is all about finding the people. It always will be."

"You're really cheering me up here."

Rae held up her keys. "Go off duty then. Take off the badge. And we'll go for a drive. The guys here can do without you for half an hour."

"In a half hour you'll have us in Wisconsin."

Rae jangled the keys.

"Can I drive on the way back?"

"Better yet, you can break it in." She offered the keys.

"How bad is the smell?"

"Your grandfather called it spoiled turnips. I think it's more like crusted rabbit droppings that you step on. You know the bad smelly source is there around you, but you just can't see it."

He accepted the keys.

Nathan caught his deputy chief's attention. "Will, I'll be out of radio range in a bit; use the cell phone if you need me."

"Not a problem, Boss. Enjoy the drive."

Nathan looked at Rae. He fully intended to.

ε☯3   ε☯3   ε☯3

Devon understood greed, lying, and betrayal. He expected all three in the men he worked with; only a fool expected loyalty in a criminal enterprise. If he had more on the other person than they had on him, he had the upper hand. And with this particular man—Devon had enough on him to get the man the death penalty. It created a certain trust by virtue of distrust that made the relationship work. He considered the steak before him and sliced into a piece. "The situation in Justice is unfortunate."

The man across the table from him kept eating. "It was the risk of a small town, and a risk accepted when we discussed the matter years before."

Devon was willing to accept the statement offered. It was a cost of doing business, the risks involved, and the cash lost in the raid. "How's the new formula coming along?"

"The drug powder is perfected, but delivery is . . . losing Isaac will set back some of the work."

"You're abandoning chocolate as your method of choice."

"Isaac is dead. Finding another with his knowledge base isn't worth the liability. I'll get back to what I do best. Pills will work; we can still stamp them *EE*, and get the drug on the market in the next month. I told you I didn't work well with a partner."

Devon had always known that, which was one reason he could tolerate this man being an employee. "Chocolates are that hard to figure out?"

"If you want the drug visible as white specks in the chocolate, and the pieces tasting a bit like chewing sand, I can do it. But if I raise the preservative being used to a level I can get this powder to dissolve into the chocolate, the samples kill people. Isaac had figured out something different for getting the powder into the melted chocolate without changing its properties, and he wasn't sharing his secret. For all I know he was turning the chocolate into a powder too and then flash heating the two together somehow and immediately chilling it. I know he went through a lot of ice. But I never figured out what he was doing."

"You shouldn't have shot him."

The man shrugged. "Isaac doesn't know you. He knows me. You weren't around figuring out the risks when you realized this kid decided to get scared and run rather than just go home and sit tight a few days and let the matters in Justice chill out again. I'm just relieved he called me before he called the cops. I got him to clean out the locker I didn't know where was, and I made sure he was dead. You should be grateful I cleaned up the mess the way I did."

"You'll be moving?"

He nodded. "Friday, if things stay as they now are. I'm covered. There's a new address for folks to have and a pretty good story now working around town for my coming absence. I'll need a new name and documents so I can start over cleanly with the move. I like the sound of Victor for this set of documents."

Devon nodded. "I'll get them for you. So, a month to put the product onto the street?"

"I'll need another full list of precursor chemicals for the new lab." He finished eating and reached over for a mint.

"Hand the list to your supplier. He knows I'm good for the funding. He can make the pickup anytime."

"I appreciate that." He rose to his feet. "I'll get this dealt with, Devon. Your budget line will start coming in positive again."

Devon didn't bother to push the reality of what would happen should his money keep funding failures. This man understood reality. "We'll meet in a month to look at the marketing data. Leave by the back entrance; a van is waiting for you there."

He nodded and left.

Devon more slowly finished his own meal and thought about matters. A month, and this man would likely become expendable too.

47

The Fine Chocolates Shop had a closed sign in the windows; *Back After Reporters Go* the block printed sign said in fluorescent red. Shades were pulled down to block the view into the store. Rae could understand that sentiment. She'd had her fill of reporters asking her questions in the last three days.

She pulled into a parking place a few spots down from the front door of the Chapel Detective Agency and retrieved her briefcase. She could hear water dripping and realized the sun was warming the ice on the roof and it was beginning to drip along gutters. It was a nice sound, the first reminder that spring was around the corner in a few more weeks.

She walked into the agency and back through the hallway, humming as she went.

"Rae?" Bruce called.

"It's me."

She walked past her office and leaned against the doorpost to Bruce's office. "Cleaning house?" She could smell the sharp cleaning agent he was using to wipe down his whiteboard. His case list was growing shorter. There wasn't a need to tail Henry any longer. The guns had been found.

"It's going to be a slow week by the look of this work list," Bruce agreed. He looked past her down the hallway. "Nathan's here."

Rae turned to see the sheriff walking toward them.

"Nathan, great timing," Bruce called. "I've got a house for Rae to look at this afternoon and you should come along. She can't live in a hotel forever."

"The Horton place?"

"That's the one."

"I heard you were asking the Realtor about it. You can't be serious."

Rae looked between the two men as Nathan joined them. "Why?"

"My great-great-something-grandfather used to own the place," Nathan explained. "It was built in the early 1800s and shows its age. It frankly needs to be leveled and replaced with something new on that property."

"It's stone, Rae. Lots and lots of stone and brick and practically shatter-proof by weather or flood or earthquake. And sitting on its own forty acres of land, most of it timber," Bruce noted.

"This place I have got to see. I'm already interested."

"That timber is such a dense patch of underbrush on steep slopes that you can't walk through most of it. If it wasn't such a huge deal to keep land in the family, it would have been sold off decades ago. Rae, the guy who bought the property from my father took only five years before saying enough. It's not worth your interest."

"I don't know. I like the idea of owning something so connected to the Justice past—your family, as well as the town."

"A place in town, Rae. A place near grocery stores, shopping, and a nightlife that won't eat you up in bug bites," Nathan suggested instead.

She just laughed. "If the house out east sells, I have to buy something. Bruce volunteered to help me look around. Seriously, come along if you don't have something pressing on your afternoon's calendar. You know this town; I'd like your input."

"I've got the time. Will kicked me out of the office. He said I couldn't come back for seventy-two hours. He said everyone in the office needed a break, and if I was around the guys couldn't blow off steam like they should or some such nonsense."

Rae grinned. "You're having a pity party that you're the boss and can't join in their bad jokes and numerous excuses to take a break at the watercooler."

"Two years ago, I was leading those war stories, not getting kicked out so they can tell them without me," Nathan noted.

Bruce pointed to the hall. "Go. We're right behind you. This agency has a closed sign on the front door and you can turn it for all three of us. We'll go start searching for where to spend Rae's money. It will cheer you right up."

"Absolutely." Rae tugged Nathan's hand to get him to start moving. "Who knows, maybe we'll find your grandfather and talk cars for a while too. I heard a rumor you want to inherit that Porsche."

"Better believe it. Have you seen that thing eat up a highway? I've been chasing it long enough to appreciate its handling."

Rae settled in between the two men, not sure if she was ready for this afternoon spent with both of them, but figuring it would at least not be boring. Nathan turned the sign of the Chapel Detective Agency to closed.

She pointed to her car. "I'm driving."

She saw the two men look at each other, but neither said a word as they crossed over to her car. "Thank you."

"I'm still going to hold me nose when you're not looking," Bruce replied, sliding into the back.

Nathan just smiled at her.

Rae clipped on her seat belt and started the car, pausing just long enough to return Nathan's smile and then look back at Bruce. "One perfect house, gentleman. Character being the best word to describe it. Let's see what you can both recommend in Justice that fits that description. The Horton place first?"

"Take a left at the next street," Nathan directed.

"You're going to like living in Justice, Rae. You won't want to settle anywhere else," Bruce predicted.

"We're about to see." She followed Nathan's directions, wondering if when this search was done, she would find a place in Justice she would be comfortable calling home.

About the Author

Dee Henderson is the author of fourteen best-selling novels, including the acclaimed O'Malley series and the Uncommon Heroes series. As a leader in the inspirational romantic suspense category, her books have won or been nominated for several prestigious industry awards including the RWA's RITA Award, the Christy Award, the ECPA Gold Medallion, the Holt Medallion, the National Readers' Choice Award, and the Golden Quill. Dee is a lifelong resident of Illinois and is active online. Visit her at www.deehenderson.com.

BOOK DISCUSSION GUIDE
Before I Wake

The word *Justice* is both the name of a town and the name of its sheriff. Does this seem like an appropriate name to you? Explain.

In the prologue, we meet Rae Gabriella. What are your first impressions of her? of Bruce?

What might make Rae think she can "disappear" in Justice? Do you think that Rae will succeed in escaping her past by moving there? Why or why not?

What is Bruce's motivation for taking Rae on as a partner? In Chapter Four he tells Nathan that she was a good cop and that it will be useful for him to have a female on his team. Do you think his motivation goes deeper than that?

What are some things Rae does to get familiar with her new surroundings? How does her approach, as a trained undercover cop, differ from that of a typical newcomer?

Nathan and Bruce are both dedicated to uncovering the truth in Justice: one as a sheriff, the other as a private investigator. How did each of them land in their present positions? When do their responsibilities complement each other? When might they clash?

Discuss Nathan and Bruce's friendship. What do they have in common? Are their feelings for Rae a potential source of tension between them?

Discuss the significance of a labor strike in a town like Justice. Why are emotions running so hot? What are the issues from the workers' point of view? from the management's point of view? Explain the looming threat of violence.

Have you ever personally observed or experienced a labor strike? If so, what was it like? Did it achieve its objectives?

Many people are surprised to learn that the underground drug culture is not just an urban blight, but also a real problem in small towns—from marijuana to methamphetamine to heroin. What might be some of the advantages and disadvantages of small-town connections to someone making or selling drugs?

What qualities make the "EE" designer drug nearly a perfect formula, as far as illegal drugs go?

Nathan has an interesting relationship with his grandfather. Why has Nathan asked Bruce to monitor his grandfather's activities? Do you think that was the right thing to do? Why or why not?

Both Bruce and Rae feel that they have changed a lot in the past several years. Do they feel they've changed for the better, or for worse?

How did the event in Washington, D.C., affected Rae's confidence in her skills? What questions of faith has it raised for her?

In Chapter Fifteen Bruce says, "I'm walking around proof that people can change." What—or whom—does he credit with the change? Have you seen evidence of this kind of change in your own life or that of someone you know?

In Chapter Forty-Two Rae asks, "How can God let us get so hurt if He loves us?" What is Nathan's response? Do you agree with his response? Why or why not?

Do you think Rae will eventually rekindle a romantic relationship with Bruce? begin a new one with Nathan? Neither? Explain.

DANGER IN THE SHADOWS

THE SUMMER STORM LIT UP the night sky in a jagged display of energy, lightning bouncing, streaking, fragmenting between towering thunderheads. Sara Walsh ignored the storm as best she could, determined not to let it interrupt her train of thought. The desk lamp as well as the overhead light were on in her office as she tried to prevent any shadows from forming. What she was writing was disturbing enough.

The six-year-old boy had been found. Dead.

Writing longhand on a yellow legal pad of paper, she shaped the twenty-ninth chapter of her mystery novel. Despite the dark specificity of the scene, the flow of words never faltered.

The child had died within hours of his abduction. His family, the Oklahoma law enforcement community, even his kidnapper, did not realize it. Sara did not pull back from writing the scene even though she knew it would leave a bitter taste of defeat in the mind of the reader. The impact was necessary for the rest of the book.

She frowned, crossed out the last sentence, added a new detail, then went on with her description of the farmer who had found the boy.

Thunder cracked directly overhead. Sara flinched. Her office suite on the thirty-fourth floor put her close enough to the storm she could hear the air sizzle in the split second before the boom. She would like to be in the basement parking garage right now instead of her office.

She had been writing since eight that morning. A glance at the clock on her desk showed it was almost eight in the evening. The push to finish a story always took over as she reached the final chapters. This tenth book was no exception.

Twelve hours. No wonder her back muscles were stiff. She had taken a brief break for lunch while she reviewed the mail her secretary had prioritized for her. The rest of her day had been spent working on the book. She arched her back and rubbed at the knot.

This was the most difficult chapter in the book to write. It was better to get it done in one long, sustained effort. Death always squeezed her heart.

Had Dave been in town, he would have insisted she wrap it up and come home. Her life was restricted enough as it was. Her brother refused to let her spend all her time at the office. He would come lean against the doorjamb of her office and give her that look along with his predictable lecture telling her all she should be doing: Puttering around the house, cooking, messing with the roses, something other than sit behind that desk.

Sara smiled. She did so enjoy taking advantage of Dave's occasional absences.

His flight back to Chicago from the FBI academy at Quantico had been delayed due to the storm front. When he had called her from the airport, he had cautioned her he might not be home until eleven.

It wasn't a problem, she had assured him, everything was fine. Code words. Spoken every day. So much a part of their language now that she spoke them instinctively. "Everything is fine"—all clear; "I'm fine"—I've got company; "I'm doing fine"—I'm in danger. She had lived the dance a long time. The tight security around her life was necessary. It was overpowering, obnoxious, annoying . . . and comforting.

Sara turned in the black leather chair and looked at the display of lightning. The rain ran down the panes of thick glass. The skyline of downtown Chicago glimmered back at her through the rain.

With every book, another fact, another detail, another intense emotion, broke through from her own past. She could literally feel the dry dirt under her hand, feel the oppressive darkness. Reliving what had happened to her twenty-five years ago was terrifying. Necessary, but terrifying.

She sat lost in thought for several minutes, idly walking her pen through her fingers. Her adversary was out there somewhere, still alive, still hunting her. Had he made the association to Chicago yet? After all these years, she was still constantly moving, still working to stay one step ahead of the threat. Her family knew only too well his threat was real.

The man would kill her. Had long ago killed her sister. The threat didn't get more basic than that. She had to trust others and ultimately God for her security. There were days her faith wavered under the intense weight of simply enduring that stress. She was learning, slowly, by necessity, how to roll with events, to trust God's ultimate sovereignty.

The notepad beside her was filled with doodled sketches of faces. One of these days her mind was finally going to stop blocking the one image she longed to sketch. She knew she had seen the man. Whatever the cost, whatever the consequences of trying to remember, they were worth paying in order to try to bring justice for her and her sister.

Sara let out a frustrated sigh. She couldn't force the image to appear no matter how much she longed to do so. She was the only one who still believed it was possible for her to remember it. The police, the FBI, the doctors, had given up hope years ago.

She fingered a worn photo of her sister Kim that sat by a white rose on her desk. She didn't care what the others thought. Until the killer was caught, she would never give up hope.

God was just. She held on to that knowledge and the hope that the day of justice would eventually arrive. Until it did, she carried a guilt inside that remained wrapped around her heart. In losing her twin she had literally lost part of herself.

Turning her attention back to her desk, she debated for a moment if she wanted to do any more work that night. She didn't.

As she put her folder away, the framed picture on the corner of her desk caught her attention; it evoked a smile. Her best friend was getting married. Sara was happy for her, but also envious. The need to break free of the security blanket rose and fell with time. She could feel the sense of rebellion rising again. Ellen had freedom and a life. She was getting married to a wonderful man. Sara longed to one day have that same choice. Without freedom, it wasn't possible, and that reality hurt. A dream was being sacrificed with every passing day.

As she stepped into the outer office, the room lights automatically turned on. Sara reached back and turned off the interior office lights.

Her suite was in the east tower of the business complex. Rising forty-five stories, the two recently built towers added to the already impressive downtown skyline. She struggled with the elevator ride to the thirty-fourth floor each day, for she did not like closed-in spaces, but she considered the view worth the price.

The elevator that responded tonight came from two floors below. There were two connecting walkways between the east and west towers, one on the sixth floor and another in the lobby. She chose the sixth floor concourse tonight, walking through it to the west tower with a confident but fast pace.

She was alone in the wide corridor. Travis sometimes accompanied her, but she had waved off his company tonight and told him to go get dinner. If she needed him, she would page him.

The click of her heels echoed off the marble floor. There was parking under each tower, but if she parked under the tower where she worked, she would be forced to pull out onto a one-way street no matter which exit she took. It was a pattern someone could observe and predict. Changing her route and time of day across one of the two corridors was a better compromise. She could hopefully see the danger coming.

Sara decided to take the elevator down to the west tower parking garage rather than walk the six flights. She would have preferred the stairs, but she could grit her teeth for a few flights to save time. She pushed the button to go down and watched the four elevators to see which would respond first. The one to her left, coming down from the tenth floor.

When it stopped, she reached inside, pushed the garage-floor parking button, but did not step inside. Tonight she would take the second elevator.

Sara shifted her raincoat over her arm and moved her briefcase to her other hand. The elevator stopped and the doors slid open.

A man was in the elevator.

She froze.

He was leaning against the back of the elevator, looking like he had put in a long day at work, a briefcase in one hand and a sports magazine in the other, his blue eyes gazing back at her. She saw a brief look of admiration in his eyes.

Get in and take a risk, step back and take a risk.

She knew him. Adam Black. His face was as familiar as any sports figure in the country, even if he'd been out of the game of football for three years. His commercial endorsements and charity work had continued without pause.

Adam Black worked in this building? This was a nightmare come true. She saw photographs of him constantly in magazines, local newspapers, and occasionally on television. The last thing she needed was to be near someone who attracted media attention.

She hesitated, then stepped in, her hand tightening her hold on the briefcase handle. A glance at the board of lights showed he had already selected the parking garage.

"Working late tonight?" His voice was low, a trace of a northeastern accent still present, his smile a pleasant one.

Her answer was a noncommittal nod.

The elevator began to silently descend.

She had spent too much time in European finishing schools to slouch. Her posture was straight, her spine relaxed, even if she was nervous. She hated elevators. She should have taken the stairs.

"Quite a storm out there tonight."

The heels of her patent leather shoes sank into the jade carpet as she shifted her weight from one foot to the other. "Yes."

Three more floors to go.

There was a slight flicker to the lights and then the elevator jolted to a halt.

"What?" Sara felt adrenaline flicker in her system like the lights.

He pushed away from the back wall. "A lightning hit must have blown a circuit."

The next second, the elevator went black.

THE NEGOTIATOR

DAVE WAITED UNTIL KATE'S brother Stephen disappeared up the stairs. "Why didn't you tell me yesterday? Trust me?"

"Tell you what? That I might have someone in my past who may be a murderer?" Kate swung away from him into the living room. "I've never even met this guy. Until twenty-four hours ago, I didn't even have a suspicion that he existed."

"Kate, he's targeting you."

"Then let him find me."

"You don't mean that."

"There is no reason for him to have blown up a plane just to get at me, to get at some banker. We're never going to know the truth unless someone can grab him. And if he gets cornered by a bunch of cops, he'll either kill himself or be killed in a shootout. It would be easier all around if he did come after me."

"Stop thinking with your emotions and use your head." Dave shot back. "What we need to do is to solve this case. That's how we'll find out the answers and ultimately find him."

"Then you go tear through the piles of data. I don't want to have anything to do with it. Don't you understand that? I don't want to be the one who puts the pieces together. Yesterday was like getting stuck in the gut with a hot poker."

He understood it, could feel the pain flowing from her. "Fine. Stay here for a day, get your feet back under you. Then get back in the game and stop acting like you're the only one this is hurting. Or have you forgotten all the people who died?" He saw the sharp pain flash in her eyes before they went cold and regretted his words.

"That was a low blow and you know it."

"Kate?"

"I can't offer anything to the investigation, don't you understand that? I don't know anything. I don't know him."

"Well he knows you. And if you walk away from this now, you're going to feel like a coward. Just what are you so afraid of?"

He could see it in her, a fear so deep it shimmered in her eyes and pooled them black, and he remembered his coworker's comment that he probably didn't want to read the court record. His eyes narrowed and his voice softened. "Are you sure you don't remember this guy?"

She broke eye contact, and it felt like a blow because he knew that at this moment he was the one hurting her. "If you need to get away for twenty-four hours, do it. Just don't run because you're afraid. You'll never forgive yourself."

"Marcus wouldn't let me go check out the data because he was afraid I would kill the guy if I found him."

Her words rocked him back on his heels. "What?" He closed the distance between them, and for the first time since this morning began, actually felt something like relief. He rested his hands calmly on her shoulders. "No you wouldn't. You're too good a cop."

She blinked.

"I almost died with you, remember?" He smiled. "I've seen you under pressure." His thumb rubbed along her jaw. "Come on, Kate. Come back with me to the house, and let's get back to work. The media wouldn't get near you, I promise."

Marcus and Stephen came back down the stairs, but Kate didn't look around; she just kept studying Dave. She finally turned and looked at her brother. "Marcus, I'm going back to Dave's."

Dave gave in to a small surge of relief. It was a start. Tenuous. And risky. But a start, all the same.

have you visited
tyndalefiction.com
lately?

Only there can you find:

- ⟿ books hot off the press
- ⟿ first chapter excerpts
- ⟿ inside scoops on your favorite authors
- ⟿ author interviews
- ⟿ contests
- ⟿ fun facts
- ⟿ and much more!

Sign up for your **free** newsletter!

Visit us today at: **tyndalefiction.com**

Tyndale fiction does more than entertain.

- ⟿ *It touches the heart.*
- ⟿ *It stirs the soul.*
- ⟿ *It changes lives.*

That's why Tyndale is so committed to being first in fiction!

TYNDALE FICTION